This book is dedicated to my grandparents,
Hilda and Wilfred Hanslow.

Chapter One

Monday, April 14th

His eyes fixed on the sword and started to travel its length, down from the black handle, over the plain hilt and along the two-inch wide shaft to where it penetrated the young woman's mouth. Beneath her head the pillow and sheet were stained a mix of red and black.

Detective Superintendent Colm McEvoy hitched up his creased trousers and eased his six foot three frame down onto his haunches. He tipped his upper torso sideways, careful not to place his hands on the floor, and looked under the bed. The sword had exited the mattress and the bed's thin base and was embedded in a floorboard. A crown of splinters had erupted around the tip and a dark puddle snaked across the boards.

He levered himself back upright and took another look at her naked body. Her smoky blue eyes were open in a glazed stare. The sword was aligned to the shape of her mouth, the blade biting a centimetre or so into the cheek on either side, widening her grimace. Some of her brown hair had escaped from a ponytail, curling over her forehead, down past her ears and onto her neck.

Her thin arms were placed by her side, hands clenched tight; her skinny legs closed. Her pale, almost translucent, skin was pulled tight over her ribs, her breasts slight. She looked as if she had been starving herself.

There were no signs that she had worn make-up and her fingernails were short and clean of nail polish. Whatever blood had been on her face and body looked to have been wiped away carefully. There were no tie marks on her limbs, no evidence of bruising, or that she had struggled.

It was almost as if she had welcomed the killing – made her peace and simply swallowed the sword.

He forced himself to look away and examined the room, his gaze tracing over every surface. Except for a small, brown shoulder bag that lay on the only chair the space seemed empty. No clothes, no shoes, or any other visible possessions.

He stared back across the room at the young woman's face. She looked no more than 18 years old. He massaged his temples and sighed. He wanted to wrap her up and take her away, to protect her from what was about to unfold; give her some measure of dignity in death. Instead he took a plastic cigarette from a box, placed it between his lips, and stepped out into the corridor.

Detective Inspector Barney Plunkett shuffled listlessly from one foot to another, impatient to start the investigation. Occasionally he shared a quizzical look with Detective Sergeant Kenny Johns, a fellow member of the NBCI – the National Bureau of Criminal Investigation – the branch of the gardai that investigated Ireland's most serious crimes including murder and organised crime.

Mostly Johns picked at imaginary lint on an immaculate, well-tailored, dark blue suit, and tried to catch his own reflection in the fire glass in the door at the end of the corridor. His hair was slicked back with gel and his aftershave filled the enclosed space.

Plunkett gnawed on his fingernails, brushed back his sandy hair, and stared out of the window at the melee of guards, staff and guests congregated on and around the grassed courtyard of the Glencree Centre for Peace and Reconciliation and beyond that down the Glencree valley, its green fields and conifer forests framed by the yellowy-brown of the Wicklow Mountains. The sky was shades of grey, rain threatening to fall at any minute. He wasn't looking forward to viewing the murder scene. Blades usually left a bloodbath and carnage that he found hard to forget.

The emergency call had been received at just gone ten o'clock that morning reporting that a young woman had been stabbed to death sometime during the night. The local superintendent had called in the NBCI shortly after arriving and inspecting the scene – this kind of murder was their territory not his. He'd followed procedure and had summoned a local doctor to pronounce death and take initial room and body temperatures, then left the scene alone.

Plunkett swung round at the sound of the door creaking open. With tired eyes McEvoy gazed out at his two colleagues, his mouth an angry line punctuated by the cigarette. He plucked the plastic stick from his lips and held it cupped in his right hand as if sheltering the tip from a wind. With his left hand he rubbed his short and thinning hair. Bought before he'd recently lost two stone in weight, his dark grey suit hung off his shoulders over a crumpled, light blue shirt and loosely knotted tie.

'Jesus,' McEvoy muttered to himself. 'It looks like the poor girl's been sacrificed. Some sick bastard placed a sword in her mouth and then rammed it through the back of her head. I've never seen anything like it. It's … It's …' he struggled to find the right word. He shook his head in disgust and stared out of the window, pausing before continuing. 'She was just a child; a teenager.'

He took a couple of steps away from the door, his voice taking a softer lilt. 'Here, you'd better take a look, see what kind of monster we're dealing with. You know the score – keep to the entrance and don't touch anything – we don't want to mess things up for the crime scene people. Have they arrived yet?'

'I saw them pull up in the yard a couple of minutes ago,' Plunkett replied, stepping forward to peer through the bedroom door. 'They should be up shortly.'

Hannah Fallon could hear Colm McEvoy listing instructions as he descended the flight of stairs above her. They turned the corner.

'Ah, Hannah.' McEvoy nodded a greeting, drawing to a halt, waiting for her to join them on the landing.

'Colm. Barney.' In her late thirties and neither thin nor fat she was wearing black trousers and shoes, a chocolate brown, long-sleeved top, and no jewellery or make-up. Long, curly, auburn hair covered her shoulders. She was carrying a broad, brown leather case and a pair of stepping plates. 'How's it going so far?' she asked.

'Badly,' McEvoy stated flatly. 'She's on the next floor up, through the corridor on the left.'

Hannah nodded, climbing the rest of the steps in silence. 'How's Gemma?' she asked as she reached them.

'She's okay,' McEvoy replied, the edge leaving his voice. 'Well, as okay as she could be, I guess. She's 12 this week. I've no idea what you get a 12-year-old. Maggie always looked after that kind of thing, y'know. I'll find something.'

'And you?'

'I've been better,' McEvoy conceded. Everything was better when Maggie was alive, he thought, before the cancer ate her from the inside out and slowly drained of her life, stealing her away from him and his daughter. 'I don't imagine this case is going to help much.' His voice changed timbre, shifting back to business. 'It's not good up there, Hannah. The sick bastard pushed a sword through her head.'

'It's never good.' Her face creased with concern. 'You haven't contaminated the crime scene have you?'

'We just stood in the doorway,' McEvoy tried to reassure. 'It'd already been disturbed by the person who found the body, the first guard to arrive, the local doctor, and God knows who else. This is the main stairwell. Several people have used it already today going to and from bedrooms.'

'Right, okay, well this will be the route of access to the crime scene,' Hannah said, her voice betraying her annoyance. 'I'll need the other doors sealed off. We're going to need to set up at least three cordons – an inner one sealing the room, a middle one sealing the building, and an outer one sealing the whole site. Can you organise the outer one if I do the inner two?'

'No problem. I'll get someone on it right away.'

'And do you know if the building's empty?'

'I'm not sure. As far as I know. We'll check it out.'

'Don't worry, I'll get Chloe to do it,' Hannah said referring to one of her assistants. 'She'll know what to look for. I don't want some idiot messing up potential evidence. Not that I'm calling you …' she trailed off. 'You know what I mean.'

'Yeah, I know,' McEvoy said, aware that he shouldn't have entered the bedroom.

'While I'm thinking about it,' Hannah continued, 'if there're bedrooms in the other buildings they're also going to need sealing off. If the killer was staying here he'll have taken evidence with him – blood, hairs, whatever. I'm also going to need fingerprint and DNA samples from everyone staying and working here last night.'

'Consider it done,' McEvoy promised. 'We're trying to round everybody up and we should start interviewing them shortly. I'd better get down there. Give me a call if you find anything significant, okay.'

'You'll be the first to know.' Hannah slipped past them and started to climb the next flight listening to them descend, McEvoy continuing to give Plunkett instructions.

McEvoy shook hands with Superintendent Peter O'Reilly, whose ruddy and poorly shaved face and ruffled, grey hair, marked him out as a man who enjoyed a drink or two. He was wearing a well-worn uniform that had last seen an iron the day it was tailored.

'Peter,' McEvoy stated, stepping back slightly to make space for a round-faced man in his late twenties, his hair shaved close to his head. 'You keeping well?'

'As well as can be expected,' O'Reilly replied with a Cork accent.

'This is Detective Sergeant John Joyce. John, Superintendent Peter O'Reilly.'

The two men shook hands.

'Myself and Peter go way back,' McEvoy explained. 'John's our bright young thing. Has a doctorate from Trinity in sociology, which sharpened the mind but didn't exactly provide a career path, if you know what I mean.' He wasn't really convinced that Joyce had entered the gardai for the right reasons, but there was no denying he was good at the job. 'I want you to work together on the questionnaires. We need blanket coverage for at least a couple of miles, maybe further given how isolated this place is. We'll also need any CCTV footage for last night reviewed.'

'You think it was a local?' O'Reilly asked, doubt in his voice.

'I was going to ask you the same question. You know of any likely candidates?'

'Only murder we've had recently was a domestic in Enniskerry. Banker killed his wife for having an affair with his brother. We have the usual cranks and petty criminals, but nobody fits the profile for this.'

'That figures. Well, whoever did this had to get in and out, and someone must have seen him. We need to know if anyone saw any strangers or anybody acting suspiciously.'

'The road out the back goes up onto the top of the mountains and then drops down into Dublin,' O'Reilly explained. 'There's not a house on it for miles. He could have easily gone that way in the dead of night and not have been noticed.'

6

'He had to park up somewhere though,' McEvoy countered. 'Someone driving around might have seen something. Just do the best you can. If you get no joy through the questionnaires organise a search of the moorland, see if we can find any of her personal effects. The killer stripped the room clean; he must have dumped them somewhere.'

McEvoy sat across the desk from Janine Smyth, the centre's director. She was a small, wiry woman with a pinched face that was painted with too much make-up – pale foundation, rouge blusher, thick black mascara, pale green eye shadow, painted eyebrows, and dark red lipstick. Her hair was cropped short and highlighted blond. She wore a dark green trouser suit over a white blouse. An enormous silver brooch, in an abstract design and studded with painted stones was pinned above her left breast. She kept glancing out the window up at the imposing barracks that formed the west side of the centre's quad, clearly unhappy that the space had been invaded by the police.

McEvoy followed her gaze. The barracks were three storeys high and 60 metres long. At either end stood a four-storey tower, slightly wider than the main frontage, so that building would look like a giant letter I if seen from above. Behind the building was the derelict wall of a similar building and a row of trees screening the bog and gorse beyond.

The barracks had been built by the British. Completed in 1806, it was one of a set of strongholds strung out along a military road that snaked across the Wicklow Mountains. It had been constructed to keep the rebel Irish in line, though it was defunct almost as soon as it was built following the defeat of France, Ireland's ally, and the end of the Napoleonic wars in 1815. From 1858 until 1940, it had been St Kevin's Reformatory School, an isolated site in which to transform orphans and problem children into model citizens. After the Second World War it had been used until 1950 by the Irish Red Cross as a refugee centre for starving German and Polish children, before falling into dereliction. The peace centre had started to restore the building in the mid-1970s. More a prison than a place for children, McEvoy reflected. Then again, for nearly 100 years, it had been a prison for children.

He turned his attention to the office walls, which were covered in framed photos of Ms Smyth standing next to leading politicians from all persuasions, drawn from across Northern Ireland, the Republic, the UK, and United States. Ian Paisley, Bill Clinton, Tony Blair, Bertie Ahern, John Hume, David Trimble, Gerry Adams, and others beamed down at him. Finally he broke the silence. 'You put through a call at just after ten this morning, was it you that found the body?'

'No,' Ms Smyth said tersely in a Northern accent, turning to face him, clearly unhappy that the centre had been taken over by the guards. 'It was Andy. He was cleaning the rooms. He thought hers was empty so he let himself in. He got a hell of a shock.'

'He came to you?'

'He rang me using an internal phone. I went over to check it out, then I rang you.'

'Did you know the girl?'

'No. She was part of the group staying here.'

'So you don't know who she was?' McEvoy pressed.

'Laura. The group said she was called Laura. I hadn't met her.' She softened her voice. 'I can't believe this happened here. People come here to feel safe.'

'Do you have an idea who might have killed her?' McEvoy asked, failing to warm to her, trying to keep the interview on track.

'No.' Her voice hardened again. 'As I said, I didn't know her and I didn't know the group.'

'And the group were?' McEvoy prompted.

'Some homeless kids from Dublin. The Dublin Homeless Co-operative brings a group out every year. They do workshops and try to help them out. It's so isolated up here they can't really disappear – it's four miles to the nearest village.'

'And do you have details about the group? The names of those staying here? We're going to have to try and round up those that have scarpered.'

'All we have are their first names and what rooms they were allocated to. The book is in the reception area. Even if I did have details, I'm afraid I couldn't give them to you; they're confidential.' Janine Smyth saw McEvoy's face harden slightly and offered an explanation before being prompted. 'We're a peace and reconciliation centre, Superintendent. People come here to discuss things; to work through problems. We offer them an anonymous space in which to do that – no names, no cameras. We've had everyone through here, paramilitaries, politicians, ex-prisoners, you name it.'

McEvoy leaned forward slightly in his chair. 'Look, Ms Smyth, with all due respect, I don't care who you've had through here or what you've promised them. If it doesn't look like the murderer is part of the homeless party or your staff we're going to have to look at who's stayed here previously. That will mean looking through your records.'

'I've told you, they're confidential,' Smyth said firmly.

'Don't worry, I'll get a search warrant if necessary,' McEvoy threatened. 'But I *am* going to catch this killer. The job will be a lot easier if you work with us rather than putting obstacles in our way.'

'Any obstacle is there for good reason, Superintendent. Confidentiality is part of the deal; part of the peace process.'

McEvoy sighed audibly. 'Look, I know you do great work here, but let's try and get a little perspective, shall we? The girl's murder takes priority over everything, including the peace process. And don't give me any "we have friends in high places" nonsense either.' He gestured at the walls. 'Nobody's going to prioritise ex-prisoners over the murder of a young girl.'

The centre's director stared back at him coldly, but said nothing.

McEvoy stood up and headed for the door. He turned at the entrance. 'I'm going to need a list of all the staff working here, with those here between six last night and ten this morning highlighted. One of my colleagues will come and collect it shortly. I'd appreciate your co-operation.'

Barney Plunkett stood in the reception area of the low building bordering the east part of the square. He was talking to a tall, thin woman in her late twenties, with long, dark hair, who was clearly distressed.

McEvoy exited an office a couple of yards down the corridor and made his way to them. 'Sorry to interrupt, Barney. Can I have a word?' He moved over to one side.

'Just give me a minute,' Plunkett said to the woman apologetically. He followed McEvoy.

'The director's going to be a pain to deal with,' McEvoy started. 'She's more concerned with her centre and the peace process than this murder.' He shook his head in frustration. 'I'm going to need to talk to the person who found the body.'

'He's in an office just here,' Plunkett pointed to a door two down from the director's. 'Kelly's with him.'

'Okay, good. Who's your one?' he nodded towards the woman Plunkett had been talking to.

'Angie Jenkins. She's from the DHC. She was in charge of the group. She says the girl's name was Laura. She doesn't seem to know much about her except she was from England and that she kept herself to herself. She'd been on the street a few months. She thinks she used to hit the bottle rather than drugs. Might have done a bit of on-street prostitution, but that's only speculation. She thinks she was about 19 or 20.'

'Okay, good. See if you can find someone who knew her a bit better.' His mobile phone rang and he held up a hand of apology. 'McEvoy.'

'What's your verdict, Colm?' Detective Chief Superintendent Tony Bishop asked without introduction.

'Just give me a second, Sir.'

McEvoy headed back to the reception and left the building. A garda car coasted into the car park, an unhappy looking teenager sitting in the back seat; one of the homeless kids who'd fled after the discovery of Laura's body.

McEvoy spoke into the phone again. 'Sorry about that – too many people around. The victim's a young girl who was forced to swallow a sword. No obvious sign of a struggle or sexual assault, but we can't be sure until the pathologist's had a look. It looks like it was some kind of sacrifice. The crime scene people are in there now, we're interviewing staff and guests.'

'Any obvious line of enquiry?'

McEvoy imagined Bishop pacing his office, nervously rubbing his short red hair. 'Not yet,' he replied evenly. 'Looks like he was careful.'

'He'll have made a mistake. They always do. Just make sure you find it. You probably already know,' he said changing tack, 'but the press have found out about the killing. Nobody's to talk to them until I say so, okay? We're just going to issue a holding statement for now. Peter O'Reilly, can deliver it. It can be his little moment of fame,' he added dismissively.

'I'll let him know.' McEvoy shook his head at Bishop's spitefulness. 'Any news on Elaine Jones?' he asked, referring to the state pathologist.

'Hannah Fallon's already been on. Hopefully she'll be out to you in the next hour or so. She's been tied up with a house fire. Two young kids died.'

'Jesus,' McEvoy said, exhaling. 'What ...' he stopped, realising that Bishop had ended the call. He pocketed the phone and entered the building again. The reception area was empty. He knocked once on the office door and entered without waiting for an answer. A man was sitting with his back to him, facing Kelly Stringer. Behind her a window provided a view down the Glencree valley to the conical peak of the Sugar Loaf.

Stringer was dressed in a plain white blouse, covered by a grey cardigan with a ruffled collar that extended down along the buttons, a royal blue, knee length skirt and black, flat shoes. Her dark brown hair was pulled into a tight plait and a pale blue silk scarf was wrapped round her neck. The look made her appear nearer 40 than 28.

McEvoy nodded a greeting, rounded the man and stood next to her, gazing down at the seated figure.

The man's brown hair was long, greasy and uncombed, his face unshaved and scarred with acne. He wore a pale grey The Strokes t-shirt over a long-sleeved black top, blue jeans, and dirty white running shoes.

'Sorry to interrupt,' McEvoy said, breaking the silence. 'My name's Detective Superintendent Colm McEvoy. I'm in charge of the investigation into the young woman's death. You're Andy?'

The man nodded, briefly holding McEvoy's eyes before lowering his own.

'I know you probably don't feel like answering any more questions, Andy, but I need to ask you a few. Okay?'

The man shrugged, acknowledging that he didn't really have a choice.

'You found the body this morning?' McEvoy asked.

'I was on cleaning duty,' Andy replied in an American accent. 'I thought the room was empty so I let myself in.' He paused. 'I practically jumped out of my skin. She was just lying there, the sword pinning her to the bed,' he said flatly, shaking his head, trying to dislodge the memory.

'Did you enter the room at all?'

'No, no.' He raised his hands to emphasise the point. 'I got the hell out of there and called Janine from the phone in the stairwell.'

'So you didn't touch anything or take anything from the room?'

'No.'

'And did you know the girl at all?'

'I'd seen her around, y'know, in the last couple of days. She was with the group, but I hadn't spoken with her. She seemed kind of withdrawn.'

'So this morning was the first time you'd been in her room since she arrived?'

'Yeah. We only clean the rooms on the days that people leave.' Andy looked up, alarmed. 'You don't think I did it, do you?'

'I don't know, Andy. Did you?' McEvoy asked, returning the question, his eyebrows raised.

'No, of course I didn't!' the American protested, his body language becoming defensive. 'I didn't even know her.'

'So do you have any idea who might have killed her or why?'

'No! It was as if she'd swallowed the sword, y'know,' he muttered, his eyes glazing over. 'Just … swallowed it.'

McEvoy re-read the note through the clear evidence bag, aware that his blood pressure was rising. It had been found nestling at the bottom of the brown shoulder-bag left in Laura's room.

The Rules
Chapter One M: Choosing a victim R

"The vast majority of killers know their victims. A select few choose to kill people of whom they had no previous knowledge; they simply had the right profile and were in the wrong place at the wrong time. Such killers are much more difficult to identify because there is seemingly no motive, and no means to link them to the victim beyond the crime."

1a. Choose a victim at random.

1b. Have no prior interaction with the victim before the kill. They should simply be chosen because they were in the right place at the right time.

1c. Take no account of age, sex, looks or any other characteristic in selection.

Master rule: Patterns provide psychological purchase. Avoid patterns.

'He's breaking one of his own rules – a so-called master rule,' he observed bitterly. There was little doubt in McEvoy's mind that the killer was male. All the criminal statistics showed that women rarely took another life except for revenge or self-defence and even then they tended to do it simply – either a frenzied attack, usually provoked, or a straightforward slaying such as poisoning. They didn't undertake such an elaborately crafted murder as Laura's death.

'Leaving the body and the note gives us psychological purchase. He killed her the way he did to make a point – that he's in control; that he's thought it all through. He thinks he can afford to toy with us because he won't be caught,' he said, anger and frustration in his voice.

'You think it's genuine?' Hannah asked sceptically. 'The killer didn't just leave it to deflect us? Make us think this is about something else?'

'I think it's unlikely,' McEvoy answered. 'You've seen how well planned her murder was. The way she was killed, how the body was prepared, how clean he left the room. If he simply wanted her dead, he would have killed her and then got the hell out of here. This is the genuine article, not some elaborate attempt at deflection. And he's probably followed his rules. She's a random victim.'

McEvoy looked out the window and down the valley. 'Whoever killed her almost certainly doesn't work here and probably wasn't staying here either. We'll follow procedure to make sure we're not being double-bluffed, but we also need to make sure everyone is asked about seeing strangers or anything unusual. We'll also need to check past employees and guests. He obviously felt comfortable killing here.'

'There'll be something from forensics,' Hannah offered. 'He'll have left something behind, impossible not to, even if he was suited up and took precautions.'

'Yeah, but how many different people have used that room in the last year?' McEvoy observed. 'You'll probably end up with samples from tens of people. Perhaps 30 or more. Who knows? And what if we've got nothing to match it against? There'll have to be something else to put someone in the frame. Unless he has a prior conviction, forensics are just going to cement the case if we catch the bastard. No offence, Hannah.'

'None taken. We know the limits.'

'Do you have any ideas about the quote?' McEvoy asked, changing tack. 'His own or from something?'

'Easiest thing to do is type it into Google and see if anything pops up,' she suggested. 'Do you think it's important?'

'I've no idea,' McEvoy stated. 'How about this M and R business?' he asked, pointing to the header. 'Chapter One M.'

Fallon shook her head and they stood in silence for a moment reflecting on the note.

As far as McEvoy was concerned it was big trouble. Whoever had committed the murder had crafted the note in advance of the killing. He'd spent time planning it, thinking it through, creating his *modus operandi*.

'When do you think he's going to strike again?' Fallon asked, breaking the quiet. 'Assuming he does strike again.'

'He'll strike if we don't catch him,' McEvoy predicted, certainty in his voice. 'Maybe in a couple of days, maybe a year or longer. Impossible to predict. The only thing we can do is get on with the case and hope we catch the bastard before it happens again.'

McEvoy sat down opposite a short, thickset man who looked to be in his late thirties. His brown hair was thinning on top and he had two-day stubble. His eyes were red, under which sat two dark crescents.

'I'm Detective Superintendent Colm McEvoy. I'm in charge of the case …'

'Dermot Brady,' the man interrupted. 'I'm an outreach worker at the North Quays drop-in centre.' His voice was a flat version of upbeat, as if trying to contain a more sunny personality. 'We thought this would be a good change of scene for them. Instead this happens.' He threw his arms out wide to make his point.

'I guess things don't always turn out as planned,' McEvoy replied. 'Certainly not for Laura. How well did you know her?'

'Not very,' Brady answered frankly. 'I don't think anybody really knew her. She kept herself to herself. You know the kind?' He didn't wait for McEvoy to reply. 'She only used to come into the centre to get something to eat or to keep warm. She often never said a word and she always tried to sit on her own. For a while she started to come with a dog, but after a few weeks it disappeared. I was surprised when she came out on the trip. We all were. She's never turned up to any of our other events.'

'She didn't seem close to anybody?' McEvoy asked. He was warming to Brady. He seemed to have a bit of verve about him.

'Not really, no. The only person she seemed to talk to was Karen, but she rarely dropped in. She was nearly always on her own.'

'Is Karen here?' McEvoy leant forward in his seat. 'Did she come on the trip?'

'Karen! God, she wouldn't be caught dead on a trip like this. No, Karen tends to avoid us do-gooders. She prefers to fend for herself. She lives in a squat off the North Circular Road. Scrounges off her fellow squatters and occasionally does a bit of street work. She's an addict – heroin mostly, but anything she can get her hands she'll take. The only time we see her is if she's really down on her luck – she comes in begging.'

'That how Laura survived? Bit of prostitution?'

'I don't know.' Brady shrugged theatrically. 'I never saw her out soliciting when we did the late-night rounds, but that doesn't mean it was off-limits. She didn't seem the type though; too withdrawn; too closed in on herself.'

'How about drugs?'

'I think it was just alcohol. Mainly cheap vodka. It deadens the pain and cold. She also smoked. Marlboro Lights if she could afford them, roll-ups if she couldn't.'

'Do you have any idea where she was from? Or what she was running from?'

'I'd say Liverpool,' Brady said, imitating a Scouse accent. 'Maybe not the city, but nearby. She never spoke about her past though. Never spoke about anything, to be honest. I don't know why she left the place she did or how she got to Dublin.'

'How long has she been going to the drop-in centre?'

'About a year, maybe.' Brady pulled a face of indecision. 'Definitely over nine months.'

'What about accommodation?' McEvoy asked, reclining back in his seat. 'She sleep rough or did she use the hostels or have some other arrangement?'

'I'd say she mostly slept rough,' Brady hazarded. 'She didn't seem the kind for the hostels. Probably had some little hideaway on a bit of wasteland or in a derelict building. We never saw her on our patrols round the streets.'

'Would anyone know?'

'I doubt it. Perhaps Karen. She really did keep herself to herself, Superintendent.'

'But she came on this trip,' McEvoy said, contradicting Brady's assertion.

'As I said, we were all shocked. She turned up at the bus a few minutes before we set off. We were hoping she'd come out of her shell a bit. Maybe turned a corner; decided to get her life back into some kind of order.'

'And how was she?' McEvoy prompted.

'The same really to be honest.' Brady leant back in his chair, relaxing a little. 'She was always on the margins. She never contributed to the discussion. There's always one or two like that. They seem to drift around in their own little worlds.'

'How about last night? When did you last see her?'

'I don't know.' He shrugged. 'Maybe ten o'clock. We had a get together in the den. It's in the building the centre's staff stay in. It was a cash bar for cans of beer and bottles of wine. They had an allowance of ten euros each and whatever they'd brought themselves.' He noticed McEvoy arch his eyebrows in question. 'They wouldn't come if they were going to be strictly policed,' he explained. 'That's why some of them are on the street. Treating them like children won't help. Anyway, she sat on her own in the far corner with a bottle of wine. A few of the lads tried to talk to her but she just blanked them.'

'Do you know what time she left the den?'

'I don't know.' Brady shrugged and splayed his hands. 'She left earlier than the others, I know that. I'd say shortly after I last saw her. Someone must have seen her leave. She would have had to walk the length of the room to get out.'

'And you didn't see her after that?'

'No. I hung around until about half-one to see the last of them out and up to the dorms, then I went to bed myself. I was sharing a room with Tom, one of the other leaders.'

'And do you have any idea who might have killed her? Maybe somebody from your group?'

'No.' Brady shook his head to reinforce his answer. 'Look, the kids we brought out here are not exactly saints, but I don't have any of them pegged as murderers.' Brady squirmed nervously in his seat and leaned forward. 'Look, Superintendent, I'm going to come clean, okay.'

McEvoy started to sit up in his chair.

'I've done time.' The warmth and theatre of his conversation had disappeared. 'Eight years in Mountjoy, out in five. If I don't tell you now, it'll only come back on me later. I know how these things work. I didn't kill that girl. I swear I didn't. I'll take whatever test you want me to. I've paid my debt and I continue to pay it. Every day. That's why I help out at the drop-in centre. I'm serving my community; trying to help others.'

'What did you do time for?' McEvoy asked, keeping his voice neutral. Dermot Brady had suddenly become a lot more interesting.

'Manslaughter,' Brady said matter-of-fact. 'Hit and run when I was blind drunk. Killed a small boy and his mother. He was five, she was 28. I was 23 at the time. I was young and stupid and I got what I deserved. Got less than I deserved. It's haunted me ever since.'

'And have you been in trouble since you got out?' McEvoy asked, thinking that if he'd killed once, he could do it again. Just because he was drunk it didn't mean it hadn't been deliberate.

'No, no. I've kept my nose clean. I don't drink, I don't drive, I go to church every week, and I try and lead an honest life. The only time I come into contact with the guards is when I'm trying to help out one of my homeless friends.'

'You were right to tell us now, Dermot. Better to do this informally rather than under caution. One last thing. Do you have a last name for her?'

'No. She never said. She just used the name Laura.'

'Okay, thanks, I think we can wrap this up for now,' McEvoy said calmly, keeping his thoughts from his voice and expression. Brady might have killed in the past, but he couldn't see him as Laura's killer. The man had repentant do-gooder written all over him. That or he was a hell of an actor.

The imposing black gates to the centre opened and the driver eased his way through. A hustle of journalists and cameramen descended on the car.

'Keep driving,' McEvoy ordered. They were like a pack of vultures feeding on other people's misery, he reflected. They'd pick apart Laura more thoroughly than the pathologist.

The car sped up slightly, rising up the driveway past the small church, and swung right onto the narrow road that wound its way down the valley to Enniskerry. Fifty yards later it stopped at an entranceway.

McEvoy exited the car, followed by Hannah Fallon and Barney Plunkett. He showed his card to the local guard. 'Nobody's to follow us in, okay.'

'Sir.' The man nodded in affirmation.

He pushed open a small gate and hurried up the path. 'You know anything about this place?' he asked.

'Came here when I was a kid,' Hannah replied. 'It's where German servicemen who died in Irish territory during the first and second world wars are buried.'

The path led into an old quarry. The floor had been flattened and laid out across its surface were three beds of heather – small plaques laid flat on the soil indicated who was buried beneath. Six sets of low, double stone crosses were scattered across the beds. To one side there was a small grotto where four guards stood chatting.

'Detective Superintendent McEvoy,' McEvoy announced. 'Where am I meant to be looking?'

One of the guards stepped forward. 'They're over there, Sir,' he said, pointing to the nearest set of double crosses.

Stuck on the top of the left-hand cross was a business card. McEvoy scanned the other sets. One cross of each of the six pairs sported a card.

Plunkett leant forwards, careful not to step out onto the heather. '*The Rule Book*,' he read out. 'A self-help guide for would-be serial killers. In all good book shops soon. There's a picture of a bird as well. Looks like a crow or a raven at a guess.'

'The bastard's trying to taunt us,' McEvoy stated flatly. 'We have chapter one. You think there are six more to follow?' he speculated, pointing at the crosses.

'Possibly' Hannah replied, shrugging. 'Are they all the same?'

Plunkett edged his way along the path, leaning out to each set of crosses. 'Yeah.'

'Jesus,' McEvoy muttered. 'You'd better get a team up here, Hannah, see if they can find anything useful.'

The man held the filthy blouse aloft then buried his face in its thin cotton, drawing in Laura's pungent, musky body odour and the debris of Dublin's city streets. Killing her had been mechanical; clinical. She had put up no resistance – no fight, no screams, no drama. She had simply followed his instructions, undressing passively and lying on the bed.

He removed the blouse from his face and threw it onto the open fire recalling her final moments. She had held her arms tight to her side and opened her mouth wide, staring through him rather than at him. She had been his mirror, displaying as much emotion as he himself had felt. It was as if she had already departed to another world and he was acting outside of himself, his anger centred and benign; both of them in a different space and time.

The sword had been slightly too wide and its weight difficult to balance above her. He'd nodded at her once, she'd blinked – the first sign that she'd noticed him and what was happening – and he'd thrust the sword down, pulling hard on the hilt, ramming it through her neck, the mattress, and into the floorboard below. Her spine had severed easily, the sword widening her grimace, her eyes bulging with reflexive shock, her limbs involuntarily jerking.

He was surprised at how little blood there had been. Except for the soaking of the sheets and the pools snaking across the floorboards, there had been very little; just the occasional spray across her face and upper torso, a little onto the walls. He had cleaned up carefully after himself, gently wiping down and cleansing her body, taking his time, doing a thorough job. There had been no elation or euphoria, no sorrow or regrets; no anything.

He pulled her dirty white bra from a plastic bag and held it aloft, gazing at the worn and frayed lace frill, recalling her slight breasts and rosebud nipples. He drew the bra to his face and savoured the smell of fear and self-loathing. He smiled to himself and lowered it slowly onto the open fire, watching raptly as the lace twisted and shrank to black wisps as it encountered the flames.

The dining hall had been re-organised into an incident room. On one side of the room three computers had been set up along a wall, each staffed by a guard. Above them, tacked to the wall were two patchwork quilts, each small panel stating a message of peace and hope. On the opposite wall was a row of old, wooden tables, file boxes stacked on top. On the table nearest the door were two flasks, a stack of polystyrene cups, and a basket of biscuits.

A scattering of orange plastic chairs occupied the middle of the hall. Hannah Fallon and Fay Butler, the DS in charge of the room, were sitting together chatting quietly; John Joyce, Peter O'Reilly and Kenny Johns were standing nearby, lost in their own thoughts, swirling the coffee in their cups.

At the far end of the room a map of the area had been taped to the wall, a whiteboard standing nearby. McEvoy was standing in front of the map, mentally tracing the different ways the killer could have got to and from the centre.

Barney Plunkett entered the room and headed for the refreshments table. He pressed the top of a flask, squirting hot coffee into his cup and grabbed a couple of biscuits.

Sensing that the team was now complete, McEvoy turned to face the others. 'Right okay, let's make a start,' he announced more harshly than he intended.

The assembled team finished off their sentences, the four men pulling up chairs and sitting down.

'We need to review where we're at,' he instructed, 'swap notes and make a plan of action. I want to catch this bastard, hopefully before he can kill again. That poor girl was sacrificed. I ...' McEvoy hesitated, 'well words can't describe ... let's just say that I haven't seen anything like it in 20 years and I never want to see it again. So, what have people got? Hannah, how about we start with you?'

Hannah brushed her auburn hair off her face and glanced round at the others. 'We're still processing the scene. I won't have anything concrete until we've run the tests in the lab. We're still waiting for Elaine Jones to arrive, so nothing on the body I'm afraid. It looks like he was very careful. Probably wore gloves, hairnet, whatever. There are no footprints, despite the amount of blood, just smears. It's as if he was wearing socks over his shoes, though that's just a guess. We're also going to get a lot of noise from previous occupants; God knows how many people have slept in the room in the past couple of years. We've only just started work on the cemetery.'

McEvoy looked up from scribbling a note on a pad. 'Any questions?'

'Was he suited up before or after the killing?' Fay Butler asked. In her mid-forties, with dyed blonde hair cut in a bob, she was wearing a well-cut, dark blue trouser suit. A large, plain silver cross hung round her neck, resting on top of a round-necked, cream top. 'If it was before, he would've probably had to have made his way to the room already suited up – difficult to change while he's assaulting her. That or he'd have had to restrain her, then change; but then he'd have risked leaving traces in any struggle before she was subdued.'

'It doesn't look like she was physically restrained,' Hannah replied. 'We'll have to wait for Elaine Jones for confirmation, but that's my assessment. It might be that he broke in first; then got changed while he waited for her to return,' she speculated.

'In which case,' McEvoy said, 'that would mean the murder was probably committed some time shortly after Laura returned from the drinking session. What time did people go down to the den? We need to know if anyone was spotted entering the building around that time.'

'I don't think anyone was mentioned in the interviews,' Kenny Johns replied. 'I'll re-check the statements.'

'How about the room?' McEvoy asked. 'Any sign that it had been broken into?'

'No,' Hannah replied, 'but by the look of the door and the lock it wouldn't have been difficult to get in undetected – hardly Fort Knox.'

'Right, okay,' McEvoy said slowly, 'any more questions for Hannah?'

The room stayed silent.

'Kenny, how about the interviews?'

Johns adjusted his tie and tugged a shirt sleeve, his hand staying in place to play with his cufflink as he started to speak. 'We have preliminary statements from all of the centre's staff and the homeless group. We're still working on cross-checking their stories and eliminating people, but just about everyone seems to have an alibi – mainly that they were sharing rooms. I have a couple of the team checking on previous convictions, but my guess is that it's all going to be stuff like burglary or drugs, maybe drunk and disorderly, not violent crimes. There's a few shifty characters okay, and we need to re-check a few things, but I get the sense our man isn't amongst them.'

'How about the missing five?' Plunkett asked.

'We're still waiting for them to be tracked down,' Johns replied. 'Once they are, they're top of our priority list.'

'Anyone obviously hiding anything?' John Joyce asked.

'Just about all the homeless group – dealing with the guards is well down their things-to-do list. Let's just say they kept things to a minimum.'

'Did any of them claim to be friends with the victim?' McEvoy asked.

'Not that I'm aware,' Johns said. 'I'll ask round the team but anyone I spoke to said she was a loner. She kept herself to herself; hardly said a word to anyone. I got the impression they didn't really know how to react. They were sorry that she was dead, but they're not really in a position to grieve; they didn't really know her. Plus they have their own problems and demons to worry about.'

'If she hadn't been killed here,' Joyce stated, 'no one would have known she was dead.'

'And we don't know who she is yet either,' Butler added. 'All we have is the body and a first name. Laura.'

'We know a young life was taken too early and that's enough,' McEvoy said firmly. 'Did no one hear anything? The sound of a struggle? The thud of the sword hitting the floor? Jesus, that must have made one hell of a noise.'

'Nothing other than a few of the lads having a drunken party in one of the rooms,' Johns replied. 'If your man was waiting for her to return then, as you say, there was probably no one around to hear the killing.'

'We can't take it that he broke in first for granted,' McEvoy responded. 'But if no one heard the sword then it's more probable that she was killed after she left the den but before the others did.'

'Unless they mistook it for a slamming door,' Plunkett offered.

'Which is another possibility,' McEvoy conceded. 'We need to try and get an approximate time of death from the body. Anything else from the interviews?'

'I don't think so,' Kenny replied.

'Okay, tell the centre staff and DHC they're free to go, but to leave contact details. Explain to the DHC that we're releasing the homeless kids into their care. Ask them to try and set up hostel accommodation or something. We don't want them scattering to the four winds. Peter, John, how are the questionnaires coming on?'

'I've got 40 officers out,' Peter O'Reilly responded. 'Thirty doing the door-to-door, ten scouting round the site looking for anything he might have dumped – a couple of them picked up the business cards. I'm looking after the door-to-door, Detective Sergeant Joyce the search work. We're surveying every property within a five-mile radius. We've not got too much so far. Sightings of strangers, but then the place is full of strangers given the number of tourists and people coming into the mountains to walk.

'News is filtering out though, and we're starting to get asked questions. And the rumour mill's already at work. One woman had heard that a girl had been killed as part of a satanic ritual; that those staying here had drunk her blood while calling forth the devil. I think we're gonna need to nip that in the bud, it's only going to be counter-productive down the line.'

'Fair comment,' McEvoy responded, 'though it's not far off the mark. A sword through the head and a killer on the loose is hardly going to reassure the public. Anyone got anything else?' He paused before continuing. 'Okay then, now we're up-to-date, let's work on what we've got.'

He moved to the whiteboard, picked up a marker and turned back to face the small group. 'First, this was carefully planned. The killer knew what he was doing and he knew his way around. Either he was familiar with the place or he made himself familiar. He turned to the whiteboard and spoke as he wrote, '"1. Past guests. Former employees. Strangers."' He swung back round again. 'We need a full list of everyone who stayed or worked here in the last five years and descriptions of any strangers.

26

'Second, our killer was accomplished. He had composure. He didn't lose his temper or panic. He killed Laura in cold blood then arranged her body and cleaned the room. That doesn't sound like a first-time killer to me.' He turned back to the board. '"2. Convicted or suspected killers. Violent offenders. Sexual assault." We're going to need a list of all freed murderers and suspected killers in the last 20 or 30 years. See if any names tally with the guest lists. Given the number of ex-prisoners and paramilitaries that have passed through this place there's bound to be a few. They all need to be checked out and eliminated.'

'Jesus,' Plunkett muttered, acknowledging the size of the task.

'Third, he had to get to and from here,' McEvoy continued, ignoring the interruption. 'The centre's miles from anywhere so the chances are he didn't walk. That, or he's still here, and I doubt that. "3. Vehicle." We need to identify all vehicles that have been parked near to or in the centre's car park over the past two weeks.

'Fourth, we have some obvious pieces of evidence. "4. Material evidence – sword." That sword had to come from somewhere. It's either been purchased, stolen or it's a family heirloom. "– note." We need to trace the quote. Also, see if he's copying the rules from some other source. "– business cards." Did he make them himself, or did he get them printed? If they were printed, then where?

'Finally, the victim. Why did he choose her? Was it just a random selection or was there more to it than that? Was he after a young woman? Did he know her? We need to piece her life together – who she was, who her friends were, who she knew. "5. Victim."'

He placed down the marker and took a couple of steps back. 'Anyone got anything to add to that?'

'The stuff he cleared out of the room,' Butler suggested. 'Her belongings and his clothes, he must have disposed of them somewhere.'

'"6. Crime scene artefacts." Good point. Anyone else?'

The group remained silent, staring at the whiteboard, thinking through the work that needed to be done.

Professor Elaine Jones pushed open the door onto the corridor and headed for the victim's room. Her shoulder-length grey hair was pulled tight into a short ponytail, her eyes framed by crow's feet, her bright red lips by laughter lines. The bag she carried seemed half her size.

A young, tall, thin, bald-headed man with sunken cheeks pushed open the corridor door and lurched after her.

Hannah Fallon stepped from the room, a grim look on her face.

'What a day!' Elaine breezed, starting to pull protective clothing from her bag. 'First two dead children, now this. They'd been sprayed with lighter fuel before the house was set on fire. Can you believe that?' She looked up, grimacing. 'They didn't stand a chance.'

'I believe anything at this stage,' Fallon replied. 'And this'll be another one to add to your collection. The poor girl was made to swallow a sword.'

'What, like down the throat?'

'No, no, straight out the back of her skull.' Fallon did a thrusting motion past her head to illustrate. 'She's laid out like a sacrifice.'

'Jesus. Three sacrifices in one day.' The pathologist shook her head and tugged on a glove. 'The devil's been busy.'

'Well, if the note's anything to go by, it's the first in a sequence.'

'And I was hoping for a holiday,' Professor Jones said, keeping her voice buoyant and rolling her eyes. She wanted the mood serious but light. Death was a sombre, depressing affair and she found quips and playful teasing the best way to combat the sober funk that could envelop an investigating team. 'How you getting on, Igor?'

Her assistant, Billy Keane, started to pull on his protective suit. 'Not a bother,' he replied. 'I'll be ready when you are.'

'How's the room?' the pathologist asked Fallon.

'We've cleaned a pathway over to her for you. The killer has washed the room down and bathed the body. Once you're done and the body's removed we'll finish up.' She looked at her watch. 'Probably tomorrow at this stage. The local doctor pronounced her dead this morning before we arrived; we have his notes for you.'

'Thanks. You ready then, Igor?' Elaine Jones pulled a mask down over her nose and mouth.

Billy hung a camera round his neck. 'Yes, ma'am.'

'How many times do I have to tell you? I'm not your mother. Look at the size of you.' She stood next to him, her five foot one frame dwarfed by his six foot five. 'You'd have split me in half if I'd tried to give birth to you! If you get the chance, can one of your team get us some coffee,' she said to Fallon. 'It's all that's keeping us going at this stage.'

'Bishop!' the chief superintendent snapped.

'The rumour mill's starting to work,' McEvoy said without introduction. 'I think we need to release a fuller statement to the media. We need to straighten them out on a few things and fill in a few blanks. We also need to appeal for witnesses who might have seen strangers in and around the area in the last few days. The usual stuff.'

'I've already had someone working on it. You want to check it through before I talk to the media?'

'You're talking to the media?' McEvoy asked, confusion in his voice. 'I thought it was to be Peter O'Reilly's five minutes of fame?'

'There's been a change of plan,' Bishop said firmly. 'This thing's going to be international news. A young girl made to swallow a sword. The UK dailies have already been on, plus a couple of the US stations – Fox, CNN. We'll be running this out of the national press office.'

And it'll be your five minutes of fame, McEvoy thought, unsurprised by Bishop's change of plan.

'Look, Colm, I know you're not a great fan of media work, but I'd be grateful if you'd be available tomorrow morning for half an hour. They'll want to talk to the senior investigating officer.'

'Would Peter O'Reilly not be better?' McEvoy hazarded. 'This is his patch.'

'No, I want you to do it. It'll be you they'll want to talk to, not some local yokel.'

'Okay,' McEvoy said reluctantly. Whatever Peter O'Reilly was, he wasn't a yokel. Anyone who made superintendent had to have some guile and wits.

'They may be a real pain sometimes,' Bishop explained, 'but it's best to keep them onside. You never know when you might need them, like now.'

'What time?' McEvoy conceded.

'Ten o'clock in the Phoenix Park. And wear your best suit and tie. Not one of your worn-out specials.'

'I'll dig them out.' The last thing he wanted to do was to spend the morning in garda headquarters talking to the press.

'Aye, do that. And remember to shave. Look, I've got to go. I've got to see the assistant commissioner. Remember, ten tomorrow.' Bishop ended the call.

McEvoy stared at the phone for a few seconds, shaking his head. Bishop could be a cold, calculating bastard when he wanted to be – which was just about all the time. He scrolled through his mobile's phone book again and pressed connect.

Three rings later a woman's voice answered. 'Hello?'

'It's me,' McEvoy said matter-of-factly.

'We heard the news bulletin,' McEvoy's sister said. 'Don't worry, I can look after her.'

'Are you sure?'

'Is there anyone else?'

'I guess not,' he conceded. Maggie's family all lived down the country or abroad and her parents weren't up to it in any case. His two brothers lived in London, one of his sisters in Cork and the other in Toronto. His parents were holed up in cottage in Conemara. There was only Caroline in Dublin. Thankfully she was happy to help out. God knows what he would do otherwise.

'Don't worry. We'll get a DVD if we get bored. You don't mind if Jimmy comes over?'

'No. No, that's fine. Is she there?'

'I'll put you on now.' He could hear her turn away from the phone. 'Gemma, it's your dad.'

He heard her reply from upstairs. 'Okay.'

A few seconds later the extension phone was picked up.

'Dad?'

The other handset was switched off.

'Hiya, pumpkin. You heard the news?'

'Which one are you investigating,' she said as if it were routine, 'the burnt children or the woman in the Wicklow Mountains?'

'The woman in the mountains. I'm not going to get back until late tonight.'

'Well, at least it's not in Cork or somewhere. Have you had anything to eat?' she asked, motherly.

'I'll get a Chinese on the way home.'

'You need a proper meal,' she warned. 'We'll put it in the fridge for you. You've got to look after yourself now that Mam's gone.'

'I know. I will,' McEvoy promised, embarrassed that the roles had been reversed. 'Look, I've got to go, the pathologist has arrived. I just wanted to check in. I'll be back later on, okay. I love you.'

'I love you too. And remember to drink something. You know how dehydrated you get when you're working. You forget to drink.'

He could hear Maggie in her voice. It was like she was speaking from beyond the grave.

'I will, I will,' he conceded, realising that all he'd had to drink since lunchtime was a cup of coffee.

'And don't smoke either,' she chided him. 'You're giving up remember?'

'All I've smoked all day is my plastic substitute.' His hand curled round the packet of ten Silk Cut in his pocket and then let go. Maggie's brand. 'Look, Caroline's going to stay with you until I get home,' he said, trying to change the subject. 'She said she might get a DVD. Nothing rated more than a 15, okay.'

'Okay.'

'And Jimmy might come over.'

'She's already asked.'

'Right, well okay. Be good.'

'As if I wouldn't be.' She ended the call.

McEvoy stared down at his phone and then out the window. The sky was starting to darken. It was frightening how fast she'd grown up since Maggie's death. Sometimes it was like she had become the ghost of her mother.

He placed the plastic cigarette between his lips and sucked down a lung full of fresh air. He tried not to think about how much he wanted to open the packet nestled in his jacket pocket.

Barney Plunkett looked up from the desk he was leaning over and ran a hand through his sandy hair as McEvoy approached. He scooped up the sheets on the table and held them out towards him. 'Laura Schmidt, aged 19. Lived in Meols on the Wirral.'

McEvoy took the sheets and looked down at the photo. The girl in the picture was wearing jeans and a pale pink blouse, pulling an ironic smile, pretending to be happy. Her face in general looked like Laura's, though it was fuller, less hollowed out.

'That's the peninsula that sticks out between the Mersey and the Dee,' Plunkett continued. 'Meols is on the North Wales side, not the Liverpool side. Apparently it's quite a well-off place. She ran away from home 20 months ago. Her parents thought she might have headed to London. She'd run away a couple of times previously and on both occasions she went there. I've spoken to a local officer familiar with her file and he told me that the family had been investigated by Social Services. It seems that the father might have been abusing her. She'd confided in a friend, who'd gone to a teacher, who'd gone to the authorities.'

'She escapes the abuse to be killed here.' McEvoy shook his head at the injustice. 'What a world.'

'Nothing was proven, apparently,' Plunkett said, obviously not believing the father's innocence. 'Though it seems her personality changed quite a bit when she was about 13. She became quieter, more withdrawn, stopped hanging around with her friends, and her grades started to drop. Before that she was a straight A student. She went to the local grammar school and was planning to go to university to study engineering. I'd say it was odds on he was sexually abusing her.'

'And it's definitely her?' McEvoy asked.

'She has matching birthmarks on the back of her left leg. One is halfway down her thigh, the other half way down the calf. I spoke to Hannah while you were on your way down here. Professor Jones has checked it out and she has the marks.'

'Right, okay.' McEvoy placed the papers back down on the table. 'We need to arrange for someone to go over and talk with the family, act as liaison and to find out if there was any reason why she might have been killed.' He glanced down at the photo again. 'Her name is Schmidt,' he stated. His faced creased in thought. 'I thought you said Smith. That German, you think?'

'I guess so,' Plunkett shrugged.

'And the business cards were left in the German cemetery. A coincidence?' He shrugged.

'You mean she might not have been a random victim?'

33

'It has to be a possibility,' McEvoy conceded. 'Maybe he's trying to play games with us?'

'You want me to go back up to that graveyard and see if there are any Schmidts buried there?' Plunkett offered.

'I guess we'd better at least check it out.'

Elaine Jones was standing with Colm McEvoy and Hannah Fallon outside Laura's room giving them her assessment before she headed off to Loughlinstown Hospital to conduct the autopsy.

'All I can go on here is the lividity, the stage of rigor mortis, and the body temperature readings taken by the local doctor this morning and myself this afternoon. On that evidence I'd say she was killed somewhere between ten and one last night.'

'Nearer to ten than one?' McEvoy asked.

'I can't really say. Probably before midnight is as far as I want to go right now.'

'What about the killing? I assume she was killed by the sword?'

'There's nothing to indicate otherwise, unless she was drugged in some way. We'd need to do some tests to rule that out. I'd say though, if she was drugged, the sword followed quickly – her blood pumped over the sheet and body. Once we get to the hospital I'll do a full autopsy. There doesn't appear to be any other signs of physical attack. And it doesn't look as if she fought back either. We'll do the usual checks under the fingernails, just in case.'

'She just swallowed the sword,' Hannah said.

'It looks that way,' Professor Jones agreed. 'Dead in an instant.'

'How about sexual assault?' McEvoy asked.

'I don't think so.' The pathologist shook her head. 'It's difficult to say ahead of the autopsy or moving the body, although she was almost certainly naked when she was killed; the killer wasn't as thorough a cleaner as he thought. Beyond that you'll just have to wait.'

The man smiled to himself, turned the news off, and tightened the grey scarf around his neck. Laura's death was headline news, the reporter breathlessly relaying the gory details of how she had been found and warning the public to be vigilant against a dangerous killer on the loose. They could be as vigilant as they wanted, he thought, it would make little difference; everything was already scripted.

He tugged on a dark blue waterproof coat and headed for the door. He felt oddly calm; his emotions still contained; his perspective detached. He knew what he was about to do and how he was going to do it. He had no doubts. Taking the next life was simply a task to be completed, a means to an end. It was nothing personal, nothing to get worked up about. As far as he was concerned, killing a person was different to killing an insect in only one respect – nobody cared enough about the insect to try and take away the killer's freedom for doing it.

That was the challenge – to kill without being caught; to out-wit all the forces and resources that would be thrown at the case. And that was the thrill as well; the fuel that fed the adrenaline high; that made him feel alive.

He was confident he could meet the challenge, even if he wasn't following all of his own rules. After all, he had written the book. He closed the front door and set off at a brisk pace.

McEvoy leant against the cool bricks of the barracks and sipped piping hot coffee from a polystyrene cup. His mobile rang and he snatched it from his jacket pocket. 'Barney?'

'There's a Schmidt in the graveyard,' Plunkett said hurriedly. 'Walter Schmidt. Died in 1941.'

'And Fay Butler has confirmed that her father is German; the mother is from Mayo. They're on their way over to identify the body, the poor bastards.'

'If he hadn't been abusing her in the first place, she probably wouldn't be dead,' Plunkett said bitterly.

'True,' McEvoy conceded, 'but I bet her death's still torn him apart,' he said, imagining what it would be like to be told his daughter had prematurely joined his wife.

'My heart bleeds for him,' Plunkett muttered without sympathy. 'I just hope he doesn't take it out on the mother. If he was abusing his daughter, there's a good chance the wife has experienced the same treatment.'

'I'll talk to Family Liaison,' McEvoy offered, knowing that Plunkett was probably right. 'If he so much as lifts a finger against her we'll bring him in. About the cemetery, do you still think it's a coincidence?' he asked, changing the subject.

'If it is, it's a pretty big one. He kills a girl called Laura Schmidt and then leaves his calling cards where one is buried. Chances of that must be pretty small; miniscule even.'

'Well, if it's not a coincidence, then whoever killed her must have known her in advance and also known that she was coming out here,' McEvoy reasoned, letting a thought unfold, 'where there just happens to be a German cemetery with her namesake buried in it. Unless you organised the trip, the chances of Laura being anywhere near that cemetery are practically zero. Especially when this was the first time she'd been on anything like this.'

'You think the killer might be one of the DHC organisers?' Plunkett asked. 'You said one of them did time.'

'Yeah, Dermot Brady. Hit and run. Killed a mother and her young son. Now claims to be whiter than white.'

'Well he helped organise the trip. Maybe he talked her into coming?' Plunkett hypothesised.

'Possibly,' McEvoy said cautiously, mentally starting to unpick his own speculation. 'Finding a person with the same name as someone in the cemetery and getting them to come on an annual trip is a difficult ask though.'

'What do you want me to do?'

'Just note down Schmidt's details and then head home. Tomorrow's going to be another long day. We'll need to run a check on your man in any case and see what comes up. We're gonna need to review all the DHC staff first thing. If there is a connection then our killer is either so clever he thinks he can outwit us or pretty stupid.'

'You don't think it was Brady?' Plunkett sounded disappointed.

'If it was then he's not giving himself much chance of writing the other six chapters,' McEvoy stated flatly. 'What do you think?'

'I think I'm going to head back to the incident room to pull up what I can about him.'

'If that's what you want. I'll talk to you later, okay.' McEvoy disconnected the call. He took another sip of coffee and instinctively placed his plastic cigarette between his lips and inhaled deeply. He snatched it away and looked at it in disgust, before slotting it back. He needed to get rid of the pack in his pocket; they weren't going to stay un-opened much longer. And he needed a drink; a proper drink. Something to deaden his thoughts; let him sleep the night through without thinking about Maggie or Laura Schmidt, the cold sword sticking up out of her mouth. The door a few feet away opened and Billy Keane's back emerged, his arms holding up the front of a trolley laden with a body bag.

Barney Plunkett and Fay Butler looked up as McEvoy entered the room, looking tired and dishevelled. Somehow his body seemed to have gotten smaller inside his suit, his skin paler and tighter to his bones.

'I was just going to come and find you,' Plunkett said as a greeting. 'We've being going through Dermot Brady's file. Except for the hit and run and his time in Mountjoy his record is clean. In fact he's helped us out a few times with incidents involving homeless folk. Seems like he's turned a new leaf. There's one interesting thing though.'

'There always is,' McEvoy muttered.

'He worked in Germany for a year and a half in his early twenties. Did casual labour on the building sites in and around Cologne. He'd only been back in Ireland for four months when he killed the mother and son.'

'Another coincidence, you think?'

'The manual says that multiple coincidences equal a probable link. I think he's worth a closer look.'

'Okay, then,' McEvoy nodded.

'You don't think so?' Plunkett asked, sensing McEvoy's doubt.

'No, no, absolutely, find out everything you can about him. It's … it's just it doesn't seem to fit.' McEvoy scratched at his cheek absently. 'If you wanted to write a whole book, why give away so many clues in the first chapter?'

'He's a bad author?'

'Everything else though is so clinical – the cleaning of the body and room; the laying out of the cards. Having too many coincidences would be sloppy. It's a manual on how not to get caught. You'd have thought he would have thought it all the way through. At least for the first killing while he's got time and space to plan things.'

'So you're saying we should leave him be?'

'No, I'm saying we should check him out fully, but don't rush in thinking it's definitely him. We need to keep an open mind.

Let's pull together what we can and see where that leaves us. We also need to check out whether there's a link between Laura Schmidt and the Schmidt in the cemetery. Were they family or do they just share the same name?'

Dr David Hennessey strolled along the lime tree avenue at the rear of Maynooth University approaching a ten-foot-tall crucifix adorned with the body of Christ. The crucifix stood at the head of a row of ancient yew trees lining a little laneway to the seminary's cemetery. The sky was fading fast toward twilight, a cold wind blowing in from the east. The lights surrounding the seminary flickered into life, illuminating the long, dark walls with an orange glow, accentuating its Gothic look. The spire of the church reached up into the sky, a murder of crows circulating round the bell eaves.

He started to zip up his navy blue coat. His greying hair kept being lifted by the breeze and falling in odd ways. He tried to pat it down along the parting, but it was immediately ruffled again.

A figure was walking towards him along the path. He took little notice – the circuit was used by people from the town in the absence of a park, and also by staff and students from the university and the priests and their trainees from the seminary. He'd already passed four people on his first loop round the grounds.

The person had a baseball cap pulled down low across his brow. His head was scrunched into his shoulders, the collar on his weatherproof jacket turned up, a thin grey scarf buried underneath trying to keep the wind out; faded jeans covered the top of blue hiking boots, his hands sheathed in black leather gloves.

As the walker came within a few feet, Hennessey nodded an acknowledgement. 'Chilly night,' he said as a way of greeting.

The walker didn't reply, simply lowering his head so the cap covered his whole face.

Hennessey shrugged to himself.

As the person drew level, the blow hit the lower left side of his head just at the base of the skull. His brain exploded into light and pain, immediately cancelled out by darkness and unconsciousness. He hit the ground hard, his head thudding into the broken tarmac, his glasses spilling forwards.

The assailant pulled a surgical face mask up from under the scarf, placing it over his mouth and nose, and dropped down to his haunches. He rolled the lifeless Hennessey onto his back, grabbed him under the arms, and dragged him quickly in under the nearest yew tree. He looked out along the path, checking for witnesses, but nobody was in sight.

Happy he was alone he drew a plastic bag from a coat pocket, shook it out and slipped it over Hennessey's head, tying the handles round his neck. He moved to the end of the body and dragged it underneath the branches, out onto the path between the yew trees, and then along it toward the silent cemetery.

The graveyard was dark and silent. McEvoy was not surprised to find he was the only occupant given that gates had been locked earlier in the evening. He stared down at Maggie's grave. He could barely make out the inscription in the poor light. He knew it by heart in any case. 'Margaret McEvoy. 1965-2007. Loving wife of Colm and mother of Gemma.'

'Jesus, Maggie,' McEvoy stated slowly, 'where do I start. It's been a hell of day. We found a girl who'd had a sword thrust through her head. Can you believe the things people do to each other?' He spent the next 20 minutes reciting his day, gently puffing on his plastic cigarette, craving to replace it with a real one.

Eventually he started to bring his monologue to a close. 'I guess I'd better get going. I haven't been home yet. I need to see Gemma. Our Gemma. I'll see you tomorrow, okay?' He waited momentarily for an answer then reluctantly headed for the gate and his car, wondering if the pain and grief of Maggie's death would ever dissipate, knowing he'd have a fitful night after the day's events.

Chapter Two

Tuesday, April 15th

Gemma was sitting at the kitchen table dressed in her dark green school uniform. Her long, brown hair fell over her shoulders, her left hand held a book open, her right spooned Rice Krispies from a bowl to her mouth. She looked up as she heard the door opening. 'You can't go like that,' she said, mock horror in her voice.

'Like what?' McEvoy asked, looking down. A dark blue suit hung loosely from his shoulders, slightly rumpled. A poorly knotted tie fell over a creased, light blue shirt. As he looked up a wisp of tissue broke free from a shaving cut and fell onto his tie. He swatted it away.

'Like that.' Gemma pointed at him with a spoon.

'This is my best suit.' McEvoy poured water from a filter jug into a kettle. He had slept fitfully and felt tired and washed out.

'But look at the state of it,' Gemma cried. 'It's all crumpled. And your shirt's all wrinkled.'

'It'll be fine,' McEvoy said half-heartedly. 'The cameras will be on the chief super. I'm just wallpaper. Have you got every-thing ready for school?'

'Yeah,' Gemma intoned as if McEvoy had asked a stupid question. 'At least my stuff is ironed.'

'I'll have my jacket on, no one will see.' McEvoy placed two pieces of bread into the toaster and glanced at his watch.

'It'll be better if your shirt is ironed and you don't wear a jacket.' She dropped the spoon into a near-empty bowl and let the book fold shut. 'Come on, give me the shirt and I'll iron it for you.'

'You're not ironing my shirt. We'll be late.' McEvoy took the butter from the fridge.

'You can't appear on television dressed like that! That suit's too big for you.'

'No one's going to notice the suit. They're there to hear about the murder I'm investigating.'

'They'll judge you on appearances. Everyone's judged on appearances. It's the age we live in. Come on, take it off.' Gemma pulled at her father's suit. 'It'll only take a minute.'

'Gemma, we don't have time for this,' McEvoy protested, thinking, where the hell does she get this stuff – 'the age we live in.' 'Did you do your homework?' he asked, trying to deflect the conversation.

'We didn't have any.' She pushed him away. 'I'm going to go and get one of your other shirts from the wardrobe.' She headed for the door. 'Mam wouldn't have let you go out like that!'

The kitchen door closed shut.

McEvoy went to shout after her but stopped. He took a deep breath and then trailed after her. He stopped at the bottom of the stairs. 'Be careful with that iron, okay. And remember to unplug it.'

'I know what I'm doing,' Gemma shouted back. 'Go and finish your breakfast, we don't want to be late. Next Saturday we're going to buy you two new suits. Nice ones.'

McEvoy headed back into the kitchen. He dropped a tea bag into a cup and filled it with boiling water. Then he plucked his toast from the toaster and dropped it onto a plate. He started to butter each slice. He was being looked after by his soon-to-be 12-year-old daughter. 'Jesus,' he muttered to himself, 'I need to get my feckin' act together.'

McEvoy stared out at the line of traffic snaking out in front of him, sucking on his plastic cigarette. 'For God's sake,' he muttered to himself. In recent years the city had, for periods of the day, become a giant car park. He remembered a traffic cop who'd told him that Dublin was officially the slowest moving city in Europe. The average speed was around five miles an hour. That's what happened if, in the space of a few years, a couple of hundred thousand people moved to the city and you doubled the number of cars using an old road system without building new roads or vastly increasing public transport provision. He glanced at the time on his mobile phone and then tapped in a number. After five rings it was answered.

'Hannah Fallon.'

'Hannah, it's Colm,' he said into the hands-free system. 'Any progress?'

'Not really. There's nothing on the sword. No prints, no hairs, no anything. There probably was a maker's mark but it's been carefully polished off. We've been trying to find a way of recovering it, but nothing so far. To tell you the truth, it's remarkable in its plainness. No decorations or obvious identifying features.'

'Any chance I can take it to the press conference? Be better to show it than a photo. Someone might have sold it or had it stolen.'

'Shouldn't be a problem. We've nothing else to go on. The bag was free of prints, as was the note. It was printed on a laser jet of some kind. We might be able to match it to a specific machine, but not unless we find it. We're waiting for the other samples to come back from the lab.'

'How about the cards?' McEvoy edged his car forward 10 yards.

'Probably home-made. You could appeal to see if anyone produced them for him.'

'I think we'll keep them to ourselves for now. We don't want to start a panic. Anything else from the centre?'

'No. My feeling is, whoever killed her almost certainly didn't hang around. He killed the girl, cleaned up, and then snuck out into the night. The rest of the team are already on their way back out there. They're going to work through the rooms more thoroughly. I'll be heading there shortly, I've got to tidy a few things up here first.'

'Can you check out the room of Dermot Brady for me,' McEvoy instructed. 'I want to make sure he's clean.'

'You think he did it?' Hannah asked.

'I've no idea,' McEvoy replied. 'I doubt it, but we'd better make sure.'

McEvoy walked down the short, magnolia-painted corridor towards Elaine Jones' office in the Department of Forensic Medicine in Trinity College. A brass plate outside a door announced 'The Office of the State Pathologist'. He walked past it, bypassing the secretary, and knocked on a heavy wooden door.

'Come in,' the pathologist instructed.

He gently pushed open the door and poked his head through the gap. 'You ready for me, Elaine?' he asked.

'As ready as I'm going to be,' she replied, tiredness in her voice. She was sitting behind a large, mahogany desk, inlaid with green leather. Three piles of neatly stacked papers were lined up on one edge, a laptop was open in front of her, her fingers hovering over the keys. She was wearing a tight black, full sleeve top, black trousers and black flat shoes. An amber necklace was draped round her neck, dipping into her cleavage. 'It was a long night and another early start. Come in. Stop hovering.' She beckoned him into the office.

McEvoy pushed open the door and crossed the room towards her, extending a hand across the desk. 'I'll try not to keep you long, I'm needed up at garda headquarters for a press conference.'

She slid her hand into his and shook it limply. 'When are we going to become continental and do the whole cheek kissing thing? We're embracing everything else European.' Her eyes sparkled, but she couldn't quite shake the exhaustion from her voice.

'What would the nuns think of that?' McEvoy replied. 'The guilt would crush us.'

'The nuns should lighten up. Only the Irish would invent a style of dancing where you keep your arms by your side and you don't touch anyone. And don't give me "it's a catholic thing" answer. The Spanish are catholic and they practically sleep with each other when they dance.'

'If you want to start a campaign, Elaine, then I'll sign your petition,' McEvoy offered.

'I want you to kiss me on the cheeks each time we meet, not sign a petition. Come on, you can start now.' She pushed herself up off the chair and leant forward across the desk.

McEvoy shifted awkwardly on his feet, unsure of whether this was part of the banter or whether she was being serious.

'Come on,' she goaded. 'I'm not going to bite. It's a social greeting, not an infidelity.'

McEvoy reluctantly arched his frame across the table, feeling like an idiot, his frame dwarfing hers. He gently kissed each cheek, as she did his. He stood back and sat heavily into a chair.

'And I expect the same every time I see you,' she said to him.

'Er, right,' McEvoy said, blushing, uncertain of how to deal with the way the conversation was unfolding. 'What can you tell me about Laura's death?' he asked, trying to get things into a familiar frame of reference.

'Well, we did the full autopsy out at Loughlinstown late last night. The body's still there. It'll take a while for some of the tests to come back from the lab, but my estimate is she died around eleven o'clock, give or take an hour either side. And it

46

was the sword that killed her. It punctured the back of the throat, cutting off her tonsils and severing her spinal cord just below the base of the skull before exiting. She was almost certainly conscious at the time, but would have been killed instantly.

'The rest of the body wasn't touched. She had a few small bruises and a couple of cuts but they were old, certainly from a couple of days before she was killed. And there's no evidence of sexual activity, although she was naked when she was killed. There were a few small droplets of blood on her body that the killer hadn't cleaned off fully. They wouldn't have splattered the way they did if she'd been clothed or if they were dripped on later.'

'So he must have persuaded her to undress,' McEvoy added.

'That would be my conclusion. There doesn't appear to have been any struggle. We don't have the clothes to know whether he ripped them off her, but if he did, that would have probably left some marks. And there's no skin or blood under the fingernails. She probably removed them herself under the threat of the sword.'

McEvoy shook his head, disgusted at the world. A final humiliation, probably knowing that she was about to die or be raped.

'The killer had done a pretty good job of cleaning the body,' Professor Jones continued. 'It was probably more than she'd done for herself for a while. I doubt her hair had been washed for a few weeks. Maybe longer.'

'Probably had nowhere to wash,' McEvoy said. 'It's not like the corporation provide facilities to the homeless.'

'But the homeless organisations, hostels and halfway houses do,' Professor Jones countered. 'She obviously chose to steer clear of them. She either wanted to avoid too much contact with others or she was past caring about her appearance or health. My guess is the latter. And she was staying in a room with an en-suite shower for heaven's sake, yet she'd ignored it. My reading is that she was beyond caring; given up on life. She only weighed 42 kilos – 6½ stone in old money – which for someone her height and bone structure is massively underweight. She either couldn't find enough to eat, or didn't have the will to eat.

'She could find the will to drink though. She was drunk when she died. And from the look of her liver, I'd say she's been getting drunk almost every night for a good while. Drinking to get paralytic drinking, not a social tipple. She probably had little comprehension of what was going on.'

'But enough to know to strip off and do what the killer wanted,' McEvoy noted. 'The sword must have sobered her up. Most drunk people wouldn't have been so compliant; they would have needed coaxing into understanding the situation. In my experience, drink tends to make people a bit thick. He would have had to push her around and threaten her to get her to do what he wanted. She'd have probably fought back.'

'Well, she seemed to have her faculties about her,' Professor Jones replied. 'Maybe it's from living on the street? You get drunk to keep the cold out and forget, but you have enough of an instinct to be alert to any danger? Or she might have just given up. Resigned herself to death. Did what she was told and waited for the world to end.'

'Possibly. That or she knew whoever her attacker was. Knew that it was best to comply or maybe she trusted them.'

'Would you trust someone who was carrying a sword and asking you to take your clothes off?' Elaine raised her eyebrows signalling sarcasm.

'No, but if she was drunk …' McEvoy stopped, his head dropping. 'None of it makes any sense. The killer's note says this was a random act to a random person. But the person he killed shouldn't have been there, she put up no resistance, and her namesake is in the cemetery where the business cards were found. It just doesn't add up.'

'Her namesake?' Elaine asked.

'There was a Walter Schmidt buried in the cemetery.'

'Could be just a coincidence,' she reasoned.

'That was my feeling, but … look,' he said, changing his tone, becoming more business-like. 'I'd better get on and get to this press conference. When you get the rest of the test results in let me know if there's anything interesting in them.' He pushed himself up off the chair.

'You'll be the first to know,' she promised. 'Look, I hope you don't mind me saying this, Colm, but you could do with a good feed yourself. And a good night's sleep as well. You don't look your usual self and that suit's hanging off you.'

'Don't you start as well, Elaine. I've already had this conversation with Gemma this morning.' He opened the door.

'It's only because we care about you. You need to look after yourself. You'll be no use to anyone if you go off work sick.'

McEvoy ignored Elaine's concern and let the door close behind him. He made his way out of the building onto a drizzle soaked Pearse Street. Elaine was right. He looked terrible. And what's more he felt it. He hadn't eaten or slept properly in months, from well before Maggie's death. He just couldn't muster an appetite and insomnia regularly kept him awake until the early hours. He seemed to stagger round in a tired stupor he couldn't shake off. He fished his plastic cigarette from a pocket and wedged it in his mouth, checked his mobile for the time and messages and picked up the pace to his car. He hoped the worst of the traffic had passed or he was going to be late.

McEvoy stared across the top of the 20 or so journalists and cameramen at a fire extinguisher at the far end of the room, tuning out the statement Chief Superintendent Bishop was reading. He felt out of place on the podium; he was a street cop not a television presenter. He'd been on the media training course, but all it had done was confirm his suspicions that the press wanted a good story, not the truth. They wanted to become partners in the investigation. To nose around and do their own detective work, often messing up lines of police enquiry at the same time and tainting the possibility of getting an impartial jury. They would offer friendship, but were quite happy to stab you in the back if things didn't work out well, pointing out the failures in the investigation, critiquing the approach taken, and telling you how it should have been done with the benefit of hindsight.

Movement to his left caught his eye and he swivelled his head to see the press liaison officer pull the sword from a bag. The officer held it out, balanced between his two palms. Cameras clicked and flash bulbs popped. Several of the photographers moved position, trying to get a better shot.

'Please, ladies and gentlemen,' Bishop said. 'We can set up a blue screen afterwards so you can get a better shot. Please settle down.' He waited for the room to quieten a little. 'We need help in tracing this sword. We need to know who it belonged to. As you can see it is quite plain and any distinguishing features have been erased. Is it a family heirloom? Was it sold recently? Or was it stolen? Any information can be given in confidence to our officers on our hotline.'

Bishop paused, waiting for the majority of journalists to stop scribbling. 'Well, that's it for now. Any questions? Yes, Claire.' He pointed to a short, thin woman in her mid-thirties.

'Do you have any idea who the girl was? Or why she was killed?'

'The girl went by the name of Laura. She was homeless and living on the streets of Dublin. Once the family have formally identified the body we'll be releasing full details. We'll need help in trying to retrace her last few days.'

'Do you know why she was killed?' asked a balding and overweight man, who sat on the right of the room.

'It's not very clear at present,' Bishop replied. 'It could be simply that she was in the wrong place at the wrong time.'

'So she was a random victim?' the man continued.

'We don't yet know that. We don't know if the victim knew her killer. It's part of the investigation.'

A tall thin man, with short black hair and a goatee beard, stood up at the back of the room. 'My sources are telling me that there was a note left at the scene, along with several business cards, that state that this girl's murder is the first in a set of killings.'

Bishop and McEvoy shared a look, trying to decide how to deal with the question.

'We do have a note and some business cards,' Bishop said hesitantly, 'but at this stage there is no indication of their veracity. They might simply be a decoy to confuse our investigation.'

'Does that mean that you think this is a one-off murder?' the journalist continued. 'Perhaps by a family member or someone she knew?'

'It means we have an open mind on things while we sift through the evidence. It's too early to jump to any conclusions.'

'But what if it was the first of set? What are you doing to protect the public?'

'We're trying to catch the killer,' Bishop hissed a little more harshly than he intended. He changed his tone. 'I'm sorry ladies and gentlemen, that's it for now. Barry here,' he motioned to the press liaison officer, 'will set up the blue screen for photos of the sword. He also has copies of the statement and can arrange for you to receive further statements via email.'

'Can you tell us what the note said,' the journalist called out, starting to make his way to the front of the room.

Bishop stood and walked behind McEvoy, down the couple of steps from the podium and out the door. McEvoy retrieved his jacket from the back of his chair and trailed after him.

Bishop stopped a few feet down along the corridor and turned, his face flushed red. 'I'm going to kill the stupid bastard who told that fecker about the note and cards. I want his name, okay.'

'There's 80 to 100 men working the case between our lot and the locals. Gossip travels through the ranks and into the pubs. It's just the way it is,' McEvoy tried to reason.

'Well it's time that changed,' Bishop snapped. 'Come on, let me walk you to your car and you can fill me in further on where you're at.' He turned and set off again without waiting for a reply.

McEvoy rolled his eyes and sighed silently, then took off after Bishop, falling into step at his side.

McEvoy leant against the door of his blue Mondeo, Tony Bishop standing on the other side of the wing mirror, his gold braided cap wedged under his arm.

'So, what are you going to do now?' Bishop asked, his face still flushed red.

'I'm going to get hold of Barney Plunkett and see how things are progressing. Then I'm going to go and find Laura's homeless friend, Karen, and see what she knows.'

'Whatever resources you need, just ask, okay. If he starts a killing spree then we're going to come under a lot of pressure – from the public, the media, and from the politicians. I'll do my best to protect you, but you have to play the game my way.'

'What's that mean exactly?' McEvoy asked cautiously.

'It means that you keep me in the loop on everything. You ask my advice on anything sensitive or any key decisions. You leave the press work to me, which is something that you probably want to avoid in any case. And you bring me in when you need to talk to anyone important or you've snared the bastard. In return I'll watch your back and give you the resources you need.'

McEvoy nodded, but stayed silent. What Bishop meant was he'd do all the donkey work, be the brunt of any criticism, and the chief super would get the limelight and a share of the glory at the end. If he messed up, he'd be cut loose to fend for himself.

This was why he was never going to make chief super. He just didn't have the political ambition to play institutional politics and climb the greasy pole. He was more interested in the job than the career. At least Bishop was being open. Half the time the bargain was assumed but left unsaid, meaning you never really knew what was going on or who to trust.

'Well?' Bishop prompted.

'Sounds fine to me,' McEvoy said, feeling like a cheap fool. He needed a cigarette. His hand played with the still sealed packet in his jacket pocket.

'Good,' Bishop said. 'I'll let you get on.' He turned on his heels and headed back to the building without looking back.

McEvoy opened the door and sank into the driver's seat. He sat for a few moments trying to collect his thoughts and calm himself a little before taking his mobile phone from his pocket. He pulled up a number.

It was answered on the third ring. 'Plunkett.'

'Barney, it's me. How are things?'

'Slow. Very slow.'

'Anything significant to report?'

'Not really. We're still trying to piece together everyone who's stayed here who has a violent, criminal record. So far it's got 18 names on it. I hate to think how long that list is going to get. Half the republican and loyalist prisoners must have been through this place on reconciliation courses. My guess is it going to be a who's who of The Troubles. Plus they've had victim support meetings up here – some of Mountjoy's finest have wandered through.

'It doesn't help that a good portion just used their first name to register. We've managed to fill in some of the blanks by cross-checking the register with the centre's paperwork – sometimes there's a manifest for the group. Their filing though is all over the place. Sometimes there's material to match the register, other times not. We've started to use the accounts files to contact some of the organisations that brought people here to see if they have records. Many of them are in the North and they're not the keenest to help out. In fact, most of them have told us to get lost.

53

'Jesus,' McEvoy muttered. 'Just do the best you can. Maybe try and narrow it to people who have killed in cold blood and at close range, or have seriously injured someone. Maybe with a knife or gun, rather than those that have set off bombs.'

'Okay,' Plunkett replied, uncertainty in his voice, 'we'll do our best, but there's still going to be loads of them. With the amount of punishment beatings in the North, there's bound to a whole bunch of them that fit that profile.'

'I know, but whoever killed Laura has probably killed before and he was familiar with that centre. If nothing else we have to try and eliminate them from the enquiry.' McEvoy paused and stared out at the grey sky. 'That bastard really knew what he was doing, didn't he? He knew we were going to have sift through all the lowlifes and scumbags that went through that place.'

'We'll get him, don't worry,' Plunkett replied firmly. 'He'll have made a mistake; then we can reel him in.'

'I hope so, Barney. If we don't catch him and he carries out several murders we're going to be in all the history books for all the wrong reasons. Have we found our missing four homeless people yet?' McEvoy asked, changing tack.

'We've got one more. I reckon the other three have headed out of town. We've done a few sweeps at this stage.'

'Keep trying. We need to find them. How about our friend, Dermot Brady?'

'He's been out helping some of our lot trying to find those missing three. He dropped into the DHC centre this morning, but that's it. Nothing out of the ordinary.'

'No surprise there, I guess. Anything from the questionnaires or the search round the centre?'

'A lot of noise from the questionnaires. Several different cars parked on the side of the road near to the centre over the past few days. Red this, and white that, with no registration details beyond county identification. Probably all hikers wandering about on the moorland. Nothing from the search. If he dumped the stuff from the room, he did it a long way from the centre.'

'How about the Schmidt connection?'

'I've had someone checking things out with the German embassy, but it's going to take a few days to try and work out the family tree of Walter Schmidt. It might prove impossible – Schmidt's a really common name. Plus the loss of records during the war and the post-war upheaval isn't going to help things.'

'Jesus! We've got bugger all!' McEvoy snapped, frustrated with his morning – the traffic, the press conference, the lack of progress, Bishop's pact. 'For Christ's sake!' He tipped his head back against the headrest and stared up at the car's roof.

'Something'll turn up,' Barney tried to reassure. 'How did it go with the media circus?'

'I think I was the clown. The usual stuff. Someone had told one of the reporters about the note and business cards; Bishop saw red. We'll see if it does any good beyond generating noise. Look, keep plugging away at your end and I'll ring you later this afternoon.'

'Okay, I'll speak to you later.' The call was disconnected.

McEvoy pulled the packet of cigarettes from his pocket and ripped off the cellophane wrapper. He flipped open the lid, teased a cigarette from the pack and jammed it between his lips. He fished a lighter from his pocket, lit it, and sucked down the smoke.

He blew it out slowly, savouring it and regretting it at the same time. He closed his eyes, listening to the rain starting to patter against the windscreen and roof. He took another drag and popped smoke rings, his mind sifting through the past 24 hours trying to find a fresh angle on the case.

McEvoy pulled the car to the kerb and looked across the road at the red brick, terrace housing. The properties looked tired, battered doors, paint peeling from window frames, and litter spread across the wet pavement. One of them had its windows boarded-up, a large padlock hung below the door handle. It had probably been bought by a property developer buying up stock for future re-investment. A couple years' time and the whole area would be gentrified, a different set of people mixing with and pushing the older residents out.

He crossed the road to the boarded-up house, pulling up the collar of his suit jacket as if that would stop the light drizzle. There was no obvious way in. He headed right to where an alleyway led in past the end terrace. It was the smell, rather than the boards, that told him when he'd reached the right spot – the stench of rotting rubbish heavy in the air.

The dark green, wooden gate had been wedged shut. He pushed on it, testing its strength and then gave it a hard shove. It creaked open a few inches, enough to let him squeeze past into a yard piled high in household waste, some of it bagged, some of it thrown loose. A rough path had been kicked from the gate to the back door and he crept his way along it.

He grabbed the handle and let himself into a kitchen that looked as if a bomb had exploded in it. He waded through the debris and into a hallway. There were two doorways and a set of stairs leading upward. He opened the first doorway and stuck his head through the gap. In the dull light he could see a man of indeterminate age lying on a tatty, blue sleeping bag on top of bare floorboards across which were scattered beer cans and cigarette butts. In one corner of the room were a handful of used syringes, jutting at odd angles.

'Fuck off,' the man spat.

'Where's Karen?' McEvoy demanded.

'Who am I, her fuckin' keeper? Upstairs.'

McEvoy closed the door and headed up the stairs, two at a time. There were three doors open off the landing. One led into a stinking bathroom. The door opposite the top of the stairs was slightly ajar. He pushed it open. The room was dully lit, the boarded-up window blocking out the sunlight.

A skinny woman was sitting on top of dirty blankets, her back wedged into the corner facing the door, her knees drawn up to her chest. Her thin face was drained of colour, strands of her long, black hair hung across it, her eyes downcast looking at his shadow. She was wearing a purple vest and grey jogging pants. Her arms were bare and she was shivering. Even in the poor light, McEvoy could see the tracks and bruising along the inside of her arms.

'I don't have it,' she muttered, barely audible.

'You don't have what?' McEvoy asked.

'I don't have your fuckin' money,' she hissed. 'I'll owe you. I'll do whatever you want, but you've got to give me some. You've got to.'

'I need to know about Laura.'

'What?' She looked up. 'Who the fuck are you?' she asked, her voice changing tone.

'Detective Superintendent Colm McEvoy. You're Karen?'

'What d'ya want?' she replied, ignoring his question, her body language becoming both anxious and defiant at the same time.

'I need to know about Laura,' he repeated.

'I don't know a Laura.' She drew her knees tighter to her body, lowering her eyes again.

'That's not what I've heard. We found Laura's body yesterday morning. Someone had rammed a sword through her head.'

Karen flicked her eyes up at him and then closed them. 'I told you, I don't know a Laura.'

'We need to catch him, Karen. He's going to kill again.'

'Go fuck yourself,' she murmured.

'I know you knew her, Karen. She thought you were her friend.' McEvoy threw a cigarette onto the bedding.

She grabbed at it, digging a lighter from between the folds in the blanket. She lit the cigarette and inhaled deeply.

'Tell me about Laura,' McEvoy asked evenly.

Karen stayed silent, letting the smoke trailed from her nostrils.

'Karen?' McEvoy prompted.

'Like what?' she answered sharply.

'What was she like?'

Karen shrugged. 'She kept herself to herself.'

'But you were friends?' McEvoy pressed.

'I hardly knew her. Nobody did.'

'Where was she living? She must have been sleeping somewhere. Here?'

'No, no. She wouldn't come here. Didn't trust the others. She was a loner.'

'So where?'

'I don't know.'

'Come on Karen, where?' McEvoy said, frustration in his voice.

'I don't know,' she spat. 'She never told me; didn't tell me anything.' She sucked greedily on the cigarette.

'On the street? In a hideaway? Another squat? On a derelict site?'

'I don't know,' she hissed. 'I told you, I hardly knew her.'

'Well who did? Did she hang around with anyone? Did you see her with anyone else?'

'No. She was always on her own. I never saw her with nobody. I need to go.'

'Did she talk about anybody?' McEvoy continued. 'She talk about any friends?'

'I told you, she didn't say anything. She was just some lost kid.'

'How about drugs?' McEvoy pressed. 'She take them?'

'Never saw her. She just used to sup her vodka or gin. She could sink a bottle, no problem. She fuckin' loved the stuff.'

'Where'd she get the money for that?'

'Begging. She used to hang round Connolly Station or sometimes O'Connell Street. Just sat on the pavement holding out a cup.' She shifted her body. 'That's all she did. Just fuckin' sat there.'

'She do anything else, maybe a bit of prostitution?'

Karen stayed silent, drawing on the cigarette.

'Karen?' McEvoy pressed again.

'I don't know.'

'But she might have done?'

'You'd have to ask her.' Karen crossed her arms and hugged herself. 'I ain't her keeper.'

'I would, Karen, but she's dead. Someone put a sword through her head,' McEvoy said matter-of-fact.

Karen didn't respond, trying to look strong, but appearing more like a petulant child. She sucked in another lungful of smoke and stared at the blanket.

McEvoy pushed himself off the windowsill and headed for the door. 'I hope you're not hiding the killer from me, Karen. You never know, you could be next.'

She stared up at him with defiant eyes, trying not to shiver.

He closed the door and headed back down the stairs. He shook his head at the squalor, kicking aside junk. How did anyone end up in such a mess? Shooting up shit; trying to block out the world; living like shadows. He thought of Gemma and vowed to find some quality time with her. He slipped out through the kitchen and back into the dull light and drizzle.

The man jerked his head back out of sight and then eased it forward slowly, peering through the dense foliage at McEvoy's tall, lean figure emerging from the alley. It hadn't taken the superintendent long to make his way to the squat. Perhaps he should have taken Laura last not first, but there was no point worrying about that now. What was important was to make sure *The Rule Book* was published in full.

He watched McEvoy ease himself into his car and a few moments later pull away from the kerb, heading away from him. It had been stupid to follow him – against all the rules. He was putting himself at unnecessary risk, yet he'd felt compelled to see what was happening – to judge how well the guards were getting on; to see that everything was still going to plan; to try and control and shape things. He knew he needed to back away and let things unfold as they should.

At the minute the guards still seemed to be concentrating on Laura, the body in Maynooth not yet discovered. Instinctively he glanced at his watch. He hoped he wasn't going to have to give them a pointer; it wouldn't do for the third chapter to be released before the second. The second body would also send them into a flatspin, dividing their attention and resources. He headed back to his dark blue Ford Fiesta and trailed after McEvoy, driving slowly past the squat, staring up at the boarded-up windows.

The second killing had almost been a textbook affair. The victim had known nothing of the attack except for the brief millisecond between the satisfying, hollow thwack to the skull and unconsciousness. The only worry had been controlling his anger as he had approached Hennessey. It bloomed as a bright red sun, threatening to boil over and consume him. It had taken all of his self-control to keep it in check, to manage and harness it, rather than be engulfed by it.

He was now its master, not the other way round. Not like when he was a child when he would fly into fits of uncontainable, blind rage-driven tantrums. As he'd grown older, become a teenager, he'd learnt to manage his anger, found ways to vent it in controlled ways, although occasionally it welled up and exploded into violence. Now he knew how to cultivate and harness it, draw strength from it.

Once the figure had hit the tarmac he'd easily suppressed his fury. After that it had been easy, slipping the bag over the bloody and lifeless head and pulling the dead weight down through the yew trees to the cemetery wall.

As he stripped the clothes from the body he'd felt as he imagined a pathologist or funeral director would do when they worked with the dead – cold, distanced, measured. He felt nothing for the victim; seemingly felt nothing at all.

McEvoy was signalling right, waiting for a gap in the traffic. He approached slowly and as he pulled to a halt McEvoy darted out, slipping into the traffic. He smiled to himself and turned left, heading to the site of the next attack. He wanted to make sure everything was as it should be before he headed to work.

Dessie Carthy threw the tennis ball in the air and swung the hurley in one motion. The ball sliced off the face of the stick and shot between the lime trees, across the moss-ridden tarmac and through the second set of trees that lined the path. A blur of golden retriever bounded after it, snatching the ball out of the air as it bounced through the undergrowth on the edge of a yew tree avenue. As the dog started to head back it veered off, its nose to the floor, disappearing under the yew trees.

Dessie took little notice, expecting the dog had caught the scent of a squirrel or rabbit. He continued to trail along the edge of a football pitch back toward the seminary buildings, the church steeple reaching up high, and in front of it, the four-storey, Gothic façade – grey, cold and seemingly devoid of life – dominating the landscape.

After a minute or so he looked over to where the dog had disappeared. He bellowed out. 'Syrup! Come on. Oi, Syrup!'

There was no sign of the dog.

'Jesus,' he muttered to himself, changing course to try and track it down. 'Oi, Syrup, where are you, you daft bugger. Syrup!' He looked at his watch and winced to himself. He needed to get going, his shift started at two o'clock.

The dog barked a few times, but did not come into view.

Dessie passed under the first row of lime trees and onto the tarmac path, heading for the last place he'd seen the dog. He ran his hand through his short, brown hair, scratching at his scalp.

'Syrup! Stop messing about. Come on! I need to get to work.'

The dog barked again in response.

'Will you get out of there,' Dessie half-shouted into the yew trees. 'Come on. Syrup!' He swung the hurley at twigs and other debris, snapping them and sending them scooting across the surface.

When he reached the tree line he bent down slightly to gaze under the lowest branches. He could see the dog away to his right in behind the trees on the far side of the avenue near to the cemetery wall, sniffing at something on the ground.

'Leave it alone. Come on, Syrup.'

The dog barked in reply, asking him to come and take a look.

'Jesus!' Dessie crouch-walked quickly between the lower branches of two trees and hurried along the tree-enclosed path toward the dog. As he neared the cemetery entrance he lowered himself to his haunches. Through the second row of trees he could see a foot.

He shifted to one side. A man's naked body was laid out on the ground between the stone wall and a slight mound of earth. The body was parallel to the wall, his feet pointed towards him, a white, plastic bag tied round his head. The body had been daubed with blue paint; a wide line circled each nipple and belly-button, carelessly covered the man's flaccid penis, edging his upper things, and thick streaks ran down the outside of each upper arm and the thigh of each leg.

'Holy Mother of God,' Dessie hissed, backing away and struggling to pull his mobile phone from his pocket. 'Get away from there. Syrup! Come here.' He gestured at the dog, patting his thigh, trying to tempt him away from the body.

The dog stared at him and then back to the body, a quizzical look on its face.

'McEvoy.'

'I've been told to inform you,' said a female voice, 'that they've found another body out in Maynooth that fits the profile of the Glencree killing.'

'What? Oh, Jesus Christ!' McEvoy muttered, the news slowly sinking in. 'Right, okay, tell the local super that I'll be there shortly. And make sure the crime scene people are on their way out there and the pathologist has been informed.'

'Yes, Sir. I'll ...'

'Good, thanks,' McEvoy interrupted, disconnecting the call, flipping on the blue lights hidden behind the radiator grill.

His mobile rang again. He snatched it up. 'McEvoy.'

'Colm, I want a full update when you get there, okay,' Tony Bishop instructed without introducing himself.

'Absolutely. I'm going to need a second investigative team.' It was standard practice that each murder would be investigated by a new team. Each crime would involve thousands of hours of searching, interviewing, sieving, checking. It was unrealistic that one team would try and do this several times over and simultaneously. The trick was to link and stitch each separate investigation together. That was McEvoy's job – to work with the officers in charge of each strand to weave an overall tapestry.

'I'm sending Charlie Deegan out to you. I've been onto him already. He's ...'

'Are you sure that's a good idea?' McEvoy interrupted, caution in his voice. Charlie Deegan was an ambitious, up-and-coming detective. While he had the potential to be a good investigating officer he cut corners, always following the most obvious line of enquiry. He wanted *a* result, not necessarily the right result. Given that most of the time the obvious line of enquiry was the correct one, he'd closed cases quickly, successfully and, of appeal to senior management, cheaply.

To make it worse, Deegan was determined to rise up the ranks as quickly as possible. As a result, he was quite happy to stand on anybody who would lever him upwards, to take credit where none was due, to push blame onto colleagues who didn't deserve it, and to generally employ any tactic that would get him noticed as a high flyer and cast his colleagues as bumbling idiots. At the same time, he cultivated friendships with those higher up the system that could develop his career and secure him promotion.

'I know Deegan has a bit of a reputation and him and Plunkett aren't exactly best buddies,' Bishop continued, 'but they'll just have to work with each other. Deegan might be a bit of a loose cannon sometimes, and he might have his head stuck up his own arse, but he knows what he's doing.'

'Right, okay,' McEvoy muttered, disappointment in his voice, unable and unwilling to challenge Bishop's decision.

'Clunk their heads together if they get a bit thick,' Bishop advised, as if managing things would be as simple as admonishing them and moving on.

McEvoy ended the call and pocketed the phone, feeling deflated. He was going to get squeezed from above and below, sandwiched between egotism and antagonism.

McEvoy ran his hand over his close-cropped, thinning hair as he turned left onto Maynooth's main street. He needed another cigarette. And a good night's sleep. Instead he shoved his plastic stick between his lips and made do. He drove down between the small, two-storey, terraced houses, the ground floors a gaggle of shops, cars jammed in narrow parking spaces in front of them, the street lined with pollarded lime trees.

A hundred yards later he passed through a set of traffic lights and the ruins of the 15th century castle, and approached the front gates of the university. The place had once been described to him as being like an Oxford college dropped in an Irish field, though he'd never actually ventured onto the campus to see for himself, despite passing through the town numerous times. Its location, like Glencree, was the result of events in France.

Before the French revolution of 1789 the British had denied Irish Catholics the right to operate a seminary to train their priests. Instead seminarians travelled to France to be educated. With revolution and the subsequent wars with Austria and Britain, the British became afraid that the fledgling priests would bring similar ideas and actions to Ireland. In an effort to thwart an Irish revolution, in 1795 an Act of Parliament gave permission for a seminary to be built in Ireland and the Duke of Leinster donated lands on the edge of Maynooth village not far from his Carton estate. Despite its establishment, in 1798 the Irish rebelled, but without military help from their French allies were soon defeated. The seminary, however, had continued to operate. From 1910, St Patrick's College had been part of the National University of Ireland, and in 1997 the seminary and university had become two separate entities, sharing the same campus, but with their own administrations, structures, procedures, and degrees.

A local guard stood between the light grey pillars, a grand manor house with long, cream-coloured residential wings behind him. Slightly off to the right, a tall steeple climbed into the grey sky. Just inside the gate, a couple of local security men stood by a wooden hut looking slightly lost.

McEvoy lowered the window and held out his identification. 'Detective Superintendent McEvoy,' he announced. 'National Bureau of Criminal Investigation.'

The guard glanced at the card and nodded in acknowledgement, stepping out of the way. 'Round to the left, Sir. Keep going as far as you can.' He pointed along the roadway. 'Go past the orchard and park in on the right.'

McEvoy nodded back and accelerated through the gates, swinging to the left. He followed the road up and passed another manor house and a Boston ivy covered building. He slowed as he approached a crossroads, passing straight across and between some workshops, a sign for the staff dining room, and into a small car park. In front of him was a two-storey set of classrooms and off to the right was the imposing, drab grey of the seminary building.

A little laneway ran out the far side alongside an old orchard, its trees let grow, their branches old, long and gnarled. He drove up the laneway and turned right into a large car park that ran the length of the school-like building and the seminary buildings beyond. It was filled with a dozen or so cars and vans, some painted in garda colours, and 15 or so people. A uniformed guard directed him to a parking space. He parked the car where instructed and eased himself out into the shadow of the building.

Off to his left a few guards were milling around a large crucifix affixed to the top of what seemed like a mound of earth. The crucifix was placed at the end of a row of yew trees, 40 or 50 yards long leading off to the left. He pulled his collar up against the chill wind and set off towards them, slowing puffing on his plastic cigarette, passing an aqua-coloured health and safety sign warning that dogs should be kept on a lead, and a short low wall on which were fixed two taps.

As he neared the crucifix he could see that it rose out of a low rockery. Atop of the cross was a small roof. You nail a man to a cross, McEvoy thought, and yet you shelter him from the rain? Someone had their priorities mixed up.

The four guards stood at the foot of the crucifix were all local. They occasionally swapped a few words but mostly they looked lost, waiting for orders. One of them kicked at some glass on the tarmac as they watched the tall figure, wearing a suit a couple of sizes too big, approach.

'Detective Superintendent McEvoy,' McEvoy announced. 'Where's the body?'

'Down there,' one of the guards pointed along the yew tree avenue, 'on the left near to the cemetery wall.'

McEvoy looked down between the trees, the branches from each row knitting together to create a darkened tunnel 30 feet high. He could see two men standing together talking by the archway framing the entrance to the cemetery. He muttered a 'Thanks' and strode past a metal fence and in under the yew tree canopy.

As he approached the men turned to watch him. McEvoy recognised one of them as Dermot Meaney, the local Superintendent. Meaney was almost the total opposite to Peter O'Reilly. Tall, thin, uniform immaculate, shoes polished, well groomed. The other man was younger, shorter and more thickset, and not as well turned out.

As he reached them McEvoy extended his arm taking Meaney's hand, shaking it. 'Dermot. How's it going?'

'It was going fine until this.' He jerked his thumb over his shoulder, before realising that he needed to introduce the second person. 'This is Tom Bacon, the local sergeant. Tom, this is Detective Superintendent Colm McEvoy of NBCI.'

McEvoy shook the sergeant's hand. 'Good to meet you, Tom. So what have we got?' he asked the pair.

The two men shuffled out of McEvoy's line of sight and he crouched down to get a better view. The body was poorly hidden from the path, but well screened from the car park because the area in between contained hundreds of saplings, 3 or 4 feet high, the grass high around them.

'By the look of him, he's been dead a while,' Meaney offered. 'Some time in the night is my guess. A local man found him an hour or so ago – out walking his dog. It's a pretty quiet spot despite everyone being on campus. He hit his ball near to the trees and the dog ran in underneath and found the body.

'Do we know who he is yet?' McEvoy asked.

'Not at the moment,' Meaney replied. 'All of his clothes seem to be missing. We need to get the bag off his head – no other way of telling. No one locally has reported anyone missing in the last 24 hours, unless he's from somewhere else and the body's just been dumped here?'

McEvoy nodded and took a step forward onto the edge of the path. 'We'll need to get that checked out. How long until the crime scene people get here?'

'They're on their way. I spoke to them five minutes ago. They were just passing Lucan on the motorway.'

'How about the pathologist?'

'She's on her way too. She was just leaving. He left his cards in the cemetery.' He moved towards the archway. 'Obviously the same madman that killed the girl up in Glencree.'

'Looks that way,' McEvoy said, his mind wandering elsewhere. Two victims killed, potentially five more to go. They'd barely got started on the investigation into Laura's death and now there was another to deal with. One that looked equally bizarre. He followed Meaney through the archway, noticing the plaque listing names and dates embedded in its 4-foot thick wall. Another uniformed guard was stationed on the far side of cemetery, blocking access in over the low wall, a hedge behind it.

In front of them was a tall, plain, Celtic cross. To the right was what looked like a small stone chapel with a heavy wooden door. To the left was a cluster of 20 or so low, stone Celtic crosses. Meaney led them past the tall cross and a couple more low stone crosses to a set of dark, plain, metal crosses, five in a row. Stuck to the top of them were the business cards.

'You can only be buried here if you lived and worked in the seminary,' Meaney explained. 'These would have probably been students who died while they were studying for the priesthood.'

McEvoy looked at the cards and then cast a glance around the graveyard. 'Any sign of a note?' he asked.

'Nothing beyond the cards,' Meaney replied. 'We haven't done a search of any kind, we were waiting for you and the crime scene team.'

McEvoy nodded at three rows of gravestones, each 15 or so long, opposite the metal crosses. 'What the hell has happened to those?' Many of the small crosses attached to the top of the small triangular stones had been knocked off.

'Local vandals,' Bacon explained. 'It's obviously good craic to smash up memorials to the dead,' he said sardonically.

'Jesus Christ,' McEvoy muttered, anger boiling up in him. If anyone did this to Maggie's grave there would be hell to pay. The little feckers would wish they hadn't been born. He wandered over to one of the smashed gravestones. What was the sense in breaking it? The man had been dead over a hundred years.

He turned back to the other two. 'Right, okay. Who's the head of security here.'

'Martin Cleary,' Bacon answered. 'Used to be …'

'I know Martin,' McEvoy interrupted. 'We worked together a few times when I was starting out. I wondered what had happened to him when he retired. I always thought he'd head back out west. He still a cantankerous old bugger?'

'You could say that,' Meaney replied sourly.

'Good,' McEvoy said, 'I always thought it suited him.'

He set off for the car park. As he neared, a bright red sports car drove in through the orchard gate and pulled to a stop. Charlie Deegan eased his well-toned frame out of the car, brushed a hand through his thick, dark hair, and cast his gaze over the other vehicles. He spotted McEvoy, shut his car door and headed towards him, beeping on the alarm.

'Sir,' Deegan smiled.

'Charlie,' McEvoy stated flatly. 'The victim is next to that set of yew trees, by the cemetery wall.' He pointed behind him. 'The crime scene people should be here any minute. Take them up there and have a look yourself – see what a sick bastard we're dealing with. Dermot Meaney's the local super, he'll help work the questionnaires, and Tom Bacon's the local sergeant. They're stood by that crucifix with some of their men. Who's your team at the moment?' McEvoy asked, seeking confirmation that things were as usual.

'DSs are Grainger, Murphy and O'Keeffe,' Deegan replied, a slightly amused look on his face. 'They're on their way. They left right after me.'

At least the core team were all sound, McEvoy reflected. Good guards with plenty of guile. All he hoped was that their common dislike of Deegan wouldn't hinder the investigation. He needed everyone pulling in the same direction. 'And did Tony Bishop brief you?'

'Yes, Sir.'

'Good. I'm going to talk to the head of security here, Martin Cleary. See what he has to say. I suggest you introduce yourself to the locals; I'll find you again afterwards to see how things are going.'

Deegan nodded and set off towards the crucifix.

McEvoy watched him for a moment then turned back towards the car park. He hoped Deegan was going to behave himself.

Martin Cleary was leaning against the bonnet of a white van, its side emblazoned with the crest of the National University of Ireland, Maynooth. His thick, white hair was stuck up in tufts, his face round, cheeks ruddy, and his green tweed suit crumpled. He looked as if he had fallen out of bed after a long night. He was talking to a middle-aged woman. She in contrast was immaculately dressed in a blue trouser suit and black shoes with a slight heel. Her long brown hair framed a stern looking face. They stopped chatting as McEvoy approached.

'Martin, long time no see. How's it going?' McEvoy extended a hand.

'I'm surviving, Colm.' Cleary pushed himself forward and shook McEvoy's hand warmly. 'Don't tell me you're in charge of this rabble?'

'For my sins,' McEvoy said. 'I'm Detective Superintendent Colm McEvoy,' he introduced himself to the woman.

'Clara Russell,' the woman replied in a clipped accent, 'health and safety officer for the university.'

'They made you a detective superintendent,' Cleary said, doubt in his voice. 'They must have been desperate, Colm.'

It was always difficult to tell whether Cleary was joking or not. McEvoy's policy had always been to think that the cantankerous old sod was speaking the truth dressed up in jest. The only way to deal with it was to reciprocate the compliment. 'Not as desperate as when they made you one, Martin.'

'You insolent young pup!' Cleary stated, an amused edge to his voice. 'I was sorry to hear about Maggie, Colm,' he said, changing his tone. 'Cancer's a terrible thing. A terrible thing,' he repeated. 'Colm's wife recently passed away,' Cleary explained to Clara Russell.

'I'm sorry,' Clara said, without sounding it.

'It's okay,' McEvoy said. 'We just take one day at a time. So, Martin,' he said, becoming more businesslike, 'you have anything that's gonna help us solve this murder? Any CCTV?'

'Only bit we have on this side is inside this place.' Cleary jerked his thumb towards the seminary building. 'The north campus is pretty well kitted out at this stage, but I'm still trying to convince the stupid buggers to install it on the south campus too. Same problem as ever. Money.'

'So you have no footage of the grounds? The entrances in and out?'

'No. Though he could have got in and out over one of the walls easy enough. The perimeter must be a couple of miles long and it's all fields and the canal on this side.'

'How about any of your team? Did they see anything?'

'Nothing out of the ordinary. Campus like this, there are people wandering around all the time. Quite a few people walk round the circuit here in the evening; getting a bit of exercise. We shut the library gates around ten o'clock, the main gates at eleven. Plus there are guests staying in campus accommodation and seminarians who live on site.'

'So he could have easily come and gone without anyone seeing him?'

'He could have walked out the front bloody gates and we'd not have a record of it,' Cleary said, a touch of anger in his voice.

'Jesus. Right, okay.' McEvoy spotted Cheryl Deale and her team walking down the path towards the crime scene. Just as there was a new investigative team, there was a new crime scene team. A lawyer would have a field day if he knew the same team had processed both sites. Any evidence could have been carried from one site to the other. It didn't matter that they wore disposable, protective gear, there was a hint of doubt, and that was enough to open a chink into the prosecution's case.

Charlie Deegan had broken off holding court with the local guards and was heading to meet them. 'Look, Martin, can you work with the locals to keep this site secured? Maybe pacify everyone being detained while we take statements?'

'No bother. You have a madman on your hands, Colm. We saw the body.' He nodded at Clara. 'Anything you need just give me a call.'

McEvoy met Charlie Deegan at the crucifix.

'My lot have arrived,' Deegan explained. 'I'm going to bring them up here so they can see what they're dealing with then I'll get them set up. I've spoken with Meanbag and Bacon Roll and a couple of their lads. I mean Superintendent Meaney and Sergeant Bacon,' he corrected himself. 'Sorry about that,' he continued disingenuously.

McEvoy did his best not to roll his eyes. Deegan wasn't sorry in the slightest. He was letting McEvoy know what he thought of the locals, which wasn't a lot. He'd obviously decided that none of them were going to be of any use in building his career.

'Keep an eye out for Elaine Jones,' McEvoy instructed, letting Deegan's insubordination slide. 'She should be here by now.'

'Will do.' Deegan set off back to the car park to meet his DSs.

McEvoy shook his head and strolled down the yew tree lane-way. Up ahead he could see Cheryl Deale and her two team members getting suited up.

'How're things?' he asked the team in general.

'Somebody's already fucked things up,' Cheryl Deale replied, agitated, not bothering with any pleasantries. The paper suit covered her slight frame and hair, just her face showing. Her eyes were bright blue above a small button nose. She held a camera in one hand; a video recorder hung round her neck.

'What?' McEvoy said, confused. 'No one's been near the body.'

'No, but people have been tromping all over its path. Can you see here?' She pointed into the low undergrowth. 'This is where he was dragged in.' She turned and pointed at the entrance to the avenue. 'He was probably killed down near that crucifix, pulled in under the trees, across onto the path, along it towards the cemetery,' she traced the route with her finger, 'and then back out the other side and into this hollow.'

'So he was dumped here?' McEvoy asked.

'Do you want the sarcastic answer to that?' Cheryl said caustically. 'I've just told you, he was dragged down the path.'

'Jesus, Cheryl, calm down.' McEvoy knew she was feisty, bullish even, but he thought her reaction was a little over the top. His hand instinctively played with the packet of cigarettes in his pocket. 'Is it going to make a difference?'

'Of course it's going to make a difference,' she snapped. 'Any bloody material is going to be contaminated.'

'Well how about the body?' McEvoy asked calmly.

'Give us a chance, we've only just got here. The body might have been stripped here – a lot more private than out on the path. We might pick up something.'

'Is there any chance we can get the bag off his head so we can identify him?' McEvoy added. 'We need to get started. We need to catch this bastard before he kills number three.'

'As soon as we get a clean route in, we'll do that,' Deale said, calming a little. 'The pathologist should be here shortly.' She moved away to one of the bags of equipment.

One of her two colleagues, the taller of the two men, sidled over to McEvoy. 'She's only in this mood because she hates Charlie Deegan,' he whispered. 'Anything goes wrong it's our fault, otherwise he claims all the credit. He's shafted us a few times.'

'Brendan,' Cheryl interrupted sharply, 'can you trace back the route of the body, tape it off, and see if you can find anything.'

'I'm on it,' the man said, pulling a tight smile at McEvoy. He plucked a role of blue and white tape from a bag and started to follow the edge of the yew trees, searching for the body's path.

McEvoy stood to one side and watched Cheryl Deale and her other colleague start to work. Behind him he could hear Charlie Deegan and his three DSs approach. His mobile rang again.

'McEvoy.'

'Dermot Brady hasn't been out of our sight since yesterday,' Plunkett said, 'except for when he was in his apartment.'

'So he couldn't have killed our man here then,' McEvoy replied.

'Doesn't look like it. Not unless he managed to sneak out,' Plunkett answered. 'I'd say he's off the hook.'

'Seems that way.'

'Should we keep a team on him?' Plunkett asked. 'Just in case.'

'What?' McEvoy asked, his mind wandering. 'No, no. There's no need. We know where he was. Look, I'd better get off. Keep in touch, okay.' McEvoy ended the call.

He turned his attention back to Cheryl Deale.

'Haven't you got anything better to be doing,' she asked, looking up, 'than watch us?'

Colm felt his face start to redden. 'I'll … I'll just go and see if Elaine Jones has arrived yet,' he said, embarrassed, feeling like a spare part.

Cheryl Deale stood with her feet wide apart, well away from the body, and leant over the victim's head. She cut one of the handles of the plastic bag with a scalpel and took hold of the corners and eased it back over the man's blue-grey face and slightly greying hair. Pulling it free she dropped it into a clear bag held open by one of her assistants.

The man's eyes stared up at them, wide and vacant rather than surprised. His lips were slightly parted, the bottom of his top teeth just visible. His forehead was grazed, grit still embedded in the wounds. There were two pinch marks at the top of his nose where his glasses usually rested. Deale shuffled her feet back a little and stood clear of the body.

McEvoy waved Martin Cleary forward from where he waited a few yards away with Charlie Deegan. He took a couple of steps and leaned towards the body, his hands shoved deep in tweed suit pockets.

'David Hennessey,' he growled. 'Worked in the politics department. I used to see him around. Liked a pint and a bit of a flutter, but nice enough man.' He leant back and looked at McEvoy. 'Don't know what he could have done to have deserved this, poor bastard.'

'Probably nothing,' McEvoy replied. 'Probably just another random victim. Do you know where he lives? Anything about him?'

'I doubt it's random, Colm,' Cleary said. 'Too much thought has gone into this. The place, the time, the way the body is painted. It's lots of things, but it ain't random.'

McEvoy pursed his lips, thinking about what Cleary had said. The man might of retired, and he might be a cantankerous old git, but he'd a lot of experience to draw upon.

'Personnel will be your best place to start,' Cleary continued. 'They'll have a file with his personal details in. Maybe a staff photo you can use.'

McEvoy nodded and turned to where Deegan stood. 'Charlie, you'd better …'

'… go and see what personnel have got,' Deegan finished quickly, clearly frustrated that McEvoy was in charge of things. 'I'm on it.' He started to head briskly back towards the car park.

'Right, well. I guess I'd better leave you to it,' McEvoy said, unsure what to say. He took one last look at the body and started to trail after Deegan, Martin Cleary in tow.

'This is a bad business, Colm,' Cleary said. 'A bad business.'

'I know.'

'And you need to watch that Deegan. He's only interested in glory. He'll be running his case, not yours. He'd dump you in the shit without hesitation if he thought he could fill your shoes.'

'I know that as well.'

'Just so long as you do, Colm. Just so long as you do. You've enough to be worrying about without watching your back. You need your people in here, not just his.'

McEvoy nodded, but didn't respond.

From behind them Cheryl Deale shouted out. 'Sir.'

McEvoy looked over his shoulder. She was waving for him to come back.

He set off, Cleary staying where he was, waiting to see if it was worth the effort of returning.

Cheryl Deale held a small plastic bag using a pair tweezers. 'It's a second note,' she explained. 'It was placed in his mouth in what looks like a sandwich bag.'

'Can you see what it says,' McEvoy asked, moving towards her.

She held the bag up level to her face. The bag had slightly unfolded but was still creased and there was condensation inside. 'Not really,' she said. 'I need to flatten it out.'

'Just pull the bag tight,' McEvoy suggested.

'The condensation might ruin the note.'

'Can we take the note out and put it in a new bag?' he suggested.

'I guess.' Cheryl nodded. 'Brendan, I'm going to need two evidence bags – one for the note and one for the bag.'

Brendan reached into a box and handed her a second pair of tweezers.

Gently Cheryl pulled the note free and dropped it into a bag held by him. She then put the sandwich bag into another bag. She took back the bag with the note in, handing the tweezers to Brendan. She peered through the clear plastic and read aloud.

The Rules
Chapter Two A: Motive D

"Murderers know, to varying degrees, that they are constructing a world of their making, a world different to that of their fellow citizens. They are driven by an imperative to act on their deviant desires. Many hold some notion that they have the right to play out their fantasies, or envisage themselves on a mission for God or some other entity that conveys on them the right to torture and kill. Yet others believe that their victims deserved the terrible crimes done unto them."

2a. Have no reason to kill beyond murder. The motive should be death itself. Nothing else.

2b. Do not let sex, money, religion or power cloud things. Pathology will be your downfall.

Master rule: Do it because you can, not because you have to.

'That's all it says,' she finished.

'All the same, sounds like he has it all worked out,' Cleary said, having walked back to the group when it was clear McEvoy was not going to re-join him. 'He understands the nature of motive; that the most difficult crime to solve is a motiveless one.'

'Can you get a copy made as soon as possible,' McEvoy instructed, ignoring Cleary. 'Give one copy to Deegan, the other to Barney Plunkett. Tell Barney to see if he can locate the quote. Is it the same source as before or a new one? And if you find anything else let me know. I want to nail this bastard. And we are going to nail him.' McEvoy sucked in a breath and pumped it back out through his nose.

'I'll do it straight away,' Cheryl said. 'Then we're going to do a wider sweep and also process where he left the cards. We're then heading back to the lab. I'll ring you the moment we get anything.'

'He thinks he's being clever,' McEvoy continued, 'but the perfect serial killer is the one who kills and no one even knows it's happening. People just disappear and are never found. He's leaving us notes and he's leaving us the bodies, which means he's leaving us evidence. We just need to make sense of it.'

McEvoy stood outside an old manor house and sucked deeply on his plastic cigarette. A sign stating 'Personnel Office' was pinned over a doorway. He watched Martin Cleary walk off towards the front gates and pulled his mobile from his pocket.

'Barney, it's Colm. Can you go through the centre's records and see if a David Hennessey has ever been through the place. Also check with Janine Smyth.'

'Who's David Hennessey?'

'The second victim. He worked here in the university in the politics department. Martin Cleary has just identified him. I want to know if there are any links between the victims.'

'You think there is a link?' Plunkett asked sceptically.

'I've no idea, but if there is then that's an opening. Look, I'd better be going. I need to catch up with the team here.'

'Is it going okay? Deegan behaving himself?'

'I'll talk to you later, Barney.' McEvoy disconnected the call and opened the door. Through an opening to the right he found a door marked reception. He knocked and entered. A woman in her forties was sitting behind her desk. A man wearing a garda uniform was standing behind her, looking over her shoulder. The two other desks in the office were empty.

The woman spoke. 'Can I help you?'

'I was looking for an officer,' McEvoy stated. 'DI Charlie Deegan?'

'And you are?' the guard asked.

'Detective Superintendent McEvoy. I'm the investigating officer for the murder up beyond.' He gestured to his right. 'I wanted to know what he found out about David Hennessey.'

'He left a couple of minutes ago, Sir,' the guard said, standing up straighter. 'He went off with the head of personnel – Carl Fahy – to Dr Hennessey's office. DI Deegan wanted me to stay here with Margaret while she searched through some files.'

McEvoy nodded. 'I think I'll catch them up. Can you tell me where Dr Hennessey's office is?'

McEvoy strode from the manor house and took a diagonal path leading towards the seminary buildings and the church. A couple of hours in and he was already feeling like a spare part. A tetchy spare part. Bishop was pulling strings but it was his investigation. Now things seemed to have drifted. Deegan was doing his own thing and he had no idea where the incident room was. He was running around on his own trying to catch up. He needed to either get hold of things and take charge or get off site and let them get on with it. He knew which Deegan would prefer. Deegan wanted this for himself. He'd run his own separate investigation competing, rather than collaborating, to catch the killer.

He slowed to a stop and pulled out his mobile, calling up Deegan's number. 'Charlie,' he barked into the phone. 'It's McEvoy. Where the hell are you?

'I'm over on the other campus checking out the dead guy's office,' Deegan replied coolly.

'Did you not think to call to update me? That I might want to see the office as well? I need to know what's going on.'

'Hang on a sec,' Deegan said.

McEvoy could hear a muffled apology and a door close.

'I was just trying to find out more about him,' Deegan continued, exasperation clear in his voice. 'The head of personnel offered to bring me over, so I came.'

'And what's the story on David Hennessey?' McEvoy continued. 'Does he have any family? Do we have any more details on him?' He watched two garda cars drive past him heading slowly back towards the main gate.

'He lives locally in one of the estates,' Deegan said, clearly unhappy with the tone of McEvoy's call. 'Lives on his own apparently. He's not married and he has no kids. I don't know if he has a partner or not. I'm going to talk to a couple of his colleagues and see what they know. His file says he was 52. He joined the university 20 years ago. Before that he'd worked at UCD for a couple of years. The guy was a plodder. He only got promoted to senior lecturer a few months ago.'

Dead wood for someone like Deegan, thought McEvoy. If you weren't near the top of the tree by 52 you were pretty much a failure. 'Where the hell is the incident room, Charlie?' McEvoy asked, changing subject.

'It's in the bottom of Rhetoric House.' There was a touch of frustration in Deegan's voice. 'It's one of the ivy covered buildings on the right as you head back to the main gate. There's a passage next to the swimming pool – it's just through there. They're at the end of the building setting up in a classroom and computer lab. Grainger should have called you.'

Simon's for a roasting, McEvoy thought. 'I want a team meeting there in ten minutes,' he stated. 'Sort out a full plan of action now we know who the victim is.'

'We have a plan of action,' Deegan stated. 'Grainger is

80

managing the incident room, Jane Murphy is doing interviews and managing witnesses, O'Keeffe is organising a search of the site and running questionnaires, and I'm looking after David Hennessey.'

'And I'm in charge of *two* murder investigations,' McEvoy snapped, irritation rising in him again. This wasn't like him, he knew, but he was tired and the stress was starting to build.

'It's going to take me more than ten minutes to walk back,' Deegan complained. 'I still need to look over his office and talk to a couple of his colleagues.'

'You can talk to his colleagues later. Just get back over here.' McEvoy hung up before Deegan could reply. He took a deep breath and blew it out slowly. That whole call was probably a mistake. It was most likely going to push Deegan further away. Make him more determined to run his own investigation rather than do McEvoy's bidding. He shook his head, frustrated at his own petulance. If Deegan was going to be a problem, through his making or not, he needed to make sure that Grainger, Murphy and O'Keeffe knew where their loyalties should lie. He glanced around looking for Rhetoric House.

'McEvoy,' he answered flatly into his mobile as he pushed open the heavy door into Rhetoric House. He hadn't come past a swimming pool. Instead a football pitch was set out in front of an old, three-storey, ivy-covered building. He hoped he was in the right place.

'Three things to report,' Barney Plunkett stated.

'And they are?' McEvoy stood in a short, tall hallway. On the wall on either side large pairs of curtains were hanging. At the far end the passageway split left and right.

'First, David Hennessey had been out to Glencree, the last time a couple of months ago. He bought a bunch of postgraduate students out here for a training weekend. He's brought them out here every January or February for the past four years. He's also been involved in a couple of courses they've run here on restorative justice. Apparently he's done a lot of work on this in the North recently. He was definitely in Janine Smyth's good books. She thinks the stuff he did was "really moving things forward in a positive way".' He said the last bit in a mocking manner.

'And do we know who were on those courses?' McEvoy pulled back the curtain on the right-hand side. Behind it was a large, old map, its delicate looking paper covered in faded, coloured ink.

'Problem kids, ex-paramilitaries and community development workers. We're putting a list together. I've also spoken to Angela Jenkins at the DHC. Seems David Hennessey was well known there amongst all the staff. He did a piece of work a couple of years back for Combat Poverty on policy and action concerning homelessness. He went round all the homeless agencies to see what they were up to. Seems he specialises in disadvantaged youth. He's been back a few times to catch up on their work and offer advice in tackling particular issues and sourcing monies.'

'Hence his interest in restorative justice in the North,' McEvoy observed. 'It's mainly aimed at youths in disadvantaged areas. So we have two links between the victims. They were both familiar with DHC and they both had visited Glencree. Do we know if he knew Laura? Did their paths ever cross?'

'Might still be coincidence,' Barney hazarded, ignoring McEvoy's questions.

'Might be, but they're not the kind of places that most people would have visited. There might be something in it.'

'I'll get myself down to the DHC and see what I can find out.'

'Good idea. Also, tell Fay to keep working the lists. There might be someone on them that shares their connection. And the third thing?' McEvoy prompted.

'Kenny's found one more of the missing homeless kids.'

'No sign of the other two yet?'

'No. I doubt we'll catch up with them for a while. Disappeared into the underworld.'

'Right, okay. If you get anything interesting call me.'

McEvoy ended the call and the phone rang almost straight away.

'McEvoy.'

'Colm, it's Elaine. We're just putting Dr Hennessey into the van. We're going to take him to Naas Hospital for the post-mortem. My first estimate is that he was killed last night sometime between nine and eleven. He was hit hard at the base of his skull, probably with a stone – something solid with a lot of force behind it. He then smashed his face on the tarmac when he fell. I'd say the bag followed that and he died of asphyxiation. I doubt the blow killed him; just knocked him unconscious. He died shortly after though. Sword through the mouth, now a bag over the head. Looks like he doesn't have a preferred mode of killing,' she observed.

'I don't think he cares as long as they're dead,' McEvoy stated.

'I'd say he cares very much. A lot of thought has gone into these killings, Colm, including how to kill them.'

McEvoy nodded to himself.

'I'll talk to you later, Colm,' the pathologist said, tired of waiting for a response, and terminating the call.

The killer had it all worked out. Where and when he was killing them, how he was doing it, and how he'd leave the bodies. The whole thing had been choreographed. The question was whether the victims were planned as well, or were they simply in the wrong place at the wrong time as the first chapter suggested?

McEvoy was standing next to a small platform leaning against a wooden lectern. Off to his right Charlie Deegan was sitting on the edge of a desk, removed from his own team who were sitting on a cluster of chairs to McEvoy's left. Cheryl Deale sat in the no-man's land between them. She was now free of the paper suit. She wore dark brown trousers, a pale blue round-neck shirt, and a darker, smoky-blue cardigan. Her hair was dark brown and plaited together into a long tail. McEvoy noticed that she seemed much older now that more than just her face was visible, somewhere in her mid-to-late forties.

He took a sip of water and cleared his throat. 'Right, okay, let's make a start. The first thing, this isn't a single incident murder. It's the second of a pair, and if we don't catch the killer, probably the second of a series. That means we need co-ordination and dialogue across the teams, not separate investigations.'

To his right, Deegan shifted his posture, bristling with hostility, his gaze fixed on the cheap carpet.

'I've been talking to Barney Plunkett,' McEvoy continued. 'It seems that David Hennessey was a regular visitor to Glencree and the Dublin Homeless Co-operative drop-in centre on Gardiner Street. So we have two points of connections between our two victims. The question is, did they know each other and did they also know their killer?'

McEvoy paused and looked round the group. He could almost hear the cogs whirring. He continued. 'Simon, I'm going to need you to liaise closely with Fay Butler and Barney Plunkett. Anything that comes in here you cross-check with them, especially names. Who else has connections with both DHC and Glencree? Were any of the DHC people out here last night? The killer claims they were random victims, but they don't look that way to me. They share common acquaintances. They look like they've been selected, along with the time, place, and method. Both attacks have been carefully planned. Which means familiarity.

'Charlie, I want you to go back over to Hennessey's office. Find out what you can about his work in Glencree and the DHC

– names of people attending the courses, collaborators, any correspondence. And talk to his colleagues. Find out whatever you can about him and try and fill in his movements yesterday.'

Deegan gave him a look that said 'I was about to do all of that before you hauled me back over here, you feckin' moron'.

McEvoy ignored him. 'Cheryl do you want to …' His mobile phone started to ring. He fished it out of his pocket, stared at the screen and decided he'd better answer it. 'McEvoy.'

'We're going to need to hold a press conference as soon as possible,' Bishop stated.

'What?' McEvoy spluttered. 'Why?' He held up a hand apologetically to signal to Deale, Deegan and the others he needed to take the call.

'Because he's sent a bunch of his feckin' business cards and the first two chapters of his so-called self-help manual to the media. They've nicknamed the son-of-a-bitch The Raven. Or he's chosen the name himself.'

'Makes sense, I guess,' McEvoy said, threading his way through the group and out into the corridor.

'What?' Bishop replied tetchily.

'He had a picture of a bird on his card and the raven is something to do with death in mythology. They transport you to the afterworld or something like that,' he hazarded. 'I'll get someone to look into it.'

'Whatever the meaning,' Bishop said, frustration in his voice, 'we need to decide what we're going to do about what he's sending to the media. They're bombarding the press office with questions.'

'They knew about the cards and the notes in any case,' McEvoy said.

'But they didn't know what was in them! And they shouldn't have feckin' known about them in the first place!'

'Can't we just issue a statement?' McEvoy suggested wearily. He didn't want to have to deal with this. It was way down his list of priorities. 'I don't have time to come in for a press conference; I'm tied up here trying to co-ordinate two investigations.'

'Which is why they want to talk to you!'

'Surely you're the best person to deal with this?' McEvoy said, hoping that Bishop would take the bait.

Bishop stayed silent thinking the situation through.

Unsure about what to do, McEvoy filled the silence. 'Maybe the best thing to do is ask for an embargo on printing the material? Or maybe they could talk about the material without actually publishing it verbatim? Printing the cards and books are just going to cause a panic. Everyone will know there are more murders to come. That's what he wants. He wants to create a panic.'

'There *are* more murders to come if we don't catch the bastard,' Bishop snapped. 'If people knew that then maybe they'd look out for themselves; protect themselves.'

'That's not going to stop him,' McEvoy said patiently. He wasn't handling this well. 'There'll still be people who will leave themselves vulnerable. What can we do, shut down the whole the country?' It was a facetious statement and he knew it.

'No, we can catch the son-of-a-bitch! But if we don't catch him and we don't alert the public then there'll be hell to pay. We're going to have to do something.'

'I still think a statement is the best thing,' McEvoy persisted. 'It means we can set out exactly what we want to say. There'll be no confusion.'

'You're still going to have to talk to them at some point, Colm.' The edge started to fade out of Bishop's voice now that they seemed to have a plan. 'I'll deal with them for today, but I'm setting up another press conference for tomorrow morning. Early. Say 9 a.m. You're going to need to discuss the Hennessey murder in any case. And I don't want any excuses. Just make sure you're there and that you look presentable. Dig your uniform out if needs be.'

Charlie Deegan closed the office door and strode down the corridor and out through the automatic doors. He'd looked through Hennessey's office and interviewed three of his colleagues: a pretentious prick, Miss Prim-and-Proper, and a saucy old cow. As far as Deegan was concerned they were living safe and cosy lives, locked in their ivory towers thinking they knew something about the world, but really knowing nothing about hardship, or poverty, or crime; about the sharp end of the stick. How could they with their heads stuck in books and living boring, middle-class existences in the suburbs? He'd rushed through the interviews, still angry at being belittled by McEvoy at the meeting. And in front of *his* team.

He wanted to get back over the other side of the campus to check on progress; to make sure that things were being run as they should be; to make sure they knew whose team they were playing for. Besides, he would end up doing a better job than McEvoy. The guy was a washout. The only reason he was there was they needed a superintendent. It wasn't like he was any kind of genius and Deegan would soon make the rank. There was no question of that; he was the rising star of NBCI. They might as well have given the case directly to him. Still he'd better give McEvoy a call. Play along with the idiot. He pulled up his number.

'McEvoy.'

'It's DI Deegan,' he said, businesslike. 'I've just finished over at Hennessey's office. His diary shows that he was out at Glencree in January. He's also visited the DHC twice this year. Once in January and once in March; both for just a couple of hours. The name in the diary is Angie Jenkins. I'll get someone to go through his machine, look at his email. His colleagues weren't much help. They didn't seem to know much about what he did or his personal life. They all said he was a quiet, pleasant person who got on well with students, was a good colleague, and was social enough. The usual kind of stuff,' he said disingenuously as if no one could be as nice as people said. 'All they knew about his home life was that he was a confirmed bachelor and that he had a brother living in Dublin, a sister in Fermanagh and another in the US somewhere. I'll get Jane to take full statements from them.'

'Did any of them work with him on any projects?' McEvoy asked.

'No. Seemed he liked to do things on his own. He'd work with groups and government and that, but he did all the writing himself,' Deegan clarified. 'He put in the hours; regularly in here until 7-7.30, and at weekends.'

'Right. Right, okay.'

He could almost hear the cogs going round in McEvoy's head. 'So what now?' he pressed.

'We work the search and the questionnaires, we liaise with the other team, and we see what comes up.'

'I'll check in on the others. I'll talk to you later on.' Deegan ended the call before McEvoy could say anything in response.

He smiled to himself and dropped the phone back into his pocket. He looked down at the notepad, wrapped in clear plastic. The top sheet had Dermot Brady's name scrawled across it and circled. He wanted to check that out himself. Brady's name had already come up several times. He had all the appearances of a prime suspect. Which meant he was the logical place to start. Deegan knew if he could crack this case then the promotion to superintendent was as good as in the bag.

'Hello?'

'Hi, it's me,' McEvoy said.

'I've heard the news,' Caroline replied. 'You want her to stay over?'

'Please,' McEvoy said with apology in his voice. 'I'm not sure how long this is going to go on, but I'm going to be flat out until we catch the bastard. He's going to keep killing until we stop him.'

'Look, don't worry, I've already got the spare bedroom sorted. She'll be grand. She's stayed over loads of times.'

'Tell Jimmy that I'll treat you both to a weekend away in a hotel somewhere down the country,' McEvoy offered. He knew Jimmy didn't mind Gemma staying over, but at the same time he wanted the fact to be acknowledged; that they weren't being taken for granted.

'He'll be happier with tickets to Old Trafford.'

'I'll work on it,' McEvoy said without any idea about how he'd source them. 'Look, thanks for doing this, Caroline. I really appreciate it.'

'It's no bother. What's family for? Just make sure you catch him.

'I'll do my best. We're doing our best. I'll call you later to talk to Gemma,' he ended, guilt filling him with regret for the lost time, for not being there, for letting her down; knowing that he would always be doing so given his job. Often he would be away from days or weeks at a time if a murder was committed elsewhere in the country, away from Dublin.

'McEvoy,' he answered distractedly, staring down at a witness statement.

'It's John Joyce. I've looked up the raven in mythology as you requested. Do you want me to send you the file?'

'No, no, you can give it to me later. Just give me the edited highlights for now.'

'Well,' Joyce paused, gathering his thoughts, 'the raven appears in a whole load of different religions and myths – Norse, Celtic, North American, Greek. It's associated with death in all of them. It's either the messenger of death, or a medium of communication with the underworld. It's also considered by some to be the bringer of war or misfortune, mainly because it hung round battlefields and ate the dead. Er, let me see.' There was a slight pause as Joyce skipped through his notes.

'In Irish folklore, the raven is omniscient, all seeing and knowing. It's linked to a couple of mythical characters – the Celtic goddess Morrigane and the war goddesses of Badbh, Macha and Nemain who took the form of ravens. For North American Indians it seems that the raven appears as a deity and is a powerful shapeshifter, being able to transform into anyone or anything to get what it wants. Or he's a trickster, fooling people into giving him what he wants, something that might be of great personal harm.

'According to Wikipedia,' he quoted, 'a "raven can be a magician, a transformer, a potent creative force, sexual deviant or ravenous debaucher but always a cultural hero". The "raven has also been described as the greediest, most lecherous and mischievous creature known to the Haida" – a tribe on the pacific coast,' Joyce elaborated, "but at the same time Raven always helps humans in our encounters with super natural beings". That's it really. Basically, it's a dark bird. An eater of flesh. A bird that tricks and cheats, but sometimes for people at the expense of gods. The collective noun is unkindness,' he added, almost as an afterthought. 'An unkindness of ravens. Though I found it called a terror in one source. I've printed off a few webpages I found using Google.'

'Jesus,' McEvoy said, exhaling. 'The bringer of death, a god, a messenger, a trickster, a shapeshifter. He thinks he's invincible.'

'He's bound to have made a mistake,' John Joyce offered. 'He's not as clever as he thinks he is. Nobody is.'

'Perhaps not, but he's definitely put a lot of thought into this. Look, I'll see you later at the team meeting. Thanks for the update.' McEvoy terminated the call and tumbled the pack of cigarettes in his pocket. Whoever The Raven was, he'd spent months preparing for these murders, carefully constructing the plot, writing the chapters, developing a profile for the media, planning the slayings; making sure it all hung together as a coherent whole. This wasn't about killing, this was about notoriety. He was probably already in place for the next slaying.

McEvoy cast his gaze round the room. Both teams were present. Barney Plunkett, Fay Butler and Simon Grainger were huddled together swapping notes and ideas, standing next to two notice boards onto which were stuck photos, victim details and sketch maps. Padraig O'Keeffe, Jane Murphy and John Joyce were sitting together chatting and gesturing at a pile of photofits. Kenny Johns and Charlie Deegan stood halfway down the room trying to out-pose each other while tracing the room every now and then with conspiratorial gazes. Hannah Fallon stood by a hot water urn making herself a cup of coffee, surveying the scene, an amused smile on her face. Cheryl Deale and Dermot Meaney hovered nearby sipping from white mugs.

McEvoy looked at his watch – 7.50 p.m. – and tried to ignore the rumbling of his stomach. Twenty-four hours previously David Hennessey was probably just getting ready to head off on his last evening's walk. He rapped his knuckle on the blank whiteboard placed just to the right of the lectern. 'Okay, okay, let's make a start.' He waited while they shuffled to their seats. 'I think the best way to do this is for each team to give an update then we'll take it from there. We'll take the Glencree murder first. Barney, you want to start?'

Plunkett stayed seated. 'It's been a slow day. John continued the search of the surrounding area for any evidence – dumped bags and the like – but nothing so far. Kenny's managed to track down another of our homeless abscondees. There are still two missing. God knows where they are. Fay's been working through the centre's records trying to make an inventory of everyone who's stayed or attended one of their courses. It's a thankless task. It seems as if every criminal on the island has been through their doors.

'I've been talking to Laura's family and also to the DHC about David Hennessey. He'd been in to see them a couple of times in relation to research projects he'd been doing. It all seems in order. He'd had a grant from Combat Poverty to do the work. As far as anyone knew Hennessey had never come into contact with Laura. That's about it really. We're just running the usual routines trying to spot a way in.'

McEvoy nodded. 'Charlie?'

People twisted round in their seats so that they could see Deegan. Like Plunkett he stayed seated. 'I've been through Hennessey's office and his computer. Nothing much to report from that. The guy was anally retentive – liked everything neat and tidy; obsessively so if you ask me.' He didn't mention the five emails to Dermot Brady arranging to go for a few pints after the DHC meetings.

'O'Keeffe and Murphy have had more luck with the witness statements and door-to-door. They've managed to put together a timeline and a photofit. Seems there was someone well wrapped up hanging around the place – baseball cap pulled low, scarf hiding most of his face. The description's a bit vague – anywhere from 5 feet 7 to 6 feet tall; slim and well-built; but it's a start. Hennessey was seen walking in the university grounds between 8.30 and 9.00, but he disappears after that. Nothing else to go on at the minute.' Deegan drew to a close.

'Cheryl?' McEvoy prompted.

'Same as earlier. We're still processing materials from the site. We'd hope to get something more concrete for tomorrow. We're waiting on the lab. There's not much to go on to be honest. He cleaned up after himself; left us the minimum to go on.'

'Same for us,' Hannah continued. 'We're still waiting for results to come back from the lab. It's just a waiting game at the minute.'

'We need to work at the links between Laura Schmidt, David Hennessey and the DHC,' McEvoy stated, turning to the white-board. He drew a triangle with the letters L, D and DHC at the points. 'I'm not convinced that the victims were picked at random as the first note says. The killings were meticulously planned – they were not spur of the moment murders. I think that both Laura and Hennessey came into the orbit of the killer well before either of them were killed. They were known to him in some way. How? Who did they both know in common? I want to know.

'Barney, I want you to take charge of that angle.' He noticed Deegan start to bristle. 'Charlie, I want you and your team to concentrate on finding out who the mystery man in the photofit is.' Deegan didn't look any happier. 'Also talk to David Hennessey's family. Try and find out as much as you can about him, who he knew, who might hold grudges against him; the usual stuff.'

Deegan looked away, a sour pull to his face.

'Kenny, keep looking for those homeless kids. Try the other cities and spread the word around. John, I need you to concentrate on identifying the two quotes he used on his notes. Where are they from and is the source significant? Also liaise with the media and see if we can trace where he posted his letters to them from. If nothing else it might give us a fix on his movements.'

'Simon, Fay, I want you two to continue to work closely together. Keep building the files, but also try and identify the links between them. It's the connections that are going to lead us to him. It doesn't matter how small or seemingly insignificant they are, work them through. The tiniest of things might crack this whole thing open.'

They both nodded their heads in confirmation.

'Anyone got any other observations or questions?' McEvoy paused, but no one spoke. 'No? Okay, let's get back to it. People will now be home after work, there'll be a new batch of people to survey.'

Charlie Deegan walked up past the orchard heading for his car. He pulled up a number on his mobile and pressed call.

'Yeah?' said half as accusation, half as question.

'It's Charlie. How you getting on?'

'I, er,' the voice hesitated. 'I lost him about 15 minutes ago. Don't worry, I'll find him again. He gave me the slip near Middle Abbey Street. I think there might …'

'For fuck's sake,' Deegan interrupted. 'I only asked you to do one feckin' thing.'

'Yeah, as a favour Charlie,' the voice said unhappily. 'As a favour.'

'Just find him, okay.'

'What do you think I'm trying to do?'

'If this fucker kills again …' Deegan let the sentence hang.

'If you think this idiot's the killer, why have you only got me tailing him? Does Colm McEvoy know what you're up to? You'd better know what the fuck you're doing Charlie, because if I get into hot water, I'm dragging you in with me,' the voice threatened.

'Just find him, okay.' Deegan terminated the call. 'For fuck's sake,' he hissed to himself. Dermot Brady was running round loose. If anything happened and that note or the emails came to light he'd be in big bloody trouble. On the other hand, if he collared Brady, and he was the killer, no one would care how he solved it, just that he had. The next promotion would be in the bag and he wouldn't have to take any more crap off of McEvoy. It was worth the risk.

He was confident nobody had followed him to the edge of the park. He turned off the engine and switched off the lights. The side street was quiet, the street lights dim, the houses hidden behind high hedges.

It was time again. He unclipped his seatbelt and pulled on a black polo neck sweater, tugging it down over his ears. He reached across the passenger seat and dragged a black coat towards him, slipping into it. The park would be cold at this late hour.

Since the discovery of David Hennessey's body and the second chapter the story had been the centre of the media's attention. He was confident, however, that as long as he kept moving, they would not be able to keep up. The third slaying would add further confusion and division and without a definite line of enquiry, he could operate with impunity.

He'd expected to be interviewed by a guard – perversely welcomed it – and it had been as easy as he'd expected. He'd scripted everything in advance and he'd just stuck to the script. The guard had hurried through his questions with only half his attention seemingly on the process and he'd then left him alone.

He'd taken a risk following McEvoy earlier that morning, but he would stay away from them from now as much as possible. After all, there was no point having rules if one was going to constantly keep breaking them; he needed to play his own game not constantly worry about theirs.

He pushed open the car door and eased himself out. From the back seat he collected a small, black rucksack and a red baseball cap. His body tingled with anticipatory tension, his controlled rage starting to pin-pick in crimson bursts. He took a deep breath, letting it out slowly, collecting himself, pushing the anger deep down into the pit of his stomach, well away from his focused mind. He needed to manage his fury, harness it, and not lose himself in it. That would lead to mistakes.

He closed the car door and set off towards the darkness beyond the gates.

The light was fading fast and the Phoenix Park was becoming quieter. An irregular stream of cars coasted along the main thoroughfare; a couple turned off to find a secluded spot out of the view of prying eyes. A few late walkers bundled along in pairs trying to burn off calories; some took a more leisurely pace, throwing balls for dogs. A handful of cyclists kitted out in the lurid colours of some team sped around doing laps. A handful of runners in one or twos pounded wearily around their circuits, their legs trying to match the rhythm being pumped into their heads via earphones. The sound of the surrounding city could hardly be heard beyond the park's walls.

Lurking in the dark shadows of the trees, away from the path, a figure pulled his baseball cap lower across his eyes, checked both left and right and stepped out quickly across a dirt path that ran parallel to a paved one just a couple of yards away, a road immediately beyond that.

He placed the looped end of a black-coated, steel wire around a tree trunk at chest height, fed the rest of the bunched wire through the loop, and retraced his steps back across the path to the nearest tree, feeding out the wire. He passed the free end of the wire around the trunk and pulled it tight. Keeping the tension, he spun the steel cable round twice more and tied it off. Visible for barely a couple of seconds, he backed away into the shadows and lay flat on the ground, blending into the dark, a pair of wire cutters clutched in his hand.

Twenty seconds later a runner came into view. The man was pounding out a steady rhythm, his feet slapping against the tarmac of the path. He ran past where the wire was primed, oblivious to its presence, and disappeared into the dusk.

After a short while a second runner appeared. Rolling from side to side, gasping for air, her eyes focused on the dirt path three yards distant. Robbie Williams, singing Rock DJ, urged her on via earphones snaking from the pink iPod mini strapped to her upper arm. She wore a light grey t-shirt with the letters UCSB written across the front in blue, the underarms and neck dark grey with sweat, a pair of black, tight-fitting Lycra shorts that stopped just short of her knees, and a pair of white running shoes.

She had last been in reasonably good shape ten years ago when she had played hockey while studying in the United States. She was now three stone heavier and a long way short of fit. She was hoping that the stitch in her side would ease shortly. That or she was going to have to stop for a breather. She shouldn't have pushed so hard earlier on, she should have taken a more measured approach. She'd only been running round the park for two-and-half weeks, setting out every other night. The first time she had only managed one circuit, sucking in air while her heart threatened to break through her ribs.

The wire caught her high on her chest just under her collarbones. The air shot out of her lungs, her face twisting into a look of surprise and pain, legs running through empty space. She fell almost horizontally, slamming into the ground heavily, her head thumping off the packed earth.

Her assailant darted out onto the dirt path, glancing left and right. He slammed the wire cutters into the stunned woman's face, breaking her nose and shattering a cheekbone. Satisfied she was pacified he threw the cutters toward the base of the nearest tree and grabbed the woman by the shoulders, dragging her quickly off the path, away from the road into the darkness of the trees. His gloved hands closed round her throat and squeezed tightly. Off to his left a car swept round the roundabout and carried on down the avenue.

The woman, dazed and confused, managed to raise one arm and half-heartedly clawed at her attacker's hands, trying to relieve the pressure on her neck, her head feeling as if it were going to explode. With her other hand she tried to hit out at him. She tasted blood in her mouth and a few seconds later she gave up altogether, her arms falling limp.

The figure maintained the pressure, watching the woman's eyes bulge, white foam forming at the corners of her mouth, a trickle of blood escaping from her already bloodied nose. A minute later he checked for her pulse but found none. He quickly retrieved his wire cutters and wire and a small rucksack. Taking a heavy, dark sheet from the bag, he laid it over the body. He could hear another runner approaching through the gloom. He dropped to the ground, heart thumping, grasping the wire cutters. The feet slapped by and receded into the night.

McEvoy sat in his car, his head tipped back, plastic cigarette clenched between his lips. It was taking all his willpower not to replace the stick with a real smoke. He was exhausted. Totally shattered – physically, mentally, emotionally. He wasn't programmed any more for back-to-back 15-hour days or for trying to run parallel investigations on horrific murders. He doubted he ever was. The stress was eating him up, gnawing at his innards. He glanced in the car's rear mirror at himself. Forty-one years old, pushing 60. He was a shadow of what he used to be. His face was hollow and grey, his eyes sunken. He needed to start taking care of himself. He just couldn't work up the motivation or energy any more.

He should have headed off a couple of hours ago. Gone home, tried to relax, drunk a couple of whiskies and let things tumble around inside his head; allow the connections to float to the surface. Instead he'd tried to force them to rise, spending the last two hours looking through witness statements, trying to spot anything that might give them a breakthrough, determined to be the last to leave the incident room. Simon Grainger, Jane Murphy and Barney Plunkett had pulled out of the car park five minutes earlier. Calls were being diverted to a central call centre, the incident room guarded by a couple of locals.

He'd gotten so wrapped up in things he'd forgotten to ring Gemma, let her know his plans. No point now, he might as well just drive straight there. He sighed and tipped his head forward, started the car, and reversed back from the space. He'd visit Caroline's and see Gemma. Then ring his mother, and then maybe onto Maggie's grave, before returning home where he hoped his exhaustion would override his usual insomnia.

He stared off to his right through the gloom along the lime tree avenue. He could barely make out the crucifix with its little roof. It was nearly 48 hours since Laura Schmidt had been killed and they didn't have a single solid lead. There had to be something lurking in the jumble of samples and witness statements, some wisp of evidence that would show them the way. The problem was that it might take them days or weeks to unearth it and by then the killer would have struck again.

He needed some sleep. Maybe it would help clear the fog in his mind. And a nip of whisky. And a few cigarettes. He switched on the headlights and drove out slowly through the gate and past the orchard. As he reached the main gate his mobile rang.

He slowed to a stop and answered it. 'McEvoy.'

'Sir, you asked for any missing persons cases to be reported to you.'

'Yes.' He tipped his head back again and closed his eyes. He knew what was coming.

'A man has just reported his wife missing. She was jogging in the Phoenix Park. He's tried calling her on her mobile phone and he's been out looking for her but he can't find her. She always did the same circuit.'

'How long has she been missing?'

'An hour; hour and a half. She was due back at their house between 8.30 and 9 p.m. She's never been late before.'

'And she hasn't run off anywhere or met a friend? She's only been missing a short while.'

'We've told him it's too early to start a search, and I wouldn't be bothering you, but, you know, you requested …' she trailed off, before continuing. 'He says she would've never have switched off her mobile phone. She was only wearing a t-shirt and shorts. She would have rung if she was doing something else.' The dispatcher paused. 'He's very worried, Sir.'

'And she was running in the Phoenix Park?'

'Yes.'

'Okay, what's her name and age?' McEvoy asked, giving in, knowing that he had to check it out for his own peace of mind.

'Grainne Malone. She was 32. Married with no children. She lives on Benburb Street in an apartment block. It's next to the Collins Barracks.'

'Right, you'd better send out a couple of patrol cars,' McEvoy instructed. 'Tell them to go down every road and pathway and see if they can see anything. Give them a description. There's CCTV cameras at every gate, get a photo and get someone to check and see if you can spot her leaving. Find out what gate she would have been using. I'll be there in about 20 minutes; I'm still out in Maynooth. I'll meet them near the zoo entrance. Tell the husband not to panic and to tell us the minute she turns up.'

'He's worried she's been abducted.'

'She's probably met a friend and gone for a drink,' McEvoy said, a deepening pit opening in his stomach. 'Tell him we're sending someone round for a photo and that we've sent a couple of squad cars out to have a look for her. Reassure him that we deal with cases like this all the time and people usually turn up in a couple of hours with a tall story. We'll get back to him shortly.'

'Okay, I'll get onto it right away.'

McEvoy disconnected the call and accelerated towards the gate switching on the blue lights. Usually they would put the husband on the long finger for at least 24 hours, but he had a bad feeling about this. At over 1700 acres the Phoenix Park was one of the largest enclosed city parks in Europe, a large wedge of land stretching from the city centre to the old outer suburbs. It was about as isolated a spot in the city as you could find, with open rolling pasture, forests and gardens. It seemed to fit the modus operandi of the killer – a public space yet isolated and open. Except for the fact that it also contained Deerfield House, the American Ambassador's residence, Áras an Uachtaráin, the residence of the President of Ireland, Farmleigh House where guests of the state stayed when they were visiting the country, and Garda Headquarters, along with the offices of the Ordnance Survey Ireland and Dublin Zoo.

But these were only pockets of high security; little islands in the park's vast size. The killer probably relished the challenge of murdering within their shadow, though given the size and terrain the risks were no more than Glencree or Maynooth, and it would be easy to stick to the shadows of the trees and vault a wall rather than use one of the gates. As long as the killer stayed away from the high security sites he could wander round the park to his heart's content and no one would be any the wiser.

They were walking slowly along the dark, tree-lined roadway tracing the missing runner's route. A male guard was on the far side of the road, McEvoy and a female guard together. They crept along the tarmac path, their torch beams penetrating deep into the darkness, the trees rising above them. All they'd spotted so far was litter.

McEvoy sucked on the plastic cigarette, plucked it from his lips, and held it as if sheltering the tip from a wind. He checked his watch again. Ten to midnight. His tiredness had caught back up with him, along with a morose funk. He swivelled his neck and rolled his shoulders trying to ease the stiffness.

'Trying to give up, Sir?' the woman asked, seeking to start a conversation and fill the cloying silence.

'Trying,' McEvoy mumbled. 'Half succeeding.'

'I used the patches.'

'Did they work?' he asked, a fraction interested.

'Except for when I drink,' she replied. 'And when I'm stressed out or nervous.'

'Are you asking me whether I have any cigarettes?' he replied cupping the packet in his pocket and pulling them free.

'I've not been drinking, Sir,' she said, teasing a cigarette from the box.

McEvoy dropped the plastic cigarette inside the box and plucked one out for himself. He sparked a lighter and held it out to the woman. She lit her cigarette, her face glowing orange shadows, and he did the same. He drew the smoke deep into his lungs and they moved on in silence, their torch beams dancing in the gloom beneath the canopy.

Five yards further along the path the woman's beam stopped and moved back a few degrees. 'Sir!'

McEvoy swung his beam to find hers. Up ahead, off to the right was a low, dark mound. If the whole area around it hadn't been flat, they probably wouldn't have paid it a second glance. As it was, it was patently out of place.

'Do you think it's her?' she asked.

'We'll soon find out,' McEvoy replied, already knowing the answer, his stomach knotting with the knowledge.

They headed along the path until they were perpendicular to the mound. He swept his torch beam across the ground between themselves and the suspected body. It was clear where she had been pulled from the dirt path and through the grass, the blades flattened and previous year's autumn leaves dragged aside.

'I'm going to go back up a bit and cut across,' McEvoy said to the woman, indicating with his arm where he meant. 'Keep your torch fixed on the mound so I know where I'm going.'

'Okay,' she mumbled, an involuntary shiver running up her spine.

'And get rid of this for me.' McEvoy handed her his smouldering cigarette. 'Don't leave it on the ground.' He took a pair of sealed, rubber gloves from his suit pocket, opened the packet and slipped them on. A few yards along the path he headed in under the trees. The grass, wet from dew, soaked his shoes and the bottom of his suit trousers. He eased his way forward, scanning carefully his route before veering left toward the mound.

As he neared, he slowed to crawl, worried about disturbing any evidence. He lowered himself onto his haunches and, holding the torch in his right hand, lifted the heavy plastic sheet with his left. A bloodied foot and ankle came into view. The toes had all been severed crudely.

He let the sheet drop, moved to the other end and lifted the sheet again. The woman's eyes were bloodshot and bulging in their sockets, the middle of her face a bloody mess, the residue of froth stained the edges of her mouth. Her hair was half-pulled from her ponytail. He pushed his left elbow in under the sheet to tent it above the body, the torch beam illuminating the temporary chamber he'd created. He could see that she was still wearing her t-shirt and shorts; an iPod was strapped to her arm, though the headphones seemed to be missing. With his right hand he checked for a pulse. He couldn't find one.

He let the sheet fall back into place and closed his eyes, massaging them through the lids. Three days, three dead. There'd be another tomorrow; today in a minute, given the time. He hoped to God that the killer had left them more to go on with this victim than the previous two. It was all they could do to process the crime scenes and potential witnesses in a day, let alone stop another murder taking place.

He swivelled slowly on the balls of his feet and shone the torch beam further into the darkness. A few feet away a tree trunk reflected back a small, white oblong. Hung beneath it was small, clear plastic bag that looked to contain one of the missing toes and a folded note.

'Are you okay, Sir?' the female guard asked, concern in her voice, unnerved by McEvoy's silence. 'Is it our missing runner?'

'You'd better ring it through,' McEvoy replied flatly, levering himself back upright. 'We're going to need a crime scene team out here. Arc lights, the lot. Also get the gates shut and round up anyone still in the park. I want this whole place locked down. And get somebody to call through to Áras an Uachtaráin and the ambassador's residence and let them know what's happened.'

Feeling nauseous and impotent, he started to retrace his steps back to the path.

Chapter Three

Wednesday, April 16ᵗʰ

McEvoy stepped back onto the tarmac path. Both of his companions were on their mobile phones carrying out his instructions. He pulled his own phone from a pocket. The call was answered after several rings.

'Bishop.'

'It's Colm McEvoy. We have another body,' he said steadily. 'A woman in her early thirties killed whilst running in the Phoenix Park. He strangled her to death.'

'Jesus Christ,' Bishop muttered, still struggling to escape from his sleep.

'He cut off all her toes and left his calling card. We found her hidden under a sheet.'

'I think Jenny Flanagan's the next available DI,' Bishop said, trying to think through the situation. 'I'll give her …'

'It's okay,' McEvoy interrupted, taking control. 'I'll give her a call now. I just wanted to let you know that he's killed again. And that he's going to kill one person each day until he's finished his task,' he finished balefully.

'I, er,' Bishop mumbled, unsure what to say. After a pause he continued. 'Look, you know what to do. We have a press conference in the morning. I'll need to be fully briefed on this murder and the one yesterday.'

'I'll be there an hour beforehand,' McEvoy replied.

'Good. I'll see you then. Good luck, Colm,' Bishop said and ended the call.

McEvoy stared off through the trees and wondered whether Bishop would be able to go back to sleep now or whether the new death would eat into him like a cancer, gnawing at his brain through the long hours of the early morning.

A garda patrol car turned at the roundabout and shot towards them, its siren howling, its blue lights sweeping the trees. It pulled to a stop, its siren dying, the blue lights continuing to flash, a beacon for the other approaching vehicles.

He placed the call to Jenny Flanagan. It was answered almost straight away.

'Hello?'

'Jenny, it's Colm McEvoy. I'm afraid I'm the bringer of bad news.'

'He's killed again,' she predicted, an anxious delight in her voice.

'The body's in the Phoenix Park near to the papal cross,' McEvoy confirmed. 'You can't miss the blue lights. Round up the rest of your team and I'll see you shortly.'

'We'll be there as fast as we can,' Flanagan replied eagerly.

Another garda car pulled to a halt followed by an ambulance.

He had a clear view through the nightscope across the expanse of the park. In various shades of green he watched a figure walk to the edge of the car park and come to a halt, staring out into the darkness. Behind him the flashing lights of a garda car span, pulsing out its call sign.

His heart was thumping in his chest, his breathing laboured from his trip around the park. He was amazed that they had found the body so fast. It was probably still warm to the touch. He'd been expecting it to lie there until first light when an early runner would have pounded along the path to discover his night's work. He could live with their good fortune; they'd have a small head start on that part of the investigation, but he was still safe in his anonymity.

There had been something more satisfying about this killing. The woman had tried to fight back and it had been more visceral, more real. He could actually feel the life being wrung out of her; see the panic and confusion in her eyes. She had wanted to hang onto life, unlike Laura. But while it might have been more gratifying, he knew that he could not take that risk again. The remaining victims needed to be rendered incapacitated immediately, unable to defend themselves.

He took one last sweep of the park and lowered the scope, placing it back into the rucksack, and retrieved a small sandwich bag at the same time. He placed the sandwich bag in the crook of a small tree and headed back to the wall of the park, comfortable in the security of the dark. He needed his sleep and to re-check his plans for the next murder. He'd leave the rest of the night to the guards.

McEvoy stood at the edge of a large car park used during the day by numerous coach companies to offload tourists. A metal bar blocked access, a sign attached to it stating that it was padlocked at nine o'clock each evening. At the far corner, a short distance beyond the car park, the tall cross rose tall into the sky, silhouetted against the dull, orange-tinged clouds. Over a million people had gathered at its base in 1979 to hear Pope John Paul II say Mass. Now it cast its shadow over a murder scene. He could hear another car approaching those parked along the roadside and turned to examine the new arrival.

Elaine Jones' diminutive figure stepped out onto the pavement, her eyes drinking in the scene, trying to get her bearings.

McEvoy started to head towards her and called out her name. 'Elaine!'

She glanced left, noticed him approaching and waited.

'No Billy?' he asked as he neared.

'Decided not to disturb him.' Even at this hour she sounded chirpy. 'Lad needs all the beauty sleep he can get.'

'Yeah, sorry it's so late,' McEvoy apologised. 'We found the body at around midnight.'

'Well, it can't be helped, can it? You find them when you find them. It's better to look at her now than in the morning. Ah, ah,' she admonished him as he pulled to a halt. 'The cheek kissing business. Come on.' She patted a cheek with her index finger. 'I'll get you trained yet.'

McEvoy rolled his eyes, leant forward and kissed her on both cheeks.

'Doesn't hurt, does it,' she teased. 'And it puts me in a good mood. So, where am I heading?' she asked, moving to the back of the car to retrieve a bag.

'The body's in under the trees covered by a sheet.' He gestured with an arm. 'A runner doing a couple of circuits. I think she was probably attacked out at the path and then dragged into the darkness. There's a trail evident through the grass. One of paramedics has confirmed she's dead and took some temperature readings. He's over in the ambulance there.' He pointed along the road and they started to walk toward the crime scene.

'I'll talk to him afterwards. Just make sure he doesn't disappear on me, will you,' she instructed. 'So, any ideas as to how she died?'

'Well, her face has been smashed in and her toes cut off. I'm not sure if they killed her though. It was dark and I didn't want to mess things up too much. I just made sure she was dead.'

'Her toes cut off?' Elaine repeated.

'He left one pinned to a nearby tree with a note.'

'First the sword, then the paint, now toes. Well, he's certainly creative.'

'He's a sick, depraved bastard, is what he is,' McEvoy stated, a quiet anger in his voice.

'That as well,' Elaine agreed, keeping her tone light-hearted. 'Do you have any lights so I can see what I'm doing?'

'We're waiting on the crime scene people to arrive with some arc lights. I'll find two volunteers. They can go across with you and hold a couple of torches each. How's that sound?' McEvoy hazarded.

'Well I guess it'll have to do for now,' she conceded, clearly not happy with the arrangement, liking things to be performed professionally.

A dark Audi pulled up on the far side of the road. A woman with long, dark brown hair eased out of the driver's seat and smoothed down the jacket of her well-tailored, mid-grey business suit. Beneath the trousers she wore flat black shoes. Under the jacket was a white blouse with stiff collars, open a couple of buttons to reveal a small, gold cross on a chain. She surveyed the scene, picked out McEvoy and headed over to him.

'None of my lot here yet?' she asked as a greeting.

'Not that I'm aware of, Jenny,' McEvoy replied. 'You ready for this?' he asked, aware that this was Jenny Flanagan's first case as a detective inspector. The transfer to NBCI had only taken place a few days earlier, though she had previously worked for the unit as a detective sergeant. 'Our killer's a very sick bastard.'

'Don't worry, I'm ready. I've been waiting my whole career for this; to lead a murder investigation.'

'Well, they're obviously paying you good money,' McEvoy said, nodding at the car.

'It's not mine, it's Brian's. I've left him with my Peugeot, not that he knows it yet. I'm still hoping he might swap on a permanent basis.'

'Fat chance. Look,' he said, the pleasantries over with, 'what I want you to do is take charge of the crime scene. Make sure it's all taped off properly and that people know what they're doing. Someone will need to go and talk to the victim's husband. You if needs be. We need to find out everything we can about her – what she was like, where she worked, who her friends were, everywhere she'd been in the last two weeks, whether she knew Laura Schmidt or David Hennessey – the two other victims. Anything you can think of. Something links these murders together. We need to know what it is.'

'You want me to interview her husband?' Flanagan asked, aware that if she was doing that then she wouldn't be able to co-ordinate things at the murder site.

'I don't care who does it, as long as it's done,' McEvoy said, knowing that he didn't want to do it. They were too emotionally charged; too depressing.

Flanagan nodded in acknowledgement. That would land on one of the DS's lap.

'We're still waiting for the local superintendent to turn up,' McEvoy continued, 'and also the crime scene people. Can you try and find out where the hell they are. We need to get some arc lights from somewhere and we also need the site processed. He's left us another note and I want to know what the hell it says.'

'I'll get on it right away,' she replied, pulling an ultra thin phone from her pocket and starting to move away.

Two more cars turned up in quick succession. Two of Flanagan's DSs – Diarmaid Savage, wiry and athletic with a shock of black hair just past the stage of needing a haircut, and Declan Greer, stocky, with a gut just starting to hang over his waistline.

McEvoy sat, head tipped back, in the front passenger seat of a garda car, the seat pushed as far back as possible to give his long legs room and reclined a little from its normal position. There was a light tap at the window. He rolled his neck slightly, but didn't open his eyes. The tap was repeated. He tipped his head to the left and opened his right eye. Michael Foster, the crime scene manager, gestured through the window. McEvoy wondered how long he'd been asleep. Whatever it was, it wasn't enough.

He pulled himself forward, pushed open the door and looked up at Foster. It was raining now, a steady drizzle.

Foster was wearing a luminous yellow jacket, his collar turned up, his short, grey hair wet with the rain. 'We've processed the note,' he said. 'It's a quote plus what looks like a grid reference.' He held out a clear plastic evidence bag.

McEvoy reached out and took the bag. He read through the plastic.

The Rules
Chapter Three I: Planning K

"Serial killers who kill for years plan their every move. They are rarely impulsive and despite their internal conflicts, unstable emotions, and rage at the world, they can present themselves as an ordinary member of society. They construct 'murder kits' containing essential items such as their weapon of choice, duct tape, gloves, and a change of clothes. They select their site of attack and plan their routes to and from the scene. They enjoy the planning and they revel in the duplicity of killing an innocent victim and getting away with it." 53,21,41.72, 06,19,31.88

'Jesus!' McEvoy whispered sharply. He read it again. 'He's telling us that he thinks he knows himself; knows exactly what he's doing. That he's enjoying this whole sick episode – the planning, the killing, the chase. Everything. The guy's a complete psycho.'

McEvoy paused and read the note a third time. 'We need to know where he's getting these quotes from.' He slapped the bag. 'You got anything else?' he asked, easing himself up and out of the car. He pulled up the collar on his suit jacket, realising his coat was in his car back at the start of Grainne Malone's circuit. Off to his right he could see the murder site covered by a canvas gazebo trying to keep the rain off, though it was soaked in dew in any case. The whole area was lit by bright arc lights.

'Seems it was the little toe of the left foot in the bag,' Foster said. 'We've got a few other bits and pieces – blood and hair samples. Maybe the victim's, maybe not. A few good footprints.'

'How about the numbers? Do we know where they refer to?'

'We're working on it. We think it's latitude and longitude, rather than a grid reference. He's pointing us to another site.'

The business card had been found pinned to a lime tree near to Áras an Uachtaráin, the President's palace. A clear, plastic sandwich bag was pinned to the tree, a severed toe nestled in a corner, the folds of a note resting on top.

McEvoy read the note through an evidence bag.

```
3a. Plan meticulously from start to finish.
53,21,27.63, 06,19,23.92
```

He pursed his lips and scratched at his scalp, thinking through its significance. 'He's trying to lead us on a merry dance, trying to waste our time by chasing after your one's toes and his damn notes; giving himself more time to get on with planning and executing his next murder.' He paused, staring off across the park, before focusing his gaze back on the note. 'Well, I guess we haven't got a choice, have we?' he muttered, shaking his head in disgust. 'For feck's sake!'

Jenny Flanagan headed towards McEvoy as he approached the murder scene. As they neared each other she started to talk. 'We've found another toe and note. Over there by the outer wall of the ambassador's house, pinned to a tree – right at the end of the walkway leading up to the papal cross.'

'Another's been found up by Áras an Uachtaráin,' McEvoy answered. 'He's left us a trail to follow. Parcelling his feckin' chapter out in bite-size chunks.'

'Well he certainly has balls, killing someone within a hundred metres or so of two of the most prestigious addresses in Ireland. Addresses with some of the best security arrangements.'

'You sound like you admire him,' McEvoy snapped. 'He's a cowardly bastard who kills innocent victims.'

'I … I wasn't,' Flanagan stammered, a red blush rising from her collar. 'I didn't mean …'

'Forget it,' McEvoy said, annoyed at himself for lashing out at a colleague. 'What did the note say?'

'It says it's a master rule. Something about analysing all mistakes, not repeating them or trying to correct them. It's over with Michael Foster.'

They walked to where the forensic officer stood, talking to a uniformed guard.

'You've found a note?' McEvoy asked, halting their conversation.

'I didn't,' Foster answered. 'One of the local guards did,' he gestured his hand at his companion.

McEvoy nodded in thanks and continued. 'What does it say?'

'It's in the van.' Foster walked the few metres to a white Ford transit, opened the rear door and passed the note to McEvoy.

McEvoy read through the clear plastic bag.

```
Master rule: If you make a mistake, however
small, do a full analysis and do not do it
again. Do not try and correct it. Any attempt
```

at correction is likely to lead to more problems
than it solves.

He stared at the sheet in silence, his mind a complete blank, reading the words but unable to give them meaning. Eventually he lifted his head and said to Foster, 'You'd better let the others know you've found this in case they're hunting for it later.' He handed the note back. 'I'm going to get a coffee,' he said to no one in particular. He could do with a rest not caffeine; there was no question of sleep, however, the clock was already counting down to the next murder. He glanced at his watch – ten minutes past six – wondering whether it was too early to ring his daughter. He'd better leave it at least another hour.

'We've just found the fifth toe and note,' Diarmaid Savage said, 'but there was no business card. I thought I should let you know. We've had a good scout around, but there's no sign of it.'

'Four makes sense,' McEvoy said. 'There's four more murders to go. He's counting down. I doubt you're going to find any more. What do the notes say?'

Savage read them out.

```
3b. Scope out the victim as little as possi-
ble - enough to feel confident that things will
work out as planned, but not enough that you
get noticed.
53,21,02.47, 06,18,57.60.
```

```
3c. Do a full reconnaissance of place and es-
cape routes. Make sure all options are tried
and tested.
53,21,05.07, 06,20,03.72.
```

```
3d. Have contingency plans for all stages of
the murder.
53,20,51.21, 06,20,03.87


3e. Do not confide in anybody. Ever. You might
be able to trust your own mouth, but you can
never trust anybody else's. 53,21,03.04,
06,20,34.74.
```

'That's it. We're going to head on to the next point. He seems to be leading us round the park. The third point was way off towards the Wellington Memorial, up on top of a small hill opposite the fort. We're now down near the Chapelizod exit.'

'Right, okay. Keep going,' McEvoy instructed. 'I'll talk to you later.'

McEvoy ended the call. He leant back against the car's bodywork and felt the clammy, cold sweat on his brow with his palm. There was a dull ache behind his eyes, the start of a headache forming higher up in his forehead. His suit was damp from the light drizzle, his shirt sticking to his back. They were going too slow. He was going to kill again soon. And what were they doing? Wasting time trying to locate toes hidden around the Phoenix Park! He needed to be doing something, but had no idea what.

He moved his hand down and rubbed his eyes through their lids. All he wanted was the murders to stop and a couple of days' sleep. That and a cigarette. Maybe he was going to have to try the patches. He pushed himself forward and moved off, hunting for someone to talk to or something to do.

'Hello?'

'Caroline, it's Colm.'

'Where the hell have you been?' she snapped. 'You could have called. We've been worried sick. So's Mammy. You didn't call her.'

'Yeah, sorry,' McEvoy conceded. 'I decided I'd drop in on the way home, but I got another phone call. I've been in the Phoenix Park all night. This time it was a jogger.'

'God almighty,' Caroline whispered, her anger re-directed away from McEvoy. 'Are you any nearer to catching the bastard? He should be strung up in front of their families,' she said with vigour. 'Strung up,' she repeated.

'We're still working on it,' McEvoy answered neutrally. 'He's not leaving us much to go on and he's moving too quickly. It's difficult to keep up.'

'And have you managed to get any sleep?' Caroline asked, mothering him, knowing that he wouldn't be looking after himself.

'A quick doze here and there. Look, I haven't got long, is Gemma there?'

'Yeah, I'll get her. Take care of yourself, okay? You're no use to anyone ill.'

'I know, I know,' McEvoy conceded, stifling a yawn.

There was a brief pause.

'Has there been another murder?' Gemma asked, already knowing why her father hadn't contacted her.

'At about nine last night. I'm still at the scene. Look, are you okay?'

'I'm grand.' She said it as if there was no reason why she shouldn't be, that it was perfectly natural for her father to be out until the early hours investigating a serial killer. 'I'm just getting ready for school. How about you? Have you been drinking and eating enough?'

'Of course,' McEvoy lied. 'I'm going to need you to stay with Aunt Caroline again tonight. I'll try and drop in so we can catch up.'

'If you can, you can, and if you can't, that's fine,' Gemma sang.

'Right. Right, okay.' He didn't know what else to say. She was in the land of normal families; he was floundering in the sick world of homicide. He wasn't able for her light heartedness after the events of the past couple of days. They were just on different wavelengths – his sombre, dark and hollow, unable to mix with her light. 'I'll see you later, okay,' he finished lamely.

'Okay. Try and catch him today so you can be home for my birthday tomorrow. Though it doesn't matter if you can't, catching him is more important.'

'I'll do my best, pumpkin,' McEvoy promised. 'I love you, okay.'

'I love you too. Look after yourself, okay.' She ended the call.

He stared at the phone for a second, wanting to be at home, away from all the madness around him. His mind drifted to Maggie. Her smiling on a beach in Clew Bay, her hair windswept across her face; she was six months pregnant and in love with the world. Then fast forward to six months ago, a forced smile through the pain and drugs, her skin grey, her hair matted and greasy from cold sweats. He wished he could bring her back somehow, make her more than just a memory. He looked up at the trees and back down at the phone and checked the time. He started to walk back toward the zoo and garda headquarters.

The woman was staring at the wall, her back to her partner. Her mind was a tangle of confusion; of suspicions and questions half-formed and desperate to be asked. Without turning she eventually found the courage to speak.

'You knew the first two people,' she half-whispered, half-spoke.

'What?' he muttered, backing into her, suddenly becoming alive inside, attuned to her coldness.

'You knew that young girl that died and you knew David Hennessey.'

'We both knew David,' he said neutrally, fighting to suppress his rising anger. 'And I don't know what you're trying to suggest, but I never knew the girl.'

'Laura,' the woman said. 'Her name was Laura. I saw you with her once. You were talking to her near to the hospital.'

'I think you must have her or me confused with someone else,' he said calmly, keeping his inner rage from his voice, rolling over onto his back. 'I've never met her. You think I'm The Raven?' he asked incredulously.

'I don't know what I think,' she said quietly.

'You really think I could have killed those people in cold blood,' he said, unable to keep his voice neutral. 'I mean, why would I? How could I?' He placed a hand on her hip. 'I don't know where you've got this crazy idea from, but I'm not The Raven. I don't know who is, but it isn't me.'

She stayed silent regretting having said anything. If her suspicions were right she was potentially lying next to a serial killer; a deranged lunatic who thought he could kill with impunity. She was fairly confident that he knew the first two victims. She'd barely seen him in the past few days, and he'd arrived at her apartment at gone one o'clock last night, ever so slightly hyper. Through the thin cotton of her nightdress she could feel him bristle with irritation at her silence.

After a few moments she swung her bare legs out of the bed, his hand sliding onto the sheets, and headed for the bathroom. The main thing was to get away from him, find somewhere to think things through, get her thoughts into some kind of order; somewhere where she didn't feel under threat. She'd get ready for work as normal; tell him that she was sorry, that she was just being paranoid. She pushed the bathroom door shut and stared at her tired face in the mirror before bending to scoop up handfuls of lukewarm water, splashing them on her face trying to calm her inner panic.

He waited until the door closed and then followed, carefully rolling his feet to keep silent. He shut his eyes, gathering himself, trying to centre his anger, sucked air in through his nose and burst through the door.

She was bent over the sink. In one motion he grabbed hold of her hair, yanked up her head and violently shoved her face into the mirror. His anger crimsoned his vision, threatening to blossom into blind rage. He tugged her head back and slammed it forward again, the mirror cracking in a jagged pattern of concentric circles centred on the point of impact. He felt her go limp in his grasp and he managed to rein in his fury, letting her slide unconscious to the floor, blood tricking from her nostrils. Her once beautiful face a bloody mess.

He left her there and headed to the kitchen, now feeling strangely calm, his anger dissipating as quickly as it flamed. He retrieved some packing tape from a drawer and returned to the bathroom. He slipped the cotton nightdress over her head and levered her dead weight into the bath. Using the tape he bound her wrists to the handles of the bath and her feet to the taps. He then placed the tape across her mouth and wrapped it round her bloody head several times leaving her nose free.

Trust her to see through him. He'd accounted for everything except her. He didn't think he'd need to. He'd been confident that he'd left no clues to his alter-ego and his project. She would now inevitably have to die and with her disappearance he would ultimately be exposed. But that was okay; he'd just need to re-think his exit strategy. He wouldn't be able to blend back in to society; instead he'd need to disappear into the shadows. He'd planned for such a possibility; after all he was writing the rules not following them. He was even leaving a trail of clues that would lead right to him if the guards had enough brains to follow them; or perhaps they would follow his false trails instead.

He sat on the closed toilet seat and traced a finger over her alabaster skin, a red trace of pressure left in its wake. This would be a death he could savour.

Tony Bishop stared out the window and across the park. He was trying to convince himself that he was calm and collected, in control of things; that the butterflies in his stomach and the jitteriness in his blood were not real; that he could handle the bombardment of questions from the world's media. And it was going to be global coverage. Three murders by a self-proclaimed serial killer in three days, with the promise of more until his sick, little book was written. The table behind him was covered with the day's newspapers. The murders were on the front page of every one. There was little hope of keeping the cards and chapters under wraps now. One of the foreign papers would publish them and then they'd be all over the Internet.

He sucked in air slowly and let it out gently. He was dressed in a pristine uniform and subconsciously he played with the cuffs.

There was a knock at the door and he could hear it opening. He swung round, his manner turning immediately to one of irritation, his nervousness surfacing and escaping. 'For God's sake, Colm! Look at the state of you!' He gestured angrily, a flood of red rising from his collar into his face. 'What the hell are you playing at?'

McEvoy stared back impassively, then down at his attire, and back up again. His shoes were covered in blades of grass, the lower part of his suit trousers wet and dirty, his shirt and loosely knotted tie stained by coffee. He caught his reflection in the window, his face pale, skin tight to the bones and dark with stubble, crescents under his eyes.

'You look like shit and you're dressed like a scarecrow!' Bishop berated him. 'We have a press conference in an hour and you look a hurricane survivor.'

'I've come straight from the murder site,' McEvoy said as way of explanation.

'You spent the whole night there?' Bishop asked incredulity in his tone. 'Why the hell did you do that? It's called delegating, Colm. You're a manager for God's sake. You should have handed it over to Jenny Flanagan when she arrived and gone home and tried to get some sleep. Jesus! How the hell are you going to catch him if you can't think straight because you're knackered?'

McEvoy stayed silent.

'No wonder you look like shit,' Bishop stated. 'When was the last time you slept? Properly slept,' Bishop qualified.

McEvoy shrugged. 'A while ago, I guess.'

'Well, you haven't got time to go home to clean up now. You've probably only got a wardrobe of those ridiculous suits in any case. We'll just have to try and find someone who's the same size as you. Preferably someone wearing a uniform. It doesn't matter what the rank is as long as it fits. I'll get someone else to go and get you a razor and some deodorant from a local shop. I'll be back in a minute. Don't go anywhere. You understand?'

He brushed past McEvoy and out of the door. It clicked shut behind him.

McEvoy drew out a chair and sat at the table. He looked down at the papers on the table and then stared up at a Yeats print. He didn't need to read the papers, their half-truths, conjecture and psychobabble analysis. He knew the reality of what was happening; he was living it. It was bearing down and crushing him.

His phone rang and he pulled it reluctantly from his pocket. 'McEvoy.'

'It's Diarmaid Savage. We've found all the toes and notes,' he said excitedly. 'If you plot them ...'

'What do they say?' McEvoy interrupted.

'Well, they ... er,' Savage was thrown off balance. 'Look, it's, er, not so much what they say, as what they show, if you know what I mean. I mean, if you plot the location of each toe and note and draw a line between them in the order that they were left then they draw the picture of a bird – the beak, the wings, and the tail. He's drawn a picture of a bird – a raven – across the park.'

'A raven,' McEvoy repeated, trying to make sense of Savage's news.

120

'And where the murder occurred forms the eye,' Savage said.

McEvoy stayed silent trying to digest the information. 'You'd better tell me what the notes say,' he muttered eventually.

Savage read them out.

```
3f. Do not draw attention to yourself. Act like
an ordinary member of the public. 53,21,10.43,
06,20,13.78


3g. Never become complacent.
```

'He's underlined, never,' Savage explained before continuing.

```
53,21,34.31, 6,20,54.18

3h. Do not create patterns - vary timing, method
of killing, method of disposal, and so on.
53,21,28.02, 06,19,39.53.
```

'Plus the master rule.'

'He's got it all worked out, hasn't he,' McEvoy said quietly. 'The cocky bastard. You'd better let Jenny Flanagan know. I've got to go.'

He ended the call, wanting to process the information, to sit in silence. He stared up at the ceiling. The press were going to have a field day with the killer's sky writing of his supposed emblem. The Raven was feeding the machine, developing a recognisable persona that would ensure he would be remembered well after he was caught and jailed. He lowered his eyes back to the Yeats print.

McEvoy slipped off his shoes and started to strip off his clothes, hanging them on a clothes hook. The borrowed uniform hung two hooks along the rack. His mobile phone rang and he dug a hand into his trouser pocket to retrieve it.

'McEvoy.'

'Colm, it's Elaine. Do you have a minute?'

'Sure, but it'll have to be quick. I've got to have a shower and a shave. This press conference is in 20 minutes' time.'

'She was killed by asphyxiation caused by strangulation. He used his hands rather than a tie or rope, gouged his fingers deep into her throat. She had some deep spots of haemorrhaging under the skin, damage to her larynx and thyroid cartilage, and her hyoid bone had been fractured. Interestingly, she has a horizontal stripe of abrasions and bruising high across her chest. Up near her collarbones.'

'A stripe?' McEvoy repeated.

'I'd say she'd been caught across the chest by a rope or wire. If I was to guess what happened, I'd say she was running along the path when she ran into a wire that whipped her legs from under her bringing her to the ground. Our killer then bashed her in the face to stun her and then strangled her. The blow to the face broke her nose and fractured her right cheekbone, but just stunned her. He hit her with something long and wide in shape – the blow fell across her face, rather than being concentrated into one point. The toes were cut off after death, which I can confirm as being around nine o'clock give or take half an hour. They'd been cut off with something sharp, but not serrated. Probably shears or pliers, bolt-cutters or something similar. She was also pregnant. I'd say she was about eight weeks' gone.'

'She was pregnant?' McEvoy repeated, sitting down on the wooden slatted bench in his underpants and socks.

'Just a few weeks,' Elaine replied.

'None of the people who've been talking to the husband told me that.' McEvoy stared at the changing room's tiled floor. Now they were investigating four deaths – three lives and one future one.

'The husband might not have known. She might have been saving it, waiting until she was a bit further into the pregnancy when there was less likelihood of miscarriage before telling him.'

'Jesus,' McEvoy muttered.

'Look, have your shower and do the press conference. If you've got any other questions come back to me, otherwise it'll be in the report. And get some sleep.' She ended the call.

McEvoy pulled each sock off, stood, pulled down his underwear and crossed the room to the showers. It was going to take more than water and soap to make him feel clean.

The uniform was a better fit than his suit, but it was still a size too big. McEvoy felt uncomfortable wearing someone else's clothes, inhabiting their space, his hands straying into foreign pockets. He jammed a finger between his collar and neck trying to make space, though there was plenty of room.

He was sat on a small stage, sitting behind a cloth-covered table. Multiple microphones crowded the surface, their necks ringed with network logos. Off to his left was a small podium, which Bishop moved to and cleared his throat.

'Please, ladies and gentlemen, if we could make a start.' Bishop waited for the room to descend to a hush. He then started to read out a prepared statement. 'It's my unfortunate duty to inform you that Grainne Malone was murdered yesterday evening whilst running in the Phoenix Park. She was attacked and then strangled some time around nine o'clock. From items that were left at the scene we believe that she was killed by the same person who murdered Laura Schmidt and David Hennessey. We are appealing for witnesses who were in the Phoenix Park last night to come forward to help us with our enquiries. We are also still seeking to speak to anyone who was in the grounds of Maynooth University on the night of Monday the 14th, and visited Glencree Peace and Reconciliation Centre on the night of Sunday 13th of April.

'All available resources are being directed at catching the killer of Laura Schmidt, David Hennessey and Grainne Malone.

It is clear, however, that we are seeking a very dangerous individual who is preying on people who are alone and vulnerable in public places. We are therefore advising all members of the public to be extra vigilant in the coming days and not to move about at night unaccompanied unless absolutely necessary. Until caught, there is every likelihood that the killer will try to strike again. If anyone sees anybody acting suspiciously or in a threatening manner under no circumstances should they approach or try to apprehend them, instead ring the gardai immediately. Any help the public can provide that will help us apprehend the killer will be gratefully received.' Bishop paused and pulled a tight smile.

The room was suddenly filled with a barrage of questions.

'Please. Please, ladies and gentlemen, one at a time. Yes, you, wearing the purple.' Bishop pointed at a dark haired woman wearing a purple blouse over a black skirt.

'The killer left business cards and chapters for his book at the scene of the last two murders. Can you confirm that he left the cards and a chapter with the body of Grainne Malone? And if so, what did the note say?'

Bishop scrunched his face, deciding how to answer the question. 'We can confirm that they were both present. However, at this time we do not want to reveal their contents as they are critical to the enquiry. If these items have been sent to the media then we would appeal strongly to you not to publish the material. We do not want any copycat murders or hoaxes that might make catching the …' Bishop paused, not wanting to say 'The Raven', 'murderer more difficult. We want the knowledge of the notes to be limited to the gardai and the killer. I know this is a difficult request to make, especially as they add meat to your stories, but I cannot express strongly enough the need to keep this material out of the public domain until he is caught.'

The air filled with questions as Bishop ended.

'Please. Please, ladies and gentlemen, one at a time. Yes, madam, fourth row back with the red scarf.'

'Hi, yes,' the woman said with an American accent. 'Ireland's not noted for its serial killers. In fact I'm not sure you've had to deal with one outside of maybe gang or paramilitary in-fighting, and I'm not sure they really fit the mode of what we might call a serial killer, more like hired assassins. Do you think you have the expertise and the resources to deal with catching a serial killer of this type? I notice for example that you don't employ a criminal psychologist or something similar.'

McEvoy shifted uncomfortably in his seat and glanced over at Bishop.

Bishop's face had flushed a deep red, his body language becoming defensive. 'We have a highly skilled police force with many specialist officers. They have many years' experience of solving murders and other serious crimes and we are confident that they are doing the best job possible. If we need to bring in other specialists, whether that be criminal psychologists or forensic anthropologists we do that. We are not shy about asking for help from experts in Ireland or from elsewhere – Europe or North America. We are a small country of just over four million people with a low murder rate, nearly all of which is domestic or gang-related in nature. We do not have the need for such full-time staff. Yes, they would be useful now, but we would no doubt be criticised by the media for wasting resources on un-needed personnel any other time.'

'Does that mean you'll be hiring in such staff?' a red haired man asked, quickly.

'I'm not sure we have such plans at the moment. Colm, per-haps you can answer that?'

McEvoy looked up from the doodle he was pencilling on the pad in front of him, startled by the use of his name.

'I, er, it's a possibility,' he conceded, his mind foggy with tiredness. 'Forensic evidence would, however, I think, be more useful. Rather than a set of possibilities, we'd be looking for a specific individual. He has killed one person a day for the past three days. The balance of probabilities says he will kill again today. A profile is not going to stop that. Specifics, not generalities, will stop that. We are working on establishing the specifics that will identify the killer.'

'So, how confident are you that you'll catch him before he's finished all his chapters?' an overweight, bald-headed man asked sceptically.

'We're doing our best. We have hundreds of gardai working on the case.' It was not the answer the man was looking for, but it was the best McEvoy felt he could offer. There was no point lying; if he said that they would catch him and they didn't, then they would never hear the end of it. It would be used to whip the gardai for years to come. That said, if they didn't catch him, they'd suffer the same fate. They were damned either way.

'That's not very reassuring,' the man replied predictably. 'What the public wants to hear is a "yes".'

'There's no point making promises that we do not know we can keep,' McEvoy said, shrugging his shoulders. 'We are doing our best to catch him. We can only do our best. Until we catch him, we're asking people to be extra vigilant.'

'The woman at the back wearing the blue blouse,' Bishop said, trying to re-grab the initiative, hoping that she was going to ask about something else.

McEvoy eased on the jacket of his stained and creased suit. The press conference had lasted another five minutes until Bishop had brought it to a close. The questioning had become demanding, more critical, loaded with expectations that were unrealistic and undeliverable. It was becoming clear that however the case unfolded they would receive bad press. If they caught the killer in the next few hours, the question would be why they hadn't caught him earlier; that they had allowed three deaths to occur. If they didn't catch him until all the chapters were released there would be questions about resourcing, effort and strategy.

He could already feel Bishop starting to distance himself from the case, making sure that people knew that it was McEvoy in charge of the investigation.

'Go home, Colm,' Bishop said, breaking the silence. 'Go home and get some rest. The others can cope for a few hours.'

'We need another team meeting. I need to catch up on Laura Schmidt and David Hennessey's murders.'

'That wasn't a suggestion, Colm. That was an order. The team meetings can wait. Give the teams their heads for a while.'

McEvoy nodded reluctantly.

'Ring your DIs and tell them not to bother you for a while,' Bishop paused. 'He's making fools of us, Colm. He's playing the press against us. There's no way we're going to be able to keep the lid on the cards and notes. They're going to be everywhere by this afternoon now the international media are covering things. They won't give a shit about our case; they're just interested in the story. Then it'll be the public and the politicians. You wait and see. They'll want their pound of flesh as well.'

McEvoy pulled a tight smile, but kept silent, letting Bishop have his rant.

'Go home, Colm, and pray the sick bastard makes a mistake.' Bishop pulled open the meeting room door and exited, leaving McEvoy with the prints and the view of the Phoenix Park.

Simon Grainger walked across the incident room to where Charlie Deegan was standing staring at a newspaper.

'Sir?'

'Have you seen this?' Deegan asked, stabbing his finger at the sheets. 'They've spelt my fuckin' name wrong. They're missing an e.'

'Dermot Brady was one of Hennessey's students,' Grainger said, ignoring Deegan's bluster. 'Hennessey gave a character reference at Brady's trial.'

'What?' Deegan said, turning, having only half-heard Grainger.

'I said, Hennessey gave a character reference for Dermot Brady at his trial.'

'Brady and Hennessey go way back?'

Grainger noted that Deegan didn't seem surprised by the connection. 'Brady studied politics here. David Hennessey was his personal tutor. He'd only left university a couple of years when he ran down the mother and child. We have a definite link now between Brady, Laura Schmidt and Hennessey.'

Deegan glanced round the room, trying to work out if they could be overheard. Taking no chances, he stated, 'Follow me,' and left the room. He pulled to a halt in the corridor. 'I'm going to bring Brady in and question him, okay,' he whispered harshly. 'I don't want you putting out an alert for him, and there's no need to contact McEvoy either.'

'Don't you think …' Grainger started to whine.

'It's my job to do the thinking here,' Deegan interrupted. 'I'm in charge of the investigation into David Hennessey's death. We're looking into a link between Hennessey and Brady, nothing else. You understand?'

'But surely we should at least contact Colm McEvoy,' Grainger suggested, feeling uncomfortable with Deegan's request.

'I've just told you, *I'm* in charge of this investigation,' Deegan stressed. 'McEvoy is just co-ordinating between the cases, I make the operational decisions.'

Deegan could see the indecision in Grainger's eyes. 'Don't try and fuck with me, Simon. Just do as I say or I'll have you back in uniform before the end of the day. I can do it and you know it.'

Grainger chewed on his lip and nodded.

'Good. If Brady is the killer and we nail him, we'll get all the credit. Don't forget that. We could all benefit from that,' Deegan said in reconciliation.

He waited for Grainger to slope off back toward the incident room then pulled his mobile from a pocket.

'Yeah?'

'It's Charlie Deegan.'

'Shit! Look, I've lost him again. He left his apartment block at 8.35, walked over a few streets, got in a dark blue Fiesta and drove off. There was nothing I could do. I was on foot. The car had a Dublin plate, 01-D-5 something. I couldn't get the whole reg.'

'What do you mean, you lost him!' Deegan said angrily. 'I need to bring him in for questioning.'

'Well put out an alert for him,' the man snapped.

'I want to talk to him, not launch a fuckin' major manhunt. Go back to where he took the car from and wait for him. He's bound to return at some point. Then bring him in for questioning.'

'For fuck's sake,' the man muttered darkly. 'You'd better know what you're doing, Charlie.'

The bungalow was set back five yards from the roads, fronted by a mature shrubbery and a lawn, the grass long, needing to be mown. To the left of the house was a gravel driveway, leading to a separate garage. The Raven cut between the garage and residence and edged along the back of the house. A wide, brick patio extended along the full length of the bungalow, dotted with groups of pots. He peered in through a window, framed by a clematis plant climbing a lattice. The bedroom was empty, the bed made, the contents tidy. The next window was frosted, a blind pulled three-quarters of the way down. He passed the back door and gazed into the kitchen. There was no sign of life.

He moved back to the door, shifted the grip of the hammer in his right hand, his skin sweaty inside the thin rubber gloves. With his left hand he checked that the surgical mask was correctly in place and then carefully twisted the door handle. As expected, the door clicked open, and gently he pushed it wide, entering the kitchen. He stood stock still for a moment.

A television or radio was on toward the front of the house, the volume turned up loud. He moved toward the sound, out into a hall. In front of him the passageway led to the front door, to the right it extended toward the bathroom and bedroom. The blare of an advert for a car came from the door to his left. He raised the hammer, pushed the door open and darted in.

The man was sitting where he always was; on the dark red sofa immediately inside the lounge door. He had barely started to swivel his grey-haired head to see who the intruder was when the hammer landed a heavy blow on the top of his skull, followed quickly by another. He slumped to one side, his chin on his left collarbone, blood oozing from his wounds, snaking down between the bridge of his nose and eye socket.

The Raven walked to the window, its frame almost the full height of the room, the windowsill near to the floor. He laid the hammer on the carpet and pulled four tea-light candles from his pocket, placing them at intervals on the floor along the length of the curtain, the wicks a couple of inches below the fabric. He struck a match and lit each candle, then he grabbed the hammer and retreated from the room, gently pulling the door closed so that the draft did not extinguish the flames. It would take a few moments for the flame to bite into the wax and grow. A few more for the material above to heat up and catch fire. He had already exited the driveway before the first streaks of gold and orange were visible through the front window.

The mobile phone was ringing. Eventually the noise penetrated McEvoy's sleep, digging in at his unconscious, prodding him awake. After a moment's confusion, the ringing finally registered and he snuck a hand from underneath the quilt. He grappled around trying to locate the phone, finding it just as it stopped ringing.

He withdrew his arm and tried to cling to the last of the dream; to will himself back to sleep. He had lain awake for a long time before finally falling into fitful dreams. Now he was going to have to repeat the trick. He pulled the quilt tighter to himself. The phone started to ring again.

'For God's sake,' he muttered. He snaked a hand out again and grabbed the phone. 'This better be good,' he stated flatly.

'I, er, Detective Superintendent McEvoy?' a woman asked hesitantly.

'Yeah?'

'There's been another death, Sir. A man burned to death out at Rathmoylan, County Meath. Chief Superintendent Bishop asked me to ring you.'

McEvoy slowly pushed himself up, emerging from the covers. 'Another death?' he repeated.

'Yes, Sir. He told me to tell you that The Raven has killed again. Detective Inspector John Cronin is on his way to the scene. The fire brigade and gardai from the local station are already there.'

'What time was the fire brigade called?' McEvoy swung his legs out of the bed and looked at the clock. 1.46.

'Just after one o'clock. A neighbour noticed the blaze and called it in. The whole house is apparently gutted. They've found three of his business cards.'

'Jesus. Okay, thanks. I'm on my way. Can you let DI Cronin know I'll be there shortly?'

'I'll ring him now.'

'Thanks.' McEvoy ended the call and started to get dressed. He glanced at himself in a mirror – a gaunt face, black rings beneath the eyes stared back. He barely recognised himself.

McEvoy pulled to a halt behind a marked garda car on the narrow road and edged the passenger door as close into the hedgerow as he dared. He was close to the village of Rathmoylan, just off the road to Trim. It might have been within 30 miles of

Dublin, but he was deep in rural Meath.

Along the laneway he could see the flashing lights of the fire engines, wisps of dark smoke still rising from their right, dissipating in the stiff breeze. He levered himself out of the car, rubbed his short hair, and slotted his plastic cigarette into place. Fields stretched out beyond the hedges, long grass to the left, dark, furrowed soil to the right. The sky was tall, grey, racing clouds across snippets of blue, the threat of April showers at any minute. He glanced at his watch – 14.28 – and set off up the road.

The small bungalow was beyond repair. The roof had collapsed in on itself, taking half an outside wall. The wind lifted ash and smoke, dark water pooled on the driveway, red and grey hoses snaking from the road. Firemen milled about, their faces ringed by soot and sweat. He looked for someone he recognised.

DI Johnny Cronin stepped away from a small group of men. His short, black hair was cropped close to his scalp, his upper lip sporting a dark moustache. 'The victim's name was Billy Mullins. Sixty-four, a widower and recently retired; used to work in the insurance business. He'd been in a bad way for a while – rheumatoid arthritis; practically made him immobile. His family had been considering putting him in a home. They had a schedule worked out so someone visited him every day, and friends and neighbours also dropped in and kept an eye on the place, but it was becoming unsustainable – they had too many other demands on their time. They feel as guilty as hell now for even thinking it. He would've been young to get shunted away like that; 64.'

'Anyone see anything?' McEvoy asked, ignoring Cronin's observation.

'We're still checking for witnesses.'

'And was he attacked beforehand or was he burnt alive?'

'We don't know. He might have been, but he probably wouldn't have been agile enough to get out anyway. They found him sat on the sofa in the front room. They think the fire started there. We're still waiting for Professor Jones to arrive.'

'Fear would have made him move,' McEvoy stated. 'It might have hurt like hell after, but he'd have shifted. My guess he was knocked unconscious or killed beforehand. Any cards or mementos?'

'Three cards and chapter four. They're laid out on the lawn just inside the gate. Here, I'll show you.' Cronin led McEvoy in through the entranceway, past a metal gate, painted black, and a large hebe. He stepped onto the lawn. On the far side of the bush was what looked like a small, home-made shrine. Three small, mini crosses were planted into the grass, spaced a few inches apart, The Raven's business card affixed to the top of each. Inside their crescent was a large, dead, black bird. Clutched in its claws was the top roll of a note. Holding it unfurled was a small, clear glass container, a tea light candle glowing inside, fighting with the breeze to stay alight. McEvoy kept his distance, leaning forward and over to read the note.

The Rules
Chapter Four X: The Murder V

"The victims were vulnerable in many different ways. Their assailant had found a time and
place where he could prey on such victims at
will. He then took their lives without mercy
or guilt."

4a. Keep things simple.

4b. Be prepared to walk away if the situation changes. Improvise only in exceptional
circumstances.

4c. The place — choose a location where there
are no or few potential witnesses; where there
are no cameras; where there is a good chance of

contamination of evidence.

4d. The weapon – non-traceable and an everyday item. Never use a gun or anything that can be traced to a point of purchase.

4e. Do not give the victim the chance to fight back. Do not explain what you are going to do to them; kill them while they are still confused and trying to work out what is going on.

4f. Never give the victim the opportunity to escape.

4g. Ignore their pleas, should they have opportunity to voice them.

Master rule: at all times do not panic and stay in control of how things unfold.

McEvoy wandered along the driveway by himself, surrounded by personnel from the emergency services, yet alone. He surveyed the charred wreckage of the house, a lifetime's collection of possessions destroyed, trying to marshal his thoughts. Billy Mullins was not a random victim killed in a public place, he was a specific individual murdered in his own home. It was not a chance occurrence that he'd come into the orbit of his killer. Something had drawn them together. Something tantalisingly out of reach.

His mobile phone rang. 'McEvoy.'

'It's Cheryl Deale,' she said quickly. 'We've a positive match for a hair sample from Hennessey's murder site. It was stuck to the paint on his left thigh. It belongs to Dermot Brady.'

'Dermot Brady,' McEvoy repeated, doubt in his voice. 'Are you sure?'

'Absolutely positive.'

'Jesus.' Brady was the killer. McEvoy felt physically sick, his legs weak. They shouldn't have pulled the surveillance team off of him. He'd killed twice since then. Twice. Two lives extinguished because of his error in judgment. He leant against the front wing of a parked car and held his temples between thumb and forefinger.

'We'll keep processing the samples,' Deale said into the silence, 'see if we can get some corroboration.'

'Okay. Okay, thanks for the call.' He mind started to race. He needed to put out a full alert for the arrest of Dermot Brady. They had to get him into custody before he murdered a fifth victim. He pushed himself back to standing and pulled a number up on his phone.

'Dispatch. How ...'

'It's Detective Superintendent McEvoy, NBCI,' McEvoy interrupted, taking command, 'I want a full nationwide alert for the arrest of Dermot Brady, DI Plunkett has his full details. This needs top priority, you hear? I want every available unit on it. He's wanted for four murders.'

'He's The Raven?' the man asked.

'Yes, he's The Raven,' McEvoy snapped. 'And he's dangerous, okay, so I don't want anyone risking their lives for a moment of glory. Call in a full arrest team if necessary. And I want to know the minute he's caught. The absolute first to know, you understand?'

'Yes, Sir.'

'Good. Right, get on with it then.' He ended the call and pulled up Bishop's number.

'Bishop.'

'It's Dermot Brady,' McEvoy said more calmly. 'Brady's The Raven. Cheryl Deale found one of his hairs stuck in the paint on David Hennessey. I've put out a full alert for his arrest.'

'Dermot Brady,' Bishop repeated.

'I can't believe I've been so ...'

'And do we know where he is?' Bishop interrupted.

'I've put out a full alert for his arrest.'

'Well, he's not going to remain at large long with every guard in the country looking for him. Give it an hour or so and if he hasn't turned up then we'll ask for help from the public. Keep me informed, okay? Remember our pact, Colm. I've protected your back on this.'

'I haven't forgotten,' McEvoy said to a dead line. He might have misjudged Brady, but if there was one thing he was sure of, it was that Bishop was going to shunt him to one side and claim the credit for The Raven's capture. McEvoy would be left holding the responsibility for not arresting him earlier.

His phone rang. 'McEvoy.'

'Dermot Brady was brought in for questioning half an hour ago,' the dispatch controller said. 'He's been taken to Harcourt Square. DI Deegan has just started to interview him.'

'Deegan?' McEvoy repeated, trying to process the information.

'Yes, Sir.'

'Okay, thanks.' McEvoy terminated the call and pulled up Deegan's number. It rang once and then swapped to the answer service. He pressed stop immediately and thumbed through his address book looking for Simon Grainger's number.

'DS Grainger.'

'What the hell is going on, Simon?' McEvoy demanded.

'I, er, I,' Grainger floundered. 'What do you mean?' he rallied.

'I mean, why has Dermot Brady been arrested? Why is Charlie Deegan interviewing him? And why wasn't I feckin' well told about it?'

'I, er, we, that is, we, er …'

'Heads are going to roll here, Simon,' McEvoy growled. 'This is a team game and I'm the manager, remember? Have a go at saving yours.'

'Well, er, we found out that, er, Dermot Brady used to be a student of David Hennessey. Hennessey was his tutor and, er, gave him a character reference at his trial.'

McEvoy set off towards his car. 'So, Deegan thought he'd pull in Brady, give him a verbal grilling, did he? See if he'd crack?'

'Well, er, I guess, something like that,' Grainger admitted. 'We've since discovered emails between Hennessey and Brady. They used to meet up for drinks occasionally when Hennessey came into Dublin. The last time was last week. I ... I think, DI Deegan already knew that.'

'He did, did he? Jesus Christ. Which pub, Simon?'

'The White Horse, it's on George's Quay near to Tara Street Station.'

McEvoy opened the car door and slid in. 'And why hadn't I been told?' he asked, starting the engine.

'He said there was no point disturbing you over a routine enquiry.'

'Routine enquiry!' McEvoy said angrily, pulling away from the hedgerow. 'Why the hell wasn't a full alert put out for Brady?'

'I ... I don't know.'

'You don't know? What do you mean, you don't know!' McEvoy exploded. 'He's the prime suspect for four murders! For fuck's sake! He's killed another person while you've been playing games. You know that, don't you? He burnt the poor bastard to death.'

'I ... I got the impression that DI Deegan knew where he was,' Grainger said, trying to deflect McEvoy's wrath.

'He knew where he was?' McEvoy repeated. 'How the hell did he know where he was? Did you have a surveillance team on Brady?'

'I ... I don't know. I didn't know about one. Not that ...' Grainger tailed off.

'Jesus Christ! I'm on my way in to Harcourt Street. Do *not* tell Deegan I'm on my way. I want to hear all this straight from the horse's mouth and I don't want him primed. You understand? If you mess with me, Simon, you'll be in deeper shit than you already are.' He ended the call.

Fuckin' Charlie Deegan flying solo; trying to bathe himself in glory – playing God with people's lives for the sake of easing up the greasy pole a little faster than he would have otherwise. Well his scheming was going to come back and haunt him now. He was going to need all his big-shot friends to save him after McEvoy had finished with him.

Five minutes later his mobile phone rang.

'Yes?' he snapped as way of a greeting.

'Colm, it's your mother, we're coming up to Dublin.'

'What?' McEvoy said, trying to shift his mind away from Deegan and pulling to a stop.

'I said we're coming up to Dublin. Your father is driving us down once we're packed. I've spoken to Caroline and she says you're not coping, that she's having to look after Gemma while you're chasing that lunatic. And well, she and Jimmy are both working and so I said we'd come and help. We're coming down at the weekend in any case, so it's not like we're making a trip that we wouldn't have.'

'I'm coping just fine. There's no need for you to come up.'

'I've seen you on television, Colm. You look terrible. You need a decent meal.'

'Look, I can't talk to you right now, Mam. I'll call you later, okay,' McEvoy replied, frustrated at his mother's call. 'But I don't want you coming down tonight.' He ended the call, too angry and preoccupied to negotiate with her.

Deegan left the interview room, clearly frustrated that he'd been disturbed. He bounced through a set of fire doors to discover McEvoy waiting in the corridor.

'Can't this wait?' he snapped at McEvoy.

'No, it can't,' McEvoy stated. 'What the hell do you think you're playing at, Charlie?'

'What do you mean?' Deegan responded defiantly. 'I'm not

playing at anything! I'm investigating David Hennessey's murder.'

'You're interviewing Dermot Brady,' McEvoy said, sidling past Deegan so that he was between him and the interview room. 'You had him brought in for questioning without informing me.'

'He's helping us with our enquiries. It seems he knew Hennessey quite well. They were good friends. I wanted to talk to him about it, find out about their relationship.'

'So why the hell wasn't I told about that?' McEvoy pressed. 'You knew that Brady's name has come up with respect to the murder of Laura Schmidt. You knew that I would be interested, but you kept it to yourself. I'm the senior investigating officer on this case, Charlie, and I need to know what the hell's happening. You should have rung it through.'

'I wanted to check it out first,' Deegan stated, shifting his weight, knowing that McEvoy was right. 'No point bothering you over nothing.' He stared at McEvoy, his mouth a tight line.

'How did you find Brady?' McEvoy asked, changing tack.

'A guard spotted him getting out of a car and pulled him in. He seemed to be expecting it.'

'Why was the guard looking for him when an alert hadn't been put out for his arrest?' McEvoy asked.

Deegan shifted his gait again and looked over his shoulder along the corridor. He needed to find his accomplice and prime him before McEvoy got to him. 'Look, what does it matter?' he tried to reason. 'We've got him in custody. That's the main thing. It's just a matter of time before he confesses. He *is* the sick fuck that killed our three victims. We both know that.'

'How did the guard know you were looking for Brady?' McEvoy continued. 'And how did he know where to look? Did you have Brady under surveillance?'

'What?' Deegan exclaimed, feigning surprise and hurt. 'I'm trying to help solve a murder invest …'

'Why didn't you put out a full alert for Dermot Brady, Charlie?' McEvoy interrupted loudly, his voice becoming angry. 'You knew there was a solid connection between Dermot Brady and David Hennessey. You also knew that Brady was out at Glencree when Laura Schmidt died and that a third victim was killed last night. You knew that you needed to bring Brady in, but you didn't put out a full alert. Why?'

'If you hadn't dropped the surveillance on Brady, we could have saved the woman in the Phoenix Park,' Deegan countered heatedly, trying to fight his way out of a corner.

'That might be so,' McEvoy admitted, 'but if you'd put out an alert this morning we might have saved the old man out at Rathmoylan. I made a mistake. You failed to follow procedure. You were flying solo, Charlie.'

A look of concern flashed across Deegan's face. It was enough to tell McEvoy that he didn't know about recent developments. He didn't know about the death of Billy Mullins.

'That's right,' McEvoy hissed. 'While you were feckin' about trying to cover yourself in glory, he killed a fourth victim. Burned his house down; cremated the poor bastard. You've fucked up big time, Charlie. You're practically an accessory to murder, letting him run round when you thought you'd got him pegged for three murders.'

'That's bollocks and you know it,' Deegan spat with bravado, trying to save himself. 'You're just sore because I caught the fucker first. You're a has-been, Colm. You know it, I know it, and soon the chief super will know it.' Deegan moved to walk past McEvoy back toward the interview room.

McEvoy's arm shot out blocking his path. 'I'm sore because you fucked up. I'm in charge of this case and as of now you're suspended. You hear me? Suspended. I might be a has-been, but by the end of today I'll still have my job.'

Deegan looked over at McEvoy, anger and confusion in his eyes. He tried to brush McEvoy's arm away, but it stayed in place.

McEvoy held his stare. 'You're off the case, Charlie. There'll no doubt be a disciplinary hearing. My advice is to tell the truth

140

and plead for forgiveness. You'll be out of here, but they might just retain you in uniform. Now get out of my sight and stay away from this investigation.'

Deegan dropped his gaze, turned on his heels and walked away. He pushed open a set of fire doors and continued along the corridor to the stairwell.

McEvoy blew out a long breath of air, trying to keep his anger and stress in check. He could feel his pulse throbbing in his temples. A couple of yards along the corridor a door opened. A head peaked out and withdrew quickly. McEvoy clicked off the small, digital recorder in his pocket. It paid to have evidence if you were going to tangle with Deegan. He had influential friends.

McEvoy pushed open the door and entered the interview room. A detective constable standing opposite tried his best to hide his confusion, wondering why Deegan hadn't returned. McEvoy pulled out a chair and sat across from Brady.

Brady looked defeated, his eyes fixed on the table. McEvoy popped Deegan's cassette from the tape recorder, pocketed it, and replaced it with a new cassette. He started the recorder.

'Did you really think you were going to get away with it Dermot?' he asked, his hand sneaking back into his jacket pocket, a fingernail plucking at the cigarette box. 'Did you really think you could pull off several murders when you weren't even following your own rules?'

Brady didn't respond.

'Four lives. Five if you count the unborn baby. You might have got away with it last time, but there's no way you're getting off the hook now. It'll be life, and life will mean life. They'll throw away the key. You're the most hated man in Ireland. I'll be surprised if you last a couple of months inside after what you've done.'

Brady raised his head and looked at McEvoy with dead eyes.

'Where were you this lunchtime, Dermot?'

After a long pause, Brady answered. 'I was in Trim at a meeting. A social welfare meeting. Everyone there can vouch for me. I wasn't wherever you think I was. There were 20 different people there; they'll all confirm I was there.'

'In Trim?' McEvoy repeated, nodding.

'Yes. At a meeting. It was about rural homeless services. A friend lent me a car so I could get there.'

'Despite the fact that you no longer drive,' McEvoy said sardonically. 'Couldn't bring yourself to after killing the young mother and her child.'

'Sometimes I have to,' Brady conceded. 'Usually I get a lift. There's no other way of getting to Trim.'

'You could have got a bus,' McEvoy offered.

'The bus takes forever. I'd have spent all day travelling. I went to the meeting and I came back again. That's it. Your man picked me up the moment I parked the car.'

'And you went via Rathmoylan?'

'Rathmoylan?' Brady repeated cautiously.

'It's a small place near to Trim,' McEvoy offered.

Brady tipped his head back, stared at the ceiling, gently shaking his head.

'You drove yourself because you needed the freedom to move as you pleased.'

Brady lowered his face, his eyes coming to rest on the table again. 'I drove as I had no other way of getting there. Okay, I admit I came back via Rathmoylan. So what? I was visiting a family friend. I try and look in on him when I can. He's ill; got rheumatoid arthritis. He's the father of a friend from school. I'm on a rota to visit him; see how he's getting on.'

'Billy Mullins,' McEvoy stated.

'Yeah, Billy.' Brady raised his eyes, the penny seeming to finally drop into place. 'Oh sweet Jesus, not Billy. Why would anyone want to kill Billy?'

'For God's sake, Dermot,' McEvoy rolled his eyes, 'don't

try and act all surprised. You're crap at it. He's been dead a couple of hours and you killed him. You burnt him alive! Burnt the whole house down! Decided to add him to your list of victims along with Laura Schmidt, David Hennessey and Grainne Malone.'

'He was alive when I left him. I swear,' Brady pleaded. 'I just made him some lunch, had a chat and then drove back to Dublin. That was it. I didn't kill him. I didn't kill any of them. Why would I do such an evil thing? You've got it all wrong, Superintendent. I didn't kill any of them.'

McEvoy leant forward and held Brady's eye. 'We have you located at three of the murder scenes. You were out at Glencree, one of your hairs was found on Hennessey's body, and you were at Billy Mullins' house at the time he died. You can do as much playacting as you like, but we know you're the so-called Raven, Dermot – all those stupid cards and notes, trying to camouflage what you were up to. It was pathetic. You might have killed four people, thought you were a class act, but you're still an amateur. It was only timing that gave you an edge.'

'No, no, no, no. You've got this all wrong. I've been set up. I haven't killed anyone. Anyone,' he stressed. 'I've done my time and I learnt my lesson.'

'You really expect me to believe that?' McEvoy asked. 'You're a professional liar, Dermot! You deluded yourself you could get away with it. Tried to delude us with your games, but now you're going to pay the price.'

'I didn't kill them!' Brady said angrily. 'I'm being framed. This is … this is stupid.'

'You've just told me that you were in Rathmoylan,' McEvoy said evenly. 'You had to because there're too many people who knew you were there. Now you want me to believe that your trip there was entirely innocent despite the fact that you were also where the other victims were killed. There is coincidence and then there is pattern. These are no coincidences.'

'I was only at Glencree! I was a leader on the trip there. Of

143

course I was there! I haven't been to Maynooth or the Phoenix Park in ages. Somebody is setting me up. I'm telling you, I'm innocent.'

'They found one of your hairs stuck in the paint on David Hennessey's leg, Dermot. You weren't as careful as you thought you were when you were playing your game. You were there and the only person there before us was the killer.'

'Somebody must have planted it to make it look like I was there. David Hennessey is, I mean was, a friend. He helped me out when I was in trouble. Why would I kill him?'

'I've no idea, Dermot. Why would you kill him?'

'I didn't kill him! Look,' Brady said more calmly, trying to gather his panic, 'I didn't kill any of them. I'm being framed. Can't you see that? Somebody is trying to frame me.'

McEvoy clicked off the recording of his conversation with Charlie Deegan. 'Well?'

'Well, it seems as if DI Deegan is in hot water,' Bishop replied neutrally.

'His suspension stands?' McEvoy asked, wary at Bishop's reaction.

'Leave Charlie Deegan to me, Colm; that's my territory.'

'But he's off the case, right?' McEvoy asked, seeking at least some confirmation, some reassurance.

'His conduct will be subject to a full review.'

'You're not suspending him?' McEvoy asked, disbelief in his voice.

'I didn't say that,' Bishop said evenly.

'So you are then?'

'I'm going to review his conduct.' It seemed that Tony Bishop was wary of Charlie Deegan's network of friends in high places. 'For now I suggest that Padraig O'Keeffe takes over the Hennessey part of the investigation. He's familiar with it and he knows what he's doing. I think you should go home and get some rest. The last couple of days have been pretty intense. How much sleep have you had in the last 36 hours? Two or three?'

'I need to re-interview Brady now that his legal representative has arrived,' McEvoy said, quickly forgetting about Charlie Deegan.

'You need some rest and sleep; some time to mull things over, reflect on the case, put it all together in your mind. What I'm saying is, you can stop worrying now; you've caught him. It's over. It's just dotting the i's and crossing the t's. He thought he was being clever with his cards and chapters; thought he could beat forensics. You can't kill four people in four days and not expect to mess up somewhere along the way. He's got his comeuppance. They're going to throw away the key when they sentence him.

'Let Barney Plunkett, Jenny Flanagan and Johnny Cronin have a go at him, pick apart his story. Besides it would also give the crime scene people more time to go through his apartment, give you more ammunition to throw at him. You can start interviewing him again in the morning. Pull what all the others have done together and hit him with new stuff. If you're looking for something to do, go and get a decent dinner and buy a new suit.'

'But …'

'No buts, Colm,' Bishop interrupted, his neck starting to rise red with irritation. 'Go home, spend time with your daughter, and try and relax. You've done a good job. Let everyone else do theirs.'

'I …' McEvoy gave up. 'I guess I'd better go then.' His exhaustion had suddenly caught up with him; the energy that had kept him going over the last four days suddenly dissipating. He wanted to feel elated; instead he just felt a deep melancholy.

'Colm, it's Elaine.'

'How's it going?' McEvoy asked, placing a bag of groceries on the table.

'I've had better weeks. I hear you've caught The Raven.'

'Yeah. Sorry, Elaine, just give me a second.' McEvoy placed his hand over the phone and spoke to Gemma who had trailed in after him. 'Just give me two minutes, will you?' he asked her. 'I just need to take this call. I'll put the kettle on.'

'Whatever.' Gemma placed a second bag on the table and headed back to the kitchen door. 'I'll be watching TV.' She pulled the door closed behind her.

McEvoy lifted his hand. 'Sorry about that, Elaine. We have someone in for questioning. He works for Dublin Homeless Co-operative. He was out at Glencree and was friends with David Hennessey and Billy Mullins.' He started to empty the contents of the bags onto the table.

'Well at least my week might get better then. Might even get time to catch up on the paperwork. If I'm really lucky I might even get time on the boat, though it won't be much fun unless the weather picks up. Look,' she said, shifting tone, 'I'm ringing as I've just finished the autopsy and I thought you'd want a summary report. Billy Mullins died of asphyxiation caused by smoke inhalation. If that hadn't killed him then he might not have lasted much longer in any case. Somebody had hit him hard on the head a couple of times. He had quite severe internal haemorrhaging. Probably hit with a hammer given the concentrated nature of the fracture. It's difficult to say much else given the extent of the burning. With his rheumatoid arthritis and general poor health he was probably a sitting target; unable to get away or defend himself.'

'He didn't put up a fight?' McEvoy asked.

'From the placement of the blows I'd say he was hit from the side. I think the killer surprised him. Came through the door and attacked him before he knew what was happening. Knocked him unconscious and then set fire to the house.'

'The poor bastard.' McEvoy opened a cupboard and placed two tins of tomatoes on a shelf.

'At least it's going to stop now, now you've caught him. I'll make sure you get the full report, Colm. I'll talk to you in the next couple of days, okay.'

'Yeah, thanks, Elaine.' McEvoy ended the call.

With the exception of Laura Schmidt, Dermot Brady hadn't taken any chances. He'd killed his victims before they'd had time to react – sent them to oblivion with a casual ease.

McEvoy poured water from a filter jug into the kettle, turned it on, and finished unpacking the shopping. He couldn't believe that he had so badly misread Brady in that first interview, or that he hadn't adequately acted on his subsequent suspicions.

Gemma forked the last of the curried chicken into her mouth.

McEvoy watched her drop the cutlery onto her plate, a satisfied smile on her face. He took a sip of his Rioja and scratched at his head. He resisted the temptation to fish his plastic substitute from his pocket. 'I'm going to come clean,' he said guiltily. 'I haven't had chance to get you a birthday present. I was meaning to, but, you know, the last few days have been … well, hectic. I'm sorry. The best I can offer is we go shopping tomorrow evening and I'll buy you something you want.' He paused, wanting the earth to swallow him up. Despite everything he should have at least got something. How long would it have taken him to buy a card and a box of chocolates? 'Maybe you could bring a couple of friends along and we could go to McDonalds or the cinema?' he offered. 'Your nana and granddad will be here, they could come as well. They're travelling down tomorrow morning.'

'McDonalds?' Gemma replied, disgust in her voice. 'McDonalds is for kids. We could go to the Chinese.'

'Okay, we'll go to the Chinese,' McEvoy conceded. A couple of years ago and it would have been mayhem if they hadn't gone to McDonalds. He shook his head, thinking about how fast she'd changed in just a short space of time. Maybe he could nip to a late-night petrol station later and get a card.

Gemma started to push herself off the chair. 'I'll go and call Aine and Katie and Sarah and Susan and …'

'Whoa, whoa,' McEvoy interrupted instinctively. 'A limit of three, okay. It's not a school outing.' He was feeling guilty but he wasn't a mug.

'But everyone else has a big party,' Gemma moaned.

'We're not everyone else, are we?' God, he was beginning to sound like Maggie. A couple of years ago he'd have been all on for the party. Mind you, a couple of years ago he wouldn't have been organising it. 'It's an exclusive party, selected invitees only,' he added. 'How's that sound?'

'And we can go to the cinema as well?' Gemma bargained.

'And we can go to the cinema as well,' McEvoy repeated.

'Deal,' Gemma intoned, heading for the door, seemingly happy that she had got what she wanted.

'I'm going to see your mother in a minute,' McEvoy said to her retreating back, wondering how much the following evening was going to cost him. 'Do you want to come?'

'Just give me five minutes. I need to make some calls.'

'Five minutes max, okay? I know your five minutes,' McEvoy said, standing, gathering the plates to take to the sink. He realised he was talking to an empty room. He turned on the tap and squeezed washing-up liquid onto a scouring sponge.

He stared up at the ceiling and the shadows, the bed cold and empty next to him. Things were not going quite to plan. His own partner had realised he was The Raven after only three deaths, one of which she hadn't yet learnt of. His false trail had worked for a while, but had come to fruition a little too quickly. The guards were being much more effective than he had given them credit for, even if it looked to the world as if they were stumbling round in the dark like idiots. It wouldn't take them long to work out Brady was not The Raven; the next death would see to that.

That was a shame – he'd invested time creating the misdirection. Brady had been perfect given his past and his present circumstances.

To make things worse, killing the old man had been too easy, too impersonal, too fast. He hadn't even been aware of what was happening; dead before he could experience the fear and trepidation of suffering. He'd simply clobbered him, lit the fire and run. He hadn't even stayed to watch the house burn.

The deaths so far had served the purpose of the book, but at one level they were hollow victories. Yes, the whole world was watching and discussing his genius, but ultimately they were meaningless slayings lacking in any satisfaction. There was no terror, no begging for mercy, no bonding, no power beyond a moment. They simply served another end – a good end, the intended end, but somehow deficient.

He swung his legs out of the bed and headed to the bathroom. The woman was still lying naked in the bath, a rancid smell revealing she had soiled herself. Her eyes opened at the light from the doorway, communicating her terror and pleas, her skin goose pimpled from the cold air and fear. She lifted her head and pulled half-heartedly at the bath handles, knowing from a day of struggling that she couldn't break the bonds.

He sat on the edge of the bath, seemingly immune to the foul smell and traced his index finger along the smooth skin of her stomach. 'We need to talk,' he said quietly. 'Try and come to some arrangement.'

She nodded, trying to communicate agreement.

He reached over to the counter surrounding the sink and picked up a pack of five razor blades, tearing the packing away.

The woman's eyes bulged with panic and she squirmed hopelessly in the tub.

He removed one of the blades, pinching it between his index finger and his thumb. The woman stopped struggling, her eyes transfixed on the blade. Slowly he drew an arc from the side of her right breast to the top of her pubic bone.

The woman writhed in pain, her eyes imploring him to stop; that she'd do anything he wanted.

He smiled at her wanly then turned his attention to the wound. The thin red line slowly started to weep, the blood easing out onto her alabaster skin. He watched it with fascination as the blood eased into the tiny wrinkles before swelling and spreading.

'Don't worry, I won't touch your face,' he whispered as he drew another arc along the length of her right arm. He then put down the blade and took two sheets of toilet paper from a roll. He pressed the flesh on either side of the new wound, easing the thick red blood out, then wiped it away slowly with the tissue paper.

'You'll come to worship me, over time, you know,' he whispered. 'I'll be the god that bleeds away your sins.'

Chapter Four

Thursday, April 17th

McEvoy closed the front door gently, but it still clicked shut audibly. He cursed under his breath and headed for the kitchen. The clock on the cooker showed it was ten past seven. He placed the paper bag on the table and started to remove the contents he'd bought minutes earlier from a local newsagent – a pack of six cupcakes, a set of cake candles, and a birthday card. He tore the cellophane wrapper on the card with his teeth and pulled it free. On its cover were some lurid cartoon characters he'd once seen Gemma watching on TV, but importantly it had a badge pinned to its top right corner that stated '12 today!'

The door to the kitchen started to open.

'Out!' McEvoy barked. 'Go on, I'm busy here. Just give me two minutes, okay.'

'What are you up to?' Gemma asked hopefully.

'Nothing,' he replied, moving to the door to stop her entering, his eyes searching the kitchen surfaces for a pen. 'Look, don't get your hopes up here, okay. Give me two minutes. I'll call you.'

'Two minutes then I'm coming in,' Gemma warned.

McEvoy moved to a kitchen drawer and started to rifle through it. Toward the back he found an old biro. He quickly wrote in the card. 'Dear Gemma. Have a great day! All my love, Dad.' He stuffed it into the bright red envelope provided and scribbled her name on the front. Next he tore open the cupcakes and placed them onto a plate. Taking the candles from their pack he placed two into the icing of each.

'Thirty seconds,' Gemma called from the hallway.

'I know, I know,' McEvoy replied moving to the cooker to retrieve a box of matches. He pulled one free, struck it and moved its flame across the candles. After five candles the flame had reached his fingers. He extinguished it with a flick of his wrist, dropping the charred remains onto the table and pulled another one free.

'I'm coming now.'

'Hang on,' McEvoy instructed. 'Ten more seconds.'

He lit the rest of the candles with the match. 'Okay, right then, you can come in now.'

Gemma pushed open the kitchen door and tried to stifle a laugh. Surrounding the plate of birthday cupcakes was the debris of packaging.

McEvoy snatched at it, scrunching it up as he started to sing. 'Happy birthday to you. Happy birthday to you. Happy birthday, dear Gemma. Happy birthday to you.' He paused to lift the plate towards her. 'For she's a jolly good fellow, for she's a jolly good fellow, for she's a jolly good fellow and so say all of us.'

She blew the candles out in one go, her face flushed with embarrassment at her father's antics.

McEvoy placed the plate back down and handed her his card. 'As I said, it's nothing special.'

She pulled it free and opened it. 'Thanks, Dad.' She hugged at his waist and he placed an arm around her, bent down and placed a kiss on the top of her head.

'I've got a couple of parcels for you to open,' he said. 'One from Nana and Granddad McEvoy and one from Nana and Granddad Dacey. I've also got some cards from your aunts and uncles. I'll just get them for you.' He left the room and retrieved the items from the cupboard under the stairs. He placed them on the table in a pile. 'You can either open them now or later. It's up to you.'

'I'll do half now, and half when I get home from school.'

'Fair enough. Look, I know it's your birthday,' he said, becoming more serious, 'but I need to go to work. Once you've opened the first half can you get changed? I'll then drop you off at Aunt Caroline's? She said she was preparing a special birthday breakfast for you.'

'Sure, no problem,' Gemma replied, smiling. She stood the card on the table and reached for another envelope. 'Can I take the cupcakes with me?' she asked.

'Of course you can,' he replied, smiling at her happiness, feeling queasy inside. In five minutes' time he was going to leave this joy and innocence and re-enter the world of The Raven. He still found the transition a difficult one after 20 years; to shift from the comforts of home and family to the darkness of serious crime. He dumped the cellophane wrapping in the bin and started to gather his things.

The traffic lights glowed red. McEvoy drummed out a rhythm on the steering wheel, impatient for the sequence to change. His mobile phone rang.

'McEvoy.'

'Hi, Sir, er, it's John Joyce. I've managed to locate the source of those quotes. The one's The Raven's been using in his chapters. Well, I didn't exactly, The Guardian did, but, y'know,' he tailed off embarrassed.

'And?' McEvoy prompted.

'Right, yes, sorry. They're from a book called *Cartographies of Murder: Mapping Killers and their Crimes* by M J Draper. He's a criminal psychologist at the University of California, Los Angeles. I haven't yet managed to get hold of a copy but he basically seems to be arguing that where a murder occurs is an important component of being able to trace and track the killer; that murders don't take place in random locations but are selected by the murderer for specific reasons. Constructing a profile by analysing where he attacks people can tell you as much as constructing a profile through victim selection and method of killing. That's as much as I've got so far. I'm going to go and to see if the Garda College library has a copy. If they don't, I'll go down to Trinity; they've got to have a copy.'

'Okay, good. I guess that makes sense with hindsight.' The lights changed and he moved forward 50 metres and re-joined the queue of traffic. 'All the places where Brady's committed his murders were familiar to him; places he would have known the geography of; that he was comfortable moving around in. Perhaps the chapters were trying to tell us that? Look,' he said without waiting for an answer, 'I'm heading into Harcourt Street for a team meeting. Can you find out whether Brady owns a copy of that book. Maybe he has one in his apartment or at work?'

A mound of newspapers was piled on the desk. Someone had collected together a copy of every newspaper printed in Ireland and quite a few of the British dailies and left them for him. On the top had been a short note from the Assistant Commissioner congratulating him and his teams on Brady's arrest.

The Raven and his killing spree dominated the front and inside covers of every paper, though none of them yet revealed his real name. They simply stated that a man was being questioned in connection with the murders and that he had previously served time for the manslaughter of a mother and small child. It was clear that the papers thought that the man in question was The Raven. They had all published copies of the cards and the four chapters he had sent them.

Barney Plunkett knocked on the open door and stepped into the office. 'You reading your fan mail then?'

'What?' McEvoy said, looking up. 'Yes. Yes. Did you buy all of these?'

'Amazing how they can change their tune so much in 24 hours,' Plunkett replied, ignoring McEvoy's question. 'Yesterday they thought we were a bunch of incompetent fools in need of reform and reorganisation. They hadn't got a single nice thing to say about us.'

'Before we copped ourselves on they were right,' McEvoy stated solemnly. 'Grainne Malone and Billy Mullins would both still be alive if we hadn't dropped our surveillance on Dermot Brady.'

'Yeah, well,' Plunkett shrugged, acknowledging that McEvoy was right. 'We acted in good faith,' he said lamely.

'Once the papers get hold of that they'll change their tune again.' McEvoy slapped the top of the pile. 'They'll want to know why we didn't catch him earlier. Is everyone here? Shall we make a start?'

'Yeah, they're down in the meeting room. What's happening with Deegan?' Plunkett asked sheepishly, digging for information. 'I heard he's going back to uniform.'

'I've no idea,' McEvoy replied neutrally. 'Bishop wouldn't tell me. I asked for him to be suspended pending an investigation.'

'And is he suspended?'

'I don't know, Barney,' McEvoy said, coming round the desk. 'If I did, I'd tell you.'

There was an excited buzz in the meeting room when McEvoy and Plunkett entered. For the first time in a few days McEvoy saw his colleagues smiling. They seemed to be standing taller, more confident in their gait and gestures. The stifling pressure had been lifted off them now that Brady was caught. They knew that it wasn't over, that they had to ensure that their case was watertight, but they recognised that the hard part was over – the identification and capture of the prime suspect.

McEvoy wrapped his knuckles on a table to attain their attention. 'Okay, okay, let's make a start.' He looked round the

155

small group – the four lead investigators – Barney Plunkett, Jenny Flanagan, Johnny Cronin, and Padraig O'Keeffe standing in for Charlie Deegan; and the five crime scene managers – Hannah Fallon, Cheryl Deale, Michael Foster, Seamus Harte who processed the site at Rathmoylan, and Samantha Norrie who was responsible for searching Brady's apartment and car. They turned to face him, sitting down on chairs or the edge of desks, quickly finishing off sentences.

'I guess you've seen the papers,' McEvoy started. 'They seem to think that Brady is as good as jailed. Now that would be great if it was true, but as you well know there's a lot more to be done before that happens. What that means is we have to continue to process the evidence and build our case. I don't want this bastard getting off on a technicality, so I want to make sure it's done right, okay. I don't want anyone to cut any corners. It might take longer, but everything's to be done by the book. Everything. Understand?'

Everyone nodded their head, their face more serious.

'Barney tells me he hasn't yet confessed. In fact he's flat out denying being the so-called Raven. He maintains that he's been set up; that someone has framed him. I don't think anyone in this room believes him, but we've got to take his account seriously. Where are we at with the crime scene evidence?'

The crime scene people looked at each other, trying to work out who was going to respond. Michael Foster decided to start. 'Well, we have hair samples from three of the sites. In Glencree there were two hairs in Laura Schmidt's bedroom, at Maynooth one hair was stuck in the paint on his thigh, and at Phoenix Park we found a couple with the missing toes. We've got solid footprint matches at the Phoenix Park and Rathmoylan and partials for Glencree and Maynooth. I'd say that together they pretty much confirm he was at all the murder sites.'

'Could the hairs have been planted though?' McEvoy asked. 'Maybe someone collected some of his hair and has been parcelling it out carefully to make us think it's him.'

'The shoe size and tread matches Brady as well,' Plunkett answered, 'and when you add it to the other evidence – the fact that he knew three of the victims well, that he was familiar with all the sites, that we can place him directly at two of them, and that he has killed before – it all points to him. He's just trying to spoof us. We all know he did it. Give him a couple more days and he'll confess.'

'Is that what everyone thinks?' McEvoy asked.

Everyone nodded their head.

'And do we think that he was working by himself?'

'I think so,' Johnny Cronin replied. 'I can't see how an accomplice fits into the killings – all the evidence points to him operating on his own.'

'And do we have anything from his apartment apart from his shoes? Any cards or the remaining chapters?'

'We haven't found anything yet,' Samantha Norrie replied. 'But he might have made and printed them elsewhere, like an Internet café. He'd have known that we'd search his home if he became a suspect. There's also no trace of the victims so far, but he could have another base, somewhere which he uses to wash and change.'

'How about the car? The Fiesta he'd borrowed?'

'We've given it a thorough search, but it seems clean,' Norrie replied. 'No blood or hairs from any of the victims. No sign of any paint or anything else that links it to any of the other crime scenes.'

'If he used it for Laura Schmidt's death there had to be something,' McEvoy said, doubt in his voice.

'Maybe he only used it for Billy Mullins,' Jenny Flanagan said. 'That was pretty bloodless.'

'Maybe,' McEvoy muttered. 'We need to know if that car was spotted near to any of the other sites around the time of the murders. We also need to find the clothes he took from the victims and those that he was wearing when he killed. As Samantha says, perhaps he's got another place where he gets changed and disposes of things. Barney, can you check to see if he owns or rents any other properties.'

'No problem,' Plunkett replied, making a note for himself.

'We're going to have to construct a full time line for Brady from the moment the DHC took those homeless kids out to Glencree until he was brought in for questioning. We know where he was some of the time, but we need to fill in the blanks. Take his mugshot and show it to all the witnesses at the different sites and see if they can place him in the area at the time of the murders. Also talk to the DHC and find out when he was at work. In fact, we should re-interview all the DHC people again, talk to them about Brady, his relationship to Laura Schmidt and David Hennessey, and how he was behaving out at Glencree. Barney, can you arrange for them to come in later this morning?'

'I'll ring them straight after this. Do you want to talk to all of them or just the people who were out at Glencree?'

'Let's start with those at Glencree and then move onto the others. You should probably be around for those since you've been talking to them already.'

Plunkett nodded in agreement and ran a hand through his sandy hair.

'Well, I guess we'd better get started then. I'll leave you to brief your teams. If anything significant comes up then you're to contact me immediately. I'm going to go and re-interview Brady again, see what he's got to say for himself now he's had a night to think about things. And remember, you need to talk to each other. It's now about connections. We need to link Brady across the different victims and murder sites. I don't want anyone else running solo on this,' McEvoy warned. 'This is a team game.'

Dermot Brady shifted on his seat, rolling his wide shoulders, trying to get comfortable. His thinning brown hair was stuck up at odd angles, his face tired, two-day stubble covering skin that had an odd, pale yellow quality to it, dark crescents hanging under bloodshot eyes. Next to him his grey-haired solicitor sat bolt upright, pursing his lips and picking at his left index finger with his right thumb, his eyes boring into McEvoy. He was dressed in a well-tailored, pinstripe suit, a red tie over an ivory shirt. A blank notepad lay on the table in front of him, an expensive looking silver fountain pen sitting on top of it.

McEvoy subconsciously mimicked Brady, rolling his shoulders and leaning forward, his oversized jacket hanging open. 'Shall we make a start then?' he asked rhetorically. 'My colleagues tell me that you're still protesting your innocence,' he said evenly.

Brady stared back coldly but didn't reply.

'Forensic evidence places you at all four of the murder sites, Dermot. However careful you think you were there were hair samples and footprints that match a pair of your shoes. The chances of someone else being at all four sites are practically zero, especially since three of the victims were closely known to you.'

'Look, I wasn't in Maynooth and I wasn't in the Phoenix Park, okay,' he said firmly. 'I'm being framed for four murders I didn't commit. Why can't any of you see that? Are you all blind or something?'

'Because,' McEvoy said patiently, 'all the evidence points to you being the killer and there's nothing to suggest otherwise. Nothing. You've killed previously and got away with manslaughter, now you thought you'd have another go. Only this time you weren't as clever as your chapters suggested. Just face the facts, Dermot, and accept the consequences.'

'For fuck's sake!' Brady snapped. 'I haven't written any fuckin' chapters! And I didn't mean to kill that woman and her child,' he said expressively, holding open his hands. 'I was young, I was drunk, and I was stupid, okay. But I didn't deliberately set out to kill them. And that's the truth. I served my sentence and I ask for forgiveness every day. Every day,' he repeated. 'But

I didn't kill those four people. He's planted evidence to frame me. I'm telling you the truth, Superintendent.'

'That's not what the evidence is telling us, Dermot, and it's not what a jury will believe. What we've got is solid and whatever else we find will be as well. You lured Laura Schmidt out to Glencree, a place you knew well, to kill her. You visited a place you spent three years doing a degree and you killed your old tutor. You then killed Grainne Malone in the Phoenix Park, before killing Billy Mullins, a man you helped care for, in his own home.'

'This is ridiculous!' Brady snapped, placing his hands on the top of his head. 'I didn't lure Laura Schmidt anywhere. She came of her own free will. She turned up at the bus minutes before we set off. Yes, okay, I tried to get her to come on the trip, but then so did all the others. That's our job! And we were all surprised she came. And I would have never have killed David or Billy. They were my friends! They were people I loved and trusted. Why would I kill them?'

'I don't know, Dermot, why did you kill them?'

'I didn't kill them! Jesus, this is like talking to a brick wall. I didn't even know Grainne Malone and I haven't been to the Phoenix Park in ages. The other three all have connections to me, but I've no idea who the hell she is!'

The solicitor stopped picking at his nails and placed a hand on Brady's arm, signalling to him to take it easy, to calm down and be careful what he was saying.

McEvoy read the signal as well; aware it was as much for him as Brady. 'Okay, okay,' he said, raising his palms. 'Calm down, Dermot. You okay?'

Brady stared back angrily and snorted breath from his nose.

'Okay then, let's say what you're arguing is true,' McEvoy said steadily, 'that you're being set up by somebody else. Whoever that person is they must know you pretty well to make all the killings match your life; to make us believe that you're the killer. So, who do you think The Raven is, Dermot? It must be someone pretty close to you.'

Brady shrugged. 'I don't know. Really, I don't.' He ran his hand through his thinning hair and grabbed a handful, pulling it gently.

'You've had all night to think about it and you haven't come up with a single name?' McEvoy asked, raising his eyebrows. 'Come on, Dermot, you'll have to do better than that.'

'I don't know,' Brady repeated. 'Why does it have to be someone I know? He could have just picked me and followed me – learnt things about me. He could have known about me from the papers.'

'As you said though, Dermot, you killed that mother and child 15 years ago. It's a long time since you've been in the papers.'

'People know though. They never let you forget it. Everyone within half a mile of where I live knows I did time. They could easily look me up in the library.'

'So what you're saying is that it could be anyone living in a half-mile radius of your apartment?' McEvoy said sardonically. 'That must be over 50,000 people, Dermot. Maybe more. Are we to treat them all as suspects?'

Brady shrugged again. 'Look, I don't know who it is. All I know is that I'm being framed for murders I didn't commit. If I'm right, he's still out there and he's preparing to kill again. And you're doing nothing to stop him.'

'The fact that you're sat opposite me means he won't kill again,' McEvoy said, but there was little confidence in his voice. 'Let's take a 15 minute break, okay. I'll arrange for someone to bring you some tea or coffee.' He popped the cassette from the recorder and headed for the door of the interview room.

The door opened and Tom Cahill, Dermot Brady's room mate from Glencree, entered the interview room followed by Barney Plunkett. McEvoy stood and offered his hand. 'Thanks for coming in, Mr Cahill.'

Cahill shook it firmly and pulled a tight smile. 'Tom,' he said with a deep, gravelly voice. 'Everyone just calls me Tom.' His short grey hair sat untidily above a rugged face, deep creases defining his ruddy cheeks, strong laughter lines radiating from bloodshot eyes framed by black-rimmed glasses. He wore a mid-brown cord jacket over a red checked shirt, dark brown jeans and a scuffed pair of black shoes.

'Well, Tom, thanks for coming in.' McEvoy gestured to the seat and Cahill sat down, his fingers knitting together and coming to rest on his stomach. 'We'd like to ask you again about the trip to Glencree. That okay?' McEvoy continued.

'Yeah, that's fine,' Cahill nodded. 'I still can't believe what happened to that young girl. I haven't had a good night's sleep since.'

'Me neither,' McEvoy replied sympathetically. 'Did you know her well?'

'Me? No, no. She used to drop into Gardiner Street every now and then, but she was a quiet one. If you tried to talk to her she just withdrew in on herself. I guess if what the papers are saying is true then she had a pretty good reason to be like that.'

'And did you see her leave the den the night she died?' McEvoy asked, not wanting to dwell on Laura's life. 'I mean, did she leave on her own or with someone?'

'I've no idea, to be honest. I was probably talking to someone when she left. I just know she was sat on her own and when I looked over at where she'd been a bit later on she wasn't there.'

'And did Dermot Brady disappear at any point for a while?'

'No, but ... Look, I'm not sure what you're driving at here,' Cahill said firmly, 'but I can't see Dermot Brady as Laura's murderer.'

'Why not?'

'Because there isn't a bad bone in that man's body. He's one of the most selfless people I've ever met.'

'He's also done five years for manslaughter for killing a young mother and her son.'

'And he's prayed for forgiveness every day since. The man is genuinely tortured. It was an act of madness fuelled by alcohol. He's nobody's fool, but he'd go to the end of the earth to help you if you needed it.'

'So you definitely can't see him as The Raven?'

'Is that who you're holding? Dermot? You must be mad! There's no way that Dermot killed them. No way.'

Tom Cahill handed over the money for his pint of Guinness and his meal, took a long sup from the glass, and moved away from the bar, down a couple of steps, round the end of a long, thin table stretching the length of the pub, splitting it in two, and sat on a badly worn stool half way along its extent. He placed his pint on the pine surface, unfolded a copy of the Irish Times and scanned the front page absentmindedly.

Three stools along the table, near to the door of the pub, a man with shoulder-length brown hair, a neatly trimmed beard and stylish, thin-framed glasses nursed a glass of Coke, a paperback novel spread open before him. He was wearing a black suit over a black shirt and tie, a small black satchel at his feet. He glanced at Cahill, a sly smile forming on his lips and then turned his attention back to the rest of the pub, examining its customers and in particular the flow of people through the door marked 'Toilets'. Only occasionally did anyone pass through the door despite the pub being busy with lunchtime trade.

All of the smaller tables hugging the windows and walls were occupied, mainly by people in their late twenties through to early forties dressed in suits or smart casuals; office workers from the nearby financial companies and government offices. There were only a handful of people not eating, the majority of tables covered with wide, deep plates. A soft rock ballad was playing in the background, but it was the noise of conversation that drowned out the rumble of the traffic along the quays.

After ten minutes one of the bar staff carried Cahill's meal over to him – pan-fried minute steak on ciabatta with chips, onion rings and a side salad. He ordered a second pint and tucked into the food. A man in his early thirties brushed past him heading for the toilets.

A few seconds later, the man at the end of the table stood up. He turned his novel open to keep his page and placed it next to the near-empty glass of Coke, letting the bar staff know that he'd be back. He pulled a plastic bag from his satchel, scrunching it up in his hand and forcing it into his right trouser pocket, rounded the end of the table, bounded up a couple of steps and headed through the door to the stairs leading down to the toilets. As he descended, he pulled on a pair of thin rubber gloves and placed a surgical face mask over his mouth. He could feel his rage welling up inside and fought to suppress it, seeking a calm purposefulness. At the bottom of the steps he turned right and pushed open the toilet door.

The man in his thirties was standing at the third urinal, the one furthest away from the door and next to one of the two toilet cubicles. The walls were covered in small white tiles, adverts strategically placed above each urinal. The cubicle door was made of pine, the dividing wall between the cubicles aqua, the floor black. The man didn't turn to look at the new arrival.

The Raven headed for the cubicle next to the man, who was just starting to finish his piss. As he drew level with the man's back he harnessed his fury, shoving both of his hands hard into the man's head driving it into a silver framed advertisement for WKD drinks, the tiles underneath cracking with the impact. He savagely yanked the man's head back by his hair and slammed it forward again. The man started to slump to the floor only held upright by The Raven pressing his weight into him from behind.

He let him fall, the man's jaw smashing off the urinal lip, bucking his head back violently. The Raven stepped quickly over the prone body and dragged its dead weight into the cubicle. He struggled to get the body sitting on the toilet and then had to contort his own figure to get the door closed. He flicked over the catch locking the door and pulled the plastic bag from his trouser pocket. From within it he removed another plastic bag and a red scarf. He threw the scarf onto the man's face.

He froze. The door to the toilet had opened and someone had entered the room. A couple of seconds later he could hear the zip on the new arrival's trousers being pulled down and then the sound of the man's piss hitting and swirling round a urinal. Thirty seconds later the man zipped his trousers back up, washed his hands and then left without drying them.

The Raven let out a long breath, feeling collected and empty; his anger subsided. He pulled one of the bags over one of the unconscious man's hands, then took an elastic band from his jacket pocket and pulled it over the bag, securing it to the limp wrist. He repeated the procedure with the other hand. Next he pulled a Stanley knife from his left trouser pocket and extended the blade. Carefully he lifted up the rubber band and bag on the man's left arm and slashed rapidly and viciously across his wrist dropping the elastic band down as the blood started to spray. He repeated the exercise with the other wrist. The bags started to slowly fill with blood.

Next he took the scarf and wrapped it around the man's neck. Pulling it down slightly he slashed across the man's throat in one motion, quickly pulling the scarf up to stop the blood spraying over himself and the cubicle. He retracted the blade and placed it back in his pocket.

From the top pocket of his shirt he took two business cards which he jammed between the toilet paper holder and the dividing wall. He then withdrew the next chapter, already sealed in a clear, folded plastic bag, and slotted it past the man's flaccid penis between his underpants and trousers.

He opened the door, placed a shoelace around the lock, and stepped out of the cubicle. He closed the door, tugged on both ends of the lace and pulled over the lock, before releasing one end and teasing it free. Next he washed the blood off the rubber gloves, but did not remove them. He unhooked the face mask, checked his appearance in the mirror and straightened his hair. He then left the toilet heading back upstairs, pulling a wet wipe from a travel pack in his jacket pocket as he ascended.

He wiped the door handle leading back into the bar, pulled it open and headed back to his Coke and novel. He retrieved his bag from the floor, hanging it on his shoulder, then downed the remainder his drink, picked up the novel and wiped quickly the surface where he had been sat with the wet wipe. He then left the pub still carrying the empty Coke glass in his gloved hands.

As Cahill pushed the last of the onion ring into his mouth he shoved the plate away from himself and dabbed at his mouth with a napkin. He placed the remainder of his pint on top of his newspaper and stood up.

He descended the stairs and went for a piss. The toilet was quiet; one of the cubicles occupied. He finished, zipped up and washed his hands, blowing them dry. As he opened the door to leave he heard a soft splat sound behind him. Rather than investigate he exited and started to climb the stairs. As he reached the top he almost collided with a young man in a cheap looking, light grey suit, who was turning into the stairwell.

'Sorry,' the man said, stepping back.

'No problem.' Cahill passed the man and returned to his spot, taking another sup of his pint and turning to the sports pages.

The young man continued down the stairs entering the men's toilet. He moved to the first urinal and went for a piss, staring at the advertisement. As he was turning to head to the sinks he spotted a dark red trail starting to ooze from under the slight gap at the foot of the closed cubicle door. He moved towards it, crouching down to get a better look. 'Are you okay in there?' he asked, standing up again. 'Hello? Hello?'

He knocked on the door and getting no response tried to push it open, finding it locked. 'Hello? Are you alright?' A slight panic was starting to grow in his chest, a sense that his ribs were been crushed. He moved into the adjacent cubicle and stood on the toilet rim, leaning over to balance against the aqua partition and look down over it.

A man was sat on the toilet staring up at the ceiling, his forehead bloody but his face drained of colour, his arms hanging limply by his sides, his flaccid penis hanging out of his flies. A red scarf was wrapped around his neck, his shirt soaked in blood. A white plastic bag was tied around his right wrist covering his hand, the weight inside pulling it down. The left hand was exposed, the slash marks across the wrist clear. Beneath it a plastic bag lay on the floor, blood oozing slowly from its opening.

'Fuckin' hell,' the young man said in a flat Dublin accent, recoiling instinctively. He took another quick glance to confirm what he'd seen and bolted for the toilet door, pulling his mobile phone from his trouser pocket.

McEvoy rubbed his right eye and tried to stifle a yawn.

'He's a stubborn bastard, I'll say that,' Bishop said, pushing back his chair, standing and moving to the window. 'He must know that there's no way out of this?' It had just started to rain again, the sky a murky grey, people scurrying on the street below, pulling up collars and pushing up umbrellas. He turned back to face McEvoy. 'Whatever he tries to argue, the forensic evidence places him at the four murder sites. There's no getting out of that.'

'He insists that that evidence's been planted,' McEvoy replied wearily. 'That he's being framed.'

'And do you believe him?' Bishop asked incredulously.

'I, er …' McEvoy hesitated.

'Jesus, Colm,' Bishop snapped, his face starting to flush red, 'he's as guilty as hell! We all know he's guilty. The only person who doesn't think he is guilty is him! I want him formally charged with the murders. Do you hear me? This has gone on long enough. The press, the politicians and the public – they all want to know what the hell's going on. They want to know that we've caught The Raven. That it's over.'

'But we're still questioning him,' McEvoy replied without conviction. His time as a hero was feeling short-lived. Bishop's short fuse was easily lit and he seemed to possess an inexhaustible supply of matches. 'And we're still collecting and collating the evidence,' he added, knowing that Bishop wouldn't care; he needed something to sate the never ending appetite of the media.

'We have enough evidence to charge him, for feck's sake! The rest will show up in time. You know it will. It's just a case of doing the bloody legwork. Have you any idea what kind of pressure we're under here, Colm? Have you seen the news or the newspapers? This is a global story. And I mean global. Every feckin' news crew in the world has descended on Dublin. The Minister for Justice is on the phone to the Garda Commissioner every five feckin' minutes wanting to know what's happening! And he's then onto me. I've been doing my best to shield you from all that shit, to give you the time and space to do your job, but it's now time to move things along. I'm telling you, Colm, not asking you, to charge him.'

The phone rang and Bishop snatched the receiver out of its cradle. 'Bishop!' He listened for ten seconds or so. 'What! Are you sure? … For God's sake! Tell them to seal the place off. You know the routine.' He slammed the receiver down, his cheeks so red they looked like they would start to bleed. 'They've found another body. It's in the men's toilets of The White Horse on George's Quay. It's on the opposite bank to Liberty Hall, near to Tara Street Station. His neck has been slit and his wrists slashed.

168

There were two of his feckin' cards stuck to the wall. You'd better get down there and find out what the hell's happened.'

'They've found another body?' McEvoy repeated, rising, disbelief in his voice, his bowels shifting, feeling as if they were about to drop out from under him.

'What do I have to do, repeat everything?' Bishop snapped angrily. 'Yes, they've found another body; on George's Quay.'

'Okay, shit. Look, what should I do about Dermot Brady?' McEvoy asked, still trying to process the news.

'Fuck Dermot Brady!' Bishop shouted. 'Get to that murder site and find out what the hell's going on! And ring me the minute you get there.'

'I want Barney Plunkett as the DI,' McEvoy asked, gathering himself, 'and Hannah Fallon. I need people familiar with all of this.'

'I don't care! You can have BoBo the feckin' Clown as far as I'm concerned, just get on with it!'

McEvoy headed for the door, a mix of anger and anxiety rising in his chest. His left hand instinctively plucked at the plastic substitute in his pocket.

'I hope for your sake it's a copycat or something,' Bishop mumbled, turning back to the window, massaging his throbbing temples. 'Jesus.'

He was standing on the far bank of the river watching McEvoy exit a car, glancing around before heading into the pub. He knew that the most sensible thing to do was to disappear; to get away from the murder scene, and yet he desperately felt the need to cross over the river and nose around; to find out what was happening; to introduce himself to McEvoy and get a measure of the man; to offer himself to the investigation as a witness – he'd been in the bar at the time and had fled or he'd seen the killer leave and head up the alley. He'd now shed his disguise and knew he could mingle in the crowd without fear of recognition.

Following Cahill from Harcourt Street to The White Horse had been easy. As soon as they set off he knew Cahill was heading to his usual Thursday lunchtime eating spot; a spot that he had scoped out for a killing, along with tens of others, as part of his pattern to frame Brady. He was originally going to target Cahill as a victim, but perhaps now the focus would shift to him instead – he was out at Glencree and he knew Hennessey through Brady; he had all the connections to make him a suspect.

It had certainly been the most exhilarating of the slayings. The second man entering the toilets whilst he was still in the cubicle had added a certain edge and the fact that so many people were around had heightened the adrenaline rush. Someone might have seen through his disguise and recognised him or if things had gone wrong he would have had to fight his way out from the basement and then try and escape through busy streets. He'd killed in broad daylight in the middle of the city – he'd told the world that he could kill anywhere, any time; that The Raven was formidable and *The Rule Book* infallible. There would be a media frenzy.

He took one last look across the river. He would spend the afternoon watching the world become ever more hysterical about his work and ever more disdainful of the gardai. He turned on heels and headed away, a slow euphoria building in him. Two more deaths and his global infamy would be ensured for centuries.

McEvoy was standing in the entrance to the cubicle, his feet astride a dark pool of blood. He could feel the bile creeping up his throat, his jaw so tight that the muscles on the edge of his cheeks ached. His held his left hand up and looked at it shaking slightly, nothing he could do to stop it. He jammed the plastic substitute between his lips, it trembling between his fingers, and inhaled deeply.

Someone had forced the lock and the door was pushed open to reveal the dead man. His face was vacant, his eyes half-closed and mouth open, the bottom of his top teeth visible. His white shirt matched the deep red of the scarf looped round his neck. The slashes on the man's left wrist were deep, the bone visible through the clotted blood. The plastic bag on his right arm, hung low, almost touching the ground, the thin rubber band struggling to keep it covering his hand. He could see the two business cards poking up from the top of the toilet roll holder.

Dermot Brady was innocent unless he had a partner and McEvoy doubted that. The Raven operated alone; he didn't want the risk that someone could reveal his identity. He'd laid a credible false trail, picking places and victims linked to Brady and planting forensic evidence. The White Horse was where Brady used to meet David Hennessey. If he hadn't already been brought in for questioning, the location would have nudged them a little nearer to suspecting him.

He rubbed his right eye with the heel of his hand. Bishop would go apocalyptic when he told him, quickly followed by every journalist camped out in Dublin. They'd wasted a day chasing and questioning Brady letting The Raven plan and execute his next murder.

Barney Plunkett pushed open the door behind him. 'Well?' he asked.

'It's a bloody mess, no pun intended,' McEvoy replied, standing to one side so that Plunkett could see the body.

'And it's definitely The Raven?' Plunkett asked, blanching.

'What do you think?'

'It could be a copycat killing.'

'Come on, Barney,' McEvoy hissed. 'Of course it's him. He planted the evidence concerning Brady. He's the trickster, remember – all that raven mythology nonsense.'

Plunkett nodded reluctantly, turning away from the body.

'Leave Fay Butler and Kenny Johns working on Laura Schmidt's murder,' McEvoy instructed. 'Dr John can help you here. First thing is to make sure the place is sealed off. At least 50 yards all round. Get onto Traffic – closing the quays is going to cause chaos. And find out where Hannah and Elaine are; we need this site processed – the next chapter has to be here somewhere. Come on, let's get moving.' McEvoy brushed past Plunkett and headed up the stairs.

McEvoy spotted Cahill as soon as he entered the bar. He was sat on his own nursing a pint of Guinness, everyone else around him clumped into small groups. 'You're going to tell me it's pure coincidence you were here when The Raven killed again,' McEvoy stated as way of a greeting.

'Would you believe me if I said yes?' Cahill replied flatly. 'I come here one or two days a week for lunch, Superintendent. I used to come with Dermot Brady.'

'Well Dermot didn't kill the poor bastard downstairs. Did you?'

'Do you think I'd still be sitting here if I had? I'd have scarpered.'

'Whoever the killer is, he has strong nerves,' McEvoy countered, already knowing that Cahill wasn't the killer. It was nothing he could articulate, it was just an intuitive feeling; that The Raven was still trying to lay false trails, trying to mislead them. 'He likes to kill in public places; thrives on the risk.'

'Well my nerves are shot to hell, I can tell you.' Cahill took a small sip of the pint. 'That could have been me down there. Was probably meant to be me given who else he's killed. I'd only just come up from the toilet when that young fella over there found the body. I reckon I've just had a close escape, though that's no conciliation to the poor bastard he killed. You can do whatever forensic tests you like, but I'm not your killer, Superintendent.'

'Well, the tests will have to be done in any case,' McEvoy said, it clear in his tone that he believed Cahill. 'There's one thing you can be certain of, whoever the killer is, he knows Dermot Brady's life inside out. There's a strong probability you know him as well given how he's targeted people and places linked to the DHC – Glencree and Laura Schmidt, David Hennessey, The White Horse. I want you to think about who that might be, Tom, and whether they were in this pub this lunchtime.'

'You think that I ...' Cahill trailed off as a guard in uniform approached.

'Sorry to interrupt, Sir,' the guard said. 'DS Fallon told me to tell you that she's arrived.

'Tell her that I'll be there in a second,' McEvoy replied and then turned his attention back to Cahill.

'I've got to go, but don't go anywhere. Someone will take your statement and do those tests.'

'I'm not going anywhere, Superintendent,' Cahill replied, lowering his gaze onto the table in front of him. 'I want this Raven fucker caught.'

McEvoy's phone rang and he snatched at it. 'McEvoy.'

'You were meant to call me, Colm, as soon as you got there,' Bishop snapped.

'Sorry,' McEvoy said without apology, heading for the door, instinctively pulling the cigarette pack from his pocket. 'I've been busy.'

'Sir!' Hannah Fallon called from the fire escape door.

McEvoy glanced over from where he was talking with Barney Plunkett, dropping his cigarette butt and grinding it under foot.

Hannah Fallon pulled a tight smile as they neared. 'We've found the fifth chapter.' She held out a clear plastic bag that had clearly been folded up. 'It had been pushed into the flies on his trousers. We've also got a wallet.' She held up her other hand, the wallet wrapped in a clear evidence bag. 'His name's Peter Killick, worked for the Department of Health and Children. It's just at the end of the street.' She pointed along the side road at an ugly, 1970s tower block.

'Can you straighten the bag so I can read the note,' McEvoy asked, holding up his hands to show he had no gloves on.

She passed the wallet to Barney Plunkett and pulled the bag tight. McEvoy read the note out loud.

The Rules
Chapter Five L: Post-murder W

"The experienced serial killer will always have a post-murder routine. He will clean the site, dispose of any evidence, and depart without witnesses. He will ensure he has a cast-iron alibi and he might even seek to point evidence at someone else. He will continue with his life as if nothing had happened. He'll either not appear in the list of possible suspects or he'll be one of many in which it is easy to hide."

5a. Leave no incriminating evidence - hair, blood, semen, personal items.

5b. Do not leave anything of yourself behind, mementos that will allow them access to your thoughts and life.

5c. Slip away from the scene making sure there's no trail to your life.

5d. Do not take anything from the scene or the victim that you do not intend to destroy.

5e. Do not hang round the police investigation.

```
5f. Have no interaction with the victim's fam-
ily or friends at any time.

Master rule: Go to ground until it is safe to
kill again.
```

'Well it's definitely him.' He looked back up at the others. 'Dermot Brady's the key to all of this. Whoever The Raven is, he wanted us to think it was Brady. I'm going to go back and talk to him. Barney, you're in charge. Find out if Peter Killick was here on his own or whether he came with someone and get onto Family Liaison. I want us to be the first to contact them. And see where Elaine Jones is. She should have been here by now. Call me if you find out anything important.'

He headed away towards his car, the start of a headache forming somewhere behind his eyes.

'Do you believe me now?' Brady asked, no malice in his voice.

'I've no reason not to,' McEvoy conceded. 'Look, I'm sorry about the last couple of days, but all the evidence pointed to you. Of course you're free to leave any time you want, but we could really do with your help. The killings are all linked to some aspect of your life – Glencree and Laura Schmidt, Maynooth and David Hennessey, Rathmoylan and Billy Mullins, The White Horse and Peter Killick. Did you know Peter Killick?'

'He doesn't ring any bells. Doesn't mean I didn't know him though. I'd need to see a picture.'

'The only one that doesn't seem to fit is the Phoenix Park and Grainne Malone.'

'I didn't know Grainne Malone, but the Phoenix Park is kind of important to me because of the Pope's Mass in '79. I don't know what it was, the million people, the service or what, but it's always stayed with me. I kind of drew strength from it when

I was in prison – the memory helped me find God. It's difficult to explain.'

McEvoy nodded, the location of the third murder now making sense. 'The Raven has to be someone you know, Dermot,' he stated. 'Someone who's familiar with your life.'

'Well that could be anyone,' Brady said, opening his arms, relaxing, starting to regain some of his expressive personality now that he knew he was no longer a suspect. 'I'm pretty open about my life, Superintendent. I don't have any secrets and I draw on my own experiences all the time when I'm trying to help somebody.'

'But you must have some idea as to who it might be. Who would want to frame you?'

Brady shrugged. 'Honestly, Superintendent, I haven't got a clue. And it's no good asking to me list down everyone I know. It would be a long list – everyone from church, from the local community, at work and on the streets. Must be a few hundred people.'

'Jesus!' McEvoy mumbled. 'Come on, Dermot, you must have some idea,' he pressed. 'We need to stop him killing again.'

'Don't you think I've been trying to work out if I know him?' Brady responded, throwing his arms out wide. 'He tried to frame me for those murders. I'll help you as much as I can, but I honestly don't know who The Raven is. Let's face it, it could be half of Mountjoy. Why don't you start with them?'

'Okay, say it is someone from Mountjoy, you must be able to narrow it down. Some must be more likely than others.'

'I guess.'

'Can you give me a list?'

Brady nodded reluctantly.

'Good.' McEvoy pushed his pen and pad towards him. 'And, how about where he might strike next? He's picking places that you knew well.'

'I don't know.' Brady shrugged. 'I can have a think, but again it could be loads of places – my local church, the DHC, where my apartment is. The list is endless.'

McEvoy was climbing the stairs to the incident room carrying the two lists supplied by Brady. The first detailed the names of 26 former inmates. The second included 15 locations of possible future attacks, the residential addresses of family members and old friends, the DHC on Gardiner Street, his local church, the house he was brought up in, and his old primary and secondary schools. His mobile phone rang.

'McEvoy.'

'It's Barney. Several of the people in the pub remember a man with a beard, dressed all in black, who was sitting by himself. He was near to the end of that table that divided the bar in two and had a perfect view of the toilet door. He didn't order any food, just nursed a glass of Coke while seemingly reading a novel. He visited the toilets not long before Peter Killick was found and when he came back out he just collected his stuff together and left.'

'I always go for a piss before I leave a pub as well,' McEvoy said without enthusiasm, coming to a halt on a landing. 'Was there anything else?'

'One of the witnesses said she thought she saw him quickly wipe the table clean where he was sat.'

'And did he?' he asked with more interest.

'Difficult to know; just about every person in the place seems to have put their hands on the surface since then. It's a bloody disaster. I've got a couple of them trying to construct photofits. I think he's our man though. The way they describe how he was acting – constantly looking about the place, shifting on his seat and fidgeting; where he was sitting.'

'Right, okay, get hold of Dr John. See if we can pick this guy up walking away from the place. There were at least four cameras on that side street. They were focused on doors but maybe they caught him in any case?'

'I'll get onto him now and I'll also circulate the photofit once it's ready. We also need to appeal for anyone who was in the pub that lunchtime but left.'

'Send the photofit on to Bishop as soon as it's ready. He can use it in the next press conference. Any more on Peter Killick?'

'We've managed to track down the two people he had lunch with. They both worked with him in the Department of Health and Children. They headed back to the office when he went to the toilet. He was going on to some meeting in the Custom House so they didn't wait for him. Family Liaison is round with his family at the moment. He was married with two young children aged five and eight. Poor bastards.'

'Jesus.' McEvoy leant over the railing and stared down into the stairwell. Three more lives thrown into tragedy and chaos for no other reason than to satisfy the psychotic fantasies of a madman. 'Look, we'd better have another team meeting. Everything's changed. Can you round up the others? We just need the DIs for now.'

'Jesus Christ,' Johnny Cronin hissed. 'He had his throat slit and his wrists slashed? Thank God I didn't have to deal with that one.'

'You think it's worse than being burnt alive?' Jenny Flanagan asked.

'At least they were both unconscious, not like Laura Schmidt,' Barney Plunkett said. 'Imagine looking along that sword, wondering if the sick bastard is going to ram it through the back of your head?'

'Have you finished?' McEvoy said irritably, looking up. 'They're all terrible ways of dying. Do we know where Padraig is?'

'He said he was on his way,' Plunkett answered.

'Right, okay, well let's make a start in any case. I'll fill Padraig in when he arrives. As you all know, there's been a fifth murder. Peter Killick, aged 35, an assistant principal officer in the Department of Health and Children. He was killed in The White Horse pub on George's Quay. Dermot Brady couldn't have committed that murder because he was being held for questioning at the time. Which means he's not The Raven and our killer is still on the loose. We need to ...' McEvoy trailed off as the door opened and Charlie Deegan entered the room, a satisfied smirk on his face.

'What the hell are you doing here?' McEvoy snapped. 'You're suspended.'

The other three occupants in the room swivelled round to view the intruder.

'I was never suspended,' Deegan replied coolly. 'That was just your fantasy. As of now I'm back heading up the investigation into the death of David Hennessey. I've already spoken to Padraig O'Keeffe.' He sat down on the edge of a table.

'You're what?' McEvoy said incredulously.

'I said, I'm back heading up the David Hennessey investigation. So, where are we at? I hear The Raven's killed again.' He raised his eyebrows and pulled a wry smile.

'Don't push your luck, Charlie,' McEvoy hissed, the red mist starting to descend. 'I don't know what the hell is going on, but I'm going to find out. Don't go anywhere,' he said, heading for the door.

'Don't worry, I've no intention of going anywhere.'

The door slammed shut. Plunkett, Cronin and Flanagan turned their backs on Deegan, whispering to each other. Deegan shook his head dismissively and gazed out of the window.

Bishop's secretary jumped in her seat as the door burst open.

'Is he in?' McEvoy asked angrily, heading for the door into Bishop's office.

'He's busy preparing for a news conference.'

'Good. I need to talk him.' He knocked once on the door, pushed it open and entered the room. 'What the hell is Charlie Deegan doing back on duty?' he snapped. 'And why is he back in charge of the Hennessey case?'

Bishop looked up, startled. 'What?' he asked, confusion and annoyance in his voice.

'I said, I wanted to know why Charlie Deegan is back on the Hennessey case. I thought he was suspended.'

'Well, you thought wrong, Colm.' Bishop snapped back, his face starting to flush red. He pushed his chair back from the desk. 'I've already told you that this whole thing is bigger than just the murders! We're already under the media spotlight without one of our senior investigators being suspended from the case. At the end of the day, what did he do? He pulled in a suspect for questioning without telling you first! Someone who at the time we believed was The Raven.'

'And while he kept that information to himself another murder was committed,' McEvoy stated, the fight starting to go out of him, knowing that there was little hope of getting Deegan removed from the case.

'Look, Colm,' Bishop said, following McEvoy's tone, trying to placate him, 'it wasn't my decision, okay, but you need to see the bigger picture. We need experienced officers working on this case, and whatever you or I feel about Charlie Deegan, he's experienced and he gets results. You're just going to have to swallow your pride and build bridges with him. I've got other things to worry about, like a press conference in an hour and briefing the Assistant Commissioner. I need to get prepared and you need to find a killer.'

'Jesus,' McEvoy muttered, heading for the door. 'I don't believe this.'

'And Colm?'

'Yes?' He turned at the door.

'Next time, wait until I tell you to come in.' The implication was clear, McEvoy was lucky not to have received a different, less accommodating reaction. 'And go and get measured for a uniform some time today,' he added. 'You're going to need it. The world thinks we have a scarecrow heading up things. We need you to smarten up your act.' It was meant to sound humorous, trying to close the encounter with some light heartedness, but it came out flat.

McEvoy looked down at his ill-fitting suit, nodded and closed the door behind him. He apologised to the secretary and left Bishop's office. Bursting in there had been a stupid thing to do; something he'd never done before. No doubt it would come back to haunt him at some point. Bishop might have been reconciliatory, but he didn't forget misdemeanours.

McEvoy pushed opened the door and walked to the front of the room, refusing to make eye contact with its four inhabitants. 'So, where was I?' he asked, as if all he had done was taken a quick break to go to the toilet. He sat on the edge of a desk and ran a hand across his thinning hair. 'We need to identify the man all in black in The White Horse,' he continued, 'and to cross-check his photofit with that from Maynooth. We'll also need to release the photofit to the media, see if anyone recognises him. Forensics will also need to go back through the samples and see if they can find any other matches across any of the five sites.

'The killer has, for some reason, targeted Dermot Brady. It must be someone that knows him pretty well, knows about his life history. That could be one of several hundred people by the sound of it, but it's a start. He's supplied a list of a number of people from Mountjoy that will need checking out. We need to track them down and to eliminate them from the enquiry. It'll need rigorous checks. We also need to get somebody to sit down with Brady and make a list of everyone he knows. Get him to put them into different categories – people who were good friends, fair-weather friends, acquaintances, people he barely knew, and so on. Then get a team to start to work through that list starting with the good friends and people linked to DHC. This person also knew Laura Schmidt. Persuaded her to go out to Glencree. I want them all interviewed face-to-face. Draft in more people if you need to.

'Brady has also provided a list of 15 locations where the next murder might happen based on where the others have occurred. I've already organised that those places be put under 24-hour surveillance from midnight. Otherwise, it's just a case of carrying on with investigations, rattling people's cages and following any leads. Any questions?'

'Brady isn't working with anyone?' Deegan asked.

'I don't think so,' McEvoy said evenly, keeping his distaste in check. 'There's no evidence that he is – he's a loner.'

Deegan nodded but didn't say anything else.

'Right, okay,' McEvoy said. 'Let's get back to it. Barney, you'd better get back down to The White Horse and find out what's going on. Make sure that photofit is distributed as soon as you're happy with it. Charlie, can I have a word.'

Plunkett, Flanagan and Cronin filed out the room casting inquisitive glances at McEvoy and Deegan.

McEvoy approached where Deegan was still sitting. He waited for the door to close.

'Well, it seems you were right,' McEvoy said. 'You're back on the case. I'm hoping that we can act professionally, put our differences behind us and work together to catch this bastard.'

Deegan didn't say anything, forcing McEvoy to continue.

'But that means working as a team. And it means keeping me informed of what's going on in your investigation. No solo runs. Is that clear?' He wanted to punch the smug bastard. 'We need to support each other if we're going to stop him killing again.'

Deegan nodded slowly. 'Sounds fair enough,' he conceded.

'Good. Right, well, you'd better get back to your team.'

Deegan pushed himself off the desk and left the room.

McEvoy watched the door swing shut behind him. Deegan was about as sorry as Göring was at the Nuremberg trials. He'd just have to hope that Grainger, Murphy and O'Keeffe would put a brake on some of his excesses and keep McEvoy in the loop. He looked at his watch and cursed. It was coming up to a quarter-past six. He pulled his mobile from his pocket.

'Hello?' Caroline answered.

'It's Colm. Look, I'm tied up at the minute. I promised Gemma I'd take her out for a meal and then go onto the cinema with a couple of her friends. I don't suppose …'

'I'm already ahead of you,' Caroline interrupted. 'We're just getting ourselves ready. Mam and Dad are also here. They're coming out with us as well. Don't worry, everything will be fine. She knew you'd be tied up, she's been watching TV. It's just about the only thing they're showing on *Sky News.*'

'I'll try and meet you at the cinema. Text me the details of what you're watching.'

'Don't worry about it, Colm. You've got more important things on your plate.'

'Jesus, the least I can do is show up for some of it,' McEvoy said, tiredness in his voice. 'What kind of a father is it that misses his own daughter's birthday? Especially the first one after her mother dies?'

'Look, I'll text you the details, but she's in good hands and she understands the kind of pressure you're under. If we see you, we see you, but don't worry otherwise. We'd all sooner you caught this Raven bastard.'

'Thanks. I'll talk to you later.' He ended the call and cursed again. He should have asked to talk to Gemma. Damn it, he'd just have to make sure he met up with them later.

The pub felt strange emptied of patrons, like a space waiting to happen. It was all set up to go – the tables clear, the seats positioned, the halogen lights slightly dimmed, and the bottles all lined up behind the bar, but without people it felt pregnant with the expectation of what it could be; of being alive, humming to the sound of chatter and laughter and music. He was appreciating the silence, the stillness, standing where The Raven had sat watching the toilet door.

Barney Plunkett pushed open the outside door, letting in the sounds of the city, breaking the moment, and approached McEvoy. He was accompanied by Dr John. 'What the hell's the story with Charlie Deegan?' Plunkett asked to McEvoy's back. 'Is he really back on the case?'

McEvoy turned to face them. 'Look, Barney, direct your questions to Tony Bishop, okay?' he said evenly. 'He's back and that's it. We just have to live with it.'

'And there's nothing you can do?'

'No. Just drop it, okay. Let's just concentrate on Peter,' he waved his hand.

'Killick,' Dr John prompted.

'Peter Killick's death. Have you got that photofit?'

Plunkett handed him a rolled-up sheet of paper which he flattened on the table. A nondescript face with shoulder-length hair and a beard stared back at him.

'That's the best they could come up with?' McEvoy asked, disappointed. 'He looks like he belongs in a computer game.'

'It was difficult to get agreement,' Plunkett conceded. 'He's kind of a composite picture.'

'Meaning he doesn't look like how anyone remembers him,' McEvoy stated. 'Did nobody get a decent look at him?'

'It doesn't seem like it. He chose the perfect spot. His back is to everyone except the toilet door.'

'And how about you, John? Did you manage to get anything useful?'

'Not really, no. Nothing from the questionnaires or the CCTV. We're appealing for witnesses to come forward.'

'Jesus,' McEvoy muttered.

184

Overhead they could hear shuffling feet and murmured conversation. Hannah Fallon and one of her assistants came into view, descending the stairs from the balcony above.

'There are still two other people we can't account for who left the bar when Killick's death was announced,' Dr John continued. 'We're still trying to track them down.'

Fallon and Carter joined them.

'How have you got on?' McEvoy asked.

'I think we're just about finished for now,' Hannah answered. 'We've thoroughly screened the toilet and this floor. We'll work through the other floors tomorrow, but I doubt we'll find anything. Nobody saw him go upstairs, nor Killick. He'd wiped this whole area down with a wet wipe, but we found a couple of hairs on the table and floor. Could be his, or could be somebody else's. Problem with this place is the same as Glencree – dozens of people come here every day.'

'How about in the toilet?' McEvoy asked.

'Loads of blood, piss and pubic hairs. Every woman's fantasy,' she said sarcastically. 'We'll have to wait and see.'

'Well, it doesn't seem like there's too much for me to be doing here. I'm going back up to Harcourt Street, then I'm nipping home briefly. It's Gemma's birthday. She's 12. I've missed the whole bloody thing. Can you make sure this place is locked up tight and somebody keeps an eye on it.'

'I've already arranged it,' Plunkett said. 'Say happy birthday to her for me will you.'

'For us,' Hannah added. 'You won't be missed for an hour or so. Don't worry about rushing back.'

'Yeah, thanks. An hour is more than enough. I need to work through today's case notes.'

'There is one thing,' Dr John said, reaching into his coat pocket. 'I managed to get a couple of copies of that book, y'know, *Cartographies of Murder*. Got one from Easons, the other Waterstones.' He pulled the paperback free and offered it to McEvoy.

'Right, thanks.' McEvoy took it and stared at the cover – a black and white map of city streets, six daggers thrust in as markers, small pools of blood where they pierced the paper. He shuffled towards the door, reading the back cover.

Every one of the murder investigations had reached a wall. Instead the teams were working through the phone calls and re-mining old ground in the hope of discovering some missed gem. Nobody seemed particularly hopeful.

McEvoy left the incident room and started down the stairs, heading for his car. His mobile phone rang.

'McEvoy.'

'Please tell me you've got something positive to report,' Tony Bishop said.

'Well, er, I, we're …' McEvoy stuttered.

'I take it that's a no then?' Bishop interrupted.

'Yes. I mean no. I mean no, there's not been a breakthrough. Brady's given us a list of former inmates from Mountjoy who he thinks could be The Raven and places he thinks might be targets given where people have been attacked so far. We're checking the names out and the places will all be under surveillance from midnight.'

'Jesus, more overtime. This case is costing us a fortune. Bad press and high cost. The feckin' politicians are going to eat us alive.'

McEvoy stayed silent.

'The press conference was a disaster by the way,' Bishop continued, feeling the need to offload his problems onto some-body. 'The fifth murder and Brady's release has sent them into a flat spin. They've nothing to focus their attention on except us. We just had to sit there and take it. You'll need to be at the next one. I don't see why I should be the only poor bastard they're throwing darts at. It's at ten o'clock in the Burlington

Hotel – we've outgrown the Phoenix Park. Make sure you're there by 9.30.' Bishop paused.

'Look, Colm, one of the reasons I called is to let you know that the Assistant Commissioner has called in a profiler. Dr Kathy Jacobs. She's done a lot of work for Strathclyde and some of the other Scottish forces. Also for the Met. Seems she knows her stuff. Anyway, she arrives in tomorrow morning early from Prestwick. I've arranged someone to pick her up from the airport and bring her into Dublin. She should be with you around eight o'clock. I want full co-operation with her, okay. Full access to the files and crime scenes.'

'I'll meet with her, but I doubt she's going to be much help,' McEvoy said sceptically. 'What we need is a solid lead not speculation. She's not going to stop the next murder.'

'We need all the help we can get,' Bishop stated flatly. 'From what you're telling me we have no solid leads; we're chasing a ghost. At least she might be able to give us some ideas that might reveal solid leads. And it doesn't end with the last murders. We still have to catch him. It's not going to be a case of meeting her and fobbing her off. Understand? As of now she's a core member of the team.'

Bishop ended the call.

McEvoy shook his head and pushed open the door. Off to his right a couple of flashbulbs popped and journalists starting calling out to him, looking for information. He hurried to his car and made for the exit. Running the gauntlet of journalists and cameramen was beginning to wear thin. There were hundreds of them now in Dublin from every nation, all covering The Raven and his killings.

McEvoy pulled into a parking space at the Santry Omniplex. He glanced over at the entrance and then down at his watch. 9.30. He wasn't sure how long the film would last but it had to be over soon. God knows what Caroline had taken them to see. He hoped it was something like *The Princess Diaries*, but was probably more like *Die Hard 12* or *Mission Impossible 8*, or whatever bloody number they were up to now.

He tipped his back against the headrest. The first tear fell from his right eye, rolling slowly down between his cheek and nose to his lips. After that they wouldn't stop coming. He didn't know whether he was crying for Maggie or Gemma, or for Laura, David, Grainne, Billy or Peter, or for Grainne's lost baby, or for their families, or for himself. It didn't matter and he didn't care. His body shook with the grief and guilt, the pent-up tension and stress, the feelings of helplessness and hopelessness. He wiped at his face with his sleeves and hands, sucking in breaths as the tears flowed.

There were a series of very bright flashes to his right, blinding him. Instinctively he threw up his hand to shield his face and turned his head left. Flashes popped into the car through the passenger window.

'Fuck!'

He swung open his door angrily, slamming it into the side of the photographer, who yelped and jumped back, his camera still trained on McEvoy, it flashing as he levered himself up and out of the car.

'What the fuckin' hell do you think you're doing?' he demanded, his hands shielding his face.

'Superintendent McEvoy,' a voice said from the other side of the car, 'are you close to catching The Raven? Were you crying for all of the victims? Do you have anything to say to the victim's families?' The questions were fired at him quickly, not giving him time to answer. 'Do you know who is going to be next and are you satisfied that you're doing everything to protect them?'

The last questions were said to McEvoy's back as he half-walked, half-ran towards the entrance to the cinema. A stream of people had begun to exit, their progress slowing as they noticed him heading towards them, two people in pursuit. He could see the apprehension in their body language. The fear that he might be The Raven or some other equally deranged lunatic.

He spotted Caroline and Gemma, one of her friends at her side, off to the right, unaware of his presence. Behind them his mother and father came into view. What was he doing? He was leading the press straight to his family. He pulled to a stop. 'Shit!'

His father spotted him, smiled and waved, tapping Gemma's shoulder to redirect her attention to him. He motioned them to head back into the cinema, holding his hand up to indicate a phone.

The journalist had caught back up to him. 'Would you like to give your side of the story, Superintendent? Is he really that good or is it just police incompetence? You can name your price for the story.' The photographer had his camera trained on the front of the cinema, which lit up with a series of bright flashes, sending people scurrying either out onto the car park or back into the complex. His family hesitated, frozen in the glare of the camera flash, before his father and Caroline bundled them back into the cinema.

McEvoy pushed the journalist out of the way and ran back to his car. He clambered in, started the engine and reversed quickly out of the space, nearly hitting the photographer. He headed for the exit, trying to find Caroline's number on his phone, as his pursuers headed for their own car.

'Colm?'

'Get out of there now, before they come back to find you,' he instructed.

'What?'

'I said get out of that cinema now before the press come and find you. Do it now! I'll talk to you in five minutes.'

The journalist and his photographer would never make it to their car in time to catch up with him. As soon as they realised that they'd go in pursuit of whoever he'd been signalling to. He exited onto the main road and headed away, a slow rage building inside of him.

He slotted his key in the front door and pushed it open. Gemma burst from the kitchen and ran up to him jumping up to his chest. He clutched her to him and tried to smile. 'Happy birthday, pumpkin. How'd you get on?'

'It was great. We went to the Chinese and I had prawn crackers and spare ribs and sweet and sour chicken.' He stepped into the hall, closed the front door and carried her towards the kitchen passing a new garda uniform hanging in the hall, a note pinned to the front. 'And Katie had chicken chow mein. Then we went to the cinema to see Harry Potter. It was brilliant! And Nana and Granddad came as well.'

Caroline, his mother and father were sitting at the kitchen table, cups of tea in front of them, solemn expressions on their faces. He let Gemma down and straightened his back. 'You're getting big. And heavy.'

'Which is more than can be said for you,' his mother said. 'Jesus, Colm, look at the state of you. You look like one of them camp survivors. Y'know, Auschwitz or wherever.' She pushed her chair back and headed for the kitchen counter. 'You need to eat something.'

'It's good to see you as well,' McEvoy replied sardonically. 'Will you sit down, Mam, I'm fine.'

His mother pulled a loaf of bread from a cupboard and headed for the fridge.

'Jesus,' he muttered. 'Look, I'm sorry about before, the press must have followed me. I hope they didn't startle you too much. They're a pack of vultures.'

'No, they just scared the shit out of us,' Caroline said tetchily.

'Language, Caroline,' his mother said.

'Close your ears, Gemma,' McEvoy said, trying to bring some light-heartedness to the conversation.

'We say shit all the time at school,' she replied, smiling, confident she could get away with it on her birthday, straying over and standing next to her granddad.

'Don't be cheeky,' her nana said. 'It's not how a lady behaves.'

'Did your friends have a good time?' McEvoy asked Gemma, realising that he was going to have to leave again soon.

'Only Katie came. But she thought it was great. Especially at the end with the photographer and the chase.'

'Only Katie came?' McEvoy repeated.

'The others weren't allowed to come,' Caroline said. She shrugged. 'Their parents said it was too dangerous. You're the lead investigator on the biggest murder case in Irish history.'

McEvoy tutted and massaged his temples. 'For fuck's sake!' he muttered to himself.

'Colm!' his mother snapped. 'What did I just say about language?'

'We say …'

'Ah-ah-ah,' McEvoy interrupted his daughter. 'Don't get too big for your shoes just because you're 12 today.' He turned his attention to his mother. 'Look, Mam, will you forget about that sandwich. I've got to go back into work.'

'Now? It's nearly half-past ten, Colm,' his mother said, disbelief in her voice. 'What are you going to achieve tonight? You'd be better getting a goods night's sleep.'

'I'm not going to get a goods night's sleep, am I? I'm going to lie awake worrying. He's going to kill somebody else tomorrow. I have to go back in to try and stop that happening. I shouldn't have come to the cinema in the first place. I only came so I could see Gemma for five minutes on her birthday.'

His mother didn't respond, knowing that he was right; that waiting wasn't an option.

'Don't worry, I'll be back at some point. In the meantime, someone will be stationed out front to stop any unwanted visitors.'

'Your father can deal with those.'

'I don't want him to deal with them. I want you to get some sleep.'

'There was someone waiting for you when we got back,' his father said, speaking for the first time. 'He had a uniform for you. It's in the hall.'

'Thanks. It's no doubt meant to improve my image. Look, I'd better be going,' he said, opening the kitchen door. 'Gemma, are you going to see me out and wish me goodnight?'

He knelt on the floor leaning over into the bath. He traced the razor blade along the length of her milky white thigh, the muscle tensing, the leg twisting, trying to escape. At first the trace was invisible and then it cracked red, beads of blood oozing out, collecting into droplets before dashing over crimpling skin and dropping to the bath below.

He re-adjusted the blade between forefinger and thumb and edged another cut diagonally across the first. He didn't look at her face, her contorted features, her eyes imploring him to stop. He barely noticed the rest of her body either except where he traced his graceful arcs. His attention was focused on her silken skin, fine hairs, and the hypnotic patterns of blood spilling from fresh wounds. This wasn't torture, it was art.

He was in a different place; a calm place; his mind empty except for what was at hand. There was nothing except the blade, her skin and her blood.

Barney Plunkett levered himself back upright from leaning over a desk. 'Do you want a coffee?' he asked McEvoy.

'Thanks,' McEvoy said without looking up from the witness statements, trying to find some chink of light amongst the mundane stories of those occupying The White Horse pub at lunchtime.

Plunkett returned from an urn and placed the mug of coffee down next to him. 'Any luck?' he asked.

'Nothing.' McEvoy sat back. 'It's completely hopeless.'

'It's coming up to midnight. I'll make sure the teams staking out Brady's suggested locations are awake and being vigilant. Unless we have a breakthrough someone else is for it.'

'Good idea. I'll …' He was interrupted by his mobile ringing. 'McEvoy.'

'Superintendent McEvoy? This is Gary Bridges from The Sun. I was wondering if you could answer a few …'

'How the hell did you get this number?' McEvoy snapped. 'This is an operational line.'

'Whoa,' the journalist said, trying to placate him. 'Look, I just want to ask you a few questions. Get the story from your …'

McEvoy disconnected the call. 'Fuckin' press,' he spat.

The phone rang again. 'Yes?'

'Look, Superintendent,' Bridges started, 'I know …'

McEvoy ended the call again. 'Jesus Christ. I'm going to kill the bastard who gave them my number. For fuck's sake.'

'Look, don't worry about it,' Plunkett said. 'It was bound to happen. You'll just have to screen the calls.'

'We've got enough to be dealing with without the feckin' press disturbing us every five minutes,' McEvoy replied tetchily. He took a sip of his coffee.

'I'll go and talk to these units,' Plunkett said, pulling a tight smile and moving away. McEvoy seemed like a man on the edge, primed like a bear trap. One misplaced step and he'd snap. He'd changed over the past few days becoming more moody, distant and aggressive, less predictable and sociable. All with good reason given the stress he was under, but it was wearing. Plunkett felt guilty for leaving him alone, but any release from the tension he was fostering was a relief.

McEvoy looked out of the window at the orange-tinted city extending into the distance. Somewhere out there The Raven was preparing for his next kill and there was nothing he could do about it. Half of him wanted to place his head on the desk and sleep, the other half to throw his chair through the window and shout and rage. Instead he took another sip of the coffee and tried to turn his attention back to the statements. The slight tremble had returned to his left hand. He held it in front of his face and tried to hold it steady, but it continued to shake involuntarily. His phone rang again.

Chapter Five

Friday, April 18th

The woman ran quickly and confidently along the coastal path. Her dyed blonde hair was plaited into two pigtails, her face lean and tanned. She wore a red windproof jacket over a pair of dark, tight-fitting leggings that stopped at her ankles, and dirty, white running shoes. The cable from her earphones snaked over her chest and into a pocket, the line jumping in rhythm with her steady pace. A stiff breeze whipped in from the green-grey sea, carrying a fine spray, the waves crashing on the sand and rocks.

From his hiding place behind a red brick shelter, a structure that resembled a covered bus stop, The Raven watched her progress as she made her way around the edge of the small bay. On the opposite side of the path the ground disappeared, grass sloping steeply away for ten feet before ending at a drop of six feet down to a rocky, wave-cut platform. He pulled a mask up to his face, tugged down a plain, dark blue cap covering a hairnet, and glanced at his watch – 6.27. As she neared, her feet slapping on the path, he readied himself, his anger starting to flare.

He slightly mistimed his interception, misjudging the pace at which she was running. Rather than hitting her hard from the side, he ended up shoving her half from behind. The result though was what he intended. The momentum of her speed, the re-direction of her trajectory, and her loss of balance sent her sailing off the path, tumbling down the grassed slope, her fingers clawing at the damp sod, and down onto the sharp, grey rocks and loose stones below. She landed heavily, side-on, her right arm extended to try and break her fall. She felt the bones in her wrist snap, her head and hip smacking into the hard and jagged surface adding to the excruciating pain.

The Raven stumbled forward a step and fell awkwardly on the side of the path, starting to slip down the steep incline, but managing to stop himself. He scrambled quickly to his feet, his fury rising phoenix-like. He darted to his right, sliding down the slope where the grass almost extended to the rocks, jumping down the last couple of feet onto a narrow patch of sand and shells. He hurried over to where she lay, retrieving a length of two by four wood he'd salvaged from the beach earlier.

She lay on her side, her right arm at a funny angle behind her back, a trickle of blood running down her forehead. He noticed through his fury that she was much older than he'd thought when he'd seen her running, probably in her late forties, early fifties. She looked up at him with fear in her eyes, knowing who he was, knowing that he intended to kill her. She managed to mutter a 'please'. He smiled manically, raised the piece of wood high above his head and slammed it down hard onto the left arm she'd raised to try and protect herself. And then again and again and again, losing himself in his rage.

He slowed to a stop, sucking in air from the exertion, becoming aware that he'd lost control, had given in to his anger. He stared down at her battered head and body. Her face was a bloody pulp, nothing left of her nose, her teeth smashed to smithereens, the white of the skull visible through her bleeding scalp. He dropped the piece of wood, and staggered back a couple of steps to retrieve his cap from a pile of rotting seaweed. He jammed it back on his head and glanced anxiously round the bay. They were still alone.

He moved back to her body, tipped her on her back and pulled her by her armpits towards the sea to a small, triangular-shaped rock pool nestled in rocks stained dark grey and green from their daily soak, his feet slipping awkwardly on seaweed. He rolled her over so that her face was submerged in the salty water, then collected the piece of wood and headed along the wave-cut platform to where there was an easy climb back up to the path.

He walked back to the red brick shelter, fuming at himself. The bench that had stretched its length was missing, rusty supports jutting out from the brickwork the only evidence that it had ever been there. He pulled a single card and a folded, clear plastic bag containing a piece of paper from his jacket pocket. He wedged the card into a crack between two bricks and stepped out onto the path again. He checked that the woman was still in the same position and then threw the bag into the air, the stiff breeze catching it, whipping it over a low stone wall and across an open field towards a long, low building, a grey centre between two red brick wings.

He watched it for a second or so, twist and twirl, bouncing across the grass and catching on a chain link fence topped with barbed wire. Then he set off at a brisk pace along the path towards Portrane, looking back every few yards until her body disappeared from view. Another walker appeared on the far side of the bay and he picked up his pace, veering left, following the headland.

McEvoy took a sip of tea and looked at the screen on his phone before answering.

'McEvoy.'

'Have you seen the goddamn papers, Colm?' Bishop snapped.

'I, er, no. No, I haven't.'

'Your face is on the front cover of every single one of them. Crying. What the hell did you think you were playing at? Letting them take that photo?'

'Playing at?' McEvoy repeated, his stomach knotting on a freshly eaten bacon and egg sandwich cooked by his mother.

'The damn thing makes it looks like you can't cope with the pressures of the investigation,' Bishop continued, disregarding McEvoy's ignorance. 'That you're on the edge of a nervous breakdown. It's bad enough trying to manage them as it is without them thinking that the lead investigator is cracking up. What were you thinking of?'

McEvoy stayed silent, unsure what to say, staring down at the greasy plate in front of him, aware of his mother shuffling round the kitchen.

After a couple of seconds, Bishop spoke again, this time more calmly. 'We're going to have to meet with the public relations people and work out how to deal with this mess. Be at the Phoenix Park at nine o'clock and we'll work out a strategy before the press conference at ten. And in the meantime under no circumstances are you to talk to the media. You hear me? Stay away from them.'

'I hear you,' McEvoy muttered, feeling sick. All he'd wanted to do was see Gemma on her birthday and this was his reward – the front page of papers and a dressing down from Bishop. He massaged his forehead with his free hand. Nothing was ever simple; there always had to be some trial to make life more difficult and complicated. It was bad enough scrabbling around trying to capture The Raven without having to battle his own colleagues and the press. The craving for nicotine clawed away at his skin, his shoulders round and tight.

It wasn't until the man reached the shelter that he noticed the body on the rocks below. He was going to call out, but then noticed she was lying face down in a small rock pool. He ran back five yards and scrabbled down the grass slope and onto the layered rocks. He hurried over to her, trying to keep his balance on the slippery seaweed. The pool of water was tinged red, the back of the woman's head a bloody mess, one of her pigtails half unbraided and stained a pinky red. He knelt down beside her and rolled her over, shuffling back to make room for her body. He recoiled at the sight of her face, rocking back onto the balls of his feet and standing.

'Shit! Jesus, fuckin' fuck.' He looked around the bay seeking help and then back at the body trying to decide what to do. He moved to head back the way he had come, then hesitated and shifted back to her. She had been warm when he had knelt next to her.

He lowered himself down again and fought back the urge to vomit. He took her right wrist and sought a pulse, but couldn't find one. He moved his fingers about in case he hadn't placed them in the correct position, but still found no sign of life. There was no doubt though that she was still warm. He looked at her face. The water had washed some of the blood away, but it was still a bloody pulp, fresh blood seeping to the surface and clotting. It was almost unrecognisable as a head, more like something from a butcher's shop. Gingerly he moved forward trying to work up the courage to attempt CPR, but pulled away, running his hand through his salt and pepper hair.

'Fuck!' he spat. 'Fuck, fuck, fuck, fuck.'

He levered himself back upright and headed back to the path. Once on it instead of heading back the way he had come, he ran up a grassy laneway extending back from beside the shelter towards the red brick buildings of St Ita's Psychiatric Hospital.

He was pouring over witness statements when his phone rang. 'McEvoy.'

'Sir,' said a nervous female voice. 'They've … They've found another body. A woman battered to death on a beach in Donabate.

One of his cards was left at the scene.' She didn't need to explain whose card she meant.

'Fuck! Look, sorry,' he apologised for swearing. 'I'm on my way.' He was already out of his chair heading for the door. 'Tell them to seal off the place. I don't want the press anywhere near that site. And tell them to put a canopy over the body as soon as possible. They'll have helicopters up as soon as they hear about it.'

'I'll get back onto them straight away.'

'Good. Right, where exactly in Donabate am I going?' he asked, heading down a corridor.

'I'll have to ring you back with exact directions. The body's on a beach near to St Ita's.'

'I'll talk to you in a minute then.' McEvoy ended the call and shoved open a door, standing in its frame. Barney Plunkett, Dr John, Hannah Fallon and a couple of DCs looked over at him, startled looks on their faces. 'There's been another murder out at Donabate. Barney, I want you to take over here. Run the team meeting as usual. I'll call you.'

He pulled the door closed and then pushed it open again. 'If Charlie Deegan gives you any shit refer it up to Bishop; let him deal with it. Also, that profiler is due to arrive around 8.30. Her flight's been delayed. Show her around and introduce her to the case.' He shut the door again and headed for the stairwell, placing a call to Bishop.

It rang three times. 'Bishop.'

'There's been another murder out in Donabate,' McEvoy said hurriedly, descending toward the car park. 'I'm on my way there. Jim Whelan's the next available DI, right?' Charlie Deegan was next in the rotation after Plunkett given yesterday's precedent, but there was no way he was letting him anywhere near this victim.

'What?' Bishop replied, still trying to compute McEvoy's news. 'Yes. Yes, Jim's next up.'

'I'll ring him now then. I'll ring you when I get out to Donabate.'

'Will you slow down, Colm, for God's sake,' Bishop instructed. 'Are you sure it's The Raven? Do you have any details about the death?'

'He left one of his cards with the body. She'd been battered to death. That's all I know. Dispatch might have more details.' He burst out of the door, half-walking, half-running towards his car. 'Oh, yeah, before I forget, I've left Barney Plunkett in charge here. He's running a team meeting in five minutes.'

'For fuck's sake!' Bishop spat as if McEvoy's news had finally hit home. 'Ring me the minute you arrive, Colm. You hear me, the minute you arrive. I need to know what the hell is happening. The media are going to go mental the minute they find out about this.'

He smashed his fist on the steering wheel. He was annoyed with himself; furious with the victim. He'd lost control; lost his temper. He could barely remember bludgeoning her to death beyond the first couple of blows. He certainly couldn't remember the moment of death. If anyone had wandered down from St Itas to the beach they would have witnessed everything.

After all of his careful planning, he'd misjudged the attack and then completely lost the run of himself. He'd nearly missed her entirely; if he had there would have been little hope of catching her – it was clear that she was a serious runner. He would have had to have fled and then try to kill a different victim later in the day. The day's risk would have doubled and his perfect record been blemished.

Despite the folly he was at least confident that McEvoy and his various teams had no idea that he was The Raven. They were still chasing a shadow that was moving too quick for their light. That would still be the case once the runner's body was found.

He placed his hands flat on the steering wheel and breathed out slowly through his nose trying to calm himself. He needed to leave the area as quickly as possible. The man who'd appeared on the far side of the bay would have now found the body if he'd continued as far as the shelter. The place would soon be swarming with guards.

He turned the ignition and pulled out of the car park, heading north. He had one murder left to commit; one more death to assure his infamy and the validity of *The Rule Book*. He was so near to completing his goal now; he couldn't afford to make another mistake, especially when performing the finale – his grand statement before slipping away.

He parked next to a garda car, its blue lights still revolving, acting as a beacon for new arrivals. A small, rocky beach was visible directly in front of him on the other side of a barrier, a narrow pipeline crossing it and extending out into the swell. Five yards to the right was a squat, half-derelict, Montello tower, and beyond that, through an entranceway to a small car park, a long strand of golden sand stretched towards the estuary at Malahide, breakers sweeping in along its length. To his left was the Waterside House Hotel, a cream-coloured, two-storey, flat-roofed structure, with a wide terrace covered in wooden tables and chairs, reaching out to the edge of the beach. Several people were milling about on the terrace looking half-lost, half-concerned.

He lit a cigarette, sucking down the smoke, hoping it would take the edge off his apprehension; the knowledge that he was about to view another corpse. He let the smoke drift out through his nostrils then seemingly galvanised, opened the car door and hurried towards the hotel. The wind whipped in off the sea, carrying in a fine spray of water and sand. In his haste he'd again left his coat in the car, his ill-fitting suit jacket flapping wildly in the breeze.

He walked quickly along a cinder path edging the roped-off terrace. Beyond the hotel, the path snaked through some sand dunes before a small bay became visible. It was only a couple of hundred yards across, a sandy middle, a bank of shells, gravel and seaweed along its length indicating high tide, framed by sand dunes and rocky headlands, the dark grey-green rocks layered and jagged. The path followed the line of the dunes, never quite touching either the beach or rocks. On the far side it trailed up the gentle rise of the headland, a small drop down to the rocks below. Four people were standing on the rocks, grouped in a loose circle.

Off to the left, across a couple of fields, were the red brick buildings of St Ita's Psychiatric Hospital, dominating the land, its clock, water and round towers jutting up into the pale grey sky. To the right, the green of Lambay Island was silhouetted against a horizon where it wasn't clear where the sea ended and the sky started. Overhead two helicopters circled, the noise of their blades competing with the crash of waves. His phone rang. He checked the screen and dropped it back into his pocket.

He hurried round the path and as he neared the red brick shelter he dropped down through long, coarse dune grasses onto the rocks, making his way over to where the four men watched his progress. A white sheet was laid on the ground, flapping in the wind, the corners weighed down with some loose stones. The middle of one end was stained red.

Two of the men were in garda uniforms, hunkered down in big, dark blue jackets with flashes of luminous yellow, caps pulled low over their brows. The other two wore white cotton jackets that extended to their knees hanging open over ordinary clothes. The elder man wore a suit, the other a red jumper over blue jeans.

McEvoy extended a hand to the older-looking guard, his other holding his suit jacket closed trying to keep the cold wind out. 'Detective Superintendent McEvoy.'

'Colm, it's Neal Beatty. We've met a couple of times at events and courses.' The local superintendent pushed his cap up and eased his chin out over the collar of the coat to reveal his full face.

'Right, okay, yes,' McEvoy bobbed his head, still not recognising him. 'Good to see you again.' He looked at the other three men.

Beatty took his cue. 'This is Michael Flannery, the local sergeant, Kevin Linehan and Dr Tomas, I'm sorry, how'd you say your name again?' he asked the man in jeans and jumper.

'Krawiec. Dr Tomas Krawiec. I'm from Poland. I'm working in St Ita's.' His English was perfect with only the slightest of accents. 'We both are.' He pointed to Kevin Linehan.

'I'm the duty manager,' Linehan explained.

McEvoy shook hands with each of them. He turned back to Beatty. 'Is that the best you could do?' he asked, pointing at the bloodied sheet.

'We've never been issued with one of those canvas gazebo things,' Beatty explained. 'Or if we have, no one knows where the hell it is. One of the lads is rooting out his tent from home and bringing it in. He should be back any minute. We had to make do before those feckin' things turned up.' He gestured at the two helicopters.

McEvoy nodded, unconvinced, but didn't respond. There must have been canvas sheeting somewhere in the hospital, or they could have requisitioned an awning from the hundreds of static caravans that surrounded the area. At least she was covered, even if it was an amateur shambles. The last thing she would have wanted was for her battered remains to be broadcast into the homes of millions of people. He looked at the foaming sea, then back to the body, and lit another cigarette, not offering the pack to the others. He sucked the smoke down, his hand shaking, his whole body tense. He should have brought the coat. The chill wind was cutting through his thin clothes.

He turned to Linehan. 'Can you go back up to the hospital and bring down another couple of sheets or something more suitable? We need to replace or cover over that sheet.'

Linehan nodded and pulled a tight smile, acknowledging that they should have protected her more effectively. 'I'm on my way.' He turned and scrabbled back over the rocks towards the path.

'Well, I'd better take a look,' he said to the remaining three, rooted to spot, unable to move to her body. 'See what the bastard's done this time. We'll lift the sheet from two corners so I can look in under. Have you examined her?' he asked the Pole.

'I've done nothing more than check for a pulse to make sure she was dead,' Krawiec said. 'But there was no need really. You didn't need to be a doctor to see that. It would be a miracle if she were still alive after what he did to her.' The Pole crouched down, removed the stone from the corner nearest the red stain and held tightly onto the sheet. McEvoy finally felt compelled to shuffle to the sheet, wanting to look but not to see.

Beatty took hold of the corner at the opposite end and slowly they raised the length of the sheet by two feet creating a tent over her.

McEvoy slowly lowered himself to his haunches, his knees cracking, and viewed her battered body. Her face was barely recognisable as human. Instead it was a bloody pulp, hardly any skin still visible, the nose a messy crater, and the mouth a jumble of smashed teeth. The flesh had been tenderised and ripped from the bone, her skull visible in her bloody scalp.

'Jesus Christ.' He brought his hand to his mouth and fought the urge to vomit. He glanced quickly along her body, her ruffled and ripped clothes, the awkward lie of her arms, and turned away, closing his eyes and trying to will away the image of the dead woman. He wondered what it would be like to slip into the sea and float away, to drift off to a new life, to a more innocent place.

The two men lowered the sheet and placed the stones back in place.

'The man who found the body says he saw another man leaving when he arrived,' Beatty said. 'He was heading along the path towards Portrane. I've sent a couple of lads off to

205

investigate, but he's probably long gone. There's another car park half a mile or so down there.'

McEvoy sucked in another mouthful of smoke, stood, and massaged his face with his right hand. 'Right, okay,' he said trying to re-engage with the situation. 'Where did he leave his card?'

'Back up at the shelter there. There's just the one.'

'That's all I'm expecting,' McEvoy said, turning back towards the path.

McEvoy slipped his phone into a pocket and headed up the laneway towards the psychiatric hospital, his body cold, his ear warm from Bishop's frustration and anxiety. The press conference had been moved back to one o'clock and he was still required to attend.

Opened in 1902, St Ita's had grown to become a massive complex of imposing red brick buildings serving the North Dublin area. At one time, Ireland had the highest institutionalised rate per head of population in the world, almost double that of practically everywhere else in Europe. It was still much higher than most countries despite wide-scale de-institutionalisation during the 1980s and 90s. The legacy was a network of huge asylums, set out in massive symmetrical patterns in green field sites, miles from anywhere.

He hurried along a narrow roadway towards the clock tower, trying to remember Kevin Linehan's instructions. He scuttled across some grass and pushed open a wooden door.

A heavy-set woman with poor make-up and uncombed hair looked up from a small reception desk. 'Yes?'

'Detective Superintendent McEvoy.' He held up his card. 'I'm here to speak to Michael Dempsey. The man who found the body on the beach,' he qualified.

'Oh. Yes. Terrible.' It was as if each word had to be processed separately. 'Terrible. He's just here,' she said, rounding the desk, her brain having finally found gear. 'We've given him some valium to sedate him. He was in a hell of a state.'

'He'll still be able to talk to me though, right?' McEvoy asked with concern, reaching into his pocket and setting his mobile phone to silent.

'Yes, yes, he'll be fine. Don't worry, we only keep the strong stuff for the permanent residents.' She pushed open an office door with a thin sliver of reinforced glass running from top to bottom.

A man was sitting on a wooden chair in front of a cluttered desk. His head was held in his hands, his elbows resting on his knees.

'Mr Dempsey?' McEvoy asked. 'I'm Detective Superintendent Colm McEvoy.'

Michael Dempsey looked up with vacant eyes and tear-stained cheeks. His dark hair, flecked with grey, tufted up where he'd been holding it.

'Is it okay if I ask you some questions?' McEvoy asked, pulling a similar chair over towards him.

Dempsey barely nodded his head.

'What time did you find her?' he asked, sitting down.

'I dunno. Around quarter to seven?' Dempsey answered with a flat voice. 'She was still warm. I could feel it. I tried to find a pulse, but I couldn't. You could see she was dead.'

'And how did you find her?' McEvoy's right leg bounced on the ball of his foot. He tried to stop it first by placing his hand on his thigh, then by lowering his heel to the ground. Instead his foot started to scrunch in his shoe, desperate to relieve the tension in his body.

'I was walking along the path, y'know, from the hotel. As I neared the far side of the bay I could see something lying on the rocks. I thought it was just something the sea had brought in, but when I got nearer I could see it was a body. See her legs and arms. She was face down in a pool of water.'

'You turned her over?'

'Yes. I checked for a pulse but it was obvious she was dead. Then I ran up here to try and get some help. I thought maybe they could save her. I think they thought I was one of their patients who'd got out.' He pulled a tight smile. 'I was kind of hysterical.'

McEvoy nodded, acknowledging Dempsey's anguish at finding the body. 'And they went down to the beach to help her?' he asked.

'Yes, three of them came down – a doctor and two nurses. But there was nothing they could do.'

'Did you see anyone else when you were in the bay? Someone heading away from the body?'

'When I came in over the dunes I could see a person walking on the path on the far side; just for a second or two until he disappeared round the headland.'

'Can you remember anything about him?'

'He was a long way away. Just a small figure.'

'Right. Right, okay.'

'He was carrying something,' Dempsey continued, dredging up a memory. 'A walking stick maybe.' He paused. 'That could have been me,' he said, 'if I'd come along before her.'

'There's no way of knowing that,' McEvoy replied. 'He could have been waiting specifically for her.'

The man nodded and lowered his head into his hands.

'You did everything you could for that poor woman,' McEvoy said. 'I want you to understand that. Nobody could have saved her after what he'd done to her. You did everything right.' He levered himself up and headed for the door, closing it gently behind him.

Jim Whelan was waiting in the corridor. He was bald except for a ring of brown hair skirting across his ears and round the back of his head, a large nose dominating his face, hairs jutting out of both nostrils. In his late-forties, he was the oldest DI in NBCI and a man of very few words.

'Well?' McEvoy asked.

Whelan shrugged.

'No sign of the next chapter?'

Whelan shook his head.

'And what about Elaine Jones?'

'Ten minutes,' Whelan reluctantly muttered.

They made their way back out of the building, heading back toward the beach. McEvoy lit another cigarette, conscious that he only had two left, happy not to force Whelan into conversation.

There was a white garda transit van parked in the laneway blocking access from the hospital to the path and the beach beyond. McEvoy and Whelan eased their way down the side trying not to catch themselves on the barbed wire fence. In the field to their left a search team was starting to be organised.

Tape had been placed around the shelter and trails stretched down onto the beach from either end, flapping in the wind, held by rocks at the sea's edge. A man kitted out in protective clothing was dusting round the area the card was located.

Down on the rocks, an orange, rickety looking tent covered the body, three uniformed guards trying to hold it in place, stop it blowing away. Off to one side, just outside the cordon, two men struggled to erect a gazebo. Cheryl Deale was talking to the Polish doctor. A uniformed guard and dark haired woman dressed all in black were walking across the beach, heading for the crime scene.

'We need that van moved,' McEvoy said.

Whelan nodded assent and turned away seeking the driver.

McEvoy headed right, cutting down a steep path onto the beach. Turning back on himself, he clambered across the rocks towards Cheryl Deale. He could tell from her body language that she was giving the doctor a grilling. As he neared he could hear their conversation on the wind.

'So no one moved the body other than the person who found her, right?' It was an accusation as much as a question.

'No, no,' Krawiec said. 'He said he rolled her out of the pool. All I did, we did,' he corrected himself, 'was make sure she was dead.'

'So the people who've been near that body are yourself, two nurses, someone else from the hospital ...'

'Kevin Linehan,' he interrupted.

'The person who found her and some local guards,' she ended.

'Yes.'

'You might as well have had a fuckin' party. Lads, will you get a fuckin' move on,' she barked at the two men trying to put up the gazebo. 'It looks like Carry on Policing to those fuckers up there.' She gestured to the helicopters still circling.

'DS Deale,' McEvoy said, making her jump.

'For fuck's sake,' she snapped, turning to him. 'I'm on edge enough as it is.'

'How's it going?' he asked.

'How does it look? We look like total fuckin' amateurs. Have you seen anything as ridiculous as that?' She pointed at the orange tent the three local guards were still struggling to keep upright. 'Plus, as usual, the whole thing is as contaminated as fuck.' She'd given up trying to keep her language in check, running with the stress. 'Garda Plod, Stupid and Fuckwit have been stamping all over it.'

'Look, just calm down will you,' McEvoy said. 'Raging about it isn't going to help.'

'I know,' she conceded. 'For fuck's sake, Brendan,' she shouted as one of the legs fell off the gazebo. She turned back to McEvoy. 'Whoa, whoa. Where the hell do you think you're going?' she barked at someone over his shoulder. 'Stay on the other side of the tape.'

McEvoy turned on his heels. The guard and the woman walking across the beach had reached the tape. The woman looked embarrassed at the order. She was wearing black, flat-heeled boots, her slight body wrapped up in a black, knee length, woollen coat, a red scarf covering her neck and chin. She had black hair and eyes, her eye lashes long, her skin a light olive. The guard didn't seem bothered one way or the other, his hands rooted in his pockets, his gaze out to sea.

'Look, I'll come and talk to you later,' McEvoy said to Deale. 'If you find anything significant give me a call.'

He headed over to the woman. 'Detective Superintendent McEvoy.'

'Kathy Jacobs,' she replied with a soft Scottish accent. 'You were expecting me? I'm the criminal profiler.' She held out her hand, giving him the once over, his oversized suit in need of a dry clean, and loosely knotted tie, flapping in the wind.

He shook her limp digits. 'You were meant to go to Harcourt Street,' he stated, without welcome.

'I thought it would be better to come straight here,' she replied unapologetically. 'Get myself familiar with things.'

'Look, I'm sorry,' he said, breaking eye contact, unable to cope with the dark depth of her eyes, 'I don't really have time to go through things with you right now. I'm busy.' He jerked his thumb over his shoulder.

'That's okay,' she said, unconcerned. 'I'll hang around. I'd like to take a look at the body and maybe I can get to talk to you later.'

'If that's what you want,' McEvoy conceded, uncomfortable with her calmness, her eyes that one could drown in. 'But you'd better have a strong stomach; she's in a hell of a state.'

'Don't worry, I've seen some pretty horrific things in the last few years, Superintendent. Things as bad as anything here.'

He glanced at breakers crashing, the foam snaking up the beach. 'I've got to go back into Dublin for a press conference at one o'clock. I'll be leaving around 11. You can travel in with me then if you want,' he offered. 'Or you can stay out here. It's up to you.'

'I'll travel in with you, if that's okay. It'll give us the chance to talk.'

'Right. Good. Well, if you'll excuse me, I have to get on. We still don't know who she is.'

'Colm,' Jim Whelan called from near the shelter.

McEvoy looked up. Whelan held up a plastic bag containing a sheet of paper.

'I'll be there now,' McEvoy replied. He turned back to Kathy Jacobs. 'You might as well come up for this. It looks like we've found his next chapter.' He set off back up to the path.

His mobile rang. He checked the screen before accepting the call. 'Barney?' he mumbled. Somehow a newly lit cigarette had found its way between his lips, subconsciously taken from its box and lit. He plucked it free.

'How's it going?' Plunkett asked.

'Slowly. He battered her to death. Took her face clean off. Look, I'm glad you rang. I need you to find out if Dermot Brady's got some connection to St Ita's.'

'I'll get on it now. You think he might have been a patient?'

'That's what I want to find out. How're we getting on with his Mountjoy list?'

'They've all been accounted for. Most of them are still in prison. A couple overseas.'

'Another dead end.' He reached Jim Whelan. 'I've got to go. Did you ring for something?'

'Only to see how things were going.'

He could tell that Plunkett wanted to say something else, but he'd not given him the opportunity. If it was important he'd ring back. 'Right, well, I'll speak to you later.' He ended the call.

Whelan held out the note.

'Where did you find it?' McEvoy asked, taking it.

'On the fencing.' Whelan jerked a thumb over his shoulder.

McEvoy pulled the evidence bag tight and read through the two clear bags, reciting the text for Kathy Jacobs' benefit.

The Rules
Chapter Six H: Hindering the
Investigation C

"Every investigation is hindered by noise – massive amounts of data, the vast majority of which are irrelevant, some of which are false, and some of which are positively misleading. Witnesses can be remarkably unreliable, remembering things incorrectly or remembering things that never happened. And often the murderer himself will seek to deflect attention, disrupt the record, and send the police on a wild goose chase, trailing along a track of lies."

6a. Let them think you have made mistakes.

6b. Plant false evidence to set false trails – point the police at innocent people.

6c. Mess with the profiling – set false patterns.

6a-c give false hope, create blind avenues, and buy time, space, confusion and doubt. Remember, the media are your friends. They will report nonsense and undermine the police investigation if the results are not to the public's satisfaction.

Master rule: Do not underestimate the police – they are smart, they have experience, there are many of them, and they have a lot of resources.

'This is about Brady,' McEvoy said, stating the obvious. 'He's letting us know that he laid a false trail. Jesus. He thinks he's so feckin' clever.'

'Can I take a look,' Jacobs asked.

McEvoy passed her the bag.

Whelan's phone rang as the pathologist's van appeared over his shoulder, slowly making its way down the laneway towards them.

'Whelan … uh-huh … I'll be there now.' He returned the phone to his pocket. 'The victim was staying at the hotel,' he stated flatly.

'You go over,' McEvoy instructed. 'I'll follow in a minute.'

Whelan nodded and set off at a brisk pace along the path.

The van came to a halt. Billy Keane pushed open the driver's door sending it crashing into a barbed wire fence. He pulled a 'sorry' face through the windscreen, levered himself out and lurched towards the back of the van. Elaine Jones climbed out of the passenger door and came round to meet them.

'Elaine.'

'Colm.' She waved her hand, calling him towards her. 'Come on, like you promised.'

McEvoy could feel his face flush. He stepped forward, leaned down and kissed her on both cheeks. 'I'm still training him up,' she said to Kathy Jacobs. Followed by, 'You're freezing. Where the hell's your coat? You'll catch your death out here with this wind. And you're smoking again, Colm. I can smell them. The damn things will kill you. They killed Maggie and they'll kill you and where would that leave Gemma? Are you going to introduce me,' she added before he could answer.

'Er, right, sorry,' he stuttered, still reeling from Elaine's re-buke, knowing that she was right, but unhappy to be reminded. 'Dr Kathy Jacobs, Professor Elaine Jones. Dr Jacobs is a …'

'I know all about Dr Jacobs,' the pathologist said, shaking the profiler's hand. 'She's making quite a name for herself these days. Someone high up must have pulled a few strings for you, Colm.'

McEvoy cut across the near empty terrace, the hotel guests having retreated to the sanctuary of the hotel, and entered through a bar. He wandered into the busy reception area. Whelan was standing at the front desk talking to a hassled-looking woman in her mid-thirties.

'How's it going?' he asked, interrupting, glad of the warmth.

Whelan rolled his eyes in response.

'I just want to know when we're going to be able to get things back to usual,' the woman said to McEvoy. 'Guests need to leave, the shift is meant to change, the rooms need cleaning, deliveries are being turned away. We need to try and get things back to something like normal.'

'There's nothing normal about this morning, Miss. One of your guests has been murdered across in the bay. Her head is missing its face,' he said callously, ignoring the fact that her request was entirely reasonable and she was no doubt under a lot of pressure from guests and staff forced to stay so they could be interviewed. 'Look, don't worry; every sick bastard for miles around will come traipsing through here in a few days' time wanting to see where she was killed. You'll make up on any lost business then.'

'I'm sorry. Look that's not what I meant … I didn't mean to …' she trailed off embarrassed and flustered.

'What have you found out about the victim?' McEvoy asked Whelan.

'I've already told the inspector,' the woman replied unsure whether McEvoy was still addressing her.

'And now I want you to tell me,' McEvoy said, turning back to the woman, frustrated she'd answered a question he hadn't asked her.

'We … we think it's Shirley Hamilton,' her face flushed red. 'She's a Northerner, lives in Belfast. She was doing contract work out at the airport; staff development training, I think. She's stays here rather than the airport as she likes to run along the coast. She runs marathons. One of our bar staff does as well.

They know each other from races. We all sponsored her last year when she ran in the New York marathon. I can't believe this has happened. She was great craic. Always had a joke.'

'Did anyone see her head out this morning?'

'One of the reception staff saw her go.' She nodded at two women sat at a coffee table. 'She set off around 6.30.'

'And can you confirm what she was wearing?'

'Ausra,' the woman called out, gesturing to the younger of the pair.

The woman approached. 'Yes?'

'Can you remember what Ms Hamilton was wearing when she went out for a run this morning?'

'Ms Hamilton? I think she was wearing a ... yes maybe a red coat and blue trousers,' she replied with an East European accent. 'She had her hair in ...' She gestured with her hands.

'Pigtails,' McEvoy said.

'Pigtails?' the woman repeated, confused.

'Her hair in two strands,' McEvoy said.

'Yes, yes, two strands.'

'Ausra's from Lithuania,' the older woman explained.

'Is she okay?' Ausra asked. 'Ms Hamilton?'

McEvoy pursed his lips. 'No, I'm afraid she's dead. She was killed while she was running. We're investigating her death.'

Ausra nodded, the rumours confirmed.

McEvoy's phone rang. He signalled apology and stepped away from the counter. 'McEvoy.'

'I've just spoken to Brady,' Plunkett said. 'He was admitted to St Ita's when he was 17. He kind of went off the rails a bit. He has severe manic depression. He's been on lithium ever since. He was an in-patient for seven months. If the killer's one of his co-patients he has no idea who it is. He can't really remember them and he hasn't kept in touch with any of them either.'

'Right, okay. Well at least the location makes sense. I want you to ask him to come in again. We need to pick his brains, see if we can dislodge something useful. See if he can come in for two o'clock. We'll hold a team meeting then afterwards, around three.'

'I'll talk to him again. The meeting will have to be better than this morning's. Charlie Deegan was a feckin' disaster. He basically said he was going to run his investigation and feck the rest of us,' Plunkett stated, saying what he'd wanted to report in his last phone call.

'For God's sake,' McEvoy said, massaging his face. 'I thought I told you … It doesn't matter, I'll deal with it when I get back. Just keep plodding away for now. I'll be in after the press conference at one o'clock.' He ended the call and stepped back over to the reception desk. 'Do you have a cigarette machine?' he asked a hint of desperation in his voice.

McEvoy reversed out onto the road, swung the car around and headed back down the road towards Donabate. He sucked on his plastic cigarette and then held it between his index and middle finger, his hand resting on the steering wheel. 'So, you said you'd had a go at constructing a basic profile?' he asked, breaking the ice.

Kathy Jacobs brushed her hair off of her face and twisted her body in the seat towards him. She'd underdone the buttons on her coat and unwound the scarf to reveal a dark grey business suit over a pale blue shirt, the skirt ending at her knees. 'I've had a go on the basis of what was sent to me – some case notes and photos,' she said in her soft, Scottish lilt. 'I'll be able to flesh it out once I've seen more of the files and visited the crime scenes.'

'But you can give me the bare bones of it now?'

'As long as you appreciate it's a preliminary profile, then yes, no problem.'

He nodded his assent.

'As you probably know,' she started, 'serial killers fall into two general types – disorganised and organised. Disorganised killers are often paranoid schizophrenics. They have a hard time distinguishing reality from fantasy. They end up killing people not so much because they want to, but because at some level they're driven to. Voices tell them to, or they over-react to a set of circumstances beyond their control. They're usually people known by the system – their illness is diagnosed and they live with their parents or in institutions or on the street.

'An organised killer is an entirely different proposition. They know what they are doing and they prepare for their crimes. Whereas disorganised killers are rarely in control of their actions, and any rape and murder usually takes place in a frenzy of violence, organised killers plan things in advance, they collect together everything they need, they clean up after themselves to avoid being caught, and their violence can be calmly and sadistically stretched out over days or weeks. They themselves were probably a victim of violence when a child, developing heightened capacities for delusion, anger, denial and revenge. As adults they're driven by a deep psychosis that they try to manage and feed victims to while trying to make sure they get away with their crimes. Unlike disorganised killers, they know what they do is considered highly deviant by the rest of society.

'In both cases, but particularly for organised killers, the murders are nearly always sexually motivated or expressed. They're driven by a desire to sexually humiliate and conquer their victims. That doesn't mean rape, it could simply be tying up and torturing the victim; but it does mean sexually dominating or punishing them in some way. The murders are usually highly choreographed and the victims, to some degree, are merely disposable props in their own theatre. The victims also usually follow a pattern – the same age, body build, hair colour, and so on, so their play can be re-performed endlessly.

'The murders you're investigating are highly organised, but they differ substantially from the kinds of murder most serial killers commit. They're not about sex; at least not all of them appear that way. The victims vary in profile and the killings, with

218

exception of Laura Schmidt were quick and perfunctory and he left the scene in a hurry. They were almost like assassinations rather than serial killings.

'And your killer is similar to and yet quite different to the usual kind of people who would generally commit such crimes. I doubt, for example, he has a record for sexual offences. I also doubt he was the victim of an abusive household or sexual abuse as a child. He might well though have caught and tortured small animals when he was growing up. He would have liked the power of life and death; of controlling their destiny. There would have been some manifestation of his sadistic tendencies, however expressed.'

'So what are the murders about?' McEvoy asked impatiently, glancing over at her.

'I'm getting to that,' Jacobs said calmly, ignoring McEvoy's testiness. 'I want you to understand that The Raven is different. He doesn't seem to be driven by a sexual psychosis that he struggles to control. He kills because he can and because he wants to. Not because he wants to commit some kind of sexual revenge. And he has almost certainly killed before this week. *The Rule Book* is a public expression of his confidence in his ability to kill and get away with it.'

'He's killed before,' McEvoy repeated.

'My professional opinion is several times. You don't start your killing spree by undertaking anything as complicated as he's attempting. He's drawing on experience and a self-assurance that he knows what he is doing. *The Rule Book* explains why he's got away with them. Why he's confident that he'll continue to get away with them.'

'Jesus,' McEvoy muttered, shaking his head.

'He probably appears little different from everyone else,' Jacobs continued, adjusting the lie of her seatbelt, 'perhaps married, with children; a pillar of the local community. That said, I think he's someone who is very confident, very smart, and probably very arrogant; someone with a high degree of detached control, a lot of patience, but also a short fuse. He's prepared to spend a lot of time planning, thinking through each crime, making sure he knows exactly how he's going to perform it, on whom, how he will get away, how he will dispose of the evidence, and so on. He's educated – he can write well, he can think through a large project, and he's researched how you'll try and catch him, taking the necessary precautions – using gloves, protective clothing, disguises, whatever's needed. He likes the challenge of killing in public places but he's a calculated risk taker.

'He was relatively cautious to begin with,' Jacobs explained. 'The murders happened under the cover of darkness and there were large gaps between them. There were 22 hours between the first and second killings. 24 hours between the second and third. Only 16 hours between the third and fourth, and it took place in broad daylight, albeit in an isolated rather than public spot. By the fifth he's grown more confident again, killing in broad daylight in a busy, public place.

'The only anomaly relates to how he killed Laura Schmidt. All of the others he attacked and knocked unconscious before they knew what was happening. With Laura there's no sign of attack. I've been thinking about that. I think he knew that she wouldn't fight or struggle. I don't know why, but I think she trusted him.'

'You think that she knew him?' McEvoy asked, his brow furrowed with skepticism. 'That maybe they were friends?'

'I'm not sure friends is the right word. And I'm only going on the case notes here. I think they'd established some kind of bond; some kind of understanding whereby she took him into her confidence and him likewise. I think she wanted to die and I think she let him kill her.'

'A pact?'

'Perhaps,' she hedged. 'It's only speculation, but that's my reading given the case notes. I think she might have provided the impetus, the spark, for this whole killing spree. If he's going to kill one person, he might as well use it for other ends. He planned the other murders to follow hers.'

'Sounds a bit far fetched, doesn't it,' McEvoy said doubtfully. 'He meets a homeless girl, he befriends her, she asks him to kill her, and then he thinks, "Well, if I kill one I might as well kill seven. And while I'm at it, I'll write a book on how to commit the perfect murder",' he finished sarcastically.

'As I said, it's speculation and I'd need to talk to people who knew her and see more of the crime scene analysis, but it would explain why she seemingly just welcomed the killing and why he carried on with several more,' Jacobs persisted.

McEvoy scrunched his face up and shrugged his shoulders signalling that he wasn't convinced. 'It's a possibility, I guess,' he said. 'She could have also been too pissed to stop him; to know what the hell was going on.'

'There's that as well,' she conceded. 'There's something about that death though; something that seems at odds with the other murders. It just doesn't seem to make sense. Even if she was drunk, you'd have thought she'd have made some effort to save herself?'

'As you said, maybe she was happy to die? Had enough of life?'

'It's more than that. She undressed, laid on the bed, and accepted the sword through the mouth. It wasn't just that she accepted death, she was prepared to make it look like a sacrifice.'

'You said he had a short fuse?' McEvoy asked, trying to steer the conversation back round to The Raven. Laura's death still gnawed away at him and he wanted time to think about Kathy Jacobs' thesis.

'You saw the body back there, Colm. All the other killings were clinical, mechanical. With the exception of Laura, he knocked them unconscious and then dispatched them. Okay, some of them were a little elaborate – the sword, the paint, the cut off toes – but they were all performed calmly and efficiently.

'He'd battered that woman to death. Not clinically or systematically, but with a violent rampage, hitting her repeatedly and without pattern. Probably wasn't even aware of what he was doing, though he regained some composure at the end. Made sure she ended up face down in the rock pool to die as he intended – by drowning – and then cleaned up after himself, taking whatever it was he hit her with, and leaving the card and chapter, though he just seemed to throw the latter away. For a brief period he lost self-control.

'My feeling is it was because the attack probably didn't go to plan. He'd spent a lot of time preparing it and maybe she didn't play her part properly. Maybe he forgot some detail. I don't know. Whatever it was, it triggered a violent reaction. More violent – more frenzied and less calculated,' she qualified, 'than the other attacks.

'That's not to say that he felt any more compassion for his other victims than her. I think he sees his victims as legitimate targets in the game he's playing. Even Laura. They're simply disposable objects, not living, breathing human beings. I doubt he has any real feelings for them or anyone else. The only thing that matters is himself.

'He's selfish and he's egotistical. And there's no doubt he *is* a psychopath. But he wouldn't recognise that in himself. He would see himself as rational and reflexive – able to self-analyse and internalise his thoughts and emotions. He knows he's not like everyone else, but he also knows what he needs to do to appear like they do. To him, though, all other people are inferior.

'My sense is that he's almost certainly an over-achiever and he relishes in his own perceived superiority. But he feels that this superiority is not sufficiently recognised by others; that he's not receiving his fair dues. Perhaps he's being blocked from promotion at work, or people are simply not taking him or his ideas seriously? I don't know. What I do think, however, is that he has a desire to prove them wrong, to demonstrate how much smarter than them he is. This is what these killings are all about – ego.'

'He could have written his book without killing six people,' McEvoy said flatly.

'But he wouldn't have been able to prove that it worked. He wants the recognition, the acknowledgement, that he's a genius.'

'He's a sick bastard,' McEvoy said without thinking.

'I agree, but so far he's got away with the killings and it appears like he really is an evil genius. And if you don't catch him he will kill again,' Jacobs continued. 'He'll start a new campaign. A new challenge. Maybe not for a while – six months or a year. He'll lie low then he'll start planning – a new book, a riddle, a different puzzle; something. But he will surface again; that you can be sure of.'

'You sound very confident.'

'Read the literature, Colm. There are very few serial killers who stop killing once they start. They might pause or go dormant for a while, but they inevitably start again. And he'll feel his audience will want an encore.'

'His audience?'

'The public. The media. This is the biggest story on the planet at the moment. Every news channel, every newspaper, have reporters here. The whole world is watching, waiting to see how it ends.'

McEvoy nodded and stared out of the windscreen at the road ahead, mulling over Kathy Jacobs' assessment. Whilst informative and useful, if anything it made the investigation seem more daunting. The Raven, while probably arrogant, seemed to the rest of the world exactly like them. Except of course he wasn't; he was a psychotic egotist.

The mirror was cracked, the line running through his face, the halves not quite matching. Somehow McEvoy felt it looked appropriate. He wedged a finger between his collar and neck and jiggled it about uncomfortable with the fit now the tie was tightened. He straightened the lapels on the new uniform and ran a hand over his hair. It seemed strange to be wearing a suit that fitted perfectly after the looseness of his usual, oversized clothes. Dressed like this there was a danger people might actually start saluting and calling him Sir.

He left the room and joined Bishop, the Assistant Commissioner, Kathy Jacobs and three members of the press team in the meeting room with the Yeats prints. The press team were already sitting in a row along one side of the table, playing with their pencils and pads, worried looks etched on their faces. The morning's newspapers were laid out before them. The other three were standing together near the window, the Assistant Commissioner holding court. He had the look of a brawler, someone you wouldn't want to meet in a dark alley – thick dark hair, ruddy cheeks, big barrel chest, and giant hands with chunky fingers.

They stopped their conversation, their small circle opening to face him.

'Colm,' the Assistant Commissioner said with a solemn face, moving forward to shake his hand.

'Sir,' McEvoy replied while trying to keep his hand stiff, resisting the crushing vice.

'Shall we get started?' The Assistant Commissioner sat at the head of the table. 'We'll have to leave for the Burlington in twenty minutes or so – get ourselves set up. No doubt they'll be even more of the feckers than there were yesterday.'

Bishop sat to his right. Kathy Jacobs skipped a seat, forcing McEvoy to sit at the far end of the table facing the AC and visible to all. He was uncomfortable with Jacobs being there, but nobody else seemed to mind.

'I hear there's been another murder,' the AC prompted.

'Shirley Hamilton,' McEvoy replied. 'Fifty-three and from the North. Married with two grown-up children. He battered her to death with a length of wood out at Donabate. She lived in Dundonald in Belfast and was a regular in a hotel near to where she was murdered. She liked to run along the coast. She had her own training company and had been running staff development courses at the airport.'

'Jesus Christ, that's just what we need. The feckin' PSNI will want to join the party now,' the AC said referring to the Police Service of Northern Ireland. 'They'll be down here giving us advice, looking down their noses at us as if we're a feckin' joke. Are you anywhere near catching this so-called Raven? He's making us look like eejits.'

McEvoy looked down at the table, his gaze avoiding the papers. 'Not at the minute, Sir. He's moving too fast for us to keep up and other than his chapters he's leaving us nothing to go on.'

'And what do you need? More people? We need to catch this bastard, Colm. Half the world's media are here. The locals are telling them that we're a bunch of incompetent gobshites; that we're lazy, corrupt, badly managed and run. Every fecker who's ever had a grievance is calling for major reform and reorganisation and the Minister for Justice is on the phone every five feckin' minutes. All he can see is his popularity rating falling through the floor. So, what's it going to take?'

McEvoy shifted in his seat and scratched the back of his head. 'A mistake,' he said quietly.

'What?'

'I said, a mistake.'

'A mistake!'

McEvoy stayed silent.

'Is that what we're meant to tell the world's press? That we have no feckin' idea about how to catch him! We're hoping that he'll either make a mistake or hand himself in?'

'We're doing the best we can,' McEvoy said, his right leg bouncing uncontrollably under the table. 'We've got six teams working flat out, hundreds of officers. He's got everything planned, he's careful, he's setting up false trails, and he's not giving us time to catch up.'

'And do we have any idea where the final murder's going to be? Who the victim might be?'

'No. So far they've all been sites connected to Dermot Brady. He's provided us with a list of places he thinks might be targets. We have officers keeping an eye on them all, though he didn't identify Donabate as a possible location.'

The AC nodded and turned his gaze to Kathy Jacobs. 'I know you've only just got here, Dr Jacobs, but do you have anything that might help us at this stage?'

'I've done a preliminary profile, but I need to work through the full case notes and flesh it out. Even if I'd completed it, I don't think it would be a good idea to give it to the media unless it's tied to a good photo or photofit. All that'll happen is you'll be swamped with calls, people saying it sounds like such and such across the road. And your photofits are too weak at the minute. They barely look like each other, God knows if they look like the killer.'

'Fair enough. And what is your initial assessment?'

'I'd sooner complete my analysis than have to change my mind later. It might lead you to chase false leads.'

McEvoy glanced over at her, trying to read why she hadn't told them what she'd said in the car.

'Well, that's up to you,' the AC said, clearly frustrated. 'As soon as you're happy, we can progress from there. Right, moving on, what are we going to do about this morning's papers?' The AC gestured at the table and glared at McEvoy and the media team.

McEvoy lowered his head again. One of the media team cleared their throat. 'I think, we think, well it's Chief Superintendent Bishop's idea really,' he spluttered looking at his notes, 'that we spin the photos as positively as possible. So rather than become defensive, we use them proactively. The tears aren't because he can't cope, that he's losing control, they're because he cares. He's grieving for the victims as much as anyone. As much as everyone working on the case.'

McEvoy glanced over at Bishop, who gently rocked his head, signalling that he'd found a way to protect him; that McEvoy was deeper in debt to him.

'We need to be careful not to allow this to become a battle between Detective Superintendent McEvoy and The Raven,' the media person continued. 'It'll become too personalised, too much about personalities, rather than the crimes. The media now know that the photos were taken in Santry Omniplex and that Superintendent McEvoy was there to see his daughter on her birthday. They also know about his wife's death. The danger is they see the photos as evidence of some kind of breakdown. That the family loss, the caring for his daughter on his own, and the burden of the case has become too much emotionally and physically.'

McEvoy felt the hot flush of anger flood his face, his jaw tightening, the eyes of the others on him.

'We need to shift the focus away from him and his family to the whole investigative team. To make it clear that *all* of them are sickened by what they have witnessed. That they are all grieving for the victims. That they are all desperate to catch The Raven. And that Superintendent McEvoy's tears are not a sign of a breakdown or of not being able to cope at home or at work, but are a natural reaction to some horrific crimes.' The man stopped and looked round the table.

'Well?' the AC asked, the question clearly directed at McEvoy.

'I want those bastards kept away from my family.'

'It's already been taken care of,' Bishop said.

'You can spin this however you want, but keep my daughter out of it, okay.'

'That's exactly what we're saying, Colm,' Bishop said. 'We want to deflect the focus away from you. We want them to realise that every guard in the city cares about the victims and about catching The Raven. Don't worry, we'll protect Gemma from all of this. You can rest assured on that. If you want her to be moved to a safe house, an anonymous address, we can arrange it.'

'She's with her grandparents, she'll be fine. Just keep the bastards away from the house.'

'It's being looked after. If the situation changes we can review things. But just so we're clear, if they ask you any questions about last night, which they will, then you just say you were expressing what every guard is feeling – grief for the victims and revulsion for The Raven and his crimes.'

The large ballroom was packed with over 300 journalists. The rows of seats were full, the overspill sitting cross-legged or kneeling in the aisles, their digital recorders on, many scribbling on notepads. Cameras ringed the outer wall, their operators jostling with each other, cramped for space. Several angry hacks and crews were stalking the corridors outside trying to find a way in. They were probably breaking every health and safety rule going, but nobody seemed to care.

McEvoy and the Assistant Commissioner were sitting on a temporary stage behind a long table. The surface was covered in a white sheet that stretched to the floor hiding their legs. It was probably just as well – McEvoy's feet were tapping out a fast rhythm. His innards were weak, knotting and writhing, and he felt like he might vomit at any minute. A microphone on a mini-stand was placed in front of each of them. Bishop was off to their left standing at lectern reading a pre-prepared statement. His face was flushed red, his left hand involuntarily tapping the lectern. Behind him on a screen a data projector cast the words, 'An Garda Síochána' and its logo.

McEvoy just wanted it to end, to escape the cloying atmosphere of the room and get back to the investigation.

Bishop was starting to wrap up, explaining that it would be impossible to try and field questions from everyone; that he was only going to take questions from the front two rows. The place erupted, people trying to move forward.

'Please, Ladies and Gentlemen. Ladies and Gentlemen.'
Bishop lost his temper, wrapping his knuckles on the lectern,
his face flushing red. 'Stay where you are and SIT DOWN!
Either sit down or we'll end this now. It's crowded enough in
here without a stampede.'

The journalists shuffled back to their seats, muttering to each
other.

Bishop glanced over at the table for reassurance. McEvoy
stared down at the white cloth. The AC simply raised his eyebrows to indicate, 'good luck.'

'I'm sure you can all appreciate that there's a lot of interest
in these terrible murders. There are several news teams locked
out in the corridor. It's totally impractical to try and field questions from you all. I'm sorry, but that's the way it is. I'm sure
your colleagues on the front two rows will ask the questions
that you all want asked. And, as I've already said, we're not
going to answer any operational questions. It is not in the
investigation's or public's interest for us to do so, so please
don't waste your time and opportunity. Yes, you Madam, in
the red necktie.'

'Jackie Rollins, CNN. The Raven has so far killed six people,
what reassurances can you give the public that it's safe for them
to go about their daily business?'

'We are presently advising people not to fundamentally alter
their daily regimes, but to also be extra vigilant. Every person
killed so far was on their own in isolated situations. We are
suggesting, therefore, that people try to remain with others as
much as possible. We *have* to continue daily life though, we
can't let him shut the country down through fear. Yes, the man
in the grey suit, blue tie.'

'Gary Bridges, The Sun. I was wondering whether Superintendent McEvoy would like to comment on the pictures in
this morning's papers?'

Bishop looked over at McEvoy, who scrunched up his face
and pulled the microphone towards him, turning it on.

'To be honest, I've been too busy to read the papers today. Other than the fact that the pictures were a gross invasion of privacy, I think they show the grief that everyone working on this case feels. I've been present at all six murder sites, and I've seen what he did to those poor people, how he killed them and destroyed their family and friends' lives. Frankly, anybody associated with this case who hasn't broken into tears is heartless. All that photographer caught is what every officer has done over the past few days. Like everyone, we're all in shock and we're in grief.' He'd rehearsed the answer for the past 20 minutes with one of the media people and it had come out roughly as intended.

'So you're not having a nervous breakdown then, as some of the papers have suggested,' Bridges asked before Bishop could move on.

'Does it look like I've had a nervous breakdown?' McEvoy answered evenly, feeling as though he was teetering on the edge of one, his muscles ridged, his fingers shaking. 'I'm not going to pretend that I'm not under enormous stress. We all are. We're doing the best that we can, and we'll continue to do the best we can under difficult circumstances, stress or no stress.'

'Yes, madam, with the pink shirt,' Bishop said quickly before the exchange could continue.

The Assistant Commissioner tapped McEvoy lightly on his arm, reassuring him that he'd done a good job. Nevertheless, he was going to give the nicotine patches a go. And the gum and any other substitutes anyone was prepared to sell him.

The press conference had ended 40 minutes previously, followed 20 minutes later by one of Bishop's tirades, venting the pressure of the media circus onto McEvoy.

The brake lights of the car in front glowed red. They'd only managed to travel a couple of hundred yards since leaving the

230

hotel. McEvoy was thinking of turning the blue lights on and clearing a path ahead. They were late for their meeting with Dermot Brady. He plucked at the plastic cigarette between his fingers with his thumb and tried to resist the temptation to place it between his lips.

'Is it always this bad?' Jacobs asked, breaking the awkward silence, staring out of the window at the shops nearby.

'Pretty much. We have a chronic traffic problem and crap public transport — this is the result.'

She turned in her seat, pointing her closed knees toward him. 'Do you want to talk about it?'

'Talk about what?' he said defensively.

'About last night. The pictures in the newspapers. The reason you were crying. Your plastic cigarette.'

'No.'

She paused for a moment before continuing. 'Are you sure? It might help. I'm a good listener.'

'Look, I know you think you're trying to help but I don't need any of your psychology, psychiatry, psychotherapy or whatever the hell it is you do. I'm fine, okay. I was tired. It'd been a long day and it just happened. No one would know about it if it wasn't for the bastards who'd followed me.'

'I'm sorry. I'm just trying to help, that's all.'

'Well, I don't need any help. What I need is to catch this bastard. Why didn't you give your preliminary profile to the AC or Bishop?' he countered, trying to push the conversation elsewhere, put her on the defensive.

'Because they would have used it in the press conference. They were desperate to give them as much as they could. It was enough for them to say that I was working with you on the case. There was no need for anything else.'

McEvoy nodded. She was probably right, they were anxious to demonstrate any progress, however slight. 'But you will run the profile past Brady?' he asked. 'We need to try and progress things. We're scrabbling around in the dark.'

'How old is your daughter?' Jacobs asked, avoiding his question.

'Just drop it, okay. I know you mean well, but I don't want to talk about it.'

'I didn't mean anything by it. I was just making conversation.'

'She's 12. She was 12 yesterday.'

'Mine are ten and eight. Two boys. Joseph and Adam. Their father was killed in the Hatfield train crash. He was meant to be on the next train but managed to get away early. They stay with my sister when I'm away.'

'I'm sorry,' McEvoy said, not sure how to respond, uncomfortable in the confines of the car. He realised he didn't have a clue how to handle Kathy Jacobs. It felt like she was shifting the ground underneath him, while at the same time holding him up. He glanced left. She was staring out of the windscreen, her eyes unfocused, then she pulled her mouth tight and turned back to him.

'Joseph wants to be a pilot, Adam a deep-sea diver. One wants to go up, the other down. Did you always want to be a cop?'

McEvoy broke from her gaze and stared at the car in front unsure whether she was making polite conversation or coming at him from a different angle.

Brady was wearing a loud, orange and green, stripy jumper, blue jeans, and a serious face. 'I was 17. It wasn't a happy time, I can tell you. Prison with drugs. I was happier to get out of there than Mountjoy. At least I deserved to be in Mountjoy.'

'How come you ended up in St Ita's?' McEvoy asked.

'Had one of my turns. Ran from one end of the street to the other, except my feet didn't touch the ground. Jumped from one car to another, then went on a bit of mad spree round Grafton Street. Totally manic. If it wasn't for the lithium I'd go uppity up

then downity down. Right down into some hellish dark place.'
He motioned with his arm. 'They could have straightened me
out without locking me up.'

'I suppose everyone you know knows you were in St Ita's?'

'As I told you before, I've no secrets from people. My life's
an open book.'

'And how about the in-patients there? Any that you think
might be behind these murders?'

'I barely remember the people I was in there with. I don't
really remember a lot to be honest – just long, pale corridors,
hard beds, and the smell of disinfectant.'

'I want you to think about all the people you know, Dermot,'
Jacobs said, taking over. 'Are there really none who might be
The Raven?'

'I've been through this before. Several times. You even had
me list and categorise everyone I know.'

'And you've been a great help,' she said sympathetically, 'but
it's important. All the murders are connected to you. It's almost
certain that you know him.'

'Look, there were a lot of people a couple of capacitors short
of a full motherboard in Mountjoy. Short circuited, y'know?
Why don't you start there?'

'We have,' McEvoy said. 'We've worked our way through
your list. They all have alibis. Have you any more ideas?'

Brady shrugged. 'I put down the ones I could think of.'

'How about outside of prison?' Jacobs asked, before McEvoy
could say anything.

'I don't know. I know a lot of people, but I don't have any
of them pegged as murderers.'

'I want to give you a list of characteristics – see if it reminds
you of anybody. That okay?'

'Sure.'

'I want you to try and think of someone you know who's
ambitious, who wants to make it to the top, and will do anything
to get there. He always lets you know how well he is doing, sings

his own praises, talks about nobody but himself or things he's interested in. He rarely asks questions of others, he's simply indifferent to their lives. He can be short with people, snappy, will pick an argument, and always has to be right. Maybe has a bit of a temper. Ring any bells?'

'Sounds like an egotistical idiot.'

'Yes, but does that description bring anyone to mind?'

'About half the people walking round Dublin. Most people only seem interested in themselves these days.'

'I'm being serious, Dermot. When you think of that description does anyone in particular come to mind?'

'And so am I! Look, several people spring to mind, but I can't see any of them being The Raven. Just because you're an arrogant prick, doesn't mean you go around killing people. And what makes you think he's like that in any case? You don't know what he's like except he kills people! I'm not giving you names so you can harass innocent people.'

'He's going to kill again, Dermot,' McEvoy stated harshly. 'Tomorrow. If we have to piss a few people off in order to catch him, so be it. We're already working through your categories, interviewing everyone. All we're asking is that you put some order on the names as we've got no other leads worth a damn.'

Brady shook his head and looked down at the table.

'It's important, Dermot,' Jacobs added. 'He needs to be stopped.'

'Give me some paper and a pen. You better run through that description again.'

There were five names on Brady's list, two of which he'd crossed out. Two from his church who both worked in financial services, one from a government department that the DHC had had a run-in with, a warden from Mountjoy prison, and a friend's brother who had unsuccessfully run for TD in the last election. Amusingly, he had thought Charlie Deegan should have been on it. 'A Class A wanker, a bully with aspirations above himself,' was how Brady had described him.

He remained adamant that while the five people on the list had most of the qualities described by Kathy Jacobs, he didn't believe any of them to be The Raven, and two of them probably didn't know that much about him. They were people he'd met a couple of times at most but who'd left a memorable impression because of their self-centredness and conceit. There were others, but he couldn't remember their names.

'I'll get someone on these right away,' McEvoy said to Jacobs, the door to the interview room closing behind them. 'Arrange for them to be interviewed. See if we can eliminate them from the enquiry.'

Dr John pushed himself up off the corridor wall as they turned towards him. It was strange to see McEvoy in a uniform. And something that fitted properly. He was barely recognisable except for the sunken and worn out face.

'I've cracked the code,' he said enthusiastically, holding out a bit of paper. 'Should have cracked it ages ago, but I was playing around with letters not numbers. I thought it would spell out a name or something. Anyway, it's a location reference. Latitude and longitude like in the Phoenix Park.'

McEvoy took the bit of paper, glanced down at it and back up to Dr John. 'Are you sure you've got this right?'

'Yeah, yeah, look.' He took the sheet of paper back and held it up against a wall so they could all see. 'With each chapter he gave us two letters. For example, Chapter One M: Choosing a victim R. In total there are six chapters, giving us 12 letters. All he's done is used a simple substitution code.' He tapped the sheet.

a	b	c	d	e	f	g	h	i	j	k	l	m
3	4	5	6	7	8	9	0	1	2	3	4	5
n	o	p	q	r	s	t	u	v	w	x	y	z
6	7	8	9	0	1	2	3	4	5	6	7	8

'If all the letters associated with the chapter bit are grouped together you get MAIXLH. If all the letters with the chapter titles are grouped you get RDKUWC. If you put them into the substitution code, you get a latitude and longitude.' He tapped the sheet again, smiling.

```
MA IX LH          RD KU WC
53,16,40          06,33,55
```

'53,16,40 North, 06,33,55 West. It's a cemetery in Oughterard out in Kildare. Between Celbridge and Naas. Not far from Straffan.'

'If it's just a simple substitution code, why haven't the papers or their readers already worked it out?' McEvoy asked.

'Because the chapters sent to the media didn't contain the extra letters. They were only in the chapters left at the murder scenes. They were a puzzle for us to solve. He was testing us.'

'Jesus! For God's sake. Come on, let's get moving.' McEvoy hurried towards the exit, his skin tingling, stomach churning, with a sickening realisation that he should have had more people working on the code. 'I've got a map in the car, we can make some phone calls on the way.'

They sped along the narrow road riding the line of a low ridge, to the left the foothills of the Wicklow Mountains rolled green and brown fields, dotted with trees, one-off housing and farms. Low cloud obscured the hills beyond. Two garda cars were parked ahead beside a couple of houses, just before the road dipped away to the left, down toward the busy N7 carrying traffic between Dublin, Cork and Limerick.

Two guards watched from the entrance of a laneway, their caps down low, collars up, hands hidden by their coat sleeves, as

McEvoy parked in behind the cars. He levered himself out and hurried towards them, the stiff, cold breeze blowing at his back, shoving him forward. As he neared he could see the large iron gates painted black, 'OUGHTERARD CEMETARY' welded into the iron work, painted white. To the side was a narrow swing gate.

'Detective Superintendent McEvoy,' he introduced himself. 'I don't want anyone else up this laneway unless they're a guard, that clear?'

'Sir,' muttered the elder of the two, sharing a quizzical look with his colleague.

'Good.'

Kathy Jacobs and Dr John joined him. 'You're going to need this,' she held out his coat.

'Thanks.' He looked down at his pristine uniform and shrugged the windproof jacket on. He hoped to God he wasn't going to have to trample across fields. Bishop would have a fit.

They slipped through the narrow side gate and headed up the gravel laneway. A hundred metres or so up ahead, through the trees to the left and beyond a stone wall, he could see a stunted round tower and what looked like a ruined church. As they neared, it was apparent that half the church was missing a roof and a small tower adjoining the main structure had peeled away, it being held upright by two concrete supports. The cemetery was surrounded by a high stone wall, the entrance blocked by a padlocked gate. A set of stone steps led up and over the structure, two guards standing at its base looking cold and bored.

'You had a look round?' he asked.

'We were told to wait outside,' one of them answered.

McEvoy climbed the steps and looked into the cemetery. It wasn't large, perhaps 60 metres long by 30 metres wide. The stone wall extended all the way round, beyond it to the right the land sloped away onto the Kildare plain, hedgerow plots stretching to the horizon. The ruined church was immediately inside the gate to the left, the stunted round tower in the far corner behind it. The ground in front of him undulated in soft rounded mounds, the thick grass relatively free of gravestones, which grew in number towards the far wall.

McEvoy turned round and looked down at the others, the cold wind whipping into his face. 'I guess we'd better get started. We need to search this cemetery. The problem is we've no idea what we're looking for. It might be obvious or it might be more subtle. He could be pointing us to a family name, perhaps his own, perhaps a victim's, or maybe he's left something here for us, I don't know. If you see something that you think might be of interest call out and we'll take a look. And be careful where you tread, okay – I don't want to mess up any evidence. John, you take here to the left and the church. You two take this side,' he instructed the two guards, pointing to the right. 'Dr Jacobs and myself will take the far end. Clear?'

The four heads nodded their assent.

He swung his leg over the top of the wall and descended into the cemetery, the wind immediately dying down with the protection of the high barrier. He waited for the others and set off with Kathy Jacobs.

'There's a lot of history here,' Jacobs said. 'This place must go back centuries. These mounds are all family vaults and the stones ahead look ancient.'

'Hardly packed though is it?' McEvoy replied. 'There are only a few plots.' He looked at the names on the stones – Garnett, Higgins, Christian, Carroll, Farrell, Hanlon, Comerford, Cahill – Anglo-Irish sounding names; most dying in the late 19th and early 20th centuries.

'Sir!' Dr John called from the entrance into the unroofed part of the church.

'What?'

'There's an envelope here. Underneath a rock.'

McEvoy hurried to the archway. Dr John pointed down to the gravelled ground three steps below. Next to a gravestone embedded in the side of the ruined wall a cream envelope, wrapped in a clear plastic bag, peeked out from beneath a flat rock. McEvoy searched his pockets trying to find a pair of rubber gloves, knowing they were in the jacket of his suit.

'For God's sake! Can you run down to the …'

He trailed off as Dr John held up a thin box. 'For emergencies.'

They descended to the church's floor, McEvoy tugging on the gloves. He lifted the rock and retrieved the envelope. He teased open the bag and plucked up the unsealed flap. It contained a single sheet of paper. He pulled the sheet free inside the bag and unfolded it, a crumpled five-euro note dropping free. He read the note out loud.

```
This is my one concession. If you are in time,
this is your chance to cut the book short and
make my fame. If you are too late, then I am
already safe in my anonymity. Of course, you
could be on time and I still manage to kill the
final victims and get clean away. Enjoy a pint
of the black stuff on me.
```

'There's a picture of a raven at the top. At the bottom he lists a series of latitudes, longitudes and dates.' He showed the others.

```
53,11,56 N, 06,17,32 W, 13th April
53,22,68 N, 06,36,01 W, 14th April
53,21,30 N, 06,19,33 W, 15th April
53,27,59 N, 06,43,42 W, 16th April
53,20,50 N, 06,15,21 W, 17th April
53,28,58 N, 06,06,36 W, 18th April
53,20,59 N, 06,15,37 W, 19th April
```

'No doubt they're the locations of all of the murders,' McEvoy said frustrated. 'If this has been here all week anyone could have found it! It's like he wants to be caught.'

239

'It's hardly on the beaten track though, is it?' Jacobs said. 'I doubt anyone's been here recently, and even if they had it's unlikely they would have picked up what looks like a bit of litter and ripped it open.'

'And even if I'd broken the code earlier,' Dr John added, 'we couldn't have found his list until this or the previous murder. The grid reference was too coarse. It would have covered a huge area. Several square miles.'

'But if we, or someone else, had found it, we could have been waiting for him,' McEvoy muttered, shaking his head.

'We still can be,' Dr John said, raising his eyebrows. 'It tells us exactly where the last murder's going to happen. We just need to work out where that grid reference is.' He stabbed his finger at the bag.

'Jesus Christ!' McEvoy said, half in excitement, half disbelief. 'He's going to let us catch him. It's like you predicted,' he said to Jacobs, 'he wants to be caught. He wants the fame. His ego's too strong to let him simply walk away. That's why he's left us the clues and this note.'

'That, or he wants to prove how smart he really is,' Jacobs replied neutrally. 'He says it himself. "Of course, you could be on time and I still manage to kill the final victims and get clean away." Maybe he's confident he can kill his last target right under your noses and walk away scot free.'

'We need to find out where that grid reference refers to,' McEvoy said, moving back towards the entrance.

'Well, it seems he has a sense of humour,' Dr John said, stopping him. 'The five-euro note. "Enjoy a pint of the black stuff on me." This is why he left the envelope here. It's kind of a joke. A sick joke.' He tapped the gravestone embedded in the wall. 'Have you seen whose grave this is?'

McEvoy stepped back and peered at the engraving on the pale grey rock, difficult to read in the pale light.

In the adjoining Vault
are the mortal remains

of

ARTHUR GUINNESS

late of

ST JAMES GATE IN THE CITY

and of

BEAUMONT IN THE COUNTY OF DUBLIN ESQUIRE

Who departed this life on

23rd of January A.D. 1803

aged 78 years

He stopped reading, shaking his head, holding his anger in check. 'Next time I have a pint of Guinness it'll be to celebrate catching the sick bastard. And it won't be with his blood money. Come on, we need to find out where this grid reference is.'

The Assistant Commissioner placed a thick arm across the door. 'I'm sorry, Dr Jacobs, this is going to have to be a closed meeting. If you could wait outside, we'll call you if we need any advice.'

Jacobs did her best not to look offended and headed for a small sofa next to a coffee table, the day's papers laid out across it. As the door closed the AC's secretary gave her an apologetic smile.

The AC sat behind his desk, Bishop and McEvoy seated opposite. 'Tell me about the note,' he instructed, resting his giant hands on his stomach.

'It was left in Oughterard Cemetery next to Arthur Guinness' grave,' McEvoy replied. 'It lists the exact latitude and longitude of all seven murders. The last murder is due to take place on O'Connell Street at the spire.'

'Are you sure about that?'

'That's what the note says and I've had it double-checked. All the other references are perfect. He left us a list of every site.'

'So why didn't we break the code earlier?'

'Because we didn't have enough letters to break it and even if we did we wouldn't have been able to pinpoint the location until we'd got the most recent letters.'

The AC nodded and turned to look out of the window at the grey sky, a light drizzle flecking the windows. 'So what are you proposing to do?'

'I think we flood the area with hand-picked, plain clothes personnel. We wait until he turns up and we arrest him. There's the risk that he might kill his target but hopefully we can prevent it.'

'Hopefully?'

'I think it's a risk we have to take. He's giving us the perfect opportunity to catch him; we might not get one again. So far, we've had very little to go on. If he goes to ground it might take us months to pick up his scent again. May never pick it up.'

'What's your view, Tony?' the AC asked.

'I think it's a hell of a risk,' Bishop cautioned. 'If we leave O'Connell Street open and he manages to commit his murder they'll be hell to pay, even if we do catch the bastard. And if we don't catch him then we'll be hung out to dry. They'll be no hiding place and they'll be merciless. You've seen what they're like. Either way, the press will say we've been playing Russian roulette with people's lives. I think we close the whole area down; locked tight. We say there's been a security alert, whatever, it doesn't matter. If we do that, then we close off his opportunity to commit his last murder and finish his book. If he still turns up then we stand a better chance of catching him.'

'If we shut O'Connell Street he's still going to kill someone, somewhere,' McEvoy countered. 'He's invested too much time and energy to simply walk away. He *needs* to finish his book. Whatever happens, I think he'll try and do that. If we seal off O'Connell Street, he'll have a contingency plan. He'll just murder some other poor fecker somewhere else in the city. He'll then tell the press that the O'Connell Street reference was a bluff, a stunt to misdirect our attention, and what's more they'll believe him.

'This whole thing's about ego, it's about outsmarting everyone and proving how clever he is. I think he *will* show up on O'Connell Street tomorrow and we *should* be there to meet him. Either way he's going to try and kill someone. I'm a hundred percent confident about that. We can be there to catch him or we can let him get away with it. The press are going to crucify us whatever we do. I think we just forget about them and concentrate on him. He's all that really matters.'

The AC looked back from the window at McEvoy and then up to the ceiling, bridging his fingers.

'Well, what do you think, Tony?'

'I still think it's a hell of a risk. We've no way of knowing that he's got a contingency plan. And we've no way of knowing how he intends to kill his last victim. He might not show up at all. He might have planted a bomb on a timer, blows up half the street and kills God knows how many. There'll be thousands of people out shopping, plus all the traffic.'

'He's not going to use a bomb,' McEvoy said firmly. 'Everything so far has been up close and personal – strangling, battering, slashing, suffocating. He's not used a gun and he won't use a bomb. Unless he has specialist knowledge he'd have to source a bomb, and even if he did know how to make one he'd still has to get his hands on the materials – explosives, detonators, timers. He's a loner and he wants no loose ends.

'We could, however, undertake a tactical bomb search this evening,' McEvoy suggested, his mind jumping ahead. 'The alert will warn a lot of people off, make the place a lot quieter than it would be otherwise. We could also partially shut the street down, for example, closing it to traffic. We could say there's emergency street work taking place – a broken main or something. It doesn't matter what, as long as it looks genuine. The crew could be some of our team. If it's still open, even partially, I think he'll show.'

'Even if you're right about the up close and personal bit, we're still putting the public in the firing line,' Bishop countered. 'We're leaving ourselves wide open to allegations of serious misconduct.'

'We're leaving the public in the firing line even if we close O'Connell Street. If he wants to kill his last victim he'll just move his final attack to Grafton Street or the Powerscourt Centre or Jervis Street or the Ilac Centre or Connolly Station or Heuston Station, the list of potential targets is endless. Plus we're leaving him at large to kill again. And he will kill again. We all know that.'

'If we partially close O'Connell Street he'll know we're waiting for him,' Bishop reasoned.

'He knows we will be in any case. He left us a note telling us where each murder will take place. He's laid down a challenge and I think he'll show up as long as we don't shut the place down entirely. He's going to kill again whatever we do, this is our one clear chance to catch him.'

The room descended into silence. The AC placed his elbows on the desk, interlocked his fingers and drew them to his mouth, his gaze unfocused. After 20 seconds or so he said, 'I need to talk to the Commissioner and then probably the Minister for Justice. There's no way I'm making this kind of decision without sanction. He's got us caught between a rock and a hard place.' He paused. 'This conversation stays between the three of us, okay. And even if we do go ahead with an operation, it'll be limited personnel on a strict no-gossip basis. I don't want vigilantes or panic on the streets. Nobody's to know details of that location, especially the press. Nobody. Understand?'

There was an expectant air in the room, a feeling that they might be on the edge of a breakthrough. They all knew that McEvoy had been out to Oughterard Cemetery, that a note had been found.

'Right, okay, let's make a start,' McEvoy said, Jacobs standing next to him. 'Come on, let's quieten down.' He waited until the DIs and crime scene managers were hushed. 'I want to start with an introduction. This is Dr Kathy Jacobs. She's a criminal profiler and will be working with us to try and help focus our efforts. She's had a look through some of the case notes and will be working on the files in order to construct her profile. She's to get your full co-operation. Understood?'

Jacobs nodded at the faces staring at her and sat at a nearby desk.

'Right, as you're all aware, there was a sixth murder this morning. Shirley Hamilton, 53, a staff development trainer from Belfast. Jim, you got any updates?'

The room's occupants shifted on their seats and shared quizzical glances. They were expecting McEvoy to detail what had been found, to see how it might influence their investigations, not to simply run through all the enquiries.

'Not really,' Whelan answered. 'She was battered to death. No sign of him or the weapon.'

McEvoy sighed inwardly; getting information out of Whelan was next to impossible. He'd been working that site all day and all he could manage was three short sentences. 'How about you, Cheryl?'

'What we have's in the lab. And it's not much to be honest. We're working through it, but it's slow work. The whole place is flat out and there's a huge backlog from the other murders. It'll probably be days before it's all worked through.'

'Right, okay,' McEvoy said frustrated. 'Right, I know it's early, but has there been any progress with the five names that Dermot Brady gave us?'

'One of them was out of the country at the time of the first murder,' Johnny Cronin said, 'trying to catch the last of the snow in Italy apparently. The prison warden's dead. Road accident two years ago; drink driving. The wannabe politician has a cast iron alibi – he was at a council meeting the night of Grainne

Malone's murder. We haven't managed to track down the other two yet. I have a couple of people on it.'

'Okay, we need to make that a priority. If they don't come up with solid alibis put them under surveillance. Right then, let's work through the other murders. Barney, any progress with Laura Schmidt?'

'Nothing. We're still working through Glencree's lists and trying to eliminate possibles. We've been attempting to open a decent channel up into the North in order to put pressure on some of the groups up there to co-operate. Maybe Shirley Hamilton's death might help, I don't know. Everything else has run cold – nothing from the questionnaires, the searches or appeals.'

'How about Peter Killick?'

'Nothing so far. We're still working through CCTV footage from every camera within quarter of a mile. We've got people out showing the photofit and we're working through all the staff and customer's statements. He disappeared the moment he stepped out of the bar's door.'

'Anything from forensics?' he asked Hannah Fallon.

'We're at the back of the queue with Cheryl. There were hundreds of hair and fluid samples in that place; probably from hundreds of different people. It's going to take us an age to process them all. And I hope someone's got deep pockets because it's going to cost a fortune as well.'

'Don't worry about the cost; that's Bishop's and the Minister's concern. Charlie, how about you?'

'We're making slow …'

McEvoy's phone rang. He held up his hand to stop Deegan. 'McEvoy?'

'Colm, you'd better come back up again,' the AC said. 'We need to talk.'

'I'll be there now.' The line went dead. 'Right, okay,' he said to the room, 'I'll be back shortly. Get a coffee or something.'

The AC was standing at the window looking out across the city. Bishop was sitting in the same seat as before, a scowl on his face. The clock on the wall said it was a ten past seven. The murder that morning seemed a lifetime ago. McEvoy hovered unsure whether to sit or not.

'Take a seat, Colm,' the AC instructed, turning and sitting behind his desk. 'The last hour has, let's say, been interesting. I've spent most of it on the phone, first with the Commissioner, then with the Minister, then with his Secretary General, then back to the Minister, and finally the Commissioner again. Basically Justice has shoved the ball back into our court and have gone to talk to the Attorney General for advice.

'They think we're screwed either way and don't want any part of it. They think we should do whatever we think's best. Unless the Attorney General says otherwise, the decision about how to proceed then is up to us. They don't think a security alert, however, is a good idea. There's enough panic around as it is without people thinking they've got to worry about bombs as well. They've no objections to closing the street to traffic, however.'

The AC paused, gathering his thoughts.

'As you know, I've also spoken to Kathy Jacobs. Based on her experience and her reading of the case notes, she's strongly of the opinion that whether we close O'Connell Street or not, he's going to kill the seventh victim tomorrow. On that basis, it seems to make sense to keep O'Connell Street open and to catch the bastard.'

McEvoy let a deep breath out unaware that he'd been holding it.

'There's still the danger that he might kill someone before we can stop him, but at least he'd be caught. And while the press might crucify us if that happens, they'd vilify us if he killed elsewhere and they then found out we'd the perfect opportunity to catch him and passed it up. What that means is we need to make sure we do catch him. I know you're not happy about this, Tony, but I really don't think we've got a choice.'

Bishop nodded and lowered his eyes to the desk.

'We've got less than five hours until tomorrow starts, so the clock has started ticking. I'll leave the operational planning to you two,' the AC said, thereby devolving himself of responsibility, 'but my feeling is that you keep the team small. No more than 30 men – maybe two teams of 15. It's imperative that whoever's involved keeps everything to themselves, okay. Nobody's to tell their families to stay away from O'Connell Street. The news will travel like wildfire and God knows what that'll start. I know they won't want to put loved ones at risk, but under no circumstances are they to mention the operation. Is that clear?'

McEvoy and Bishop nodded their heads.

'If you want an armed response unit or anything else, just let me know. My suggestion is you hand pick your teams, starting with your DIs and DSs. People with experience. People you can rely on. Right, well,' he said, drawing things to a close, 'I guess, you'd better go and make a start. If I hear anything from the Minister or Attorney General I'll let you know.'

'Do you want us to run the final plan past you?' Bishop asked, already knowing the answer.

'Only if it's going to involve anything unusual. I assume you're going to close off the street to traffic and stake the place out. What more can you do?'

'Right, well you heard the man,' Bishop said, 'go and sort out a plan and pick and organise your teams. Whatever resources you need just ask and I'll get them for you.'

'I thought he said …'

'Nevermind what he just said. My job's to oversee things and protect your back. And that's what I'm going to be doing. I'm going to give you the time and space to be getting on with things, and while you organise and run that stake out, I'm going to be working out contingency plans for the press. If he does manage to kill someone on O'Connell Street, or if O'Connell Street is a bluff and he kills elsewhere, then the media are going to go crazy. The whole world is watching us, Colm. This isn't about spin, it's about protecting ourselves from criticism and any fall-out. And that needs a careful strategy.'

'So you just want me to get on with it then?'

'Yes. And since you've only got four-and-a-half hours, I suggest you make a start.'

'And do you want to see the final plan?' McEvoy asked with a hint of facetiousness.

'Do I need to? As the AC says, it's just a large stakeout.'

McEvoy headed for the door, his shoulders slumped. Talk about being set up as the fall guy. If anything went wrong and they didn't catch The Raven then he'd be hung out to dry. The AC and Bishop would squirm and squeal and they'd make sure that anybody except themselves were held responsible. But there was no one he could advocate responsibility to. The buck stopped with him. He jammed his plastic cigarette in his mouth and descended the stairs. Feck the cigarette, he felt like a stiff whisky.

Everyone's head in the room swivelled to watch him enter, tracking him as he walked to the front, trying to read his mind.

He turned and faced them, his brow creased in worry lines. 'Sorry about the delay, there's been a change of plan. Can the crime scene people leave please, with the exception of Michael. We'll finish the meeting at another time.'

His audience looked at each other and back at him. Reluctantly the crime scene managers started to gather themselves and their notes.

'Come on, we're on a clock here; if you could make your way out.' He'd have liked to have requested that Deegan join them, but it would only cause hassle. Plus there would be plenty of people around to keep an eye on him.

Once those requested had left, McEvoy sat on the edge of a desk. 'Before I start, I want to make it clear that everything I'm about to tell you is confidential. You will not divulge it to anyone including your families or anyone else. Understand? That instruction comes from the highest level.'

Kathy Jacobs, Barney Plunkett, Jenny Flanagan, Johnny Cronin, Charlie Deegan, Jim Whelan and Michael Foster shared glances and nodded their assent.

'Good. There's going to be enough to worry about without the rumour mill working its way around the city. The note out at Oughterard stated where the last murder's going to happen. After a lot of fannying about we've decided to try and catch him at the scene. The danger is that he still manages to kill his last victim before we manage to capture him. That's a risk we're going to have to take. If we shut down the whole area, he's just going to kill someone else, elsewhere. The main thing is to make sure we catch the sick bastard. Everyone follow so far?'

'Where's he planning to strike?' Plunkett asked.

'I'm getting to that. I'm just making sure you understand why you can't tell your families. They might be planning to go to where he's planning to commit the final murder. If you warn them off, then they'll warn off their friends, and so on. We'll have a place either totally deserted or full of vigilantes and press. And we can't afford to let that happen. Is that clear?'

He paused, his eyes travelling across their faces, making them know how important the issue was.

'The note says he intends to murder someone at the spire on O'Connell Street sometime tomorrow.'

'Jesus Christ,' Plunkett muttered.

'That gives us a little over four hours to try and plan things and get ourselves in place. We've no idea when he might try and carry it out – could be the early hours, late tomorrow night or anytime in between. My suggestion is we head down there now and scope the place out; work out where to set up camera surveillance and how to try and patrol the area. We have permission to close the street to traffic, but not pedestrians.

'We also need to determine how many personnel we're going to need and whether we want an armed response unit involved. All personnel involved will need to be experienced and to be vouched for by yourselves. At this stage, I'm not convinced by armed personnel, especially as it might be busy with shoppers. I think we have them waiting in reserve in case he takes people hostage. Any questions?'

'Do we have any idea who the intended victim is?' Cronin asked.

'No. Some of the victims have been linked to Brady, others haven't. He could just pick someone at random.'

'How about how he intends to kill them?' Flanagan asked.

'Again, nothing. All the note says is the date and latitude and longitude of where he'll strike. My gut feeling is that it's going to be up close given how's killed so far.'

'And he'll want to try and get away,' Jacobs added. 'This is his final challenge – to kill where and when he's expected to and to then get clean away. It'll be carefully planned and likely to be very quick. Maybe a single stab of a knife to a heart and then hurry away before it's clear what's happening.'

'Hopefully we can identify and apprehend him before anything like that happens,' McEvoy continued. 'If it does, Michael I want you and your team nearby to seal off the crime scene and collect evidence before it's destroyed. You'll also need to organise a standby medical team. Anyone else?' McEvoy asked.

The room stayed silent, each officer mulling over the task ahead.

'Right, okay then, let's get ourselves down to O'Connell Street. We'll leave in dribs and drabs rather than a convoy. I don't want the press following us down there. When you get there have a good scout around, familiarise yourself with the area, and try and put yourself in his shoes. How would you get in and out? And how should we go about organising the stakeout?

We'll meet back here by 9.30 at the latest. Barney, I want you to come with me and Dr Jacobs.'

Plunkett was driving, McEvoy in the passenger seat, Jacobs in the back.

'We're going to have to split this into teams to make it manageable,' McEvoy said. 'Each team can do a block of four hours on duty, four hours' rest. I'll take charge of one team, I want you to take the other,' he said to Plunkett.

'Are you sure you don't want Jim Whelan to do it?' Plunkett replied cautiously.

'No. You've been with this from the start and …' McEvoy stopped.

'And what?'

'And nothing.' Wanting to say that he didn't think Whelan was the right person for the job; that it needed someone with a bit more dynamism and communication skills. 'I'll take Charlie Deegan and Johnny Cronin. You take Whelan and Flanagan. His experience will counter her greenness.'

'Okay.'

'Good.' He turned in his seat to look back at Jacobs. 'Kathy, we're going to need you to tell us what to look for, what signs might help us identify him before he strikes.'

'I'll do my best, but I can't make any promises. I still need to go through the full case files to get a better sense of him.'

'I understand that, but you must have some ideas?'

'Well, for a start, I think he'll probably show all the usual signs of stress – he'll be tense, fidgety, his eyes darting about trying to see whether he's been spotted, clasping and unclasping his hands, repeating things such as checking the route he'll use multiple times. He'll be doing his best to avoid some of those, but I doubt he'll be able to suppress them all as he'll be slightly hyper with the adrenaline, pumped up with excitement and fear.'

McEvoy nodded in agreement. 'How about the victim? Any ideas as to who he might go for?'

'My guess is they'll be on their own and probably quite vulnerable. Maybe a child or someone elderly. Someone who he doesn't think will have the wits or be quick enough to deal with him. Perhaps someone with their hands full of shopping?'

'And how about the method of killing?' Plunkett asked, glancing up into the mirror.

'I don't know. I think Superintendent McEvoy's right that it'll be up close. I don't think, for example, that he'll try and shoot someone from a distance. He wants to be next to them – to see and hear and smell them. And, as I've said, it'll be quick. With the exception of Laura, every one of the murders was over before the victim knew what was happening. This will almost certainly be the same. He doesn't want to give them time to react.

'As for method, I don't know. So far he's tried to vary it – the sword, suffocation, strangling, burning, slitting, attempted drowning. He might try something else, or he might want you to think that and use something he's used before. Given the pressure he'll be under he might well go for something he knows works like stabbing. I might be able to tell you more once I've been through the files.'

They continued on in silence, lost in their own thoughts.

He was sitting on the edge of the bath, spraying her naked body with warm water from the shower head, cleansing her wounds. The smell in the bathroom was terrible, despite his attempts to wash the faeces away from under her. Rivulets of pale red water trickled down the plughole. He ignored the sprays of blood on the bathroom tiles and shower curtain.

She had her eyes closed, refusing to look at him. Her face was drawn, her skin pale and tight on her skull. She didn't look as if she would last much longer; dying of dehydration, loss of blood, and lacking a will to live. Her early wounds had scabbed over; dry, dark lines criss-crossing her torso, arms and legs, cross-cut with new wounds, the blood freshly congealing.

'It'll be over tomorrow,' he whispered. 'One more death and the book will be complete.' He turned the shower off and watched the remaining spray congregate into droplets and slide off the body to the white plastic below. 'Our fame will be assured. I'll be known as a criminal mastermind, you a tragic victim. You will be immortal. As famous as Elizabeth Short or Annie Chapman or JonBenet Ramsey,' he said referring to actress better known as The Black Dahlia, Jack the Ripper's second victim, and the six-year-old beauty queen killed in strange circumstances.

'You will have suffered, but you will live forever. Everyone will know your name; your life.'

He stroked her hair gently.

She tried to pull her head away and settled for turning her face towards the tiled wall.

'That's my gift to you,' he said, caressing her cheek. 'Immortality.'

McEvoy stood at the three metre wide base of the steel spire and looked up towards where it tapered to a thin point 120 metres above. It had been erected in 2003 to replace Nelson's Pillar blown up in 1966 by the IRA. At the time McEvoy had thought it a tremendous waste of money – it cost a fortune, you couldn't go up it, and it was boring; just a bloody big spike rising into the sky. His opinion hadn't changed with time. He lowered his face and looked around at the street-lamp lit scene, dragging the smoke from his cigarette deep into his lungs.

The spire was positioned in the middle of a crossroads, standing on a strip of pavement that separated the double lanes of O'Connell Street, one of the widest thoroughfares in Europe,

50 metres in width. Off to one side was Earl Street, a short pedestrian area leading onto Talbot Street that led down past the bargain basement shops to Connolly Station. Opposite was Henry Street full of high street, brand name shops. On the corner of Henry Street was the GPO – the general post office – a long, squat, stern-looking building with a grand central portico of six, wide classical Ionic columns, still pockmarked with bullet holes from the 1916 rising. On top of the portico, looking down onto the street, were the three statues of Mercury, Hibernia and Fidelity.

McEvoy set off on a circuit, walking to the north corner of Henry Street, then alongside the drab, four-storey shop fronts, the dark brown portico of the National Irish Bank, up as far as McDonalds, still doing a brisk trade to gangs of teenagers and bewildered-looking tourists, then across to the central reservation again. Standing next to a giant statue of a running hare set on a wide plinth, part of a temporary exhibition of Barry Flanagan's sculptures running the length of O'Connell Street, he looked back toward the spire through some thin trees just gaining their new leaves.

The area was still relatively busy. Buses and taxis trundling their way up both sides of the reservation, office workers heading home after a few Friday night drinks, early revellers disgorging from buses and traversing between bars, tourists fresh in on weekend city breaks wandering aimlessly seeking the sights and the craic, and a handful of plain clothes guards trying to get a sense of the space.

He weaved his way through the traffic to O'Brien's sandwich shop and headed back towards Earl Street, pausing to look down its length, past the entrances to Boyers' and Cleary's department stores to the smaller shops beyond, and then right at the spire blocking the route to Henry Street, people waiting at the traffic lights to cross, a timer counting down the seconds until the lights would change. It reached zero and the pedestrians surged forward, across onto the central reservation, streaming either side of the spire, heading for the far side.

He continued down O'Connell Street, past Abrakebabra, the smell of cooking meat and fries wafting out onto the pavement reminding him that he'd once again barely eaten all day, the saucy underwear in Ann Summers' window display, to the imposing frontage of Cleary's, mimicking the GPO opposite with 12 flat columns along its length, a large black and gold clock hanging above the entrance. Restrained neoclassical style buildings, their fronts a mix of limestone, granite, red brick and Portland stone, their roofs capped with copper, stretched down the rest of the street to the Liffey. He crossed the road back to the central reservation at the statue of radical labour leader, Jim Larkin, his hands held aloft, behind him the spire rising up through them. He drew to a stop and looked at the way he had come and then across to the GPO.

Barney Plunkett and Kathy Jacobs joined him.

'So, what do you think?' Plunkett asked.

'I think it's going to be bloody difficult. It's a huge space. Even if we created a box 20 or 30 metres either side of the spire, the street must still be 50 or 60 metres wide. That's means over 2,000 square metres to keep an eye on; almost the size of a football pitch. That size of space filled with hundreds of shoppers, tourists and traffic is going to be almost impossible to police.'

'But we can shut the street down for traffic?'

'Yeah, but there has to be an excuse and I doubt we'll manage to get the diggers in before dawn. Even with just pedestrians it's going to be difficult.'

'Maybe we could use the road works as a way of channelling them, limiting the space they can use?'

'Yeah, it's a possibility alright, but then we might end up funnelling them together in such a way that we can't see what's happening – they're too closely packed. If that happens, the danger is we'll lose him in the crowd.' He shook his head, lit another cigarette and blew out the smoke. 'I think we're fucked.'

'Even if he does manage to kill someone, if we've got an

outer cordon we should be able to pick him up,' Plunkett said trying to remain optimistic.

'Well, hopefully, we can grab him before he has chance to kill,' McEvoy said without conviction, rubbing his face, exhausted. His left hand had started to shake again. He tried to still it, but it wouldn't respond to instruction. All of his muscles felt tight, aching with tiredness and stress. He tried to roll his shoulders to ease the pressure thinking that if someone was to tap him with their knuckle he would probably sound a middle C.

'Hello?'

'Caroline, it's Colm. Is everything alright?'

'It's better than it was. They've been moved back from the front of the house and most of them have given up – there's just one or two left,' she said referring to the journalists that had been stationed outside his house all day. 'When are you coming home?'

'Well, as you've probably guessed, that's why I'm ringing. I'm not going to make it back this evening. In fact, I'm not sure when I'll be back. It might be late tomorrow evening or the day after.'

'You've tracked him down?'

'I'd like to say yes, but it's not that simple. He's going to try and kill his last victim tomorrow. It might be our last chance to catch him before he goes to ground and disappears. We're going to work on through tonight and see if we can crack things open.'

'You need to get some sleep, Colm,' Caroline warned. 'You look like the walking dead.'

'I'll sleep when all this over,' he replied, not wanting to argue. 'Is Gemma there?'

'I'll just put her on.'

'Dad?'

'Hiya, pumpkin, how're things?'

'Weird,' she said excitedly. 'You're in all the newspapers and on the TV. Your uniform is much nicer than your suits. My friends have been sending me emails and texts since I got home from school. They're really cheesed off they weren't allowed to come last night. It's like I'm a film star or something. And Nana and Grandad Dacey have arrived. They're going to stay over tonight as they're worried about us. And …'

'Whoa, slow down. Slow down. Take it easy. So, you're okay then?'

'I'm fine,' she said more calmly. 'Have you been eating and drinking properly? Everyone thinks you might have become an anorexic or whatever it's called.'

'Don't worry, I'm looking after myself,' McEvoy replied guiltily. 'I'm just ringing to see how things are and let you know I won't be home this evening. So, you're to behave yourself, okay.'

'As if I wouldn't,' she said indignantly.

'And be careful.' And don't come anywhere near O'Connell Street he said to himself.

It was approaching midnight and the space around the spire was teeming with life. Young women wearing belts for skirts, bras for tops, and high heels, young men in casual trousers and short-sleeved shirts, both sets unable to feel the cold due the alcoholic anti-freeze in their systems; older folk wandering around after an evening at the cinema or theatre followed by a couple of drinks, snaking about trying to wave down taxis; and a smattering of tourists drifting around, some pulling suitcases or carrying rucksacks, eyeing carefully those around them, trying to assess whether any might make a grab for the luggage. Cream with orange and blue trim, and yellow, blue and green, buses drifted in packs, taxis darting around them like hungry hyenas.

McEvoy stepped back from the window of the third floor

corner office of the GPO building and watched Plunkett struggling with a tripod for a video camera.

'You can help if you want,' Plunkett snapped.

'You trust me with that stuff? I think it's best dealt with by an expert like yourself.' He huffed a laugh. 'It looks like everyone's in place. Deegan's strutting around like he owns the street.'

'You should have kicked him into touch.'

'It's easier to mind him this way. We have a view of him the whole time and everything he does is on camera. God knows what he'd be doing if I'd cut him loose.'

He glanced round the room. There were two windows, one on each outside wall, each made up of nine small panels set in a dark wood. The walls were papered with a cream, vertical pattern, with a dark dado rail. The carpet was mid-green, once lush but now worn in places. Along one internal wall were positioned four filing cabinets, house plants and paper files positioned on top, along the other was a dark bookcase full of yearbooks, reference texts and knick-knacks. In front of the bookcase was an old desk with leather inlay, it's surface free of objects. Behind it was a leather office chair and in front two ordinary, modern chairs.

There was a knock at the door.

'Yes? Come in.'

Dr John, Kelly Stringer and Michael Foster entered the room.

'You wanted us to work with you up here?' Dr John stated as a question, Foster brushing past him, heading for a window, knowing he belonged.

'That's right. DI Plunkett will be here for a short while then he'll head off and relieve us at four. John, you're to work the window looking out on the Henry Street side. Kelly, you're to look out at O'Connell Street. You're to keep the video cameras operating at all times. Anyone suspicious, radio it down to the street and zoom in on them and make sure you get good head shots. There are directional microphones if you need to try and hear any conversations. If required, direct our people in. The zones are working off a clock with the spire at the centre. Up O'Connell Street is twelve o'clock. Understand?'

They nodded their heads.

'Michael, I want you to oversee the technical side of things. You probably need to give Barney a hand, he's struggling a bit.'

'Says the man who relies on his 12-year-old daughter to video things for him because he doesn't know how the damn thing works,' Plunkett snapped back.

McEvoy's phone rang. 'Yes?'

'Colm, it's Kathy Jacobs. Do you have a second? I've been going through these files.'

'Absolutely. What do you want to know?'

'I'm not ringing with a question. I wanted to remind you he's chosen the character of The Raven. That's a deliberate choice. I think a lot of thought went into its selection and he'll be well aware of the mythology surrounding it. I've been reflecting on that. I think he's probably going to be quite bold. He thinks he's cleverer than you and your teams, that he's god-like figure – invincible. He's also the trickster. That could mean that the spire is an elaborate deception or he's going to use deception to kill, for example wearing a disguise or setting up a decoy to attract your attention while he commits his crime. I think he'll use either of the latter. He'll want to fulfil the promise of his note.'

'You think he'll wear a disguise?' McEvoy repeated.

'I think he'll want to act like a raven. He'll be bold and he'll use trickery – a disguise, a decoy, or some other type of trick.'

'Jesus!'

'I just wanted to warn you, that's all. He'll have planned the last murder in detail. Expect the unexpected.'

'What does that mean?'

'It means that I'm not sure what you should be looking for or even how he'll try and kill. It means, good luck.'

Chapter Six

Saturday, April 19th

Foster had managed to rig up the video cameras so they fed directly into two flat-screen monitors placed on the desk. They'd had to move the desk to centre of the room to allow the cables to stretch, the rest of their length taped to the floor. McEvoy was sitting watching the screens, his gaze shifting back and forth between them. The chair was comfortable, but his shoulders were tight, his back stiff. His eyes unfocused as his mind drifted to think about the case.

'Jesus Christ,' Kelly Stringer exclaimed. She snatched at her radio. 'A man's pulled a knife at four o'clock. Repeat, knife attack at four o'clock. Shit! He's just stabbed another man in the stomach.'

McEvoy jerked to attention and stared at the screen. 'We're going to need an ambulance, Michael,' he stated.

'Confirmed,' a disembodied voice replied via a radio link to Stringer. 'We're on it.'

Two groups of young men, surrounded by gesticulating women, had squared off against each other. A man lay on the floor between them. The attacker waved his knife at the stabbed man's friends, taunting them, stopping them from helping him. Two of McEvoy's men burst through the women. Bravely, and perhaps rather stupidly, given the man was wielding a knife, Kenny Johns tackled the attacker, sending him sprawling to the floor. The others tried to scatter. Two more plain clothes guards grabbed a couple before they could react, pressuring them to the floor, securing them. A uniformed guard arrived and bent down to help the man on the floor, pushing his hysterical girlfriend out of the way.

'Everyone else, maintain your positions,' McEvoy stated into his radio. 'It's under control.'

The siren of an ambulance sounded from the top of O'Connell Street where it had been waiting on standby at the Rotunda Hospital. Its blue lights scattered late night revellers as it sped to the scene. It slowed to a stop and two paramedics jumped out rushing to the downed man.

'We need to get some uniforms here to take over from our lot,' McEvoy stated to Foster as he headed for the door. 'Call them in. They're all to be taken into custody and questioned. It looks like it was just a drunken fight between a load of stupid gobshites. I'm going down to find out what the hell's happened.'

Barney Plunkett knocked on the door, pushed it open and entered. Behind him Diarmaid Savage, Fay Butler and Seamus Harte, the crime scene manager from Billy Mullins' murder, trailed in.

'How's it going?' Plunkett asked.

'I've had better nights,' McEvoy replied, exhaustion in his voice. 'Great if you want to watch kids throw up and fight, but otherwise fairly tedious except for a couple who got fairly amorous in a shop doorway. They obviously couldn't wait to get home. Personally, I can't see how any of them can say they've had a great night out. Most of them probably can't remember past midnight, the state of them.'

'You telling me you never used to get drunk and stagger home eating a kebab when you were 19 or 20?' Plunkett asked.

'I'm not going to deny it,' McEvoy said pushing himself to his feet, 'but I didn't go around vandalising things, picking fights for no reason, and throwing up in the middle of the street. And I used to wear clothes, and so did the girls. And they definitely didn't fight. More than half the trouble out there has been young women screaming and fighting, throwing up and collapsing paralytic. I'm telling you, it's been bloody scary.'

Plunkett shook McEvoy's shoulder gently. 'Time to swap over, Colm.'

'What?' McEvoy replied from within the warmth of a sleeping bag.

'I said it's time to swap over. It's ten to eight.'

McEvoy rubbed at his face. He'd slept fitfully, uncomfortable on the floor of an office along the corridor and with the demons in his mind. Now that he'd found sleep, all he wanted to do was dive back under. Instead he pushed back the sleeping back and sat up, turning so he could lean against a wall.

'Are you okay?' Plunkett asked. 'You look like hell.'

'I've been better,' McEvoy replied trying to decide what he needed the most – a cup of coffee or a cigarette.

'I'll go and get some breakfast. What do you want? Bacon sandwich and a cup of tea?'

'Coffee. And a shower.' All the muscles in his body ached, his shirt clinging to his back with sweat, the room warm, the central heating having come on sometime in the early morning.

'I know a good cafe near here. Best bacon sandwiches in Dublin. You want anything else?'

McEvoy stifled a yawn and gestured 'no' with his hand.

Plunkett left the room, whistling tunelessly to himself.

McEvoy slowly levered himself upright and let the sleeping bag fall, stepping out of it. He then pulled on his suit trousers and jacket, slipped on yesterday's socks and his shoes, and headed to the bathroom and had a wash, scooping up handfuls of water to his unshaven face, brushing the sleep out of the corners of his eyes. He stared at himself in the mirror. His mother was right. He was starting to look like he could be an extra in *Schindler's List*. He needed a full wash, a can of deodorant, a toothbrush, some clean clothes and a long holiday.

He headed back to the operational room. Kelly Stringer bounced up the stairs ahead of him. Her hair was brushed, her clothes pressed. Dr John trailed behind her, looking as McEvoy felt.

'Two-year-olds,' Dr John muttered. 'I love her dearly, but Jesus. She was in at 6.30. What happened to you,' he said to Stringer, 'you take regeneration pills?'

'Slept like a log. Felt like I got the full eight hours.'

'Good for you,' McEvoy muttered disingenuously brushing past them. He knocked on the door and opened it.

Seamus Harte turned away from the monitors to look over at their replacements. The desk was covered in cans and chocolate wrappers. Fay Butler and Diarmaid Savage were sitting at the windows.

'How'd it go?'

'Deathly dull,' Butler replied. 'Hardly a soul around. We had to stand half the team down at around five because we were tripling the numbers on the street. We moved the heavy equipment in at six and closed the street off to traffic.'

McEvoy moved to the window and leaned over Diarmaid Savage to look out. A JCB had been positioned on both dual carriageways on the Liffey-side of the spire, red and white tape running from one pavement to the other, limiting access to the corners of the box. Five workmen in luminous tops were gathered together looking bored, kicking at stones, waiting for instructions.

'We didn't think there was any need to dig the street up,' Butler continued. 'We thought that we could just lift a few slabs and open up a couple of boxes. It just needs to look like there's something happening.'

'Fair enough,' McEvoy conceded.

264

'The other news is that the last two on Brady's list both have solid alibis. That's all five of them in the clear now.'

Plunkett appeared in the doorway. In his right hand he balanced a tray with four cups on top of an identical tray beneath. In his left hand he held a large paper bag. The smell of bacon filled the room. 'I have four coffees, four teas and eight bacon sandwiches,' he announced.

'Just don't get any grease on the equipment,' Harte warned.

He'd walked past the spire a couple of times, half an hour apart. He'd worn a woollen beanie and false beard the first time, a baseball cap and a scarf covering his mouth and nose the second. There was no doubt in his mind that the guards had cracked his code and found his note out at Oughterard; there were at least three of them patrolling the space. They were trying to blend in, but the fact that they were milling around seemingly with no purpose, their eyes constantly scanning around them, gave them away.

He felt a small surge of energy, of vigour. The last killing would be a real challenge. Anyone could kill someone when they weren't expecting it. He had proved that. This time though the finest of An Garda Síochána would be waiting for him and he would murder the final victim right under their noses and walk calmly away. In so doing he would demonstrate the validity of *The Rule Book* and with it the genius of The Raven; that he *was* the trickster, the great bringer of death; that the world was powerless to stop him.

He smiled slyly to himself as he headed away from the spire, up O'Connell Street towards the Rotunda Hospital. As he turned the corner into Parnell Street he nearly collided with Laura's friend from the squat.

She looked through him, rather than at him, her face a blank. She took a step back, instinctively rolling her shoulders in,

265

protecting herself, her head dropping. Then she walked past him quickly, keen to avoid confrontation.

He cursed inwardly at his stupidity and complacency. The reconnaissance had been foolhardy; an unnecessary risk. It didn't matter whether the guards were there or not. The final murder was planned for O'Connell Street. His note – his word – had promised it so. The only reason for adopting an alternative plan was if they had closed off the street in its entirety. Then they would be forfeiting the challenge and he would have no choice – he would still need to complete *The Rule Book* after all.

He needed to stay focused; to concentrate on the job at hand. One more murder and he would achieve his goal. And if Laura's friend proved a problem then she would pay the ultimate price. But there would be no problem – he had planned every last detail and he knew what he was doing; only a slight of fate would prevent the seventh murder.

The time was twenty to twelve. The room had descended into silence, the occupants tired and tense, concentrating on their jobs.

'I'm going for a walk,' McEvoy announced.

'You mean a cigarette,' Stringer corrected, without turning.

'Whatever.' McEvoy stood up from behind the desk. He stopped and dropped back into the seat. 'That's Karen,' he said to no one in particular, tapping the screen. 'Laura's friend. Kelly, can you zoom in on the young woman in black at the bottom of the spire.'

Karen filled the screen.

'What the hell's she doing here?' McEvoy muttered. He watched as Karen approached a middle-aged woman and asked her a question, trailing her for five yards while the woman kept walking, her head down, failing to acknowledge Karen's presence.

'I'm going down there,' McEvoy said, easing himself back out of the seat. 'I'll be back shortly.' He left the room and descended to the street. He lit a cigarette, sucking the smoke down, and headed up past the supposed repair works and across to where Karen was hassling an elderly man.

'Karen.'

She turned to face him, her arms hugging her chest, her shoulders pulled in protectively. Her face was pale, her dark hair greasy. Shoppers streamed either side of them, making their way between Henry and Earl Street. The elderly man took his chance to leave.

'It's Superintendent McEvoy. Remember me? I came to talk to you about Laura.'

'Fuck!' She glanced around looking for an escape route.

'Are you okay? Do you want a cigarette?' He held the packet.

She resigned herself to his presence and teased one free and he lit it.

'Did you think anymore about where Laura lived? Whether she had any friends?'

'No,' she spat defiantly, letting the smoke drift out of her nostrils.

'Do you know if she had a boyfriend?'

'So what if she did?'

'Is that a yes?'

'It's an "I don't give a fuck".'

'Karen, it's important. Someone has killed six people, starting with Laura. We need to stop him.'

'I need money.'

McEvoy pulled his wallet from his pocket. 'I only have ten euro,' he lied, taking the note and offering it to her.

She clutched it in her hand and looked at him, suspicious at how quickly and easily he'd given it to her.

'Did she have a boyfriend, Karen?'

'I don't know.'

'Well did you ever see her with a man? Perhaps someone older than her?'

She hesitated, taking a drag from the cigarette. 'No.'

'Are you sure? He kills people, Karen. He killed Laura.'

'I said, no, didn't I. She kept herself to herself. Herself and her dog.'

'What happened to the dog?'

'Look, I've got to go,' she turned and started to walk away towards Earl Street.

McEvoy trailed after her. 'Karen? What happened to the dog?'

'I don't know. I barely knew her, okay.'

'Did she have a boyfriend, Karen?'

'Will you leave me alone! This is harassment.'

People were staring at them now. Several had recognised him from the TV and newspapers. He stopped trailing her and headed back toward the GPO. He spoke into his radio mic. 'I need someone to follow that girl and keep her under surveillance.'

'I'm on it,' Cronin replied into his earpiece.

'Shit!' McEvoy snapped annoyed with how the encounter had gone, that he'd been identified. He passed Deegan who glared at him, his lips curled in an amused smile.

'Superintendent McEvoy? It's Kathy Jacobs.'

'Oh, hi. How're things going?' He rubbed his freshly shaved face and looked at his watch – 4.54.

'Slowly. I've been through most of the material and my opinion hasn't changed. I still think this is about ego and I still think Laura Schmidt knew her killer.'

'I spoke to one of her friends earlier,' McEvoy said. 'I asked her if Laura had a boyfriend. She said no, but I don't believe her. She knows more than she's saying.'

'Can I talk to her?'

'After all this has finished. I have her under surveillance right now. I couldn't leave my post here.'

'Well, actually, that's partially why I'm ringing. I was wondering whether I could join you?'

'What for?'

'Because I'm tired of these files and I want a change of scene. I thought I might be able to help.'

McEvoy paused, pondering her request. What harm could it do, he reasoned, maybe she would spot something the others wouldn't. 'Sure, come along. Just make sure you're not followed and ring me when you get here.'

'Thanks. I'll see you soon.'

McEvoy placed the mobile phone in his pocket and walked to the window facing out over O'Connell Street. It was still busy with shoppers despite the road blockage. He was feeling sick with nerves, restless and agitated, and the involuntary shake had returned to his left hand. The best part of three quarters of the day had passed and there had been no sign of The Raven or another murder elsewhere in the city. Everyone was tired and bored, the teams on the street cold and weary. At least it hadn't rained yet, despite Met Éireann's forecast.

The Raven sat near to the window in McDonalds. He scratched at his back, uncomfortable with the fit of the bra. He opened the burger carton with leather-gloved hands and looked at the sad looking roll it contained, strips of lettuce poking out. Making sure no one was watching he reached into his handbag and extracted another burger in a clear plastic bag, a bite mark shape missing. He flipped open the bun, extracted the burger, and replaced it with his own. He then ripped away a chunk of bread to match the bite mark. He slid a business card and the final chapter, wrapped in clear plastic, under a serviette, placed them beneath the bun, and closed the lid.

He ate a few fries, placed the Styrofoam carton in his handbag, and shuffled to the trash disposal, tipping in the fries and redundant burger. He left the fast food restaurant, catching his reflection in the glass in the door. Grey hair tufted out of the scarf covering his head, a black coat covered a patterned blue dress and navy cardigan. He reminded himself of his grandmother. He pulled a rye smile and stepped out onto O'Connell Street, his heart beating fast, nerves tingling with anticipation.

Crossing the road, free of traffic, to the central reservation and the sculpture of the running hare, he sat down on the plinth next to a homeless man with a wispy beard, dressed in a shabby tweed jacket, filthy jeans and battered black boots. A dirty red rucksack rested between his legs, a can of Special Brew balanced on his thigh. Taking the burger carton from the handbag he offered it to him.

'I saw you from the window.' He gestured at McDonalds. 'You look hungry. Do you want it?' He held the carton to the man.

He looked at her suspiciously – an interfering auld wan.

The Raven smiled and pushed the carton closer to him. 'It's just a burger.'

The man reached out and grabbed the carton. He opened it and stared at the bun, a single bite taken out of it, and then at the elderly woman. After a pause he fished it out and took a tentative bite, chewing for a second or two before taking another one, cramming it into his mouth.

The woman smiled, tapped his arm, stood up and headed away from the spire toward Parnell Square. After a few yards she glanced back. The homeless man was still in place, the carton and can now on the floor, the lager spilling across the pavement.

The homeless man convulsed and toppled off the plinth onto the pavement, his head smacking heavily on the concrete. A woman nearby startled and moved towards him, putting down her shopping bags, and kneeling down next to his head. His face was bright red, bread and burger spilling from his mouth into his beard. She looked up at two teenagers sitting on the plinth and at passers-by, unsure what to do. A middle-aged couple joined her, the man kneeling beside her, trying to loosen the clothing round the man's neck.

'Sir,' Dr John stated, zooming the camera in on the incident.

'What's happening?' McEvoy asked concerned.

'I don't know.'

'Person down at twelve o'clock,' McEvoy barked into the radio. 'Nearest to it investigate, everyone else stay in position. I'm going to down there,' he said to the rest of the room. He headed to the door, followed by Kathy Jacobs. 'Get an ambulance.'

They descended the stairs, exited out onto O'Connell Street and half-walked, half-ran, toward the crowd that had gathered near to the running hare. He looked at his watch – just gone six o'clock. The sound of a siren approached from the Rotunda.

McEvoy pushed his way through the crowd. A homeless man was lying on the ground, a red rucksack between his legs. A uniformed guard was down on both knees checking for a pulse. The guard looked up and shook his head, signalling that the man was dead.

To one side the three people who had tried to help looked on, their faces creased in concern. Charlie Deegan hovered nearby.

'Right, okay,' McEvoy said, taking charge. 'Come on, move back please, give us some space here. Come on! Charlie, give us a hand, we need to secure this area. Please, Ladies and Gentlemen, move back.' He moved forward with his arms spread, forcing the onlookers backwards.

A couple of people in the crowd had recognised him, hurrying away, afraid they might be next, others took out mobile phones and started to film or take photos.

McEvoy realised it had been a mistake to come down before they knew that The Raven had struck. The man might have died of natural causes, in which case the operation was compromised. He cursed himself.

'Sir!' the uniformed guard called out as an ambulance pulled to a stop.

McEvoy glanced back and the guard motioned him over. The guard pointed down to the open carton at the man's feet. The burger had spilled out onto the pavement, the serviette stuck to the bun. Inside the carton the plastic-sealed note and card were visible.

'Fuck!' McEvoy spat, his guts knotting and liquefying at the same time. The Raven had struck right under their noses and nobody had noticed a thing.

'Sorry mate, can you get out of the way?' a paramedic asked.

'Don't give him CPR,' McEvoy instructed, stepping backwards. 'He's likely to have been poisoned.' He pointed to the carton.

'You sure?' the man asked.

'Ninety-nine percent.' He spoke into his radio mic. 'Right, okay, he's struck. We need this whole area cleared as soon as possible. I want the whole street locked down. Anyone within 100 metres of the spire, shepherd them down towards the Liffey for questioning. No one's to leave before they've given a full statement. Roll back the video and see if you can see what happened. Michael, you better get down here.' He turned away and swore again.

'Come on, come on, get these people back from here,' he yelled at his colleagues. 'Quickly.' He joined them, herding the on-lookers back toward the spire. The killing had taken place right at the edge of their surveillance box, probably the limit of the latitude and longitude they'd been given.

Charlie Deegan had edged closer.

'You've really fucked up this time, McEvoy,' he gloated.

'Just do your job, Charlie.'

272

'At least I'll have a job. You're finished. Gone.'

'I said, just do your job,' McEvoy repeated.

'You're history, McEvoy. Yesterday's man. The AC is going to chew you up and spit you out. And the press will do the same.'

Something snapped inside. McEvoy's right fist landed on Deegan's cheek. He yanked it back and launched it forward onto his nose. Deegan collapsed to the pavement, blood starting to trickle from a nostril.

McEvoy stared down at him, the red mist still clouding his vision. 'Get out of my sight, Charlie, and stay out of it. You come back and I won't be accountable for my actions. You hear?'

Kathy Jacobs was tugging on his sleeve, pulling him back.

'Leave. Now,' McEvoy commanded.

Deegan gathered himself and stood unsteadily. 'You've just made a big mistake, McEvoy. Assaulting a fellow officer. And I've got witnesses.'

'Just leave before you regret staying.' McEvoy tugged his arm free of Jacobs' grasp and lurched towards Deegan, who stumbled backwards, fear in his eyes.

'You're finished, McEvoy.'

'Play that back again,' McEvoy instructed.

At the very top of their screen they watched what looked like an elderly lady cross to the central reservation and sit down next to the victim. She opened her handbag and offered something to the man. After a hesitation he took it, opened it and removed the burger, taking a bite and then another. The old woman stood up and walked back across to the pavement and out of view.

'Is there any way of zooming in on her?' McEvoy said, frustrated. 'It's impossible to see what she looks like.'

'Not here. I don't think we have the kit,' Dr John stated. 'We'd need the techies to fiddle with it.'

'Shit!' The incident had happened 40 metres from the camera and the figures were indistinct and grainy. 'How long ago was that taken?'

'About 20 minutes. She left eight minutes before he had his fit.'

'Get her, I mean his, description sent out to all units. He'll be well beyond the outer cordon by now. We need to see if we can track his route in and out of the city centre. Also get the tape from McDonald's. It was a McDonald's carton and it's just across the road from where the body was found. Maybe they have some better quality images.'

'I'll get on it now.'

'We've fucked up big time,' McEvoy said to no one in particular. 'He killed that man right under our noses and we didn't even notice. He could have sat there for another half an hour or more before we'd have picked up on it.'

Foster had placed the business card in a clear plastic bag. McEvoy studied it, reading the text aloud. '"*The Rule Book*. A self-help guide for would-be serial killers. Now published and serialised in all good newspapers." For feck's sake! How about the chapter?'

Foster handed him the sheet of paper wrapped in a second plastic bag. McEvoy read it silently, Jacobs at his shoulder.

The Rules
Chapter Seven O: The Murderer D

"At the same time that we are moving into a surveillance society, our lives more and more captured by video cameras and in databases, criminals are becoming ever more adept at avoiding their gaze. They can walk down a busy street

and just fade anonymously into the background,
all the while seeking a new victim."

7a. Live an ordinary life. Go to work, have a
partner, make friends, mow the lawn on Sunday.
Act like everyone else. Do not draw attention
to yourself.

7b. Do not drink or smoke - it impairs judgement
and makes one edgy.

7c. Always wear a full disguise. Vary this disguise depending on context. Never wear the same
disguise across victims.

7d. Always have an alibi. Make sure it is as
watertight as possible, preferably recorded in
some fashion.

7e. Never feel remorse or guilt - they probably deserved it at some level. There is no
such thing as innocence, just as there is no
Truth.

7f. ALWAYS get away with it.

Master rule: Do not get caught for anything else -
drink driving, speeding, thieving. Have no record
and no contact with law unless necessary.

'Jesus Christ,' McEvoy hissed as he finished. 'He did it right
under our feckin' noses. It's even in the bloody quote. He killed
him in the middle of a busy street. He was visible to everyone,
yet no one saw him. You said he'd been wearing a disguise,' he
said to Jacobs.

'The trickster,' Jacobs stated flatly. 'I think the title is a pun of sorts. Chapter Seven O, Murderer D. OD. He killed him with an overdose of some kind.'

His phone rang. 'McEvoy.'

'What the hell is happening, Colm?' Bishop asked.

'He's killed the final victim, a homeless man. Looks like he poisoned him, but I can't be sure until the autopsy's been carried out. He left a business card and the final chapter.'

'And did you catch him?' Bishop asked, already knowing the answer, seeking confirmation.

'No. There were eight minutes between when he gave him the poison and when we found him dead. He was long gone by then. He was dressed as an old woman. I've got the outer cordon looking for her, I mean him.'

'The press are going to have a field day. I knew this was a bad idea. They've already laid siege to the place.'

'Look, Sir, I need to go. Things are pretty crazy here at the minute.'

'That'll be nothing to the firestorm you're going to get in the next couple of days,' Bishop warned.

'If we find anything I call you, okay.' McEvoy ended the call. He turned to Jacobs. 'We need to find Karen.'

McEvoy paused in the hallway, listening for signs of life. Nothing. He climbed the stairs, two at a time, pushing open the door to Karen's room. She was lying in the same corner between dirty blankets. The man he'd encountered downstairs the last time he visited lay on top of the blanket between her and the wall. A burnt and bloodied spoon lay on ground, a lighter, a twist of tin foil, and a hypodermic needle nearby.

McEvoy knelt down next to the blankets. He rolled her shoulder. 'Karen?'

There was no response.

'Karen?' he said loudly.

'She'll probably be out of it for a while,' Jacobs said.

'Shit! I don't believe this.' He shook her roughly. 'Karen.'

'What?' The word was slow and slurred.

'Karen. Come on, I need to talk to you.' He shook her again.

'You're wasting your time,' Jacobs offered.

'What?' Karen slurred again, half opening her eyes.

'Shit!' McEvoy stood and pulled his mobile phone from his pocket, his anger and frustration rising again. 'Fuckin' heroin. We need to get her moved into protective custody.'

'Is that a good idea?' Jacobs asked.

'If she does know the identity of The Raven then I want her wrapped in cotton wool. I don't want her to suddenly disappear, either through her own choice or his.'

He pulled the wig free and smiled at himself in the cracked mirror, his face reflected back two dozen times. He'd done it. He'd walked into the lion's den, killed a man and left without anyone noticing. He'd proved the truth of *The Rule Book* and his own genius. There could be no argument. He'd outwitted all the forces of the Irish state ranged against him. He'd even told them when and where he would strike and still they had failed to ensnare him. He would justifiably be the headline news on every news station on the planet. He felt euphoric; invincible.

If it weren't for his partner, lying behind him in the bath, he could slip back into anonymity; continue his life as before. But that wouldn't be a problem. He would be safely hidden, ready to rise again at his choosing, long before anyone came to look for her.

'You would have been proud of me, Sam,' he said, running hot water into the sink, preparing to wash the make-up away. He'd excelled himself this time. The disguise had been perfect. As far as anybody who'd seen him were concerned, he *had* been an elderly woman – no question.

He turned to face her. Her eyes were closed, her face drained of any colour. 'I did it, Sam. I fuckin' did it. I'm The Raven. The Trickster. I said I would do it and I did. I wrote the rules. I wrote the fuckin' book!'

He reached out and touched her shoulder. It was cold to the touch. 'Sam?'

She did not respond.

'Sam?' He sat on the edge of the bath and stroked her cheek. 'And then there were eight,' he muttered to himself. 'The epilogue. The final chapter that will announce my name to the world.'

He slowly started to unwind the tape from around her head, his euphoria subsiding. Once he finished he balled up the twisted tape and stared at her pale, placid, innocent face. Her pain and hatred were now gone – she was in a different place; the place Laura and his other victims were now residing. Somewhere other or nowhere; here then gone.

He looked down at her lacerated body and pulled a tight smile. She had served his purpose; been the safety valve for his tension, stress and anger. She had never been anything more than a prop to create the illusion of a normal life. He knew he should be feeling something towards her – for her – but he felt nothing. He was just playing a scene for an absent audience.

He turned back to the sink and continued to remove his disguise. Once finished he left the bathroom without looking back and headed through into the living room to watch the news and bask in the rhetoric and hyperbole of panicked and flustered reporters and commentators. He felt invincible.

They were driving back to towards O'Connell Street.

'You need to try and calm down, Colm,' Jacobs advised. 'You'll make poor decisions when angry.'

'Just concentrate on The Raven and forget about trying to do your mumbo-jumbo on me, okay. He killed that man right

under our feckin' noses! Just walked in, gave y'man the burge
and calmly walked out again. I'm going to get taken to the
cleaners.'

'Well being angry isn't going to help,' she said patiently.
'You need to be calm and collected. Try and get things in perspective. You hit one of your colleagues earlier on. Even if he
was taunting you, how's that going to help? You're acting like
a bull in a china shop.'

'Listen, Kathy, I know you mean well, but will you shut the
hell up, okay. If it hadn't escaped your attention I'm in charge of
seven, that's seven, murders. That sick bastard's just committed
the seventh in broad daylight in a place where over 20 officers
were waiting for him and we still don't have a feckin' clue as to
who he is! Of course I'm angry. I'm feckin' livid!'

'All I'm saying is that you've been under enormous stress,'
she continued evenly, 'you've practically had no sleep in the last
week, and you're hyper-tense. If you don't calm down you're
going to have a heart attack or a stroke. That, or you're going to
say or do the wrong thing, something you'll regret later.'

'Kathy, shut up, okay,' McEvoy said, annoyed and frustrated,
knowing deep down that she was right, but too angry to admit it or act on her advice. It was now over an hour since The
Raven had given the homeless man the burger. It was clear that
he'd gotten clean away. They'd – he'd – been made to look a
fool. Hitting Deegan had been stupid, but he deserved it. And he
shouldn't have been there; he should have been suspended. They
continued on in silence.

His mobile phone rang and he snatched at it. 'McEvoy.'

'He left the same way he came in,' Dr John said. 'Up
O'Connell Street, along Parnell Street, up Parnell Square West
past the Rotunda, along Granby Row, across Dorset Street onto
Saint Mary's Place. We lose him after that.'

'Shit!'

'He barely entered our box. Certainly didn't go anywhere
near the spire or Earl or Henry Street. The only decent shots

279

we get of him are from McDonalds, and he keeps his face looking down the whole time. He was wearing a head scarf over a grey-haired wig, a blue dress and cardigan, a black coat, black stockings and black shoes.'

'Get the best frames released to the media ASAP. We want to speak to anybody who saw her between four and seven this evening. Get them to ring the confidential hotline. We need to know where he went after Saint Mary's Place.'

'I'll do it now.'

'Good. I'll speak to you later. We'll need a team meeting at some point to go over this fiasco. I'll let you know when.' He ended the call.

'He's disappeared off the face of the earth,' he said, filling Jacobs in on the call.

'If you don't get lucky with the hotline then I still think Laura is the place to start,' she offered.

'That's why we've just been to see Karen,' McEvoy said testily.

'I know. I'm just giving you my view, that's all – that you should concentrate your efforts there. He was close to Laura but probably only tangentially linked with Brady. He might have only met him once or twice, or knew him from a distance through Laura, but given Brady's history he got the idea of using him as a decoy. If they ever did meet, he probably put on an act, being very pleasant, friendly.'

'He'd have to have learnt about Brady's life to select the places and victims,' McEvoy stated, trying to pick holes in Jacob's thesis.

'He could have learnt that indirectly – from the archives, through Brady's friends, or following him about. I doubt he got close to Brady though. My feeling's that he's pretty much followed the advice in his chapters. There's little to link him to Brady other than Laura and the murders.'

'Oh, shit,' McEvoy spat approaching the top of O'Connell Street. A crowd of on-lookers had gathered, several members of

the press set up around them. He turned left onto Parnell Street, hoping to cut down Malborough Street to Earl Street. No doubt a similar scene would await them there.

McEvoy walked briskly towards Plunkett who was talking to a guard in uniform.

Plunkett turned to face him. 'The quays are gridlocked, the rest of the city's following suit. It's mayhem.'

'I know. I've just been up to the North Circular Road.' His phone rang. He held up a hand of apology to Plunkett. 'McEvoy.'

'I've just had Charlie Deegan in my office, followed by the AC on the phone,' Bishop said angrily. 'Deegan's pissed off, the AC's pissed off, and I'm mightily pissed off. Not only has your operation gone tits up, but you assaulted another officer! Some member of the public caught it on their mobile feckin' phone! It's now all over *Sky News*. What the hell were you playing at!'

'Playing at?' McEvoy repeated, Bishop's tirade still sinking in.

'You're on your own on this one, Colm. I've done my best to protect you, but you've fucked up big time. First, pushing for that fiasco, and then punching Charlie feckin' Deegan on camera. You've lost the plot, you bloody looper. You better get back here before you do any more damage. Is DI Plunkett with you? I need to speak to him.'

McEvoy handed the phone to Plunkett. 'It's Bishop,' he stated flatly.

McEvoy was stuck in traffic along Nassau Street. His flashing blue lights were having no effect. The cars and buses in front of him had nowhere to go. He thought of abandoning the car and walking up to Harcourt Street, but it had just started to rain heavily, fat drops hitting the windscreen. His mobile phone rang again.

'McEvoy.'

'Colm, it's Elaine. Do you have a minute?'

'Yeah, no bother,' he said flatly, a quiet rage still burning inside from Bishop's rebuke.

'I think he was killed by cyanide. There's a faint smell of almonds from the burger and his face is bright red because the tissue couldn't absorb the oxygen in the blood. I won't know for sure for a couple of days as the blood and burger samples will have to be sent to London for testing. I'm pretty certain though.

'By the look of it he'd put a couple of capsules in the burger. He probably teased them apart, took out whatever was in them, paracetamol or whatever, and replaced it with potassium or sodium cyanide. When the victim bit into the burger he would have broken the capsules. He'd have ingested some of the cyanide salts direct, some of the rest reacting with the acid in the burger to create hydrogen cyanide. He'd have lost consciousness quickly, well within a minute, and entered a coma not long after. He died of a cardiac arrest bought on by the stress to his cardiovascular system. He wasn't in good shape to begin with.'

'Poor bastard,' McEvoy muttered. 'How the hell would he have sourced cyanide?'

'I don't know. The Internet? You can buy anything on there these days. I know it's used a lot in ore extraction, electroplating, that kind of thing. Also in the production of other chemicals. No doubt you can get your hands on it if you want to.'

'Well, I don't think I'm going to have to worry about it for much longer in any case,' he said dejectedly. 'I think I'm about to lose my job or at least get demoted. He managed to commit the final murder under the noses of 20 guards and a load of technical equipment and get clean away. Plus I punched Charlie Deegan on camera.'

'Nonsense,' she said sternly. 'That arrogant idiot deserved whatever he got and there was nothing you could do about the murder.'

'That's not how the AC and Bishop see it.'

'Just stick to your guns, Colm. I'll send you the full report once I've got it typed up.'

'Well, someone will get it.' He ended the call and turned onto Kildare Street, riding up on to the pavement, getting set to abandon the car and jog through the rain.

Bishop's secretary looked up at McEvoy. His hair was soaking wet, his coat dripping onto his sopping suit trousers.

She pulled a tight smile. 'He's in with the AC. They're waiting for you.'

'Thanks.' He pulled the door closed and headed for the AC's office. He wasn't sure what his strategy for the meeting would be other than there was no way he was taking the fall for Charlie Deegan. If they wanted to remove him from the case, fair enough, but Deegan would have to be removed as well. He unzipped the coat, slipped out of it, shaking the rainwater off, and knocked on the outer door.

The AC's secretary called him in and gestured towards the inner door.

He knocked again and the AC's voice told him to enter.

The AC was sat behind his desk, Bishop in the same seat as 24 hours previously.

'Ah, the gombeen himself,' the AC said, no humour in his voice. 'I'm glad you could join us. Before we start I want to make one thing clear, you are *off* this case – suspended pending a full investigation. You've messed up big time, Colm. Big time.

'In the last half an hour the Commissioner and the Minister for Justice have chewed my god damn ear off over *your* fiasco. First, for letting The Raven kill again.' He held up a chunky finger. 'Second, for not catching him. Third, for punching Charlie Deegan on camera. And fourth for gridlocking the city. I've had Charlie Deegan in telling me he's going to press assault charges and the media are going mental. We're the laughing stock of the entire world. The government are almost certainly going to set up a full inquiry into our handling of the investigation. No doubt that'll recommend wide-scale reform and reorganisation.' He looked fit to explode.

McEvoy stayed standing and silent, afraid of what his anger might make him say.

'Well?' the AC demanded.

'Is Charlie Deegan being suspended as well?'

'Is that all you're worried about?' Bishop snapped, before the AC could reply. 'What's happening to Deegan!'

'I just want to know.'

'Of course, he's not being suspended!' the AC roared. 'He hasn't done anything wrong! You hit him, you stupid gombeen. Go on, get out of my sight. You'll be lucky to have a job after all of this. Jesus Christ!'

McEvoy turned, opened the door, and walked through into the secretary's office closing the door behind him.

She looked down at her desk, embarrassed, party to the AC's shouting.

He stood stock still, his eyes closed, clenching and unclenching his hands, trying to control the rage that was boiling inside, demanding to be vented. If he was going to lose his job, he might as well lose his dignity. If he simply snuck out of the building with his tail between his legs he'd forever regret not saying what he thought, regret failing to try and keep his post. He turned on his heels and pushed open the door again, standing in its frame.

'Listen, you pair of fuckin' cowards,' he snapped, 'while you've been fannying about trying to protect yourselves and your jobs, I've been trying to catch this fucker. At least I had the courage to try and set up a trap unlike the pair of you prima-fuckin'-donnas. Neither of you would even look at the plan for fear of tainting yourselves with it. Yes, it went wrong. Yes, I fucked up. But so did you, so don't try and wipe your hands clean and run for cover. You're in this up to your necks.

'As for Charlie Deegan, if I'm suspended then so's he. He should have been kicked into touch earlier this week when he fucked up big time, but neither of you had the balls to do it. Yes, I hit him. He fuckin' deserved it. I don't suppose you asked him what he said to provoke me, did you? He said the homeless person probably deserved to die!' he lied. 'That'll look good in the papers tomorrow, won't it!

'If I'm removed from this case, I'll be on every news channel on the planet explaining how you two set me up as the scapegoat, how you've covered up for Deegan. I don't care. What difference will it make to me? I might be finished, but I'll take you and the whole fuckin' force with me.'

He finished, his steely gaze challenging them to respond.

They stared back, anger in their eyes.

'It's your choice!' McEvoy spat and slammed the door. 'Sorry, Claire,' he said more politely to the secretary.

He closed the outer door and headed down the corridor. Strangely he felt quite calm, his anger dissipated. He might well lose his job, or at the very least be shunted into a backwater, but for some reason he didn't care. If they wanted to push him out, then he had an exit strategy and they knew what it was. It was their choice. He started down the stairs. He didn't know where he was going, just that he was leaving. They could look after The Raven. He felt free of him. He knew it was a temporary feeling, that guilt and remorse and worry would follow later, but for now it was something to hold onto.

McEvoy switched on the radio and tried to find some music. After a couple of minutes he stabbed it off again. He needed to apologise to Kathy Jacobs; needed to apologise to his whole team. He'd been acting like an idiot for the past few days – being short with people, ordering them about, giving them no slack, generally being a grumpy bastard. He'd let the stress of the whole thing get to him; let it turn him into somebody else. This evening was proof of that. Twenty years of obedience, of toeing the line, and then twice in one week bawling out Bishop. He'd even missed Gemma's birthday. At the end of the day she was the only thing that really mattered; his one constant.

He'd been blind to himself the whole week. And to top it off he'd even started smoking again after the damn things had killed Maggie. He took a pack of cigarettes from his jacket pocket and flung it onto the back seat, followed by the lighter. He toyed with throwing his plastic substitute after it, but instead jammed it between his lips.

He didn't want to walk away with bad blood. He pulled out his mobile phone.

'Kathy Jacobs.'

'Hi, Kathy, it's Colm McEvoy.'

'Colm,' she said surprised. 'You disappeared in a hurry. DI Plunkett's pretty worried about you.'

'Yeah, well, y'know,' he faltered. 'Look, if you haven't heard, I'm off the case; been suspended pending an investigation into my conduct. That's okay, I deserved it. I did everything you told me not to. I just wanted to apologise, that's all. I wasn't exactly a perfect host.'

'They've suspended you?' she repeated.

'Yeah, for hitting Charlie Deegan and letting y'man commit his final murder and get away. Look, that doesn't matter. I just wanted to apologise for shouting at you in the car, that's all. It was totally out of order. I was being … well, I was being a self-centred idiot. Look, I should let you get on. I just rang to say sorry and good luck.'

'You sound very calm, Colm, you know, given what's just happened. You're not going to do anything stupid are you?'

'I might be an idiot, but I'm not that big an idiot. I have a 12-year-old daughter and I'm not going to do that to her. Look, I'd better go. I'll apologise to the others tomorrow. If you see them, tell them I'm okay and to make sure they catch him.'

'Do you want to meet up, talk about it?'

'No, look, Kathy, I'm fine, really. It's been a long week and I'm going to go home. Thanks for the offer though; maybe some other time.'

'Okay. Well, look after yourself, Colm.'

'You too. And good luck with the case.' He ended the call, feeling better for having made it. Feeling a bit more human. He edged the car forward another 50 feet and sneezed. He needed to get out of his damp clothes.

The graveyard was bleak in the rain. It poured onto his head and trickled in under his collar. He was soaked through to the skin despite the coat. He stood at the foot of Maggie's grave, his hands clasped behind his back. A single tear rolled down his right cheek.

'I miss you, Maggie,' he muttered. 'I miss you so badly.'

The tears started to flow, McEvoy unable to stop them. His fury at Bishop and the AC was just a temporary vent – a blow out – the car journey to her grave the calm before the storm. All the emotions he'd been bottling for a week welled up inside and erupted. He dropped to his knees, his hands over his face, his body shaking with grief and rage and guilt.

He wanted to claw at the earth, dig down and join her. To be with her again. To hold her and chat and laugh and just be. He missed her smile, her warmth, her reassurances, the way she finished his sentences, her resoluteness. He missed the fact that she would have kept him steady all week, advised him on how to handle things, made sure he looked after himself, and ensured Gemma got the birthday she deserved. He missed just being with her; of sharing company.

After a while he managed to start to compose himself, sucking in air through his nose, wiping away the tears and rain from his face. He stayed kneeling.

'I'm sorry I haven't visited the last couple of days,' he said between gasps. 'Things … well, things have been …'

He slotted the key in the front door and pushed it open, feeling the warmth of the central heating reach out and envelop him.

His mother appeared in the lounge doorway. 'Jesus, Colm, look at the state of you! Come on, come on,' she said hurrying to him, 'get in out of the rain.'

Sheila, Maggie's mother, followed her out.

'I'm okay,' McEvoy said, shrugging himself out of his coat. 'It's just rain.'

'Where have you been? Look at the state of your suit – your trousers and jacket.'

'I went to Maggie's grave. I needed to talk to her.'

'I'll put the kettle on,' Sheila said hurrying to the kitchen.

His father and Des, Maggie's father, came into the hall.

'Have you caught him yet?' Des asked.

'Not that I know of. I'm off the case. Suspended.' He let his mother take the suit jacket from his shoulders.

'Hitting the fellow guard?' his father guessed.

'That and letting y'man commit his final murder and get away. Is Gemma up?'

'No, no,' his mother replied. 'She's asleep. She's on the blow-up mattress in your room. Des and Sheila are in her bedroom, we're in the back room.'

'And Caroline and Jimmy?'

'They went home half an hour ago.'

'Right. Right, okay, I'm going to get a shower and get changed. I'll be back down in a bit. Have you and Des cracked open a bottle of whisky?' he asked his father.

'We've got one on the go.'

'Good, I'll join you for one and tell you about it.' He started up the stairs.

He pushed open his bedroom door and crept in. The blow-up bed was on the far side, between his bed and the wardrobe. She had the quilt tucked up under her chin, her breathing shallow. She looked at peace.

He grabbed a pair of underpants and shirt from a chest of drawers, and a pair jeans from the back of a chair, and headed for the bathroom. He stripped and stood under the piping hot water and let it pummel his back and head, squirting shower gel onto his hands and working up a lather.

His mobile phone in his trouser pocket started to ring. He turned the water off and grabbed a towel, stepping out, picking up the trousers and yanking the phone free.

'McEvoy.'

'Colm, it's Tony Bishop. I won't keep you.' His voice was calm, measured. 'We've considered your offer. We'll see you back at work tomorrow morning. I'll meet you at eight o'clock.'

'I'm not suspended?' he asked, disbelief in his voice.

'No, but they'll be some changes. We'll talk tomorrow. Try and get a good night's sleep. You've had a long few days. No doubt tomorrow will be as well.'

'Right. Right, okay,' he mumbled, unsure what to say. 'And Deegan?'

'Don't worry about Deegan. I'll see you tomorrow morning.' The call was ended.

McEvoy stared at the phone for a while, his mind a blank bubble, then slotted it back into the pocket and climbed into the shower, turning the water back on, washing the suds away.

Chapter Seven

Sunday, April 20th

McEvoy tightened his tie and brushed down his uniform. He didn't feel comfortable wearing it, but one of his oversized numbers would just provide Bishop with extra ammunition. He felt like a naughty child hovering outside the headmaster's office. He tried to gather himself, his inner voice ordering him to be strong, to fight his corner, to not back down or accept a deal simply to maintain the peace; to make sure he retained some dignity going forward. He took a deep breath and knocked on the door.

'Come in.'

He pushed it open. Tony Bishop was sat behind his desk, Detective Superintendent Paul Roche opposite him. They both rose when he entered, Roche pulling a tight smile, looking uncomfortable. He was a couple of inches shorter than McEvoy, but broader in the shoulders, with white-grey hair, a short-haired greying beard, a pair of thin framed glasses over blue eyes, and a wide mouth. He was the senior Superintendent on the NBCI murder team, the steady hand who would soon reach retirement age. McEvoy liked him as a person and respected him as a policeman.

The desk was covered with the morning's newspapers. The banner on the one at the top read, 'KEYSTONE KOPS', a picture of the homeless man on the ground, the uniformed guard knelt at his side looking up, his face communicating that the man was dead. An inset picture showed McEvoy hitting Deegan.

McEvoy looked from Bishop to Roche, back to Bishop, and down to the newspapers, his heart sinking. Bishop was outflanking him. He wasn't suspended, but he was off the case. This was the handover. And Roche's presence would inhibit any discussion of yesterday's argument – their manoeuvring and his threats.

'Colm.' Bishop pointed to the free chair and waited for McEvoy to sit. 'After yesterday's fiasco we spent the evening conducting a review. It's the Commissioner's and Minister's opinion that we bring in a fresh perspective – somebody who can stand back and see the whole picture, who isn't too close to the action; someone who can plot a new path forward. They want Superintendent Roche to take over the investigation with immediate effect.'

Bishop had gazumped him. It wasn't Bishop and the AC who was moving him aside, it was the Commissioner and the Minister for Justice. He had no direct fight with them. He slumped back in the chair. This was all going horribly wrong.

'You are to stay part of the investigative team until Paul is fully up to speed. To the outside world it will be presented that we are adding another senior officer, spreading the load, rather than it looking like you're being kicked off the case. I know you're not going to be happy with that, but this is from the top. We need to be seen to be doing something after yesterday's disaster. That something is a change of management.'

McEvoy stayed silent, staring down at the papers.

'Colm?' Bishop prompted.

'And what about once Paul is up to speed?'

'You'll be eased out of the picture and out of the media's eye. It'll be best for you, for us, and for Paul. You're not exactly a media darling and it's hurting your reputation.'

McEvoy smiled to himself. What was good for them was good for him. They were trying to make shafting him look like a favour.

'And then what?' He wiped at his nose with the back of his hand.

'And then you go back into the regular rotation.'

'And at the first opportunity I'll be sent out to some back-water that needs a superintendent?'

'I don't make those kind of decisions, Colm,' Bishop said, his face flushing red, signalling his annoyance. 'I've no idea what the plans for you are. My view is that you're lucky to have a job after yesterday, lucky that you're not being yanked from the case right now after the damage you've done.'

McEvoy shook his head and rubbed his face. Within six months he'd be stationed in Leitrim or West Offaly, operating out of a part-time station with a leaky roof, policing local GAA games and tracking down fly-tippers.

'So?' Bishop prompted again.

'So what?' McEvoy said facetiously. 'It's not like I've got a choice, is it?'

'No.'

'Well, I guess I'll leave you to brief Paul then,' McEvoy said standing.

'Sit down, Colm, we're not finished yet. There are some other ground rules.'

McEvoy dropped back into his seat.

'First, this is now Superintendent Roche's case. You do what-ever he asks you to do. You do not make or act on any decisions without running them past him first. Second, I want to be kept informed at all times as to the progress of the case. Any major decisions will need to be okayed by me through Paul. Third, under no circumstances are either of you to talk to the media. None. All of that is now being handled by me and me only. You'll probably be pleased to know that neither of you will be required to attend press conferences either. It'll allow you to concentrate 100 percent on catching this bastard.'

McEvoy stayed staring at the papers. At least the responsi-bility was being lifted off his shoulders and he wouldn't need to talk to Bishop or the media. And he'd just have to see what happened in a few days' time. A holiday wouldn't be a bad idea. Except that deep down he wanted to catch The Raven; wanted to be there when they finally cornered him; wanted to make him pay in some small way for the misery and suffering he'd caused.

Roche shifted in his seat, remaining silent.

'Right, well, you better get started.' Bishop said, dismissing them.

McEvoy and Roche were standing just inside Roche's office.

'Look, Colm, I want you to know that I had no part in that. As far as I'm concerned this is still your investigation.'

'I think we both know that there's no way this is my investigation anymore,' McEvoy said, dejected. 'I'm a sinking ship, you'd be best to steer well clear.'

'Look, feck them, okay. We both know you've been shafted by Bishop protecting his scrawny arse. I'm going keep you involved in this as long as I can. One, it's your case, and two, you've got the best knowledge of how all of this sits together. You've seen all the victims and murder scenes, spoken to all the key witnesses; all I'm going to be able to do is go on the case notes and discussions with your investigating officers. While I get myself up to speed, I want you to carry on as you would have done.'

'I'm not sure that's a good idea, Paul. Bishop's going to be looking over your shoulder like a hawk making sure I'm behaving myself.' He blew his nose.

'Okay, well we'll play it Bishop's way. You tell me what you're going to do and I'll okay it. That'll keep him quiet. However we do it, we can't stall everything for two or three days while I try to familiarise myself with things. We need to try and keep the investigation moving. What leads have you got?'

'Nothing much,' McEvoy said flatly, unable to muster any enthusiasm. 'We know about as much about him now as we did a week ago. I was going to go and re-interview one of Laura Schmidt's friends, a drug addict called Karen. I think she knows more than she's letting on. Kathy Jacobs, the profiler, and myself both think Laura's the key to all of this. She was the first victim and Kathy thinks she might have let him kill her; a kind of bizarre form of euthanasia. Whatever happened, it just doesn't fit. There was no sign of any struggle, she lay there and he forced a sword out the back of her head.'

Roche winced at thought. 'Well, once we've had this team meeting, you go and interview her and see where that gets you.'

'You don't want to be present?'

'Look, I don't need to hold your hand and you know what you're doing in any case. I'm going to spend the day talking through each case with the DIs and their teams; see if a fresh pair of eyes can spot any new lines of enquiry. Come on, let's go and get this team meeting over with.'

McEvoy nodded and opened the door.

Roche slapped him on the back as he exited. 'Don't worry, Colm, we'll catch this bastard. It might take us a while, but we'll get him. He's left too many possible lines of enquiry. And when we do, you won't be able to get rid of Bishop with a shitty stick. He'll be your best friend again.'

'Some friend,' McEvoy muttered.

Karen was sitting at the table, staring absently at its surface, smoking a cigarette despite the signs forbidding it. McEvoy and Jacobs sat down opposite her.

'We need to talk, Karen.' McEvoy said neutrally. He didn't tell her to extinguish the cigarette, savouring the secondary smoke.

She looked up slowly. 'Was it you who had me locked up all night?'

'It was for your own safety.'

'Yeah, right. More like so I couldn't do a runner. Who's yer wan? Social worker?' She took another drag on the cigarette.

'No, she's a criminal profiler. A psychologist. Dr Kathy Jacobs. She's trying to help us catch The Raven, the man who killed Laura.'

'I've already fuckin' told you, I barely knew Laura. We just met up once or twice. And I don't know this Raven fucker either.'

'When I asked you whether Laura had a boyfriend yesterday you hesitated. Did she have a boyfriend, Karen?'

'Is that why you're holding me, over a hesitation?'

'Did she have a boyfriend, Karen?'

'Jesus! How the fuck am I meant to know? She hardly spoke. Look, this is fuckin' ridiculous, can I go now?'

'No. I want you to tell me about Laura.'

'I've told you about Laura. She was just some fucked up kid like the rest of us. I want to go.'

'Are you afraid of him?' Jacobs asked. 'Is that why you won't talk about him? You're afraid that if you say who he is, he'll come after you?'

'Not another one,' Karen said looking down at the table again. 'I don't know who you're talking about. I've no idea who this Raven fucker is!'

'Okay, so you don't know him. Did you ever see Laura with any men? Perhaps just sitting and talking? Maybe somewhere round the city?'

Karen stayed silent.

'She's dead, Karen,' McEvoy said. 'Somebody killed her. He's going to carry on killing unless we stop him. Did you see her with a man at all?'

She stayed silent for a moment. 'What's it worth?'

'Worth?' McEvoy snapped.

Jacobs put a hand on his arm.

Karen tried to appear indifferent.

'Did you see her with a man, Karen?' Jacobs repeated.

McEvoy fished 20 euros from his pocket and placed it on the table.

Karen reached across and took it, rolling it into a thin straw.

'I saw her near to the Mater once talking to someone. She hardly ever talked to anyone. And she once bought him back to …' She stopped aware of what she was saying.

'She brought him back to your squat?' McEvoy pressed.

Karen stayed silent, her thumb plucking at the note.

'Karen?'

'Yeah,' she eventually muttered.

'And did you know him?'

'No.'

'But you'd recognise him again?'

'I doubt it. He was just some man.'

'How old was he?'

'I don't know, 30, 40.'

'And what was he wearing?'

'I don't remember, okay. He was just some bloke.'

'Why didn't you tell me this before?'

She shrugged. 'What difference would it make? I don't remember him.'

'For God's sake,' McEvoy mumbled. It was something and nothing. Laura the loner had spent some time with a man; possibly The Raven, possibly not. But that was it. There were over 600,000 men in the Greater Dublin Region. 'You must remember something about him, Karen,' he pressed.

She continued to stare at the table top, plucking at the note. 'Can I go now?'

'Well, it's a start,' Jacobs said, walking back up the stairs.

'It's a long shot,' McEvoy replied without enthusiasm, sniffing. 'She's not going to recognise him; she barely recognises her own face.'

'It's something to work with though,' Jacobs pressed. 'We need to try and reconstruct Laura's life. We know next to nothing about her. It might be that the man's not The Raven, but we need to find him to confirm that.'

'Come on, Kathy,' he replied, massaging his face, exhausted and moribund. 'We've had appeals out all week for information on Laura and we've got bugger all back. She wandered the streets like a ghost. Nobody knows anything about her.'

'Look, I know you're tired and pissed off, no doubt with good reason, but you're still on the case and we need to try and catch him before he kills again. I still think she's the key.'

McEvoy nodded, conceding the point. 'Right, okay, let's go and see Paul Roche,' he said flatly. 'Maybe we could organise a few people to go round the north inner city and show people her picture; see if it jogs anyone's memory.'

'That almost sounded like the Colm McEvoy I met on the beach in Donabate,' she teased.

'Yeah, well, as you say, we need to try and find out something about her.' He pushed open the door onto the corridor and let her pass through.

The patch of blue off to the west indicated that the light drizzle might stop shortly. McEvoy huddled under a small, black umbrella, hoping for a lucky break. He'd been standing near to the Eccles Street entrance to the Mater Hospital for the last 20 minutes. So far two dozen people had recognised Laura from the papers, but not from the streets, and about half of those also recognised him. He approached a young couple hurrying towards the entrance under a golf umbrella.

'Excuse me, An Garda Síochána, I'm wondering whether you might recognise this young woman?' He thrust out the card, blocking their path.

The woman took it, staring down at the four photos, all at least two years out of date. The man looked him over.

'You're the guy in charge of this Raven case,' the man stated. 'You really fucked up yesterday, didn't you? How many's he's killed now? Seven?'

'Do you recognise the woman in the pictures, Sir?' McEvoy prompted, pointing to the sheet.

'What?' The man looked down at the card.

'How about you, Madam?'

'I've seen her in the papers and on TV.'

'How about on the street? Maybe walking round here?'

'We don't live round here, we're just visiting.'

'So you haven't seen her then? Perhaps somewhere else in the city?'

'No.'

'How about you, Sir?'

'Nah. She the one who had a sword shoved through her head? Must have been a right fuckin' mess.'

'Peter!' the woman said, disapproving.

'I'll let you get on then. Thanks for your time.' McEvoy took the card back. He shouldn't be doing this. That is what uniforms are for. But then what else was he going to do? Roche was in charge now. He was a spare part. He blew his nose thinking that an anti-congestive mightn't be a bad investment.

A man stepped out of a taxi and approached the hospital entrance while his friend paid the driver. McEvoy stepped across to greet him.

'Excuse me, Sir, An Garda Síochána. Could you tell me whether you recognise this young woman?'

The man took the card and looked at it. 'Missing is she?' he said with a London accent.

'She was murdered earlier this week. She was living rough in the city and we're trying to find out something about her life. Have you seen her?'

'I'm not sure. I might have done,' the man hazarded.

'Where do you think you saw her?'

'I don't know, I can't remember.' The man's friend hovered off to one side, his hands jammed into his pockets.

'Was she with anybody?'

'Is this what's this is about, Superintendent?' the man asked, tipping the sheet towards his friend. 'You think she might have known her killer?'

The friend whipped a small camera from his pocket and started to take photos.

'What? What the ...' McEvoy snatched the card back and lurched towards the photographer, who backed away.

'Gary Bridges from The Sun,' said the man who'd been holding the card. 'Do you have any comment on your dismissal as lead investigator on The Raven murders? Do you accept that you've made major mistakes in the investigation?'

McEvoy turned away and started to hurry along Eccles Street, his anger rising, the journalist and photographer in tow. He should have recognised the toe-rag from the press conference at the Burlington.

'Do you have any idea as to who The Raven is? Do you care?' Bridges heckled. 'What have you got to say to the victim's families?'

McEvoy stopped and turned, the journalist almost colliding with him.

'If you don't back off,' McEvoy snapped, 'and leave me alone, I'm going to arrest you for obstructing a police investigation.'

'We both know that's not going to stick,' Bridges countered. 'I'm just doing my job.'

'And so am I, now back off.' He set off again away from the hospital.

The journalist and photographer hit a high five and watched him go, broad grins on their faces.

McEvoy reached his car and slipped into the driver's seat, seething. No doubt the story and pictures would be all over the following day's papers. Bishop would go apoplectic and the chances of him making the end of the week would plummet dramatically. He'd be sent home on mandatory sick leave or some other ruse to keep him away from the investigation. He started the car, put it in gear and nosed out into the traffic. There was no point staying, once one vulture found you a whole flock would soon turn up to pick you over.

The Raven exited the taxi and walked tall into the terminal building. In eight hours' time he would be walking off a plane into a new country and sanctuary. He would then slip into the shadows and bide his time, wait for the opportune time to rise again.

The departures hall was a maelstrom of people moving at different speeds, with varying degrees of purpose. Scattered visibly amongst the throng were pairs of uniformed guards, their heads constantly swivelling, scanning the crowd. He headed for the transatlantic check-in area, threading his way through his fellow passengers, their haunted faces staring through him; a palpable tension in the air. His book might be complete but no one was sure if the killings were going to stop. Many of those around him probably felt they were managing to escape from his potential clutches.

He noticed two airport security guards heading straight for him. They seemed on edge, their hands clutching tightly the sub-machine guns hanging round their necks. He held his head high and continued on his path.

The security was much greater than he expected and he could feel his confidence slipping, evaluating the risks. He should get through okay; after all, they are not looking for him; they didn't know who they were looking for. They didn't have any positive leads. Did they? If they did they'd presently be all over him – probing, questioning, checking his story. But they were clueless.

Except for one conversation with the hapless, conceited guard on the day they found David Hennessey's body he doubted his name had arisen in the enquiry. There was no reason to think that it ever would except for Samantha's death. That was unfortunate, but necessary.

That said passing through the most security intense zone in the state, one that was on high alert, was probably not the wisest course of action; an unnecessary risk. And there was no need to go. There was no need to keep up the pretence of continuing an ordinary life. That life was coming to an end. Samantha's disappearance would see to that.

He would return to the apartment and in a couple of days resort to his contingency plan. He wasn't in a hurry. Samantha wouldn't be missed for a little while. Her family lived in Wales and she often worked at home, only occasionally heading into the department and the office she shared with two others. He could continue to enjoy the small luxuries he would be without for a while – television, newspapers, central heating, running water – and then he would vanish. And, for a brief moment, he would be the most famous person on the planet, his infamy living on for an age.

He headed for the exit and a taxi to take him back into the city.

The door to the meeting room opened and Jenny Flanagan and her team emerged. McEvoy nodded at them, pushed himself up off the corridor wall, and put his head round the door they'd exited.

Kathy Jacobs was standing to one side waiting, Paul Roche was scribbling on a pad.

'Can I have a quick word, Paul?' McEvoy asked, interrupting.

'What? Yes, yes, come in. These meetings are taking a long time.' He glanced up at the clock – ten past two. 'Half the day gone already and I'm going to have to go through them all again tomorrow. I've barely scratched the surface. What can I do for you?'

McEvoy glanced at Kathy Jacobs, uncomfortable with her presence, and back at Roche. 'I was wondering, if it's okay by you, whether it's alright to head off. My lot are out on the streets – I've tried joining them but I get recognised every two minutes and it's counter-productive. I just deflect attention from ...' he tailed off, feeling embarrassed. He started again. 'I'd like, if there's nothing else you want me to do, to go round the murder sites again now that they're free of people. I thought revisiting them might spark some fresh insight, maybe I'd spot something we missed before,' he tailed off again, feeling like an idiot, afraid it sounded as it was – a lame excuse to get away and spend some time on his own.

'Absolutely,' Roche replied. 'If you think it'll be of use, go ahead. It's still your case, Colm.'

'We both know that's not ...' McEvoy trailed off again. 'Thanks. I'll have my mobile on if you need me.'

'Good, as I might have a few questions for you.' Roche tapped his note pad.

'It's a stringy vest?' McEvoy asked, suggesting the investigation was full of holes.

'No more than any other. So far, I'd have done everything pretty much the same way. There are lots of things to follow up on, loose ends, calls from the public, the usual stuff. It's probably going to take months to work through them all.'

'Right, well, I'll leave you to it then. I'll call you if I spot anything.' McEvoy exited the meeting room heading for the stairs, wanting to leave as soon as possible.

He'd just started the engine when Kathy Jacobs burst through the door into the car park, glancing round trying to spot him. He rolled his eyes and looked up at the car's roof. He knew what was coming. He looked back down and watched her approach, her red scarf swinging across the front of her coat.

She opened the passenger door and leaned her head in. 'Is it okay if I join you, Colm? It would be useful for me to see where he killed.'

'Yeah, sure, whatever.' He waved her in.

The Glencree Peace and Reconciliation Centre was quiet, it's next set of guests not due to arrive until the following day. McEvoy was standing outside of the room Laura Schmidt was killed in, looking down the Glencree valley, the sides covered in cloud, visibility restricted by drizzle. Behind him Kathy Jacobs crouch-walked under the tape that still barred entry to the room back into the corridor.

'This place feels haunted,' she observed.

'Probably is,' he replied flatly. 'Tens of children probably died up here when it was a reform school; bullied and beaten and frozen to death.'

She stood next to him and followed his gaze down the valley. 'Poor mites,' she said eventually.

He turned and pulled the bedroom door to, the image of Laura, laid out naked on the bed, the sword slotted through her mouth, still fresh in his mind.

'I thought coming here might help,' he said absently, rubbing at his nose, trying to stop the steady trickle of the cold he'd developed.

'Maybe it will,' Jacobs offered.

'All it's done is made me feel worse. Brought back memories I'd sooner forget.' He lent forward against the windowsill and tried to gather himself.

'Perhaps we should go?'

He nodded in agreement, unable to shake free the image of Laura, and pushed himself back up straight. 'Do you want to look at the German cemetery,' he offered, heading for the fire door, 'where we found the cards?'

'If it's okay with you. I can go on my own or come back another time if you prefer.'

'No, no. We're here now.' He held open the door and let her through, following her down the stairs.

They exited the old barracks, popped up a couple of umbrellas, and headed up the laneway onto the narrow road and the 50 metres to the gate of the cemetery. The place was silent except for the cawing of a couple of crows.

McEvoy hung back at the small shelter puffing on his plastic cigarette and Jacobs wandered around the beds of heather staring down at the names of the dead. After a couple of minutes she rejoined him and they left.

McEvoy followed Jacobs along the path towards the covered crucifix, pulling his plastic substitute from a pocket, jamming it between his lips. She was staring up at it from under her red umbrella when he caught her up.

'The techies say he was hit around here,' he pointed to a spot a bit beyond the crucifix, 'then dragged in under these trees here, through onto the path and down to the cemetery.'

She nodded and set off under the yew trees towards the cemetery, McEvoy trailing after her.

'From one place of ghosts to another,' she muttered.

'What?' McEvoy said, lost in thought.

'I said, from one place of ghosts to another. This place gives me the creeps.'

'You and me both,' McEvoy replied, knowing that he was killing time and starting to feel sorry for himself.

She paused to stare at the spot David Hennessey had been found and then hurried through into the open skies of the cemetery.

From behind her McEvoy said, 'Do you think there was any significance in the blue paint?'

'No,' she said, studying the names on the crosses nearest to the entrance. 'I think that's designed to throw you and generate a bit of hype and notoriety. There's no consistent pattern or theme and they peter out towards the end of the sequence. There's the sword, the paint, the toes, the crow shrine and then it just stops. Nothing for the last three victims or at Oughterard. It's like he got bored, or couldn't be bothered. He had less time for each killing, but he could have prepared something that he just had to leave.'

McEvoy nodded, agreeing with her assessment, thinking he would be better off just leaving the case to Roche; of retiring disgracefully to some country backwater. He sucked on his plastic stick and tried to ignore his craving.

Garda tape was still stretched across the driveway, blocking access. The house already had the look of a long abandoned property, the smoke gone, the ash wet and stuck to the earth.

McEvoy stopped the car, its bonnet half under the tape. He stepped out and retrieved his umbrella from behind his seat. He was feeling exhausted again, a faint headache starting to form above his eyes.

He wiped at his nose and glanced at his watch – just gone 5.30. It was almost 24 hours since the final murder. The Raven was probably sitting at home with his family laughing quietly to himself, self-congratulating his own brilliance and police ineptitude. The longer the investigation dragged on, the less likely a lead would appear.

Jacobs was already under the tape and walking towards the house, trying to place herself in The Raven's shoes. McEvoy followed her, joining her at the window to the front room, broken glass under foot.

'He died on the sofa by the door,' McEvoy said. 'He was hit on the side of the head, probably with a hammer, and knocked unconscious. He then set fire to the house, burning him alive.'

'Jesus.' She stepped away, heading for the corner of the bungalow.

McEvoy's phone rang. He answered it as she disappeared from view. 'McEvoy.'

'Sir, it's Hannah Fallon,' she said excitedly. 'We have a second match. A small hair from Glencree with one from Rathmoylan. It was in the bottom of one of candle holders at the little shrine he'd built. I'd say they're eyelashes or eyebrows.'

'And any match with the database?' McEvoy said, looking round, slightly spooked that one of the hairs had been found where he was now visiting.

'Not yet. We're also going to check with the UK database and other agencies. He has to be him though, the house at Rathmoylan was hardly well visited. If he's pulled in for anything else and tested we'll have him.'

'Have you spoken to Superintendent Roche?'

'Yes. He told me to ring you. He said you'd want to know.'

'He was right. Look, thanks, Hannah. Excellent work.'

'We'll get the bastard yet.'

'Hopefully. Thanks for ringing.'

Kathy Jacobs appeared at the far end of the bungalow having completed a loop. 'Must have been pretty lonely living out here on your own, especially if you were pretty much immobile.'

'People came and visited him. It was probably no worse than being stuck in a house on an estate. Come on, let's get away from here.'

The rain hadn't let up all afternoon, in fact it had become heavier, the wind rising, the droplets coming in waves. Their umbrellas flexed and twisted, struggling to remain in shape. They were standing on the tarmac path a couple of metres from where Grainne Malone had her legs cut from under her before being dragged away and strangled. Several bunches of flowers were grouped at the base of a tree trunk.

'He hid the toes all round the park,' McEvoy said, pointing with his plastic substitute. 'If you linked them all together on a map they formed the shape of a raven, with this place the eye. I don't think there's much point going to them all, we're just going to get wet.'

'It's pretty bleak here,' Jacobs observed. 'We're in the city, but not really. We could be back up the mountains.'

'There's usually a lot more people around – running, cycling, taking the dog for a walk.'

Jacobs stepped forward, bending down to read the messages. 'She was pregnant, wasn't she?'

'Very early stages according to Elaine Jones. I'm not sure she knew, or if she did she hadn't yet told her husband.'

'It was her husband's baby?'

'What d'you mean?'

'Well, the husband was, you know, the father to be,' she said awkwardly.

'You think it might have been The Raven's?' he said incredulously. 'She was having an affair?'

'I don't know.' She shrugged. 'I was just asking, that's all. He seemingly knew Laura, I'm wondering if he knew Grainne Malone? Four of the victims have direct links with Dermot Brady, three of the first four. Did the other victims have links to the murderer, but not Brady?'

'It was the sites that were linked to Brady, not simply the victims,' McEvoy countered, tiredness in his voice. 'It would be a hell of a coincidence for the murderer's own victims to share Brady's sites.'

'True. I was just thinking aloud, that's all.'

'I'll drop you off at The White Horse if it's open or run you to your hotel if it isn't. I'm heading home, I'm exhausted.'

'Are you okay?'

'Yeah, I'm fine,' he said flatly. 'The last week's catching up on me, that's all. I've had damn all sleep and it's been an emotional roller coaster. I feel like I've been pulled through a mangle slowly. This cold isn't helping. I feel as if someone has stuffed my head with cotton wool.'

'Well, if you need someone to talk to just call.'

'Yeah, I will,' he replied, trying to read her face, undecided whether it was signalling earnestness or invitation.

The road shimmered orange and a bus lumbered past the parked car sending up a spray of water from a pothole. The car smelt of damp clothes and the lingering of scent of Jacobs' perfume. McEvoy tipped back his head and closed his eyes. If he wasn't careful he'd fall asleep there and then. He let his chin hit his chest and pulled up Paul Roche's number on his mobile phone.

'Roche.'

'Paul, it's Colm. I'm just checking in, well checking out actually. I've just arrived home, I'm too exhausted to keep going for now. How're you getting on?'

'Slowly. I've now met with all the teams and I'm working my way through case notes. I'll probably need to go through a few things with you tomorrow.'

'No bother. What time do you want to meet?'

'I'm not sure, I'll let you know. I've got to meet Tony Bishop and the AC tomorrow morning to give them an update. They're starting to sound desperate.'

'Yeah, sorry about that. You're the replacement captain on the Titanic, flown in after I've hit the iceberg. They see themselves as major shareholders in White Star Line.'

'That's rubbish and you know it. They're the captains, were down in the boiler house trying to bail water and get the damn thing to limp to shore. Whatever. He hasn't left us a whole lot to go on, has he?'

'Well, as he would say, he wrote the book.'

'Look, feck the book,' Roche said aggressively. 'Sorry, that came out wrong.'

'It doesn't matter. I'll see you tomorrow.' McEvoy ended the call and levered himself out of the car.

He slotted the key in the front door and entered the warmth of the house. Gemma was first out of the living room, launching herself up onto his chest. He clutched her with one arm, quickly swapping to two. His mother placed her head round the door.

'You okay, Colm?'

'Yeah, I'm fine. I've had better days, I've had worse.'

'You're dinner's in the oven. Chicken casserole.'

He entered the living room. Sheila, Des, Caroline and his father were watching *Sky News*. Tony Bishop, his face flushed red and frowning concern, was discussing progress on the case.

'Either he goes, or I go,' McEvoy said, letting Gemma down, rubbing his nose with the back of his hand.

Caroline zapped the television off. 'That's pretty much what he seems to be saying as well,' she observed.

Chapter Eight

Monday, April 21ˢᵗ

His hand scrabbled round on the bedside locker trying to find his mobile phone. 'Yeah?' said half asleep through a dry mouth, his nose blocked, head full marshmallows.

'Have you seen the papers?' Bishop said angrily.

'What?'

'I said, have you seen the papers?'

He didn't have the energy to push himself up. 'No.'

'I told you to stay away from the feckin' press. And what do I find this morning? A picture of you in The Sun with the by-line, "TOP COP SEARCHES FOR MYSTERY MAN." What the hell were you doing wandering the streets with photofits?'

'I was … I was trying to follow-up on a lead,' McEvoy replied lamely, unable to gather any enthusiasm to rebut Bishop.

'That's what the grunts are for. You're off this case as of now, d'you hear? You've become too much of a feckin' liability. I'm putting you on mandatory sick leave until further notice. If anyone asks, you're suffering from stress-related illnesses. My suggestion is you keep your head down and your mouth shut.'

McEvoy stayed silent, thinking through Bishop's orders. Was it worth countering with his threat from the other night – that he'd do precisely the opposite of keeping quiet, or would it be better to lie low and come back into the rotation in a couple of weeks, see how things developed.

'Colm?' Bishop demanded.

'Yeah, fine, whatever.' He ended the call and dropped the phone on the sheet between a pillow and the quilt. 6.32 – at least he could lie in now. Lie in all day. If yesterday had demonstrated anything, it was that the investigation was bigger than him and his supposed leadership; it would carry on and he'd barely be missed. He pulled the bedding closer and tried to remember what being human felt like. His head starting to throb.

The phone startled him, jolting him awake again. 'Yeah?' he said yawning.

'Colm, it's Paul. I've just had a call from Tony Bishop. He was pretty pissed off with the pair of us – you for going out running questionnaires and me for letting you. He said he'd spoken to you and put you on mandatory sick leave. We had a brief exchange about that and he's now reversed his decision. He wanted me to let you know.'

'He's reversed his decision?' He could feel the sneeze starting to form, his face readying itself.

'So I'll see you later on this morning as planned, okay?'

McEvoy turned away from the phone and sneezed loudly.

'Dad!' Gemma moaned between the bed and the wardrobe. 'Not at me. I don't want your lurgy!'

'Sorry,' McEvoy said, searching for a box of tissues. 'Paul?'

'Maybe you should be on sick leave?'

'It's just a feckin' cold. Are you sure you still want me hanging round?' He blew his nose. 'This is the perfect chance for you to offload. There's no point us both falling out of favour.'

'What are they going to do? I'm retiring in a year's time. Feck them. I want you working this case. I'll see you later on.'

McEvoy stared out of the window, ignoring the reports in front of him. It was going to start raining again shortly. The sky had darkened from the west and a breeze was picking up signalling a new front arriving. He wanted to head off to the canteen but was worried about how he'd be received, who he might bump into on the corridor.

He needed to find something else to do, something that would keep him out of the building, but off the street. The only things he could think of was re-visiting Donabate beach or taking the rest of the day off ill. As he puffed on his plastic cigarette his mobile phone rang.

'McEvoy.'

'It's John Joyce. We've got a witness,' he said excitedly. 'A young woman who recognised Laura and saw her talking to someone she knows. She's waiting for us at Drumcondra Station. I'm on my way there now.'

'She say who it was?' McEvoy asked, anticipation building inside of him.

'One of her lecturers. She's a student out at Maynooth University. I don't have a name yet. I'll ring you as soon as I get there.'

'Don't bother, I'm on my way. I'll see you in five minutes.' He started to run for his car.

A Citroën was parked up on the pavement under the railway bridge that crossed Drumcondra Road. Dr John was sat in the driver's seat, a young woman on the passenger side. A few feet away, near to the train station entrance, a guard was chatting to one of the woman's friends. McEvoy opened the back door and climbed in.

'So?' he asked.

'This is Aoife Ni Cairealláin,' Dr John said, turning in his seat, 'she's studying Irish and politics in Maynooth. This is Detective Superintendent Colm McEvoy.'

'Hi,' she said quietly, looking back at him, apprehension in her eyes. She looked no more than 18 or 19 with long, dyed blonde hair pulled into a pony tail, a pale oval face, dabs of foundation cream covering a couple of spots on her chin and cheeks.

'Hi, Aoife. DS Joyce tells me you recognise the girl in the photos and also saw her with someone you know?'

She nodded. 'I used to see her sometimes, y'know, just wandering about or sitting on steps, like. She looked kind of lonely, y'know. I felt bad for her, but, well ...' she trailed off.

'There's nothing you could have done, Aoife. She didn't want any help. Who did you see her talking to?'

'It was one of my lecturers, Dr Andrew McCormack. At least I think it was him. He was wearing a baseball cap, but I thought it was him.'

'How positive are you that it was Dr McCormack?' McEvoy asked, his heart pounding in his chest, wanting to leave the car and raise the alert.

'I ... I don't know,' she replied hesitantly, 'I mean, I thought it was him, y'know. I was on the other side of the street, so, I don't know. I see him round there all the time.'

'Round where?'

'Phibsborough Road.'

'How come you never came forward with this information before?' McEvoy said, thinking that Phibsborough Road was only a stone's throw away from the Mater Hospital.

'I didn't ... I don't really watch the news or read the papers, y'know. It's the first time I've seen her pictures, y'know, really seen them. I didn't think ...' she tailed off. 'I didn't recognise her in three of the photos,' she tried to explain, 'just one of them. Am I in trouble?'

'No, no,' McEvoy tried to reassure, shaking his head at her ostrich-like approach to life.

'Anything grizzly I switch channel,' she continued to reason, 'it gives me nightmares. I know that bad stuff happens, I just don't want to see it, y'know what I mean? If I don't see it, like, I don't have to think about it. She's one of the murder victim's isn't she? The Raven or whatever he's called?'

'Yes. She was the first victim.'

'And Dr McCormack's The Raven?' she said, the connection finally clunking into place.

'We don't know yet,' McEvoy said evenly. 'That's something we're going to have to check out. While we do that we're going to need you to be formally interviewed and to make a full witness statement. It should only take a couple of hours.'

'But what about university?' she asked absently.

'It'll still be there this afternoon or tomorrow. How about your friend? Does she know who you thought you saw Laura with?'

'She was there when I told the guard.'

'Okay, well she'll have to come with you as well then. You haven't made any phone calls or spoken to anyone about this, have you?'

'No. Only to you and the guard over there.'

'Good, because I don't want this information circulated. It's to be kept between us until we've spoken to Dr McCormack. If he is The Raven, and there's nothing to say he is, I don't want him to run away before we've had a chance to talk to him. If he does get away, he'll kill again. I've no doubt about that.'

'I, er, yes, okay,' she stuttered. What colour there was in her face had drained away.

'Good. You've done the right thing talking to us, Aoife. I'll just get your friend. If you want, ring your parents, let them know where you are, but do not say anything about Dr McCormack. Can you explain all that to her friend?' he said to Dr John.

'Yeah, no bother.'

McEvoy stepped out of the car, a new energy coursing through him. This was the lead they'd been waiting for, he was sure of it. There had been little reason for McCormack to have surfaced as suspect. After all, he was writing a book on how to

314

commit the perfect murder. If he had been following all of his rules, then he would not have cropped up at all. The victims would have been random selections who simply vanished, their bodies never discovered. He called up Roche's number.

'Colm, I'm in a meeting, is this urgent?'

'We have a name. Dr Andrew McCormack from Maynooth University. We have a witness who saw him talking to Laura Schmidt. He's based in the same department that David Hennessey worked in.'

'Jesus!'

'My gut says it's him, Paul. It all fits together. He knew Brady through Hennessey.'

'You'd better get back here, pronto. We need to do this properly; the last thing we need is for him to slip away again. I'll talk to Bishop.'

'You'll be better off keeping him out of this.'

'I agree, but we haven't a choice.'

'I'll be back there in ten minutes. We need to find out if he's come up before in the investigation.'

'I'll get Padraig O'Keeffe on it now. I'll also see if he's got previous form. I'll see you shortly.'

McEvoy ran to the station door, his oversized suit jacket flapping, and took the steps inside two at a time. He arrived at the incident room half out of breath, gulping down air. The room was a hive of activity but Paul Roche looked up when he entered and started to cross the floor to him.

'Let's find somewhere quiet,' Roche said, re-opening the door, letting McEvoy pass through. 'He's no previous form. He was interviewed by Charlie Deegan the day after Hennessey's murder.'

'I should have known,' McEvoy muttered, trailing after Roche. 'For feck's sake!'

'It gets worse. His interview notes were the absolute minimum. According to Simon Grainger he only bothers to write them up in full if he thinks it's going to be worth the effort. In other words, he only does it if he thinks the person's a suspect.'

'So we've no interview notes!' McEvoy said exasperated.

'No, but before you blow your lid, I've spoken to Deegan to see if he remembers him. He said McCormack was a pretentious prick, which is nicer than what he said about you. He said, he was flippant, arrogant, and up his own arse. A typical academic as far as he was concerned.'

'You sure he wasn't looking in a mirror?'

'His description seems to match Kathy Jacobs' profile,' Roche continued, ignoring McEvoy's bile.

'We could have nailed this bastard earlier in the week and saved the lives of several people. Feckin' Deegan. Unbelievable.'

'Maybe, maybe not,' Roche replied wistfully. 'We've interviewed hundreds of people in the last few days, Colm. Who knows how many of them have told us a bunch of lies? Probably a couple of dozen and not all of them can be The Raven. It might have taken us months to work through them all, double checking them.'

McEvoy stayed silent and scratched at his head, fuming inside.

'And it might not be him. Just because he knows David Hennessey and he might have been seen with Laura Schmidt does not mean he committed the murders.'

'He committed them!' McEvoy snapped. 'We both know he did. He's been leading us on a merry dance all week. He must be grinning like a Cheshire cat. He knows the investigation's barely touched him. He probably think's he's home free.'

'If he'd followed all of his rules, he would be,' Roche said sighing. 'And even if it was him, he's probably got a bunch of cast iron alibis.'

'Forensics,' McEvoy stated. 'We have the matching hairs from Glencree and Rathmoylan.'

There was a knock at the door.

'Yes?' Roche said loudly.

Simon Grainger pushed it open, looking slightly ashamed, and handed a couple of sheets of paper to Roche. 'A bit of background information on him from his website,' he said before exiting.

Roche read out selected highlights. 'Undergraduate degree from Trinity in politics and sociology, masters in political science from Berkeley, and PhD from Harvard on the Politics of the Welfare State in Ireland, 1922-1992. He then worked as a postdoctoral research fellow at Cambridge University before taking up the lectureship in politics at the National University of Ireland, Maynooth a couple of years ago. Specialises in the political science of the welfare state and the Catholic Church and the political system in Ireland. He's authored one book, edited two others and has published a bunch of articles. You want a look?' He held out the sheets.

McEvoy took them and studied McCormack's photo. He looked remarkably normal – in his early to mid thirties wearing a Red Sox cap and smiling into the camera. There was no hint of any danger or malice, nothing to suggest he might commit a series of heinous crimes. McEvoy scanned down his potted academic history. 'How do you want to do this?' he asked, keen to get on with things.

'Chances are he's either fled or he's at work or home. We send teams to both of them and do a simultaneous raid. Inner and outer cordons at both. If he's not there, then God knows where he is and I think we just put out a nationwide appeal for help.'

'You don't want to wait until he shows back up again?'

'If he's gone, he's probably long gone, and we're not going to be able to sit on the name for very long. There's a good chance that one of our lot has already leaked it for a nice fee from one of the papers or TV stations. Once it's out it'll spread like wildfire. The best thing to do will be to release his name and photo and start a manhunt.'

McEvoy nodded in agreement.

'I'll take his house – he lives in Lucan – you take the university,' Roche instructed. 'Put people at all the exits and then go to his department. Make sure you've got plenty of backup, but when you go in act decisively, we don't want him to take a hostage or kill himself. I want this to end cleanly and to go to trial.'

It had started to drizzle again as they passed through the main gates to Maynooth University. McEvoy parked the car under a large chestnut tree next to the wooden hut just inside the gates.

'I'll be back in a minute,' he said to Barney Plunkett and Kathy Jacobs exiting the car, the confidence of an hour ago having started to drain away, his mind tumbling over the rationale of his initial certainty, trying to decide whether he was guilty of grasping at a nettle too quickly and firmly.

Martin Cleary and Tom Meaney were waiting for him in the hut, the heat turned up high, designed to take the chill and damp off of bodies that had been walking around the campus grounds.

'Martin, Tom, thanks for meeting me,' McEvoy said, extending a hand, feeling awkward.

'So, what's this about, Colm?' Cleary asked with a hint of a smile.

'We think we might have identified The Raven. We have a witness who's positively ID'd him. He's a lecturer in the university. He's been interviewed before, so we're going to take the softly, softly approach initially. Routine investigation. We'll do it while classes are on so there are less people around.'

'Who is it?' Cleary asked. 'Let me guess, someone from Hennessey's department?'

'How'd you know that?' McEvoy asked suspiciously, wiping at his nose.

'Come on, Colm, if I told you it was someone at the university that killed Hennessey, where would you start? With people who knew him well. I'm beginning to wonder if they might have been desperate to give you my old job.' It was said as a joke, but it came out flat.

'Maybe they were,' McEvoy said, taking the comment at face value. 'Jesus. We've ballsed this up from the start. The lecturer's name is Dr Andrew McCormack. That ring any bells?'

'Young chap, sideburns, bit abrasive, but friendly enough,' Cleary said. 'I wouldn't have him pegged for the murders, but then again most murderers appear relatively normal until you scratch away at the surface.'

'What do you want us to do?' Meaney asked.

'Nothing. I just wanted to let you know what's happening. This might be a wild goose chase or it might be the end game. Hopefully, it will go smoothly, but if it doesn't then we'll probably need your help.'

'I'm coming with you to the arts building,' Cleary stated. 'I know this place like the back of my hand. And I know the staff in there; it'll just look I'm showing you to his office.'

'I'm not sure that's a good idea,' McEvoy said.

'It wasn't a request, Colm. I'm not having a cock-up like O'Connell Street happening here while I'm on duty.'

They swapped anxious glances then set off towards a long, single-storey building, climbing five steps, entering through a set of automatic doors into an open foyer, the doors to two lecture theatres in front of them. They veered to the right heading down a narrow corridor along which the politics department extended. Skipping the secretary's office they headed straight for McCormack's door, Cleary and Plunkett taking up positions either side.

McEvoy's chest felt it had been wrapped in barbed wire slowly being tightened. He knocked twice and tried the handle. It was locked. He knocked again.

'Shit!' he hissed. 'He's not here.'

'He might be teaching,' Cleary said. 'The secretary will have a timetable, she'll be able to tell us where he is.' He looked at his watch. 'We should be able to get to him before he leaves the lecture theatre.'

They backtracked to the first office on the corridor.

McEvoy knocked and pushed the door open, feeling heavy limbed and light-headed, his heart pounding in his chest.

The woman at the desk looked over at him, a look of mild annoyance on her face. 'Yes?'

'Detective Superintendent Colm McEvoy.' He stepped into the room. 'I wonder if you could help me?'

'Is this about David? I still can't get over the fact that he's been murdered.' She looked like she was going to cry. 'Terrible. Absolutely terrible.'

'Actually, I was wondering if Andrew McCormack was in today? I wanted to follow up on something with him.'

He followed her gaze right, Martin Cleary having followed McEvoy in.

She looked back at him. 'Andrew? No. No, he's not. He's not in all week. He's at a conference in the US. Boston, I think.'

'In the US?' McEvoy repeated, feeling sick, his mind racing.

'Yes, he was flying there at the weekend. Some big political science conference. He goes every year. He won't be back until next Wednesday. Is it urgent?'

'What? No. I mean, yes. Do you have any of his travel details? The flight bookings, the conference?'

'No,' she said anxiously, 'he does all of that himself. I can ask some of the other staff, see if they know,' she offered. 'Professor Phelan will probably know.'

'I'll ask him myself, if that's okay,' McEvoy said, trying to control information flow. 'Is he in?'

'She,' the secretary correct. 'Professor Margaret Phelan. She's in next door. She's just getting ready for a lecture, she's teaching at twelve.'

'I'll talk to her now, thanks for your help.'

'Just so you know, we'll probably let ourselves into Dr McCormack's office and have a quick look around, okay,' Cleary said.

'Is … is everything, okay? Nothing's happened to him has it?'

'No, no, everything's fine,' McEvoy said, trying to take control of the situation again. 'We'll let you know when we've finished in his office. Thanks for your time.' He headed out of the door, followed by Cleary.

'Jesus Christ!' he muttered. 'He's left the feckin' country.' He took two paces down the corridor and knocked on Margaret Phelan's door.

'Yes, hello?'

He entered the office.

An elegantly dressed woman in her mid-to-late fifties was standing behind a desk, leaning down to peer at a flat-screen monitor. She glanced over at him. 'What can I do for you? This will have to be quick as I need to get over to the other campus.'

'Detective Superintendent McEvoy. I was hoping to be able to speak to Andrew McCormack; the secretary said he was at a conference in the US. You don't happen to know which do you?'

'Is he okay?' she said, straightening up, brushing her shoulder-length, grey hair off her face.

'I've no idea, but I need to track him down so I can follow up on something.'

'Is this about David? It was disgraceful what happened to him,' she said without sincerity, pulling a coy smile, holding his gaze. 'It was a terrible shock.'

He nodded and shifted his gait, uncomfortable with her demeanor. 'Do you know which conference he was going to?'

'The New England Political Science Association's Annual Meeting in Providence, Rhode Island. He's on the Association's committee. He goes every year – end of April, early May.'

'Okay, thanks. One other thing. Was Dr McCormack promoted recently?'

'Promoted? No.' She stuffed something into her bag, hoisted it up on her shoulder and rounded the desk. 'He applied for senior lecturer, but didn't make it. He's a high flyer but it's a little early. Next year or the year after. A couple more books and a bit of research money and two or three years after that he should make professor. Fast in our system.'

'Right. Right, okay. You've been most helpful.'

'No problem. Well, if you'll excuse me, Superintendent, I have to run.' She opened the door and held it open for him to pass through. She closed it behind her and headed off, ignoring Cleary and Plunkett.

They watched her go, her hips swinging on low heels.

'Phew,' Plunkett said waving the air, 'she must have had a bath in that perfume.'

'What perfume?' McEvoy asked.

'Just be thankful you've got that cold. Where he is?'

'Providence, Rhode Island.'

'Let's take a look at his office,' Cleary said, pulling a huge bunch of keys from his jacket pocket heading towards McCormack's room.

The office was neat and tidy, the desk clear. Several houseplants were arranged along a window ledge that ran the width of the room.

Cleary sat at the desk and played with the locked drawers, trying to tease them open. 'I'll talk to one of the lads, see if he has anything to get these open with,' he said heading for the door. 'Also these.' He slapped the top of the filing cabinet nearest the door.

McEvoy worked his way round the room slowly, trying to get a measure of the man. Nothing in particular leapt out at him. He pulled his mobile from his pocket.

'Roche.'

'It's Colm,' he said, downbeat. 'He's not here. According to his head of department he's in Providence, Rhode Island. She said he left at the weekend. If he went before Saturday evening then he's in the clear.'

'Shit! I bet he flew out yesterday – probably flew Aer Lingus direct to Boston. I'll get someone to check with the airports. I'll also talk to Bishop. If he's in the US then we'll need to alert the authorities there.'

McEvoy let out a long breath. 'Jesus, what a mess. I'll find out whether he turned up for this conference or not. He might be carrying on as normal, seeing whether he's got away with it.'

'Good idea. His house looks clean by the way. Nothing obvious linked to any of the victims. I've just let the crime scene people in. It seems there are plenty of samples for DNA and they're making that a priority. We should know whether it matches the samples from Glencree and Rathmoylan by late this afternoon. And it looks like he lived alone – only men's clothes in the wardrobes and a single toothbrush in the bathroom.'

'We also need someone to talk to Dermot Brady,' McEvoy suggested, 'see if he knows McCormack and whether he knows of any link between him and Laura Schmidt.'

'I'll find someone to do that. Right, I'll let you get on with it then. I'll get speak to you soon as I hear anything.'

'Thanks.' McEvoy slipped the phone back into his pocket and massaged his temples.

If McCormack was The Raven then he had taken flight. He'd spent several years studying in the U.S. so it was familiar territory. There were thousands of illegal Irish there, plus God knows how many millions from other countries. If they could operate below the radar of the authorities then so could McCormack. He'd slip into the underworld, buy himself a new identity, and start a new life. And even if they did catch him, there would be the rigmarole of extradition. It might be years before he saw an

Irish court, especially if he had dual citizenship, which was a strong possibility.

Barney Plunkett knocked on the door and entered along with Kathy Jacobs.

McEvoy blew his nose and glanced over at them with sadness in his eyes. 'I think the bastard might have got clean away. While we were messing about going round the various murder sites he was sat on a plane to Boston.' He scratched at his head. 'Barney, I need you to find out if McCormack actually turned up at that feckin' conference. The secretary has the details.'

'I'm on it.' Plunkett hurried from the room.

'You were right,' McEvoy said to Jacobs. 'He was a high flyer and he'd been turned down for promotion. According to the head of department he'd have been promoted next year or the year after. Might have gone up to professor a couple of years after that.'

'He was impatient. He was probably angry that someone like Hennessey, someone less brilliant than him, got promoted instead.'

'So he decides to kill him?'

'Some people have difficulty judging perceived crimes and their appropriate punishment,' Jacobs explained. 'McCormack blamed Hennessey rather than the promotion panel, and he felt the crime demanded the ultimate punishment. He's developed some kind of pronounced psychosis. He's living in a different reality to you and me.'

'Jesus.' McEvoy turned and stared out of the window, his mind unable to pull coherent thoughts together.

Kathy Jacobs slipped in behind the desk and sat down. 'Is it okay if I take a look at this?' she said, pointing at McCormack's computer.

A young man in an Arctic Monkeys t-shirt and ripped jeans stood up and moved out of the way. 'I've logged on as the administrator. Once you've finished, just shut it down or give me a call.' He wrote a four-digit number on a sticky note and placed it on the desk.

'Thanks,' McEvoy said absently, Jacobs sliding into the vacated seat.

Jacobs glanced down the list of folders, McEvoy watching over her shoulder. 'Conferences', 'Current Books', 'Future', 'Grants', 'Old Books', 'Papers', 'Projects', 'References', 'Teaching', 'Website'.

She clicked on 'Current Books.' There were four folders in the new list, the third of which was entitled *The Rule Book.* She opened the folder. There were several files listed: Chapters 1 to 8, 'Card 1', 'Card 2', 'Oughterard', 'Phoenix Park', 'Addresses'.

She clicked on 'Chapter 1'. The Word program loaded and the first chapter of *The Rule Book* appeared.

'Well, that's any doubt dispelled,' she said quietly.

'Open Chapter 8,' McEvoy instructed. 'We never received a Chapter 8.'

She opened the chapter.

The Rules
Chapter Eight: Postscript

"Even experienced killers make mistakes."

ALWAYS FOLLOW ALL THE RULES

Laura or David or Samantha?
Until next time ...

'Jesus,' McEvoy muttered. 'Who the hell is Samantha?'

'I don't know. His partner?' Jacobs hazarded. 'Whoever it is, he knew he'd taken too much of a chance with Laura and David,' she said, stating the obvious. 'His first two rules were "choose a victim at random" and "have no prior interaction with them before the kill." He broke both of them. The first two murders were comfort kills – known quantities while he became more confident.'

'Plus he was leaving notes,' McEvoy observed, massaging his forehead. 'He thought he could outwit his own logic.'

'He nearly did. Except for Karen and the student who saw him with Laura we'd be none the wiser.'

'We'd have got him eventually,' McEvoy said without conviction. 'Something would have turned up.'

'Samantha probably,' said Jacobs sardonically. 'And you don't have him yet. You just know who he is.'

'I better ring Paul Roche.' McEvoy pulled his phone from his pocket. '

It was answered on the fifth ring. 'Roche.'

'It's Colm. We've managed to get onto his computer. There's a Chapter Eight there. It's a postscript. He lists three names – Laura, David and Samantha. We've no idea who Samantha is, but he knew he'd messed up – the US was his insurance policy.'

'He's not in the US,' Roche said. 'I was just about to ring you, the transport people have come back to me. He'd booked a return ticket to Boston, flying out yesterday at 11.45, only he didn't show up. There's no record of him flying anywhere else in the last two weeks from any airport in Ireland or the UK or leaving through any port.'

'He must have bottled it,' McEvoy said. 'He didn't like the idea of being on a plane for seven or eight hours not knowing if he'd be greeted by police at the other end. What did Bishop say?'

'He's about to announce a full-scale manhunt, the works. He doesn't care whether McCormack's innocent or guilty, he wants him apprehended. He's organising an emergency press conference for one o'clock.'

'Is that a good idea?' McEvoy said his determination fading. 'We'll lose any element of surprise.'

'Half the media will already know who we're looking for by now. They'll have been tipped off by God knows how many people. Besides, we've no idea where the hell he is. I've heard back from Brady as well,' Roche said, changing tack. 'He knows McCormack, but only met him once or twice. He never saw him with Laura. Look, I need to go. I'll be out there shortly, okay.'

McEvoy slipped the phone into his pocket and stared out of the window again, listening to the tapping of Jacobs' fingernails on the keyboard.

After a short while, he turned to face her. 'After the O'Connell Street murder he was last seen heading towards Phibsborough Road. That's where Aoife whatshername saw him with Laura. The squat Karen lives in is not far from there either. We need to find out if he has a place there,' he said, heading for the door, wanting to do something rather than hang around killing time. 'And we need to find out who the hell Samantha is.'

McEvoy turned back onto Phibsborough Road and started heading back towards the North Circular Road. He glanced at the clock – 1.09. 'This is hopeless,' he muttered, once again downbeat, knowing that they were driving round aimlessly, looking for a needle in a haystack. 'If he's got any sense, he'd be long gone.'

'Sense is something he probably hasn't got a lot of right now,' Jacobs replied, staring out at the pavement.

McEvoy snatched at the phone before it rang a second time. 'Yes?'

'It's Barney. I've finally found someone who knows who Samantha is. McCormack kept his is private life private. Her name is Samantha Evans. She's a postdoctoral researcher in Trinity. She lives in a new apartment block on Goldsmith's Road near to the Mater. I don't know the name of the apartment block or her apartment number, but I'm going to see if I can get a full address out of Trinity.'

'Okay, right. Call for backup will you, we'll meet them there.'

'Don't do anything stupid, Colm,' Plunkett warned.

'Just order the feckin' backup,' McEvoy said testily, ending the call. 'Where the hell's Goldsmith's Road,' he muttered, turning right onto the North Circular Road.

He'd become addicted to the news since leaving the airport. He had only left the apartment once to buy the daily newspapers. He'd barely left the sofa. He'd simply sat in front of the flat-screen television and stared at it hypnotically. The Raven and his killing spree was still the headline news – hours and hours of broadcast time had been devoted to analysing his work, speculating on his personality, his motivation, his state of mind, his identity. It was all just hot air and hokum.

The image swapped from a smarmy looking news reader to that of a dishevelled and exhausted McEvoy. The superintendent appeared as a ghost – ashen and hollow. Barely ten seconds into the report it was cut short and the news reader re-appeared looking harried.

'We've just received a statement issued by the Irish police,' he said in a clipped, English accent, looking down at his notes. 'They are seeking urgently to talk to Dr Andrew McCormack of the National University of Ireland, Maynooth.'

His picture from the university's website appeared in the top right of the screen.

'If anyone knows his present location or has seen him in the past two weeks they are to contact the An Garda Síochána immediately on their confidential hotline, 1800 666 111. Under no circumstances are members of the public to approach him. To repeat, An Garda Síochána, the Irish police, are seeking the whereabouts of …'

He slipped into the bedroom and hastily applied his disguise then dashed into the hallway and collected his pre-prepared bag. It was time to disappear; to slip into the shadows. It wouldn't take them long to link him to Sam and to head to the apartment. They might already be on their way. He should have left the country when he had the chance – it had been madness to stay in the apartment. He'd known that, but he'd been convinced he had all the time in the world – time for the media and police frenzy to die down a little; time to continue his old life.

He closed the door on his old life and headed for the stairwell. It must have been betrayal for them to find him so fast. It couldn't have been the prior connection to Laura or David – that would have taken them weeks to piece together, if they'd managed to piece it together at all, and they didn't yet know about Samantha. It had to have been Laura's drug-addled friend. It couldn't be anyone else. She must have been able to identify him some how – probably sold him out for the price of a quick fix.

He felt his fury starting to rise. Well she knew the consequences. She knew the price she would pay for such a betrayal; her betrayal of Laura. Laura, who willingly opened her mouth and swallowed the sword. Laura, who'd announced his book to the world.

At least now people now knew. Knew he was The Raven. Knew that if he'd followed all the rules he would still be anonymous. Knew and feared the genius that was Andrew McCormack. And while he lay low and bided his time they would continue to fear him, dreading the day he would decide to spread his wings again.

There was only one new apartment block on Goldsmith's Road. Two redbrick houses had been demolished from the row to make way for a new three-storey apartment block that stretched back along what had been sizeable gardens. McEvoy pulled to a stop on the road, double-parking, and stared across at the building, a metal frame climbing the outside, providing each apartment with a small balcony. A laneway to the side led to car parking spaces behind. The block appeared totally out of place. He pushed open his door.

'I thought we were waiting for backup,' Jacobs said.

'We are. I just want to make sure we've got the right place. Half the houses in this road have been split into apartments. Her name's Samantha Evans. I want to check the name plates, find out what apartment she's in.'

He clambered out and closed his door, crossing the road, heading for the front entrance, double glass doors leading into a small atrium.

Jacobs scrambled out and followed, wanting to try and rein McEvoy in and make sure he didn't do anything he'd regret later. She caught him up as the door was opened by a man in his fifties wearing a red baseball cap and black, leather jacket, carrying a rucksack on one shoulder. The man stood to one side and ushered them in.

'Are you sure this is a good idea, Colm? We should wait for backup.'

'I've already told you, we're waiting for backup,' McEvoy snapped. 'I just want to make sure we're in the right place.' He stood in front a row of metal letterboxes, each with a narrow slot, a lock just below, and traced along them. 'Here, Samantha Evans,' he said, sounding vindicated. 'Flat 3c.'

He paused as something clicked into place in his mind. He wheeled round staring back out through the front door at the empty space. 'Shit!' he spat. 'That was him, come on!' He bolted for the exit. 'He was wearing a Red Sox cap, had side-burns.'

As McEvoy made it out of the doors a dark blue Fiesta appeared from the side of the apartment, turning left onto the road without stopping, accelerating away.

'Fuck!'

As he reached his own car the Fiesta was turning left onto the North Circular Road. He was never going to catch it. By the time he'd reached the turning, the Fiesta could have headed in any number of directions. He slammed a flat hand against the car roof, pulling his mobile free with the other.

A marked garda car pulled in behind him. Two uniformed guards stepped out.

'You've just fuckin' missed him!' McEvoy snapped. 'He was driving a dark blue Fiesta, registration plate 01-D-52. I didn't catch the rest. Driver's wearing a red cap, black jacket and blue jeans. He's wearing a disguise; he look's like he's in his mid-fifties. He turned left at the top of the road. Call it in.'

The two guards looked at each other.

'Now, for fuck's sake!'

One of them ducked back in to the garda car and grabbed the radio mic.

McEvoy pulled up Roche's number on his mobile phone.

'Roche.'

'He was at Samantha Evans' apartment,' he said without introduction, heading back over to the apartment block to where Kathy Jacobs was waiting, the other guard trailing after him. 'He was leaving as we were arriving. He was wearing a disguise, like O'Connell Street. Only this time he made himself look like a man in his fifties. He was driving a dark blue Fiesta, I've called the details in. I'm going up to her apartment to take a look around.'

'Jesus Christ. If he's still in Dublin, then we'll get him, don't worry. I'm already on my way back in.'

'Look, I've got to go.' McEvoy slid the phone into a pocket and tugged at the door handle, but it was locked. There was a bank of buzzers to the left. He started to press them in turn.

'Hello?' said a crackled voice through a speaker.

'An Garda Síochána, open the door,' McEvoy demanded.

'Pardon?'

'I said open the fuckin' door! Now!'

There was a loud buzz and McEvoy shoved the door open and entered the small atrium.

'Take it easy, Colm,' Jacobs warned. 'You've gone all hyper again.'

He ignored her, bursting into a stairwell and taking the steps two at a time to the top floor. He crashed through the fire door, glanced left and right, and headed right, back toward the front of the building. Apartment 3c was the only door on the left. He knocked loudly, waited a couple of seconds and knocked again.

'Shit. Right, come on,' he said to the uniformed guard, 'we need to get this open.'

'Are you sure that's a good idea?' Jacobs asked.

He ignored her again. 'On the count of three, we slam the door. Okay?'

'Sir.'

'Right. One, two, three.' McEvoy and the guard launched their shoulders onto the door. It creaked but stayed firm. 'And again.'

This time the door gave way, the two of them stumbling into a short hallway, a small utility cupboard to the left, a tumble dryer stacked on top of a washing machine. The hall opened out into an open-plan living room, a dining area and compact kitchen at one end, a sofa and a chair at the other near to French windows that led out onto a small balcony overlooking the street. A flat-screen television was placed on the wall opposite the sofa, *Sky News* broadcasting into the room, the sound audible but turned down low. Andrew McCormack's web photo stared out from the screen.

'If we'd got here before Bishop's broadcast we'd have got him,' McEvoy said frustrated, knowing that he was more angry with himself than Bishop. He'd let McCormack exit straight past them; didn't recognise him or give chase. Both unforgivable.

'Well, the whole city's looking for him now,' Jacobs said.

McEvoy headed to the door between the kitchen and dining area. It led into a short hall. To the right was a small bedroom, a double bed, its covers thrown back, taking up the majority of space. A long sausage dog draft excluder ran along the bottom of the door to the left, jammed tight into the crack. He took hold of the handle.

'I don't think that's a good idea, Colm,' Jacobs said, sniffing, her face draining of colour.

He looked back at her concerned face, pulled a tight smile of apology, and pushed it open. Even with his blocked sinuses, he knew the room stank of death and decay. He raised his hand up to his nose and mouth and stepped into the white tiled bathroom.

The sink was clean, sunk into a counter, bottles and make-up neatly arranged around it. The seat on the toilet was down, a pale blue shower curtain pulled across the length of the bath. He took hold of the edge of the curtain, his insides knotting, knowing what he was about to find. He swallowed hard and tugged the curtain back.

Samantha Evan's slight body lay in the bath, her hands tied to the bath hands, her feet to the taps. Almost every inch of skin below her chin had been sliced with a razor blade; thousands of short and long cuts, criss-crossing her body. The bath, the curtain and tiled wall were covered in splashes of blood.

McEvoy reeled around and dry heaved into the sink, then again, the burning vomit rising up his throat and out. He was aware of Jacobs edging into the bathroom, her scarf pulled up over her face. 'Don't,' he managed to mutter before retching again.

'Jesus Christ,' he heard Jacobs mutter. 'The poor girl.'

He wiped at his face with a hand and turned the tap on, scooping up water to his mouth and chin, washing the sick away. He staggered back out to the living room, his shirt and tie stained wet.

'Call a crime scene team in,' he said to the uniformed guard. 'There's a woman in the bath. Almost certainly McCormack's girlfriend, Samantha Evans. I'd say she's been dead a couple of days.'

The guard left the room, glad to get away from the apartment.

Jacobs joined McEvoy, her face stained with tears. 'He enjoyed killing her. The other deaths might have been quick, but he took his time with her. She died slowly. Very slowly.'

'If there was ever the case for bringing back the death penalty, this is it,' McEvoy said, his stomach still weak. Everything was going horribly wrong. It was turning into O'Connell Street Mark II. He felt hypertense; he didn't know whether he wanted to collapse in a heap of tears and grief or rage and rip and kick the room to bits. Instead, he pulled his mobile from his pocket. It rang before he could use it.

'Hello?'

'It's Paul Roche. That witness you interviewed yesterday, the drug addict, Karen, she's just been killed in that squat of hers. Sounds like it's Andrew McCormack. He's also seriously injured a man. Knife attack.'

'Fuck!' McEvoy spat, heading for the door, signalling to Jacobs to follow him. 'We've just found his girlfriend's body in her apartment. She died of a thousand cuts. Been dead a few days.'

'Jesus Christ! This is going from bad to worse. We need to catch this bastard before he kills anyone else. Every guard in the city's been mobilised, all leave cancelled. I'll meet you at the squat, okay.'

It had taken them less than two minutes to drive between the two sites. Two garda cars and an ambulance were already parked outside the derelict house, two guards taping off a perimeter. A gaggle of people were standing on the road and pavement watching the scene, trying to discover what had happened.

McEvoy jumped from the car and ran across the road. The boards had been pulled back, the front door forced open. He edged his way inside. A uniformed guard was standing at the bottom of the stairs.

'She up there?' McEvoy demanded.

The guard nodded and moved to one side. McEvoy took the steps two at a time and entered Karen's room.

She was lying on her back on top of the blanket in the corner of the room. Her tracksuit top was soaked with blood. The handle of a dagger protruded from her mouth, pinning her head to the floorboard beneath. Splashes of blood decorated the walls and pools had run across the floorboards, disappearing between the cracks.

Two paramedics were kneeling in the opposite corner, working on the man he'd last seen lying on the blanket with her. He had a deep cut on a bare arm, his chest bloody. His breathing was shallow, irregular.

'Is he going to be alright?' McEvoy managed to say.

'Touch and go,' one of them replied without looking up. 'The girl's dead. Nothing we could do to save her. We need to get him to a hospital, he's lost a lot of blood and I think one of his lungs has collapsed.'

'He's come full circle,' Jacobs said from behind him. 'She was Laura's friend and he thought she'd betrayed her; her death pact; betrayed him. She paid the price, dying as Laura did.'

One of the paramedics levered himself up off his knees and hurried from the room, brushing past them.

McEvoy couldn't disengage his eyes from Karen. She had probably known about Andrew McCormack from the start and yet she had lied for him while he continued to kill. Now he knew why. She'd known what the penalty would be; she'd known that she couldn't trust the guards to get to him first.

'Colm?' Jacobs prompted.

'What?' He tried to refocus.

'I think we should go; let the paramedics get on with their job. We've seen enough death for one day.'

He nodded agreement and they headed back out to the landing.

The paramedic and a guard were climbing the stairs carrying a stretcher. McEvoy and Jacobs stood to one side to let them pass and then descended in silence. A nervous looking couple in oddly matched tracksuits were visible in the front room, sitting on a sofa, staring at the blank wall.

'He's tying up loose ends,' Jacobs said as they reached the bottom. 'The girlfriend. Karen.'

McEvoy moved to the doorway and spoke to the couple.

'Did you call the ambulance and guards?'

'She did,' the young man said without turning his head, accusation and anger in his voice, unhappy that McEvoy and his colleagues had invaded their space.

'It was a man in a red baseball cap?'

The young woman nodded.

'Did a girl called Laura ever sleep here?'

The woman nodded again.

McEvoy massaged his forehead. McCormack was still loose in the city. He headed back out onto the street, aware that a thought was hovering just out of reach, teasing him. 'What did you say to me on the stairs?' he asked Jacobs, hoping her answer might prod it forward.

'I said, he's tying up loose ends.'

'Brady,' McEvoy said, the thought revealing itself. 'Shit! Maybe Brady's a loose end as well? This whole thing's been about Brady.' He started to run to his car, brushing past a man heaving a camera up onto his shoulder.

'This whole thing has been about Laura and McCormack,' Jacobs said, setting off after him.

McEvoy had started to reverse the car before Jacobs had got her door shut.

'Jesus, Colm!'

He stabbed at his mobile.

'Hello?'

'Dermot, where are you?' McEvoy demanded, swinging the car round.

'I'm in my office.'

'Lock the door and do not open it to anyone until I get there, you hear?'

'What's going on?'

'McCormack's on the run. He's killed his girlfriend and Karen. I'm afraid he might be coming after you.'

They passed Paul Roche racing up to the scene.

'For me?'

'He's trying to tie up loose ends. This whole thing's been about you. I'm worried he might be …'

'He's … he's on his way here?' Brady stuttered, interrupting, panic rising in his voice.

'I don't know where he is. Just lock the door and don't open it for anyone except me. Nobody. You understand? He's psychotic.'

McEvoy leant with his forehead resting against the mirror, the sink at his hips. All of his adrenaline and anger had dissipated to be replaced with a hollowness, an empty yawning in his chest and stomach; another low in a day of roller coaster emotions. He was mentally and physically exhausted, knowing that the day was only half over.

He pulled his head back an inch and tapped it against the mirror. He could have caught McCormack. He'd been less than two feet away when he'd held open the door to Samantha Evans' apartment block for them. If he'd followed Jacobs' advice and hadn't been in such a hurry to enter the building he would have recognised him, could have apprehended him or at least followed him. Karen would still be alive, her boyfriend not fighting for his life.

He pulled back from the mirror and stared at his grey and sunken face, his red eyes and thinning scalp. He was starting to look as Maggie had a couple of weeks before she died; his skin had the pallid cast of death to come.

His mobile phone rang. He rubbed at his temples then reluctantly fished it out of his pocket. 'McEvoy.'

'It's Paul. Where the hell are you?'

'Sorry,' McEvoy said flatly. 'I wanted to make sure Dermot Brady was okay.'

'And is he?'

'Yeah, he's fine. I'm at the DHC offices right now. Any luck your end?'

'That's why I'm ringing. We've found the blue Fiesta out in Lucan, just off the village square. The front seat is stained with blood. We think he headed out of the city along the strawberry beds, following the Liffey. Barney Plunkett's on the scene and we've cordoned off his house in case he tries to return.'

McCormack's escape route made sense. It was only a short distance from the North Circular Road to the Phoenix Park. From the far end of the park the old main road to Galway, now little used, headed out under the M50 toll bridge, snaking along the valley floor, crossing the Liffey at Lucan.

'The plates on the car matched those Brady used to travel out to Trim on the day of Billy Mullins' murder,' Roche continued. 'We're still trying to work out whose car it really is.'

'Jesus,' McEvoy muttered, a sense of dread coming over him – McCormack was getting away. He was already out of the city.

'McCormack's own car is a silver, 04 Mercedes 180. I've put out a full alert.'

'He'll make for the border,' McEvoy said instinctively.

'Maybe. I think it's more likely he's got a bolthole somewhere. He's thought of everything else. I'm putting Johnny Cronin in charge of Samantha Evans' death, Jenny Flanagan on Karen's; that okay?'

'Yeah, whatever you want.'

'I'm heading over to Evans' apartment right now. Will I meet you there? We need a proper meeting. Bishop's blown a gasket and the media are going crazy.'

'Feck the lot of them, I don't care. Look, Paul, I can't go back to that apartment right now,' McEvoy said feeling ill again at the thought. 'Not after what he did to her. You'll understand when you get there.'

'Yeah, okay, but I think we still need to meet. How about outside the block? There's no need for you to come back in.'

McEvoy paused. 'Okay,' he muttered finally.

'I'll see you in what, ten minutes?'

'Yeah, ten minutes.' McEvoy ended the call and slipped the phone into his pocket. He turned on the taps again and washed his face for the third time, trying to wash away his feelings of guilt and shame, the water trickling down onto his tie and shirt.

The world's media were strung out across the width of the road, held back by a row of uniformed guards. McEvoy barged his way through ignoring the barrage of questions, the shouts barely penetrating his consciousness. He cut left off the pavement striding up to the front door of the apartment block. Kathy Jacobs had declined to come, instead heading back to Harcourt Street.

The door was pulled open for him by a uniformed guard who looked barely past puberty and he entered the small atrium. He hovered by the lift for a couple of seconds then headed back to the guard at the door. 'Can you go and get Detective Superintendent Roche for me?' he demanded.

'He's just upstairs.'

'I *know* he's just upstairs. I want him downstairs. I'll mind the door.'

The guard nodded and set off for the stairs.

McEvoy wandered over to the mailboxes and stared at the row without seeing them. Samantha Evans probably didn't have a clue she was dating a monster until a few hours before her torture started; probably thought that McCormack was her future until she stumbled across something she shouldn't have. Or perhaps there was no reason – McCormack just killed her because he could; because he wanted to; because he needed to. He shook his head at the pointlessness of it all.

'Colm,' Roche said behind him.

He swivelled round.

'Paul. Sorry, I couldn't come up there,' McEvoy said apologetically, staring up at the ceiling. 'I couldn't face her again.'

'He enjoyed killing her,' Roche observed, letting McEvoy know he understood, his face morose. 'He might have killed the others for the sake of his book, but they were quick and anonymous. He killed her slowly and in full control; he tortured her mentally and emotionally as well as physically. He savoured her. He's going to rot in hell.'

McEvoy stayed silent, not sure what to say, knowing that Roche was right.

'There's still no sign of him and we haven't found his own car. It's just a matter of time though. Every person in the country will be looking for him now.'

'He'll use one of his disguises,' McEvoy muttered.

'It doesn't matter, we'll get him. And when we do he'll get his just rewards. A lot of steps in a police station; a lot of psychos in prison. He'll come to understand the meaning of pain.'

McEvoy nodded. He had no difficulties with the notion of McCormack being tortured and killed. After what he'd done he deserved no less; he'd only be receiving what he deemed legitimate to do unto others.

The door to the atrium was yanked open and Tony Bishop steamed in dressed in full uniform, his cap pulled low over his eyes. 'Well?' he barked. 'What the hell's happening?'

Roche turned to face him. 'Samantha Evans is upstairs in her apartment. McCormack killed her sometime in the last few days; left her to rot in her bath. He fled here just after one o'clock and headed to a squat not far away. When he got there he killed a young drug user, Karen Kirke – a friend of Laura Schmidt's

– and seriously injured her boyfriend, before driving to Lucan where he abandoned his car. He's still on the run.'

'Jesus! I don't believe this! You could have had him,' he said to McEvoy angrily. 'You were here when he was and you let him get away! How could you have been so stupid?'

'What?' McEvoy said, taken aback by Bishop's fury.

'You fucked up again. Jesus! I should have never let you back on this case, you're a complete fuckin' liability. The press are going to have a fuckin' field day!'

'If it wasn't for me, you wouldn't even know who the hell The Raven is!' McEvoy said his anger re-ignited. 'And if you hadn't been so fast to release his name and photo to the media I *would* have got him! He only bolted because he saw himself on the news.'

'Don't try and blame me for your incompetence, you …'

'Whoa, whoa,' Roche said loudly, coming between them. 'Nobody's to blame for anything, okay? Colm did a great job in identifying McCormack. We wouldn't have a clue who he was otherwise. You did what you had to do. We needed to put out a full alert to warn the public and try and locate him. There's no point fighting each other; we need to concentrate on trying to track him down.'

Bishop pulled his mouth into an angry line and stared out of the atrium toward the road, unwilling to apologise for his accusations.

McEvoy shook his head in frustration. 'I'm going out to Lucan,' he announced, heading for the door.

'I'll talk to you in minute,' Roche said, making no attempt to stop him.

McEvoy strode to the pavement and turned right, heading for the waiting media. He didn't slow as he reached their lines instead ploughing straight into the crowd, stiffening and angling his shoulders so the reporters bounced back hard into their colleagues.

McEvoy was still smarting from Bishop's words, his mind end-lessly replaying scenarios of rebuke and revenge. He eased the car through several news teams and under some tape, parking 50 metres down the road.

The Fiesta was parked up a short alleyway next to a garage. There were no houses overlooking the spot. McCormack could have climbed out and transferred to another car without anybody seeing him except from the entrance to the road.

McEvoy stared in through the window. The seat was stained with blood, but otherwise looked empty. McCormack must have pre-selected this spot. Most probably left another car there, ei-ther his own or another, in case of an emergency.

He could feel himself starting to let go of Bishop, the puzzle of the case dulling the memory of the confrontation. He heard footsteps approaching and turned as Barney Plunkett reached the back of the car.

'We've searched all the surrounding properties. There's no sign of him and nobody saw him either,' Plunkett said slightly manically. 'The car is how we found it. It's completely empty – no clothes or knife or anything else. We haven't found anything dumped locally. He must have taken everything with him.'

'He could be anywhere at this stage,' McEvoy reflected sombrely.

'He can't have got far; someone would have spotted him. We'll get him, don't worry,' Plunkett tried to reassure.

'Come on, Barney, let's get real. Everything else has been carefully planned; do you really think he won't have planned an escape?'

McCormack closed over the garage doors and padlocked them together. His clothes and hands were covered in blood from the knife attack on Karen and her boyfriend. There were a few specks on his chin and cheek that he had failed to rub clean. He'd vented his fury and frustration on them, but he hadn't lost control as with Shirley Hamilton. He'd been detached and controlled and they had gotten what they deserved.

He picked up two holdalls, one in each hand, and headed across the small yard, clumps of grass and shrubs growing through the ancient concrete, to the entrance to the derelict labourer's cottage. The building had seen better days – the paint on its outer walls blistered and peeling, one end covered in ivy, the window frames black and rotten holding glass grey with grime and cobwebs, the roof missing a few slates, a small tree growing from the chimney pot. The yard was surrounded by overgrown hedges which screened the residence from view of the narrow, unpaved lane.

The cottage was located at the end of a thin peninsula that snaked out into a lough. Behind the garage thick reed beds extended into the dark water, a small motor boat tied to an old wooden pier. If they came for him then that would be his escape route.

But they wouldn't come. Nobody knew where he was and the cottage was more than three quarters of a mile from another residence – a holiday home barely used for more than four weeks in a year. There was no reason for anyone to venture out along the narrow strip of land; the farmland had long since been abandoned to revert to untended bog and anglers favoured the far side of the lough where the river's waters flowed in.

He could hold a party and no one would be aware of it. Even so, he would be keeping his head low, never straying beyond the cottage's hedgerows for at least four weeks – he had more than enough provisions to last that long and plenty of patience.

He should have retreated to the hideaway straight after leaving the airport. He had been overconfident. McEvoy had somehow worked out his identity; had almost caught him. A few moments of delay and he would have had to fight his way out of Samantha's apartment. He would learn from that lesson. Next time he would leave nothing to chance; the game would be played fully formed.

If he'd followed all of his own rules he would now be in Providence, Rhode Island, enjoying the conference and catching up with old friends. In a week's time he would have returned and slipped back into his life, safe in his anonymity. He would have eventually been awarded the promotion he deserved and continued to have built a successful career; and he would still be half-living with Samantha, dividing his time between her apartment and his house. But then how would anybody know that he was The Raven? That he had written *The Rule Book* and it proved its genius?

Perhaps it was better this way? Perhaps subconsciously he had intended it all along? He had ignored his own advice; he'd left a trail of misdirections and clues. He'd even invited the guards to his final slaying. He smiled to himself and entered the cottage, amused at his own follies. He'd nearly been caught, but he hadn't. Now he was safe; he was certain of it.

He would spend a few weeks here then move on; re-invent himself – bide his time and rise again. He'd done it before and he could do it again. He was, after all, the trickster. The Raven. The bringer of death. He'd spread his wings once more. Perhaps he would write a new book to be acted out to the world; a new puzzle to vex McEvoy or whoever replaced him.

In the meantime his fame would build as more and more details of *The Rule Book* murders became public. No doubt there was already an army of people working on feature articles, websites, television documentaries, and true crime books. By now his name would be known around the world; 'Andrew McCormack' exiting the lips of every newsreader on the planet; *The Rule Book* murders the topic of conversation in every home, café and pub. He started to light some candles that he'd stored in a kitchen drawer, bringing new light to the dusty old kitchen.

Epilogue

Friday, April 25th

It had just gone three o'clock in the afternoon, four days after McCormack was last seen at Karen's squat. There had been thousands of suspected sightings from all four corners of the island, from across the UK and continental Europe. Following up on them all was a mammoth task. There was no trace of McCormack's Mercedes – he'd either changed the plates or it was hidden somewhere. The small town of Lucan had been systematically searched by hundreds of gardai.

DNA recovered from McCormack's house matched the samples from Glencree and Rathmoylan and also those at Samantha Evans' apartment and Karen's squat. There had been few other breakthroughs though. They hadn't found any of the victims' belongings – Laura or Hennessey's clothes, or McCormack's disguises; the false hair and beard, the old woman's outfit. They hadn't discovered how he'd sourced the cyanide or where he'd acquired the sword; and they were still trying to piece together McCormack's movements over the course of the previous week.

Elaine Jones predicted that Samantha Evans had died approximately 48 hours before she was found, probably some time on Saturday morning. She'd been tortured for at least three days, a bloodied razor blade lodged behind the bath taps. She'd lost a lot a blood from the hundreds of cuts and had died of a cardiac arrest bought about by severe stress and dehydration. There were two main hypotheses as to why McCormack had killed her. First, that she had somehow worked out that he was The Raven and he wanted her silenced permanently, or the quick deaths of the other victims had left him unsatisfied. The later was a hypothesis Kathy Jacobs thought possible given new information from Massachusett's police.

They had been in contact and were sending a couple of people over early the following week. They suspected McCormack might have been responsible for three killings in the Boston area that they had so far been unable to solve. The murders had all occurred in the final eighteen months he'd been studying at Harvard. Each victim had been bound, gagged and tortured, one with razor blades. There was no apparent motive for the crimes or links between the victims. Cambridgeshire and other UK police forces were also examining their unsolved murder files in case he'd killed while he'd been a postdoctoral student.

If the links proved positive then *The Rule Book* had been written from experience by an already successful serial killer. Only this time he had overstretched himself, trying to kill seven people in seven days while leaving a trail of chapters. He'd become complacent, grooming one victim and picking another he'd a vendetta against. Even so, he'd nearly gotten away with it all. Until he was caught, for all intents and purposes he had got away with it.

Karen's family, a rum bunch of chancers, were suing the gardai for failing to protect their daughter's life. They would probably win, or it would be settled out of court. Her boyfriend was still in intensive care but was expected to live. He was lucky the paramedics had got to him so quickly. Five more minutes and he'd have been the tenth victim. Eleventh if you counted Grainne Malone's unborn child.

After being involved in the interviews with McCormack's family and friends, Kathy Jacobs had travelled back to Scotland

and her young sons the previous evening. On the basis of the extra information she'd gleaned she was refining her profile and trying to help predict where he might be hiding and what his next moves might be. At the moment she felt he would lay low, try to slip out of Ireland and build a new life, then start a fresh wave of attacks, most probably in a scheme as elaborate as *The Rule Book*. She was checking in a couple of times of day, to see how things were developing, anxious that McCormack be caught before he could kill again.

The story continued to dominate the news globally, hundreds of journalists still covering developments, though a few had begun to move out, heading for the next big headline. Within a week or so it would no doubt be only the Irish media and the 'real crime' book writers who would be interested, the story falling dormant.

McEvoy scratched at his thinning hair then rubbed his temples, his plastic cigarette bobbing between his fingers. He was sitting by himself in a meeting room, the reports of various sightings laid out in front of him. He was utterly exhausted having worked 16 to 18-hour days all week. The door to the room opened and Tony Bishop entered.

He looked as McEvoy felt, dark bags under his eyes, his skin pale, red hair untidy. He'd spent most of the week trying to spin the story as positively as possible, with relatively good results. His basic line was that An Garda Síochána had done what any police force would have done in the circumstances, and they were dealing with a particularly clever and dangerous individual who had carefully masterminded a campaign of terror. The fact that McCormack had probably killed several times before and had not been identified helped, especially given the resources and experience of the US authorities compared to their Irish counterparts.

'Ah, Colm. Have you seen Paul Roche?' Bishop asked.

'I think he might be with Johnny Cronin,' McEvoy replied flatly.

Bishop nodded once and turned for the door. He took one pace and stopped, swivelling slowly. 'Look, Colm, about last week, I … well, you know.' He paused. 'It was a difficult week.'

McEvoy nodded unsure where Bishop was heading.

'Difficult for all of us. Feelings were, well, feelings were running high. Tempers frayed. We were all under a lot of pressure.' Bishop brushed at his cheek nervously. 'At the start of things I said I'd look after you, protect you, let you get on with your job. That offer still stands.'

McEvoy looked down at the reports and back up to Bishop trying to decide how to react. At the beginning of the week Bishop couldn't wait to drum him out of the force. 'Does that mean I'll still be on the case next week?' he asked eventually.

'Yes. Though Paul will be staying on as well. You seem to work well as a team.'

'And I won't be packed off to some backwater?'

'No, no. Not while I'm still chief superintendent. I said I would protect you, didn't I?'

'Right.' McEvoy did his best not to look confused, trying to get a handle on the conversation.

'You did a good job identifying McCormack,' Bishop said, pulling a tight smile.

'Thanks.'

'Well. Well, I guess I better be going.' Bishop took another step to the door, again stopping, turning back. 'I think you should be leaving as well, Colm. You look like you could do with a decent meal and a full night's sleep.'

'I'm fine.'

'You'll be better with a couple of days' recuperation. Take the weekend off, come back Monday. Spend some time relaxing, eating; some family time with Gemma. We can cope for a couple of days without you. If anything turns up I'll make sure someone calls you.'

McEvoy nodded, knowing that Bishop was right but unwilling to say it.

'I mean it, Colm. I have a duty of care. That means I have to look after my staff; protect them from themselves if necessary. I'm ordering you to take a break. I'll be back round in ten minutes, you'd better not be here when I return.'

McEvoy nodded as the door shut behind Bishop. He wasn't sure he'd ever be able to fully read the man – one minute he was a tyrant, the next your best friend. He pushed his chair back and stood, gathering his oversized suit jacket. He'd take the rest of the day off – spend some time with Gemma and get an early night. He'd be fine in the morning.

McEvoy glanced sideways at Gemma walking carefully along the next row. Occasionally she stopped to read a gravestone before moving on. Another plane roared overhead coming in to land. He lowered himself to his haunches and removed a bunch of dying flowers from Maggie's grave, replacing them with fresh, pink carnations, arranging them in the pot.

Gemma approached silently from behind and tugged on his arm. 'Dad, I think we should go,' she said. 'I think you need to move on.'

Move on? McEvoy thought. Move on from Maggie or The Raven or just move on in general? How could he move on? From the moment he'd viewed Laura's body, the sword sticking up through her mouth, The Raven had become an integral part of his life. Maggie and The Raven. They defined him – the first things he thought of when he woke, the things he daydreamed about, and consumed him when he tried to sleep, fuelling his insomnia; the things that gave him nightmares when he finally slept. Somehow they had merged together; become bound in some odd way. His inadequacies entwined; his inability to stop Maggie's cancer, to stop the Raven's killing spree; to stop death.

Moving on. How could he move on?

'Dad! Come on, let's go and buy a new suit,' Gemma suggested. 'Look at the state of you. It's embarrassing.' She lifted up the flap of his suit jacket and let it flop back. 'You could fit two of you in this.'

'Yeah,' he conceded flatly, 'let's go and look at suits.' That'll move things along, he thought to himself sarcastically, sucking on his plastic substitute. Jesus, he needed to shake off this lethargy, to create a new focus to his life. He needed to make Gemma the sole centre of things; not forget Maggie or The Raven, but to put them in their place.

'Come on,' he tried to say more enthusiastically, taking Gemma's hand, 'there has to be something out there that fits better than this.' He tugged the belt that held a few inches of excess trouser and pulled a tight smile. 'And I'm sure they'll have something nice for you as well. Heaven knows you deserve it.'

They started for the cemetery exit. Thirty metres away a black bird rose from a hawthorn tree and swept low over them.

About the Author

Rob Kitchin works at the National University of Ireland, Maynooth. He has published 16 non-fiction books to date. *The Rule Book* is his first novel.

Visit his website at www.kitchin.org

Acknowledgements

I would like to thank the following people for their support and advice while writing this novel: Sheila Hones, Gerald Mills, Mervyn Kitchin, Tim O'Connor, John Driscoll, Paula Campbell, Faith O'Grady, David O'Leary, Rachel Calder, Paddy Duffy, Mark Boyle, Martin Charlton, Anne-Marie Burke, Orla Dunne, Mary Gilmartin and Kate of Kate's Mystery Books.

In particular I would like to single out three people. John McElligott, former detective superintendent with the National Bureau of Criminal Investigation, for answering my various questions with good humour. Any procedural and factual errors are entirely of my making. Brendan Bartley, who read a couple of drafts and was unstinting in encouragement and support. And finally, Cora Collins for always being there and indulging me the time and space to write.

Rob Kitchin, August 2008